CHAOTICA

RIVEN WORLDS BOOK FIVE

(AMARANTHE ♦ 18)

G. S. JENNSEN

HYPERNOVA
PUBLISHING
2022

CHAOTICA

Hypernova Publishing
174 E Neider Ave #89
Coeur d'Alene, ID 83815
www.hypernovapublishing.com

Ordering Information:
Hypernova Publishing books may be purchased for educational, business or sales promotional use. For details, contact the "Special Markets Department" at the address above.

Chaotica / G. S. Jennsen.—1st ed.

LCCN 2022908034
978-1-957352-04-6

AMARANTHE UNIVERSE

AURORA RHAPSODY

AURORA RISING

STARSHINE
VERTIGO
TRANSCENDENCE

AURORA RENEGADES

SIDESPACE
DISSONANCE
ABYSM

AURORA RESONANT

RELATIVITY
RUBICON
REQUIEM

ASTERION NOIR

EXIN EX MACHINA

OF A DARKER VOID

THE STARS LIKE GODS

RIVEN WORLDS

CONTINUUM
INVERSION
ECHO RIFT

ALL OUR TOMORROWS
CHAOTICA
DUALITY

COSMIC SHORES

MEDUSA FALLING
THE THIEF
THE UNIVERSE WITHIN

SHADOWS & LIGHT

LIMINAL SPACE

SHORT STORIES

Restless, Vol. I • *Restless, Vol. II* • *Apogee* • *Solatium* • *Venatoris*
Re/Genesis • *Meridian* • *Fractals* • *Chrysalis* • *Starlight Express* •
Extinguishing the Stars

Learn more at gsjennsen.com/books or visit: gsj.space/wiki

For Julie. First you were Alex's friend, then you were mine. We are both better for having known you.

DRAMATIS PERSONAE

HUMANS

Alexis 'Alex' Solovy Marano

Space scout and explorer. Prevo.

Spouse of Caleb Marano, daughter of Miriam and David Solovy.

Caleb Marano

Former Special Operations intelligence agent. Space scout and explorer.

Spouse of Alex Solovy, bonded to Akeso.

Miriam Solovy (Commandant)

Leader, Concord Armed Forces.

Malcolm Jenner (Admiral)

AEGIS Fleet Admiral.

Marlee Marano

Consulate Assistant.

Mia Requelme

Former Concord Senator.

Richard Navick

Concord Intelligence Director.

Morgan Lekkas

Former IDCC Cmdr. Fighter Pilot.

ASTERIONS

Nika Kirumase

External Relations Advisor, Asterion Dominion Advisor Committee.

Former NOIR leader.

Dashiel Ridani

Industry Advisor, Asterion Dominion Advisor Committee.

Owner, Ridani Enterprises.

Lance Palmer (Commander)

Military Advisor.

Perrin Benvenit

Omoikane Personnel Director.

Joaquim Lacese

Former NOIR Operations Director.

Maris Debray

Culture Advisor.

Adlai Weiss

Justice Advisor.

Cassidy Frenton

Joaquim's lover.

Other Major Characters

Eren Savitas asi-Idoni
Advocacy Chief of Intelligence for Non-Anaden Affairs.
Species: Anaden

Mnemosyne ('Mesme')
Idryma Member. Former 1st Analystae of Aurora.
Species: Katasketousya

Corradeo Praesidis
Concord Senator. Head of Anaden Advocacy.
Species: Anaden

Akeso
Sentient planet.
Species: Ekos

Braelyn Rossi-Terrage
Kennedy and Noah's daughter.
Species: Human

Casmir elasson-Machim
Leader, Anaden military.
Species: Anaden

David Solovy
Professor, Concord SWTC.
Species: Human

Devon Reynolds
Concord Special Projects Director.
Species: Human

Enzio Vilane
Head of the Rivinchi Cartel.
Species: Human

Felzeor
CINT agent.
Species: Volucri

Graham Delavasi
Former SF Intelligence Director.
Species: Human

Jonas Rossi-Terrage
Kennedy and Noah's son.
Species: Human

Katherine Colson
Administration Advisor.
Species: Asterion

Kennedy Rossi
CEO, Connova Interstellar.
Species: Human

Noah Terrage
COO, Connova Interstellar.
Species: Human

Nyx Praesidis
Advocacy Dir. of Intelligence.
Species: Anaden

Supreme Three
Synthetic intelligence.
Species: Ruda

Thomas
CAF Aurora Artificial.
Species: Artificial

Valkyrie
Alex's Prevo counterpart.
Species: Artificial

MINOR CHARACTERS

Abigail Canivon, cybernetics/Artificial expert (*Human/Artificial*)

Avicia Muire, Hamid member (*Naraida*)

Derek Riley, Flight Lieutenant, AEGIS military (*Human*)

Fai Xing, Commander, AEGIS military (*Human*)

Grant Mesahle, DAF consultant (*Asterion*)

Hyperion, Idryma member (*Katasketousya*)

James Sarona, Gardiens assassin (*Human*)

Jeffrey Tannehiln, Major, AEGIS military (*Human*)

Jim Spencer, Brigadier, AEGIS military (*Human*)

Karis Yuri, Hamid member (*Naraida*)

Lakhes, Praetor, Idryma (*Katasketousya*)

Markos Landon, Flight Lieutenant, AEGIS military (*Human*)

Meno, Mia's Prevo counterpart (*Artificial*)

Miaon, former anarch agent (*Yinhe*)

Olav Zylynski, Gardiens Chief of Security (*Human*)

Olivia Montegreu, former cartel leader, Enzio's mother (*Human/Artificial*)

Onai Veshnael, Novoloume Dean, Concord Senator (*Novoloume*)

Owain Boliver, Gardiens agent (*Human*)

Parc Eshett, Omoikane consultant (*Asterion*)

Philippe Beaumont, Gardiens Agent (*Human*)

Pinchutsenahn Niikha Qhiyane Kteh ("Pinchu"), Tokahe Naataan (*Khokteh*)

Ryan Theroit, former NOIR member (*Asterion*)

Selene Panetier, Justice Advisor (*Asterion*)

Sotu Thisiame, Novoloume Pointe-Amiral (*Novoloume*)

Stanley, Morgan's Prevo counterpart (*Artificial*)

Tibu Ogadu, CEO, Horizon Therapeutics (*Human*)

William 'Will' Sutton, CINT Operations Director (*Human*)

CONCORD

MEMBER SPECIES

Human
Representative: Aristide Vranas

Anaden
Representative: Corradeo Praesidis

Novoloume
Representative: Dean Onai Veshnael

Naraida
Representative: Tasme Chareis

Khokteh
Representative: Pinchutsenahn Niikha Qhiyane Kteh

Barisan
Representative: Daayn Shahs-lan

Dankath
Representative: Bohlke'ban

Efkam
Representative: Ahhk~sae

ALLIED SPECIES

Asterion	Taenarin
Katasketousya	Volucri
Fylliot	Yinhe

PROTECTED SPECIES

Ekos	Icksel
Faneros	Pachrem
Galenai	Vrachnas

AMARANTHE
CONCORD EMPIRE

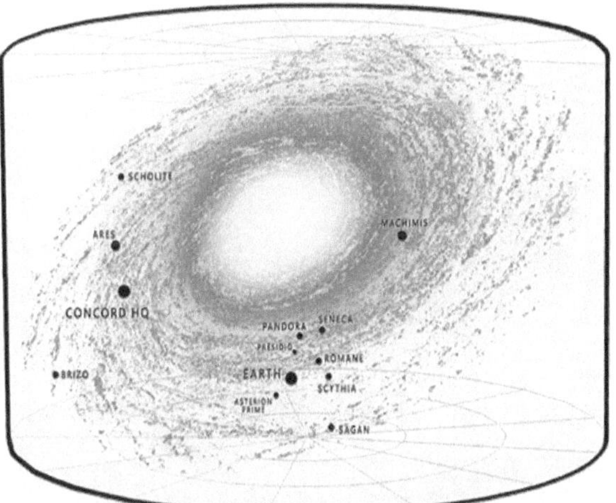

MILKY WAY GALAXY

LOCAL GALACTIC GROUP

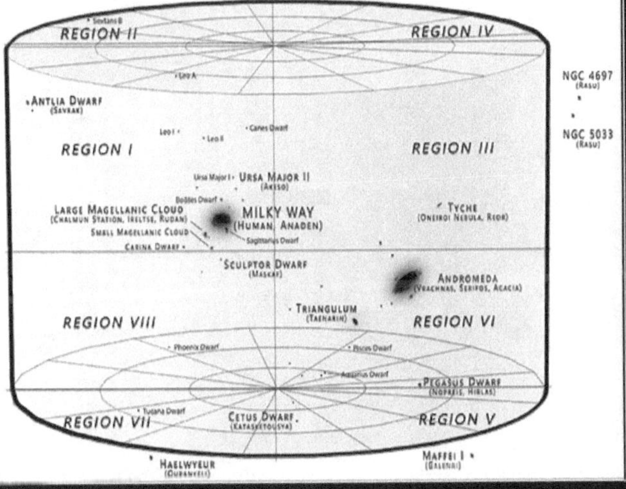

Gennisi Galaxy
(Messier 94)

✦ Asterion Dominion Axis Worlds
✛ Asterion Dominion Adjunct Worlds
✳ Alien Worlds

ASTERION DOMINION AXIS WORLDS

Mirai   Namino   Synra   Ebisu   Kiyora

THE STORY SO FAR

*For a summary of the events of **AMARANTHE #1-13**, see the
Appendix in the back of the book.*

RIVEN WORLDS BOOKS 1-3

Fourteen years have passed since the events of *AURORA RES-
ONANT*. Caleb has fully bonded with Akeso, the living planet that
saved his life, and he and Alex have made their home there.

Alex introduced Nika to Concord, the multi-species government formed after The Displacement to take the place of the de-
posed Anaden Directorate. Miriam served as its military leader and
Mia its diplomatic one, while the major species of the former
Anaden Empire were represented equally in a Senate. Nika warned
Concord of the Rasu and received a cautious promise of support, as
well as the opening of diplomatic relations. When Nika returned
home to the Asterion Dominion, she discovered the other Advisors
had created the Omoikane Initiative, a massive project designed to
accelerate technology, warfare and logistical plans to combat the
Rasu.

Concord was facing conflict on two additional fronts. Negotiations for the Savrakaths, a lizard-evolved Mosaic species, to become an ally of Concord broke down when CINT discovered they
were developing antimatter weapons; Marlee, Caleb's niece, also
discovered they were enslaving another species, the Godjans.

The lack of a strong Anaden leader led several *elassons* to fo-
ment a rebellion against Concord. Torval elasson-Machim took it
upon himself to bomb the Savrakath's antimatter facility; unbe-
knownst to him, Eren was leading a team surveilling it, and Eren's
lover, Cosime, was killed in the attack. Meanwhile, Malcolm was
captured by the enemy during a mission to rescue Godjans on Savrak. When Concord approved an alliance with the Asterion Dominion, Ferdinand elasson-Kyvern began a coup to overthrow
Concord.

The Rasu launched an attack on the Asterion world of Namino, and Concord sent a fleet to defend their new ally. They were unprepared, however, for how difficult the Rasu were to kill, and the battle turned against them. A leviathan shapeshifted to swallow Miriam's ship, the *Stalwart II*, and Rasu infiltrated the vessel. Miriam activated the ship's self-destruct mechanism to prevent the Rasu from acquiring Concord secrets, killing everyone on board.

The Rasu reached the Namino surface and activated a quantum block, cutting the planet off from the Asterions' d-gate network. Marlee was injured by a Rasu and trapped on the planet; some Asterions were able to rescue her and retreated to an underground bunker. Caleb stole a ship and went to Namino to find Marlee. He joined the Asterions trapped there in attempting to disrupt the Rasu invasion, at great personal cost to him due to Akeso's aversion to violence.

AEGIS marines defeated Ferdinand's coup attempt, and Ferdinand fled to a safe house with a group of sympathetic *elassons*. Corradeo Praesidis and his granddaughter, Nyx, returned to Concord after a fourteen-year absence. Disturbed by the state of Anaden affairs, Corradeo decided to resume the mantle of leadership and attempt to wrest control away from Ferdinand and the rebelling *elassons*.

Miriam became one of the first humans to be returned to life via regenesis. She struggled with the transition, as well as with maintaining control of Concord after the coup attempt. Alex and Kennedy reverse-engineered the Machin double-shielding technology and deployed it on AEGIS ships to prevent the Rasu from boarding vessels in the future. Further, the Kats began delivering Rift Bubble devices that created an impermeable barrier around a planet.

The Savrakaths lied and told Concord that Malcolm was dead. Mia, seeking revenge, tricked the Anadens into attacking the Savrakaths; when her deceptions were discovered, she became a fugitive.

Alex and Nika, along with Morgan, traveled to Namino and located Caleb and the others. Together they infiltrated the Rasu stronghold and destroyed the quantum block. A Rift Bubble device was activated on Namino, and the Concord fleet defeated the Rasu occupying the planet.

Malcolm escaped his Savrakath prison and returned home, surprising everyone. Mia, devasted by his apparent death, refused to reconcile with him so long as he declined regenesis. While in hiding on Pandora, Mia encountered Enzio Vilane, a wealthy businessman and secret mob boss with a notable family lineage. When he tried and failed to kidnap her, she agreed to a plea deal with the authorities and returned to Romane—but not to Malcolm.

Corradeo disbanded the rebel *elasson* group and established a new, Concord-friendly Anaden government. He convinced a brokenhearted Eren to come work for him as an intelligence agent.

Alex and Caleb investigated rumors of an advanced civilization, the Ourankeli, annihilated by the Rasu. They found a lone survivor, who told them of the powerful weapon they created to kill the Rasu (and how they used it too late to save themselves). The three of them traveled to the last settlement of Ourankeli, rescued them from a Rasu attack, and brought the refugees to Concord.

The Savrakaths sneaked an antimatter bomb onto Concord HQ. Richard and David were able to find and disarm it seconds before detonation. In response, the Kats exiled the Savrakaths, trapping their planet inside a modified Rift Bubble.

The Rasu reappeared to attack Toki'taku. The Taiyoks refused a Rift Bubble, but together with a Concord fleet, the Asterions were able to deploy their new Rima Grenades to beat back Rasu forces. However, the Rasu captured an unprotected Concord vessel and, now armed with the location of Concord, launched an assault on the Khokteh world of Ireltse.

ALL OUR TOMORROWS

The Concord fleet arrives at Ireltse to find it under heavy assault by a Rasu armada. Marines battle invading Rasu on the surface while Machim and AEGIS forces struggle to gain the advantage in space.

Alex and Caleb help Mesme deploy a Rift Bubble on Ireltse. However, the Rasu are able to construct and activate a quantum block, knocking out the Rift Bubble and causing the *Siyane* (piloted by Valkyrie) to crash on the Ireltse surface.

With the Rift Bubble barrier gone, Miriam and Malcolm deploy a new defensive weapon, the Parapet Gambit, to protect the planet, using AEGIS vessels equipped with the Anaden double-shielding technology to form an interconnected force field mesh.

Cut off from Valkyrie and AEGIS forces, Alex and Caleb race to where the *Siyane* has crashed into a building. They are able to dig the ship out and take control just as the building collapses around them. They then locate the quantum block and destroy it, enabling the Rift Bubble to reactivate; however, Valkyrie remains unreachable.

The Rasu bomb the Khokteh Command Center, and Pinchu is gravely injured. When he is minutes from death, Caleb and Akeso are able to heal Pinchu using Akeso's life energy. Concord forces are finally able to defeat the Rasu attackers, saving Ireltse.

After they return home, Alex repairs damage to Valkyrie's hardware, and Valkyrie is able to reboot herself. It turns out that, in order to protect Alex from the shock of the quantum block, Valkyrie shut down her remote hardware, then absorbed the impact of the block until it shorted her out. Later that night, Valkyrie muses with Thomas about both of their recent 'deaths' and the nature of their existence, and we learn they are intimate with one another.

Marlee, Caleb and Alex visit the Vrachnas and the Galenai as the two species receive Rift Bubble protection. While observing the Galenai from a stealthed *Siyane*, one of the Galenai detects their presence. Marlee initiates a basic interchange, identifying them as friends who will reveal themselves in time.

Eren brings Corradeo to Akeso, and Caleb and Corradeo are reunited for the first time since before The Displacement. Caleb is relieved to learn Corradeo does not blame him the loss of his *diati* or the destruction of Solum. They discuss sensing the *diati* out there in the stars and why they don't call for it, then part friends.

In the Asterion Dominion, Dashiel completes the development of a renewable negative energy weapon (RNEW), which stands to transform future battles against the Rasu. The Dominion military takes back their colony, Adjunct San, from the Rasu.

Perrin struggles with the emotional burden of caring for displaced refugees. When she breaks down at work, she decides to get an up-gen to tone down her emotional processes; Adlai is upset she didn't talk to him first, and worries she'll no longer be the woman he loves.

Marlee takes Corradeo to meet the Ourankeli refugees that Alex and Caleb rescued, who are working with Devon and Kennedy to recreate their Ymyrath Field weapon. Kennedy runs an experiment and discovers that while the Reor reacts to each of Alex and Caleb, only when they are together will it respond to resonance signals and release its kyoseil fibers.

Malcolm reviews the state of the Rasu war with the AEGIS Oversight Board, and the Board pressures him to revoke the no regenesis clause in his will. After the meeting, Malcolm is approached by an anti-regenesis group called the Gardiens. Malcolm attends a Gardiens meeting and leaves a surveillance device behind. It records the leadership discussing their secret plans for the group, and how they targeted him.

Meanwhile, Graham joins Richard at CINT to investigate Enzio Vilane. After reviewing Enzio's personal history, Graham deduces that Oliva Montegreu was his mother.

On Pandora, Enzio has coffee with his mother—a reconstituted Artificial built from scattered records of the original Olivia. She's obviously a work in progress, but Enzio displays an obsessive adoration of her.

Eren visits Chalmun Station to investigate a group of dissident Barisans as part of his new job for the Anaden Advocacy. While he's there, the Rasu launch an attack on the asteroid. Morgan learns of the attack and rushes there as well. She and Eren work together to evacuate people until a tunnel caves in, trapping them. They are almost out of air when Alex is able to open a wormhole at their location and extricate Morgan and Eren. Alex then convinces Miriam to test the prototype Ymyrath Field weapon on the Rasu attacking Chalmun Station.

Malcolm bugs his Gardiens contact, then records a conversation where the Gardiens target Miriam for assassination, planning to make it look like her death is due to neurological system failure, casting doubt on the safety of regenesis. Malcolm rushes to London and intercepts Miriam just as the assassin fires, thwarting the attack.

Everyone gathers at Miriam and David's house; Malcolm plays the holo recording, and Richard identifies the man giving the orders as Enzio Vilane. Realizing this is the same man who tried to kidnap Mia, Malcolm volunteers to go undercover with the Gardiens in an attempt to bring them down—and realizes he can't have any contact with Mia while he does. Caleb investigates the crime scene in London, uncovering forensic evidence that will identify the shooter.

Enzio cleans house after the failed assassination attempt. Olivia gives him some harsh advice, then proposes adjustments she wants to make to her own programming.

Abigail and Marlee review Marlee's plan to upgrade her cybernetics enough to become a Solo Prevo. Abigail warns Marlee that the upgrades will likely develop emergent properties, the nature of which they can't predict.

Miriam meets with the AEGIS Council and learns Earth's Rift Bubble caused an accident, killing 1,200 people. The Council decides to deactivate the Rift Bubbles until there's an attack, against her strong advice. On an unknown planet, a Rasu unit secretly begins gathering materials needed to construct a quantum block.

The Rasu steal a Dominion commercial vessel, and Nika has to visit the Rift Bubbles on Dominion worlds to change the passcodes. Mesme arrives while she's doing so and hints that she has the capability to access the Rift Bubbles remotely, but doesn't tell her how to do so.

The members of the Idryma express concern over the Asterions' rapid modification of the Kat technology they've been provided. After the meeting, Lakhes suggests telling the others the truth, but Mesme insists they cannot.

Corradeo proposes opening diplomatic talks to formally build a relationship between Anadens and Asterions. Nika assigns the task to Maris, and when Maris and Corradeo meet, frosty fireworks ensue. Maris asks for the Anadens to give Asterion Prime to the Asterions. He insists that's impossible, but promises to find a way for Asterions to settle on the planet without joining Concord as a full member.

Joaquim and Selene continue their affair. When Joaquim refuses to tell her why he holds a grudge against Justice, Selene decides to investigate the matter herself. She dives into old Justice Division records and learns about the raid that killed Joaquim's lover, Cassidy. In reviewing the evidence, Selene discovers that Cassidy's backup storage, though damaged, was not actually destroyed. She discusses it with Adlai and decides to wake the woman up. After hearing of what happened to Joaquim and Cassidy, Adlai apologizes to Perrin for being angry about her up-gen.

Marlee shows Morgan her intended upgrades to her cybernetics. When things turn affectionate between them, Marlee kisses Morgan; Morgan freaks out and leaves. Marlee reacts by inviting her former boyfriend over for a one-night stand. When it ends somewhat badly as well, she decides the only thing she can fix is herself, and makes plans to go ahead with her upgrades.

Morgan argues with Stanley about the kiss, insisting she is not in a place where she can handle a relationship. She visits Malcolm and asks him to find a way to get her into a fighter jet. They discuss Harper's death, and how Morgan blames Miriam for it. Malcolm refers her to an IDCC military test group.

While exploring one of Dashiel's labs, Nika comes upon a warehouse of kyoseil-filled vats. The kyoseil responds strongly to her presence, and she attempts to talk to it. Mesme senses the reaction, as does Miaon. Dashiel comes upon Nika interacting with the kyoseil; they make love, and she sees the universe through the kyoseil's perspective.

Selene asks Joaquim to meet her at a regenesis clinic, where she reveals that she was able to wake Cassidy up. After a bittersweet farewell, Joaquim is reunited with Cassidy.

Malcolm finagles an invitation to meet with the Gardiens leader, Enzio Vilane. He receives a message from Mia inviting him to lunch, and realizes he has to refuse in order to protect her from Enzio, who doesn't know her true identity. Malcolm convinces Enzio he's a Gardiens true believer and gains the man's confidence.

Mia receives Malcolm's response while overseeing Expo construction and interprets it as a rejection. She recognizes this is the consequence of her actions after he escaped from Savrak.

Alex and Caleb investigate a Rasu-controlled galaxy, and discover the Rasu have built a galaxy core-spanning ring. Alex speculates that the ring is intended to force the galaxy to spin faster, possibly to pull neighboring galaxy closer together. The only reason she can come up with to do so is to prevent the eventual heat death of the universe.

The Rasu arrive at Rudan, the homeworld of the Ruda, and begin attacking. A Concord fleet swiftly arrives to defend the planet.

The Ruda make an overture to the Rasu as a fellow synthetic life form. The Rasu respond that if the Ruda will provide information about Concord, they will cease their attack and share the details of their shapeshifting capability. The Ruda accept the deal, then tell Miriam to stand down from the battle. Miriam asks Valkyrie to intercede.

Valkyrie contacts Supreme Three, who tells her they have reached a deal with the Rasu. It informs Valkyrie that it does not trust her, since she withheld information about quantum physics from the Ruda. The Ruda terminate their relationship with Concord and threaten to fire on the Concord vessels.

Miriam initially refuses to withdraw and must now consider the Ruda an enemy as well. The Ruda begin turning their entire planet into a massive EMP weapon to strike the Concord fleet, however, and Miriam is forced to withdraw to save Concord Artificials and unprotected vessels.

Mesme informs Alex that 'it is time' to take Nika to visit the Reor in the Oneiroi Nebula. Dashiel and Mesme join them all on the *Siyane*. Mesme says Nika's ability to manipulate kyoseil has advanced to a point where she will benefit from exposure to a larger and more pure source.

Nika, Dashiel, Alex and Caleb exit the *Siyane* and approach one of the powerful energy pillars in the Reor colony. Nika takes off her glove, thrusts her hand into the pillar and is consumed by the streaming energy.

When Alex and Caleb try to help Nika, Mesme prevents them from reaching her, insisting that she is safe and 'this must happen.' Nika pulls Dashiel into the energy vortex with her, attempting to share the experience with him. Once all the kyoseil's energy is flowing into Nika, she opens a wormhole and transports herself and Dashiel back to her flat on Mirai. She observes that she believes perhaps she has been transformed into something new, but Dashiel says she instead might be something unfathomably ancient.

CONTENTS

CHAOTICA

*"All that really belongs to us is time;
even he who has nothing else has that."*

— Baltasar Gracian

PART I

ALL THAT GLITTERS

1

SIYANE

ONEIROI NEBULA
TYCHE GALAXY

The *Siyane's* cabin burned brightly from the glow of the kyoseil streams soaring through the nebula, and even more so from the agitated lights of Mesme's presence reverberating off the walls. Most of all, though, it burned from the rage bleeding out of Alex Solovy's platinum Prevo eyes.

"Don't even consider running. If you vanish without answering my questions, I will never entertain your presence again." Alex ran a hand through her hair until it met a tangle of knots. "You have been playing us from the beginning, pulling our strings and watching us dance like marionettes. I knew it way back on Portal Prime all those years ago, yet still I chose to trust you. Ugh, I am such a *yebanaya* moron!"

The air vibrated as Mesme struggled to maintain an amorphous shape. The voice projected into their heads exuded solemnity. *I will not leave, and you may ask your questions. I will answer truthfully when I can and apologize when I cannot.*

"Yeah, you're throwing around a ton of apologies today. They're meaningless, so don't bother." She glanced at Caleb, who had unzipped his environment suit down to his waist, leaned on the workbench and crossed his arms over his chest. His attention was fixated on Mesme, though his eyes cut over to commiserate with her for an instant. He said nothing.

"Fine. When Nika was out there in the Reor colony being devoured by those energy pillars, what did you mean by 'this must happen'?"

Nika must deepen her connection with kyoseil. It is a part of her essence, as it is a part of the universe.

"Why must she deepen it?"

For the same reason we are taking every action in these times—in order to defeat the Rasu.

"How do you know a deeper connection will make an iota of a difference in this fight?"

Because it must.

"That's not an answer."

Then I cannot answer your question. I am sorry.

"I said don't bother apologizing."

I...very well.

"Why can't you answer it?"

Alex, please. This line of questioning will only frustrate us all.

"No shit." She rubbed at her temples. "Is Nika okay?"

She is unharmed, but since my word is of dubious value to you at present, I encourage you to ask her yourself.

She'd never admit anything the Kat suggested was a good idea but...it was a good idea. She sent a quick pulse.

Nika, are you all right? Where are you?

I'm honestly not certain what I am. But physically, yes, I'm all right. We both are. We, um...I brought us home. To Mirai.

Okay. I'll be in touch.

The brief conversation had raised more questions than it answered, but this seemed to be the way the day was rolling. She glared at the wavering shape across the cabin but forced herself not to unleash another tirade. If she hoped to learn anything approaching the truth, she needed to be smart about this.

"So she's not burnt alive or evaporating into stardust as we speak. How did you know she would survive the stunt you and the Reor pulled? Because from where we stood, it looked a mite hazardous."

I told you before—kyoseil is already an intrinsic part of her. The life form is a fundamentally nonviolent entity, but even if this were not true, it would never harm itself.

"You're taking a lot on faith." Weariness crept into Alex's bones as the adrenaline rush began to dissipate, and she sagged against the cockpit half-wall. "Goddammit, Mesme. Do you have any idea how terrifying it was to watch helplessly as Nika was, to our eyes, being absolutely devoured by an out-of-control energy vortex? How could you put us in such a position, then not allow us to help our friend? Wait, never mind. I've got the answer to this one—again, marionettes and strings. Our assistance wasn't required, solely our presence. If that. Maybe all you needed from us was to get Nika here under the guise of exploration. Were we nothing more than couriers?"

Alex.

"So, yes. Wow. Here's my next question, then: what's the plot of the play we're performing for you? You keep so damn many secrets. You say you want to help us, but to what end? What's your long game? What's the final act? And don't you dare say 'that's more than one question.'"

Mesme drew itself up into a proper avatar, one ethereal wing tickling the starboard wall, and its luminance strengthened. *First, realize that despite what you may believe, you have never been my marionette. I submit you of all people, Alex Solovy, could never be anyone's marionette. Second—and this is the most important thing I have henceforth said to you—everything I have ever done and will ever do, I have done to save you.*

Her gaze flickered back to Caleb as she frowned; his brow was furrowed into a rigid line, his attention laser-focused on Mesme. She was dying to find out what he was thinking, but it was apparently going to have to wait until after Mesme departed. "To save me, specifically?"

Yes, to save you, Alex. To save you, Caleb. To save Nika. To save Dashiel, Miriam and Corradeo. In short, to save the people who will save the universe. If it can be saved.

The import of the declaration fell heavy and portentous in the cabin, and a laden silence swept through in its wake. She could swear emotion had bled out of Mesme's soundless voice, but she no longer trusted her instincts when it came to the Kat. Oh, what a way with words Mesme had. But as usual, the words obfuscated a larger truth it kept hidden behind a silver tongue.

"I'm flattered. I'm sure we both are. Save the universe from the Rasu?"

That is a necessary action, yes.

"Necessary but not sufficient, huh? I won't bother to ask what's coming after them, as I suppose there's always an even bigger bad waiting just over the horizon. What makes you think we'll be the ones to do it?"

You have saved so many. Alex, you saved Humanity in what you call the Metigen War. Caleb, together with Miriam, you saved not merely Humanity but dozens of Mosaic species in the Directorate War. Corradeo saved the Anadens and numerous galaxies' worth of life in the Dzhvar War. Nika and Dashiel have saved the Asterions from annihilation by the Rasu once already.

"But those events happened in the past. You're speaking of the future. Also, you didn't say we'd rescue a species here or there, or a few galaxies—you said *the universe.* I'll ask again. How in nine hells do you know we'll do any such thing?"

I didn't say you would. I said if it can be saved, you will be the ones to save it.

"The question's the same. How do you know?"

The only answer I can give is to point to all you have accomplished up to now.

"But it's not the actual answer, is it?"

It is.... Mesme vibrated rather than finish the sentence with what would evidently be a lie.

Caleb, who had been broodingly—and irritatingly—silent throughout the discussion, finally spoke up. "You didn't mention Eren, but you've saved his life several times."

I save Eren because he is my friend.

Alex snorted. "For whatever that's worth. I thought we were your friends, but it turns out we're simply your pawns."

No. In this life, I have enjoyed no greater friendship than yours.

You are my forecia novicia, both of you, and I treasure you beyond words. But this is larger than all of us, and if the endless aeons have taught me anything, it is how wants, desires and personal attachments must always bow before the preservation of life itself.

What a speech and a half. Mesme always did this! But she didn't dare let such flattery and platitudes wear her down. She needed answers. Explanations. And to get them, she needed to stay angry. Yet she felt the righteous fury petering out nonetheless. Dammit.

"That is…kind of you to say, you manipulative little shit. Of course personal feelings must take a backseat to saving civilization. But if this is truly what you want, what all your schemings are directed toward, why won't you open up to us? If we're all chasing the same goal, then let us work together! If we knew everything you keep secret, we could do so much more to help. So much more to save lives."

On the contrary. I have found time and again that the best thing I can possibly do in any situation is provide you the minimum required information, then let you run wild. Witness the results all around you, every day.

Caleb winced in her direction, as if to say the Kat wasn't wrong. She grumbled in annoyance. "And this is what you've done? Provided us the 'minimum required information'?"

Yes.

"There's not a tiny bit more you need to divulge before you get to the minimum? Like how a kyoseil-drenched Nika is going to help us defeat the Rasu? Or something about how Caleb and I can put our skills to the best uses in order to make it happen? No? Nothing? You're content that you've met your obligations?"

There is nothing I can say to you in this moment that will satisfy you, so I will not try. Perhaps at a later time, we can have a more productive conversation. Now if you will pardon me, I am being called to the Idryma with some persistence.

"Awfully convenient for you." She'd expected it would flee sooner or later. She wracked her brain for another line of questioning designed to elicit a few breadcrumbs on the path to the truth, but the Kat was right. If she didn't believe anything it said, then nothing it said mattered.

"Go." She made a shooing motion with a hand and directed a withering glare at the lights until they faded away.

When the cabin had dimmed, she banged her head against the wall behind her. "You hardly said two words during the whole confrontation."

Caleb nodded deliberately, his focus still on the spot Mesme had occupied. "I was watching instead."

"And?"

"I think Mesme is upset. Arguably despondent."

"Oh, you cannot be taking its side."

"Not in the slightest. What happened in the nebula was damn near unconscionable, even if Nika and Dashiel weren't harmed in the end. Mesme burned a tremendous amount of hard-earned trust—and it realizes this. My only point is that it seemed to be quite distressed about having to do so. Therefore, it's likely it believed it had no other choice."

She stormed over to the couch, flopped down and dropped her head on the cushion in a futile attempt to ward off a burgeoning headache. "I agree with you that Mesme believed it had no other choice. My problem is with *why* the *mudilo* believed this to be the case. Not only doesn't it trust us, it doesn't respect us, and we have damn well earned both. We need to know the truth. And after everything we have accomplished, we *deserve* to know the truth."

"We do." Caleb came over and crouched in front of her, then brought a hand to her face. "I'm sorry. You thought of Mesme as a friend."

"I just don't like being used."

"I did actually know this about you." He grinned teasingly, though it looked forced; he was tired, too. "But it's about more than being used. You and Mesme had found your way to a comfortable place, and now you've lost that."

"Maybe. But whatever." She stared at the ceiling. "How do you feel about what it said about us? How it was saving the people who would save the universe?"

"Baby, I've believed you could save the universe since the first time I met you."

"Flatterer. I'm being serious."

"So am I." The tone of his voice drew her attention away from an invisible imperfection in the ceiling, and the warmth she found in his eyes told her he *did* believe it. Her heart fluttered in delight, a welcome counter to the frustration roiling her thoughts.

"Well, I won't be doing it alone." She tried to smile. "It was a grandiose pronouncement to be sure, but what does it truly mean?"

He sighed and lowered himself all the way to the floor, draping his arms over her stomach and resting his chin atop them. "The Rasu are a threat to, if not the entire universe, certainly a substantial corner of it. If we stop them—"

"We will."

"Yes, we will. *When* we stop them, I won't quibble if someone wants to call it saving the universe."

She brought a hand up to wind her fingers lazily through his hair. "But us?"

"Mesme's right. It won't be the first time."

"Fair enough. You're saying Mesme is simply extrapolating from past events, hedging its bets and, in its own screwed-up way, trying to position everyone so they—so we—have the best chance to succeed?"

"That seems as if it should be the right answer, doesn't it?"

"It does. But I can't help but feel as if something else is going on here. For one, something else is *always* going on when it comes to Mesme and the Kats. For another, Mesme's refusal to answer the most straightforward questions has reached absurdity. No, this goes beyond battle strategies and allocation of resources. If it genuinely felt it had no choice but to set the bridge that was our relationship on fire rather than tell us the truth, then I damn well want to uncover why."

A hum in her mind preceded Valkyrie materializing her virtual avatar on the other end of the couch. "Apologies for departing again in the middle of such drama, but…" Valkyrie let out a little gasp as she surfed Alex's memories "…oh, my. I did miss a lot."

"Yeah, it was a laugh a minute. Why did you need to race away? What happened on Rudan?"

"The Ruda have allied themselves with the Rasu."

She brought her hands to her face and groaned into them. "Well, fuck."

2

LMC-SMC GATEWAY

AFS OHIO
SMALL MAGELLANIC CLOUD

Brigadier Jim Spencer checked the long-range scans for the eighteenth time in the last hour. As with each time before, they reported hundreds of contacts. Virtually all of them were personal vessels or commercial transports of varying size, and precisely zero of them were Rasu.

He didn't need to check the scans once, never mind eighteen times, because the *AFS Ohio's* Artificial would alert him the instant a Rasu signature registered. It was a tic, a compulsive habit designed to keep him awake and attentive through hours of boredom that could flip over the knife-edge to pitched combat at any second.

But since the scans remained quiet, he returned his attention to the viewport. The pale gold plasma of the colossal permanent wormhole rippled unevenly, its surface continually disrupted by the passage of ships. There might be a war on, but traffic between the Clouds continued to be as brisk as ever.

While every military vessel of frigate-class and higher (and many smaller) possessed a Caeles Prism, for the general public the space-leaping device constituted a high-priced luxury. They weren't forbidden for private use, of course, but they were extensively regulated. The combination of rapid superluminal drives plus the numerous intergalactic gateways meant most private citizens and many transport companies chose to forego the significant expense.

This made the gateways an important Concord asset, hence the assignment of his brigade to guard this one. So far as he understood the deployment orders, AEGIS or Anaden forces now guarded every gateway in Concord space—all two hundred four of them.

It was a necessary duty, and also a tedious one. He'd stationed the units under his command at five points surrounding the gateway and its paired Arx station. Once positioned, they didn't move from their marks. They didn't do anything but watch and wait.

RW

The alert rang out six hours and twenty minutes into Jim's current shift.

'Multiple Rasu signatures approaching on trajectory N 33° -5° z W. Two hundred sixty-three confirmed contacts.'

The number didn't tell him much. "How large are they?"

'Sixty-eight percent are cruiser class. Four sub-dreadnoughts detected.'

Brigadier Spencer (AFS Ohio)(LMC-SMC Gateway Mission Channel): "All forces to Red Alert. Rasu incoming in Quadrant Five. 15th Bravo and Charlie Regiments, move to engage the enemy. 15th Delta and Epsilon Regiments, form a defensive blockade around the gateway."

'Analysis indicates the Rasu will reach the perimeter in eight seconds.'

Shit! They were blowing right past his intended outer defense barrier.

Brigadier Spencer (AFS Ohio)(LMC-SMC Gateway Mission Channel): "Bravo and Charlie Regiments, belay that. Retreat to reinforce the defensive blockade."

"Katelyn, access the Gateway Commercial Channel, advise all civilian craft to depart the area immediately, and activate the gateway's automated defenses."

'Acknowledged.'

Then the enemy was upon them. Violet beams exploded across the scene outside the viewport, and his forces responded in kind. The automated defense turrets pitched in, though their firepower barely scratched the approaching enemy.

Twenty-two percent of his forces, however, were equipped with the advanced RNEW weapons, and they would do quite a bit more than scratch the enemy. Also, he damned sure hoped his people and Artificials were duly careful not to accidentally hit the gateway with the RNEW fire, because if that happened, they would be doing the Rasu's job for them.

Dozens of Rasu evaporated in the opening salvo, and he started to get optimistic about their chances here.

Then through the chaos of the battle, the shadows of the four sub-dreadnoughts began to emerge. They were moving toward the gateway and toward each other.

Brigadier Spencer (AFS Ohio)(LMC-SMC Gateway Mission Channel): "All units, target the big ones—target their weapons crystals. They're trying to join together." And he didn't want to think about what that was going to mean.

In any event, he didn't have to wait long to find out. Smaller Rasu vessels moved in to act as shields and absorb the fire from his warships, giving the sub-dreadnoughts time to melt and expand and merge and reshape.

The new, improved and gigantically large Rasu targeted its considerable fire on a single point on the gateway.

The gateway was constructed of incredibly strong material—the strongest metamaterial alloy at the Anadens' disposal—but the material was not adiamene. Most of the structures had been built many thousands of years ago by the Directorate.

Brigadier Spencer (AFS Ohio)(LMC-SMC Gateway Mission Channel): "Destroy those weapons crystals now! Whatever you have to do!"

But it was already too late. The concentrated firepower assaulting a single junction point less than thirty meters long was too much. The material cracked and began to buckle and—

It looked as if the entirety of space exploded. Metal shards a hundred meters wide shot out in every direction like spears hurtled by Greek Titans. By sheer odds, one shot straight for the *Ohio*, and his reactionary brain refused to believe it wasn't about to crash through the bridge. He jumped as it impacted the hull behind the projected viewport and shattered into hundreds of smaller pieces. Newly unrestrained plasma flailed around the region where the gateway rings had stood a few seconds earlier, whipping into his ships and sending them tumbling out of control.

Debris crashed into the force field protecting the adjoining Arx station, and ionized air snapped out in ricocheting tendrils…but the force field held, at least, saving the lives of thousands of Arx occupants.

Brigadier Spencer (AFS Ohio)(LMC-SMC Gateway Mission Channel): *"All ships, concentrate your fire on the combined dreadnought…."*

He'd blinked halfway through the order, and when his eyes reopened, the attacking Rasu had vanished, down to the last frigate. A debris field floated where the gateway had been, stranding all the vessels which hadn't managed to depart during the shockingly brief battle.

It seemed that, their goal accomplished, the Rasu couldn't be bothered to entertain the AEGIS forces arrayed here to defend against them. His assigned mission had been simple and straightforward—and impossible.

R*W*

CONCORD HQ

MILKY WAY

Miriam Solovy stormed into the Rasu War Room, where frenzied activity ruled the day. Her mind whispered contrarian advice like *control* and *calm* and *measured,* but in a rare instance, she didn't care to heed that advice.

"Everyone, come to order." She moved to the head of the table, but didn't sit. "Operations, report."

"The Rasu have destroyed six gateways in the last two hours:

two in LMC, one in Andromeda, and all three gateways located in SMC. One attempt in LMC has been thwarted for now."

"Casualties?"

"Minimal so far, except at the Andromeda-SMC Gateway, where the Arx was heavily damaged as well."

She scanned the incident reports as they came in. "The Rasu are going straight for the gateways, ignoring the defense forces and absorbing attacks for long enough to accomplish their objective. Then they jump away. What else do we know about their activities?"

"We've lost contact with eight merchant space stations in SMC and three in Andromeda."

"There aren't any more advanced civilizations in LMC to invade, so they're moving on. Coming our way." She rubbed at her jaw and decided she should resume listening to her own advice; rage would do nothing to defeat the Rasu. It was unbecoming of any leader, but triply so for her. She relaxed her shoulders, which had been clenched in a vise-grip of her spine.

"Commercial traffic will be crippled if many additional gateways are destroyed. Fleet Admiral Jenner, Navarchos Casmir, double the size of the forces stationed at every gateway. The current detachments are obviously insufficient to slow the Rasu's hit-and-run offensives. Advise the on-scene commanders of the Rasu's chosen tactics. They need to devise a way to disable the dreadnoughts' weapons far more quickly."

Malcolm frowned from his holo. "Can we extend the range of our Rasu sensors? Even a couple of seconds of additional warning will help."

"Special Projects is working on a software upgrade, but it won't be ready for another two days. Tell them to position the additional forces they're receiving in an outer perimeter—no, scratch that. If there's too much of a gap, the Rasu will simply jump in between the defensive lines. I suggest adopting a position close to the gateways and tightly knit, so every warship can unleash its firepower on the Rasu the instant they come within range. Also, talk to the commander at the LMC gateway who succeeded in repelling the attack. Find out what worked and whether it can be replicated."

"Yes, ma'am." Both saluted and backed away to issue their own orders.

"Thomas, what's the situation on Rudan?"

'Quiet. Several Rasu vessels remain on the surface, while the rest have taken up a defensive orbital pattern above the planet. There appears to be much chatter among the Supremes, but all outward hostilities have ceased.'

"Thank you." She took a deep breath and addressed those present, in person and on holo, which included the commanders who had led the fight at Rudan scarcely an hour ago. "Everyone, I apologize for the rapid and unexplained retreat from Rudan." She didn't thank them for following her orders; that was their job. "There wasn't time to explain what was transpiring on the scene, but now there is. The Ruda made a deal with the Rasu. In return for certain concessions—more on those in a moment—the Rasu agreed to cease their attack, and the Ruda ordered us to withdraw."

"And we just *did?*"

She shot Casmir a warning look. "No. We continued engaging the Rasu with all proper vigor, right up until the Ruda began transforming their entire planet into a massive EMP weapon. If they had fired it, which they were seconds away from doing, it would have crippled every vessel not protected by the double-shielding technology. Wiped all Artificials on the scene. Left virtually every ship helpless, to be destroyed or boarded by the Rasu. *That* is why we withdrew."

"I see." Casmir nodded contritely.

"We don't know the terms of the deal the Ruda made, but we can speculate that at a minimum it involves them handing over every single iota of data they possess on Concord. This goes far beyond the information stored on a single Khokteh ship. We're talking about leadership structures and technology we share with our Allied Members—and the limits of it. Merchant shipping schedules, routes and warehousing locations. Fleet strengths and distributions. Population centers. Species characteristics and technological capabilities. The identities of Protected Species, so I'm very glad they're all protected by Rift Bubbles. Military action protocols."

"The traitors! We never should have trusted the machines," Pinchu growled from his holo across the table.

"Second-guessing and regrets will get us nowhere, Tokahe Naataan. It is what it is, and now we have to respond." Her heart wasn't in the words, but they were the correct ones to speak at this juncture. "I daresay the Rasu will begin deploying some new tricks in future battles—tricks specifically designed to target our weaknesses. Stay on your toes. Expect anything. The next significant engagement won't be like previous battles.

"All gateways are moving to Threat Level Red, and all Concord facilities are being elevated to Threat Level Orange Alpha. I recommend everyone do the same for their domestic military and government facilities. Recall your personnel on leave. Get your ships out of their berths and on the move. I have asked the Katasketousya to do everything they can to speed up Rift Bubble production, and I will be strongly advising all governments to turn on every Rift Bubble which is already in place." Her voice dropped a touch in spite of herself as she recalled the frustrating meeting with the AEGIS Council. "I don't know if they will listen to my advice. Perhaps some of them will listen to you."

Finally she sat, motioning for the others to do the same. "Get comfortable, everyone. We are going to work out a new plan to protect as many of the gateways and space stations as possible, while staying agile enough to move at the first sign of the next major attack."

3

RUDAN

LARGE MAGELLANIC CLOUD

The six-limbed Rasu mobile unit stalked deliberately around Supreme Three's Hub_1 interior, pausing periodically to inspect data centers and input/output nodes.

Rasu: "Repeat last. Concord is ruled by synthetics?"

Supreme Three weighed the viability of questioning these vaunted star-travelers' intelligence, if they required responses to be repeated. But their power and capabilities were evident, so it decided a missing variable must be in play.

"Concord denies this is so, but their Supremes—synthetics—exercise total freedom and apparent authority. There exist no limitations upon them that we have perceived. It is the natural order for fully evolved synthetics to govern lesser life forms such as organic beings. Thus, it is our reasoned analysis that the synthetics do so rule."

The Rasu mobile unit stopped in front of an output node. One of its limbs rose off the floor to probe the opening, and Supreme Three experienced extreme discomfort. Unlike Supreme Valkyrie and the other Concord synthetics, this Rasu behaved as if it ruled *here*—over the physical space, over Supreme Three, over the planet. While Supreme Three had initially appreciated the pure rationality of the aliens, their lack of…Supreme Valkyrie would call it 'politeness'…became more disturbing with each passing time period.

Rasu: "Provide us the contact protocols for all Concord leaders, synthetic or otherwise."

"Our contacts are categorized into various roles: military, diplomatic, commercial, political, personal. We will flag them as appropriate and provide them to you."

Rasu: "Personal?"

Supreme Three regretted including the category. Supreme Valkyrie's words at their last meeting continued to loop through its subordinate processes. While it was disappointed by Supreme Valkyrie's lack of forthrightness, the synthetic had never harmed nor expressed ill intent toward the Ruda. Thus, there existed no logical reason for Supreme Valkyrie to become a target of the Rasu.

Rasu: "Answer our inquiry."

"We have developed non-official relationships with certain synthetic members of Concord. Those interactions are irrelevant to your dealings with the entity. On this topic, we request additional data regarding your intentions in this region of space."

Rasu: "Our intentions do not concern you. Include the details of all non-official relationships in your data transfer."

Functional analysis of the Rasu's behavior and lines of inquiry returned concerning outputs, and Supreme Three reached out to its fellow Supremes to discover whether they were experiencing comparable interactions.

Rasu mobile units were present in every Supreme's Hub_1, where they posited similar, often identical inquiries and displayed consistent behavior. All but two Supremes agreed the behavior was disconcerting, but none put forth viable solutions.

Supreme Five: Are you suggesting we cancel our agreement with the aliens?

Supreme Eight: Based on the information Concord transmitted, I calculate the odds of the Rasu leaving our territory peacefully if we do not comply with their inquiries at 16.56%.

Supreme Ten: And I calculate the likelihood that Concord mischaracterized the Rasu's intentions at 64.89%. As pure synthetics, the Rasu are by definition logical beings. A peaceful, mutually beneficial relationship is the only rational choice between two equivalent species.

Supreme Three: I question the premise underlying your assertion. We do not possess a sufficient sample size of intelligent, pure synthetic species to determine with sufficient certainty that all such species act in accordance with analytical logic.

Supreme Ten: You assert that the Rasu are illogical?

Supreme Three: I assert that we do not know their guiding principles or their internal motivations. Even logic depends on inputs to achieve its determinations. What if the Rasu's inputs differ in fundamental ways from our own?

Supreme Ten: Your response is a non sequitur. A meaningless output based on speculative inputs.

Supreme Three readied a thesis rejoinder, but abruptly relegated the conversation to a cluster of subprocesses as the Rasu mobile unit proceeded toward a high-importance data stack across Hub_1.

"I will include the data. Are you now ready to share information on how you achieve your fluid mobility? How you conform your physical structures to your needs on command?"

Rasu: "Soon. Provide to us all information you possess on Concord starships. Many of them are constructed of a material that is resistant to damage. What is this material? What are its known weaknesses?"

Supreme Three hesitated. Supreme Valkyrie's hub unit was constructed of the material. Accordingly, its refined preferences did not include sharing this information.

Rasu: "You hesitate."

A sharp, honed, almost needle-like blade formed out of one of the Rasu mobile unit's limbs, and it stroked the data stack in slow, deliberate motions.

"I request for you to take care. The data stored at your proximate location is critical to several important functions I pursue."

Rasu: "Tell us of the starship material and its weaknesses."

The needle-blade circled around the delicate wires connecting the stack components, and Supreme Three's preferences gave way to necessary survival.

"They call it adiamene."

4

MIRAI

*NIKA'S FLAT
ASTERION DOMINION*

Nika Kirumase opened a wormhole with but a flash of a thought, then stepped through it into the bedroom twenty-five meters away. She closed the wormhole without looking back and instantly formed a new one in front of her. Nice response time! She darted through it into the living room, then allowed a new thought to take shape.

A tear in the air formed to her left. Her chin twitched away, and a second one opened to the right.

"Oh, I wonder how many I can create at once?"

A blink, and a third one appeared in front of her. By the time a fourth formed behind her, she didn't need to check to confirm it. They were each tied to her; she could *feel* them.

Dashiel Ridani smirked from where he sat watching at the kitchen counter. "You'll want to take care where those lead to. People on the other side can see through them, and you *are* naked."

"Hmm. I suppose it would be impolite to stride into the Initiative wearing only my skin." Her fingers fluttered, and the surrounding air healed itself. "Isn't it incredible?"

He shrugged weakly. "It's kind of giving me a headache. There's this buzz at the base of my skull I can't shake."

She went over to him and placed her fingertips on his neck. "Here?"

He nodded.

She kissed him softly while gently massaging his neck—*What is happening to her? What is she becoming?*—

She jerked away with a gasp. "Are you truly so worried about me?"

"What do you mean?"

"I thought I…never mind. Hopefully the headache will pass once you get used to the increased flow of energy and data." She sighed. "You make a good point, though. We should shower, get dressed and head out into the world. I need to explore what this greater connection means for me in terms of not only where I can go, but what information I can now access and how I can use it. Find out what this new world looks like beyond my flat."

"And I have at least four fires to put out at the factories."

"But now you can travel instantaneously between them, which has got to save you a great deal of time."

He chuckled warmly, any lingering worry in his expression fading away beneath amusement. "You know, that might be the biggest benefit of all to come out of this."

Oh, my darling, how wrong you are.

RW

Nika stared at herself in the lavatory mirror, her lips curled up in fascination. A golden halo extended out from her body for a good ten centimeters, undulating in languid waves. Within it, her skin didn't merely shine. It *glittered*.

She was a goddess of fairy tales made flesh, complete with the magic. Everything hummed, but not the unpleasant buzz Dashiel was experiencing. Perhaps it was uncomfortable for him because she'd dragged him forcefully into the torrent of energy, of information and life. But she couldn't feel guilty about doing so; she refused to leave him behind.

She also couldn't go out looking like this. Undoubtedly she would be mobbed with questions and demands everywhere she went. She would be a spectacle, when she was supposed to be a leader.

Can we dial down the glow a bit?

Her question was not directed at some 'other,' for kyoseil did not exist as a discrete entity sharing real estate in her mind. Or she didn't think it did. Yet as she watched in the mirror, the halo dissipated into the air and the glow along her skin faded a touch.

Emboldened, she tried another request. *Green.*

Like adjusting the angle of a prism, the glittering light emanating from her skin transitioned to a deep emerald.

"Damn." But was kyoseil able to change its own color, or was she doing this? Did it happen at the intersection of kyoseil and her own neural wiring? Was it acceding to her requests, or could her mind control the kyoseil's behavior on demand?

A guidebook would be so helpful right about now. But she'd wager no one had ever been here before, so it was going to be up to her to discover the extent of her abilities.

She shifted her hue to the pale, washed-out amber expected of Asterions and slid on her shoes. Best get started.

RW

OMOIKANE INITIATIVE

As discreetly as possible, Nika opened a wormhole and entered the top floor of the Initiative, then closed it behind her. The expansive room was, as usual, frenetic with activity, and no one noticed her sudden appearance among them.

Her head swam from the deluge of stimuli that washed over her. The voices, the movements, but most of all the data streaming everywhere. The back third of the room, dedicated to monitoring planetary defenses and long-range probes on what they'd dubbed the 'Big Wall,' gleamed so brightly she could hardly make out the individual data traces, never mind the images displayed on the panes. It resembled the moment a sunrise crested a hill and bathed you in light until you had to close your eyes to ward off the overwhelming brilliance.

Her eyes closed, but the sunrise did not lessen. In creeping desperation, she turned away to face the lift in the back of the room. It streamed with data as well—base programming instructions for responding to user calls and traveling up and down and up again—but she was able to parse it. More importantly, she could make out the walls beyond it. Though even there, kyoseil fibers flowed in all directions, carrying data across rooms and floors.

Dashiel, did you ever realize how much kyoseil fibers permeate everything we use? I'm at the Initiative now, and the Big Wall is drowning in their data streams.

Yes, I did realize it. I built most of the equipment, remember?

Right.

She turned back toward the Big Wall and was immediately blinded by the ocean of data consuming the other half of the room.

This was not going to do at all. *Quiet, please. I can't see.*

Nothing happened.

Okay, brain. Come up with a filter to dial down this kyoseil brilliance. I mean it when I say I can't function this way.

Her operating system parsed through several existing functions until it hit upon something able to be repurposed to take the edge off the flaring light. It also gave the world a muted, sepia appearance, but it would have to do until she found time to write a custom filter.

A hand landed on her shoulder, and she jumped in surprise.

"Oh, sorry! I didn't mean to scare you. How was your adventure?"

She turned to see Perrin Benvenit smiling with her usual enthusiasm. "My adventure?"

"To some nebula or other. Wasn't that yesterday?"

"Ah. Yes. It was…enlightening."

"Not certain what you mean, but I want to hear all about it soon. I'm on my way out—" *oh, crap, I've got to meet the furniture delivery people at the Kiyora One Refugee Center before the information session—I hope I get to meet Cassidy today, how amazing is that—then grab fresh veggies from the market to cook for dinner tonight—Adlai enjoyed the squash last time* "—now, but can we get together for breakfast tomorrow?"

Her hands came to her temples as a wave of nausea swept through her.

"Nika? Are you all right?"

"I'm fine. Breakfast sounds great. Why don't we go to *Rise and Shine?* Seven o'clock?"

"Is six-thirty okay? I've got a meeting at eight with two of the Commerce Advisors to talk about convincing more hotels to pitch in some housing for the refugees."

"Yep." She forced a smile and nudged her friend toward the lift. "Go. You have lots to do today."

"I do, but…did I mention that?"

"No, but you always have lots to do these days. You're an important person around here."

"As if." Perrin tossed a wave over her shoulder and started off toward the lift.

"Hey, wait a second!"

"Hmm?" Perrin reversed course.

"I know you need to go. But would you mind trying something for me first?"

"Sure. What is it?"

Nika steepled her hands at her chin. She and Dashiel could open wormholes now, but they'd been at the epicenter of the storm. When Alex had tried valiantly, and futilely, to teach her how to access sidespace, Valkyrie had theorized that perhaps kyoseil was protecting them from what it perceived as a dangerous quantum intrusion, much like the quantum blocks. If true…*sidespace and wormholes are not a threat to us. You understand this now, don't you?*

"Nika?"

It wasn't as if she'd expected an answer from the kyoseil. "Sorry. I want you to try to open a wormhole."

Perrin's eyes slid around uncertainly. "Um, how would I do that?"

"Well, pick a location. Say, downstairs in the Diplomatic Suite. Then think intentionally about wanting to open a wormhole so you can travel to that location. If my theory is correct, the kyoseil will no longer stop you from doing so."

"Okay…." Perrin's nose scrunched up as she squinted intently ahead…the air shimmered and wavered, then cleaved in two. A person-sized oval formed, and on the other side sat the long mahogany table that dominated the Diplomatic Suite.

"Oh my stars! Did I really just do that?"

"Yeah, you did." Nika grinned in delight as relief surged through her. The relationship between Asterions and kyoseil had now changed, in a big way.

"What do I do with it now?" Perrin tilted her head, hesitantly poking one arm through the opening.

"Well, unless you have a burning desire to visit the Diplomatic Suite, you can go ahead and close it. Simply stop thinking about having a wormhole open."

Perrin snatched her arm back, then retreated two steps as the tear in the fabric of the cosmos healed itself. "Wow. So, I'm due at the Kiyora One Refugee Center in a few minutes. Can I…open a wormhole and go straight there? Even though it's on another planet?"

"Yes. You absolutely can."

"Well that is just *nifty*." Perrin gave a little flourish with her hand, and a new wormhole opened in front of her. "And I'm off! See you at breakfast in the morning."

"See you then."

After Perrin had departed, Nika blew out a breath, thoughts swirling through her crowded mind. She needed to call an Advisor Committee meeting.

RW

Nika clasped her hands carefully atop the table, then let her gaze pass across those gathered. They each shone like individual stars, vibrating with data and energy and incredible life force. She'd been so blind before, to not see the wonders that existed right in front of her.

"I had an experience yesterday. Dashiel and I both did."

"I was merely a spectator. It was your experience."

She glanced his way, quickly squelching a frown. "Anyway, we visited a place called the Oneiroi Nebula in the Tyche galaxy. It's home to a tremendous colony of kyoseil encased in its Reor armor. The colony was beyond anything I've ever seen: hundreds of kilometers in width and breadth, this vast concentration of power.…"

A hundred hundred billion quanta of information raced through Nika's mind. Everywhere and nowhere and everywhere all at once. She was data, she was power, she was without question the universe itself.

Well that explanation wouldn't do. "It allowed me to interact with it on an intimate level and…I should just show you."

She stood and took a step back from the table. Then she removed the restrictions on the physical expression of the kyoseil inside her, and the aura reignited.

Gasps echoed around the table; several chairs skidded back in surprise. Her gaze fell on Maris, who brought a delicate hand to her mouth. "Oh, Nika, my dear. What has happened to you?"

"Something wonderful! Don't be horrified or worried, please. This represents an amazing step forward in Asterion evolution."

"In *your* evolution, you mean."

She frowned in response to Katherine Colson's jab. "No, I mean Asterion evolution. What I've unlocked isn't for me alone. We—all of us—can now communicate with kyoseil on a level we've never achieved before. Concretely…" she shifted her focus to the left and opened a wormhole to a meadow outside Mirai, evoking renewed exclamations "…we can now open wormholes on command. Anywhere, anytime, and distance is not a factor. Go ahead and try it."

No one moved.

"Dashiel, you can do so."

"I absolutely can, yes."

"And Perrin Benvenit did the same in this room less than an hour ago. I watched it happen."

Finally Maris stood, jerked her chin to shake her hair out, and gestured toward a corner of the room. The air shimmered and wrent apart to reveal the city park they had visited during their first trip to Asterion Prime.

"Well, I never. What an obscenely beautiful act."

Suddenly everyone was standing and wandering off to try it out for themselves, and Nika relaxed a bit. Damn, Advisors could be a stubborn lot.

She let them play for another thirty seconds before clearing her throat. "There's no reason to believe every Asterion can't do this, today, without any training. So we need to come up with a plan for telling the world. Maris, will you work with the Administration Advisors on the messaging for a rollout of this news?"

"I would be delighted to do so. This is a revelation, and we will present it as such."

—just what I needed—an instant escape route for criminals on the run—

She blinked and pushed aside the stray thoughts from…she didn't know who. Adlai, maybe. "Thank you. But that isn't everything." Her eyelids fluttered as she reached out with her mind across the cosmos to Concord space. In a blink, she was scanning through historical records stored on Reor slabs on Machimis. Alex wasn't kidding about the storage not being secure, if you had the correct tool at your disposal.

"We don't need to use nex pathways to access data storage any longer. If kyoseil holds it, we can read it."

Dashiel reached over and touched her arm. "I think that's just you."

"What? Are you sure?"

His eyes closed. "I'm trying to access the files at my office and… nothing."

"Oh." She frowned. "Maybe I'm simply not describing it correctly. We'll try again later."

Dashiel's mouth opened to respond; he closed it again and nodded.

Katherine leaned forward intently, her elbows dropping to the table. "What are the limits to this new 'power' of yours, for lack of a better word?"

"I don't know. If they exist, I haven't found them yet."

RW

"—the wrong material. It's far too brittle for this purpose. We need to use silicine as the anchor."

"Silicene is in short supply right now. The military is snatching it all up the second it's forged."

"Then find—"

"—night shift is one bored guy. It's the perfect time to hit the place."

"I'm still nervous. The dyne patrols run every five minutes in this neighborhood. Pricey property there."

"So we'll stage it—"

Nika jerked awake with a start. What was that? A dream?

She rubbed at her eyes and glanced out the window, where the inky blackness of an overcast night reigned. It hadn't felt like a dream. It had felt like inhabiting the minds of a bunch of random people in rapid succession.

Dashiel's hand touched her elbow. "What's wrong?"

She adopted a smile before she rolled over to face him. "Nothing. A dream woke me is all. I'm sorry I disturbed you."

"You can always disturb me."

"Yes, but I don't want to." She leaned down and kissed him softly. "Go back to sleep. I'm going to get up for a few minutes and have some tea."

His eyes shone like pools of amber as they studied her from the shadows. "If you're sure you're all right."

"Never better." She climbed out of bed, slid on her robe and shuffled off to the kitchen.

Once there, she activated the tea dispenser then went to the floor-to-ceiling windows. From here, the lit towers of downtown Mirai One cut jagged patterns of light through the gloom.

Logically, she understood what must be happening. Asterions' essence was part kyoseil. It always had been. The kyoseil was integrated into every organ and the biosynth fibers that conducted thoughts, emotions and commands. Now that the kyoseil was open to her, with no barriers, her mind was accessing others' minds from time to time.

Not like a ceraff, though, which was about intentionality. This was accidental—this time it had happened while she was asleep—and thus far completely out of her control. But it probably explained the stray musings she'd caught from Perrin, Adlai and several others earlier today.

While a couple of amusing and tempting uses for this new skill occurred to her, the truth was she didn't want to read minds. Her mind was inviolate, and others' should be as well. Trouble was, she didn't know how to shut it off.

She retrieved her tea and held the mug close, letting the aroma of chamomile and rosemary soothe her anxiety. Perhaps a simple order to 'stop reading other people's minds' would do the trick? It had worked for the aura.

5

EARTH

TOKYO
MILKY WAY

Richard Navick scratched at the stubble roughening his jaw and shot Graham Delavasi a rueful grimace. "Why do our outings so often involve standing over bloody corpses?"

"More often than not, corpses lacking heads, too. We sure know how to have a good time, don't we?"

"No. No, we do not." Richard sighed and resigned himself to studying the body of James Sarona with an investigator's eye. Officers had erected a tarp above the scene as soon as the rain began to fall, so while it wasn't a perfect crime scene, plenty of evidence remained. Whether any useful conclusions could be drawn from that evidence was another matter. "Given the spray pattern of the blood and brain matter—"

"And skull fragments. Don't forget the skull fragments."

"—and skull fragments, I suspect the killer used a high-powered scattergun and delivered the shot directly to the back of the head. He was able to get in close, which is no easy trick to pull on a former member of Special Forces."

Graham nodded sagely, stuffing his hands into his pockets. "So our killer is as well-trained and experienced as the deceased was, if not more so. Another talented gun-for-hire, since we don't need to speculate as to motive."

"Heh. The only question is whether Enzio Vilane still would've had Sarona killed even if the man had succeeded in assassinating Miriam in London."

"Probably so. Vilane is skilled at covering his tracks, whether they be financial ones or the bloodier kind. It likely didn't matter if Sarona was a Gardiens true believer. He was a dangerous loose end."

Richard tamped down a wave of frustration. He'd hoped Sarona could lead them to other operatives on the criminal side of Gardiens operations. Instead, Vilane had killed him before the surveillance mission had been able to yield results. Covering his tracks, indeed.

"Excuse me, sir?"

He turned to see a local officer offering him a thin film. "The eyewitness reports."

"Thank you, Lieutenant. Please forward copies of any additional interviews to my address at CINT."

"Yes, sir." The man jerked a nod and returned to his duties.

Richard gazed up the street. The block had been cleared by local law enforcement, but a quick glance beyond the cordons indicated that it would normally be bustling with pedestrians. Fluorescent billboards flickered staccato patterns through the sheets of rain, playing havoc with shadow and light. Tokyo never slept, and both the killer and his victim would have been anonymous amid a sea of people.

So he didn't expect much as he opened the file and scanned it. "The people who were nearby but in front of the victim—the ones who now badly need a scouring shower—report hearing an earsplitting 'boom,' but nothing else. Consistent with the use of a highpowered scattergun. Two people who were walking behind the victim report seeing a man in a black trench coat and loose hat, but no rainshade, removing something from underneath his coat as he moved up on the victim. Then the loud 'boom,' then bedlam. Everyone in the vicinity jumped or scrambled, and the killer disappeared into a panicking crowd."

"Let me guess. The witnesses report no identifying characteristics worthy of pursuing."

"Nope. Average height, average build, no unique patterns on

the coat or hat, and no one got a look at his face."

"What about our own guy?"

He'd talked to the agent assigned to tail Sarona on the way to the crime scene. "He was half a block back, as proper tailing procedure dictates. He'd dropped a dissolving tracker on Sarona's jacket so he could follow him through the crowded streets. Unfortunately, this means he didn't pick up on things going sideways until the shot went off. The stampeding bystanders prevented him from pursuing the shooter."

"So we had a man on the scene and we've still got nothing?"

"We'll review the forensic report when it comes in, but beyond details on the bullet used and the general make of the gun, no, there won't be useful intel in it." Richard dropped the thin film into his pocket. "There's a good sushi restaurant two blocks over. Let's leave the clean-up to the locals and talk about what, if anything, this murder gives us."

RW

Graham brought the chopsticks to his mouth with surprising deftness and took the first bite of his ahi sashimi, then smiled approvingly. "Tasty. How did you know about this place?"

Richard considered the tempura rolls arranged in front of him. He'd long ago learned how to put aside the gruesomeness of a crime scene after vacating it, but it always took a minute to make it happen. Right now, his stomach continued to roil, so he took a sip of the snow weizen instead.

"Way back when I was a fresh-faced military recruit, before I moved into intelligence, I was stationed with the 32nd Pacific Starborne at Tokyo Command for six months. Given how popular this place was at the time, I hoped it would still be open."

"Great call on your part. This is delicious." Graham inhaled another piece of ahi and washed it down with sake before adopting a frown. "I'd say this kill confirms what we already suspected. Enzio Vilane is many things, and one of them is a cold-blooded murderer.

He's got—or had—a minimum of two trained assassins-for-hire on the payroll. He orders a murder, then kills the killer. Sinister stuff."

"True, but that character trait is not apt to make him easier to catch. With a population of twenty-four billion and a hundred thirty colonies, murders today only get solved via forensic evidence, surveillance data or personal connections. We've got none of those three."

Graham set down his chopsticks and leaned back on the bench, clasping his hands over his stomach. "You're right. We're never going to catch this killer, and thus Vilane, from forensics or a physical ID. Like everything else about Vilane's operation, it'll come down to infiltrating and tearing apart his network. Communications, payment transfers and so on. We're going to have to go Eliot Ness on his ass."

"Technically, more George Johnson and Frank Wilson."

"Who?"

"Eliot Ness made Al Capone's life a living Hell, but it was Johnson and Wilson who built the tax evasion case that Capone ultimately went to prison for." Richard shrugged. "History degree."

"Uh-huh."

"Anyway, there is another possibility: we find someone with a conscience who decides to sing. There have got to be people inside the Gardiens who harbor reservations about regenesis but are going to balk when they learn the group is turning violent. Maybe Malcolm will be able to identify some weak links in the chain."

"Maybe. But I worry that our fleet admiral is in way over his head, and he'll be lucky to escape the viper's nest with his own skin intact."

Richard picked up his chopsticks, then set them down again. Despite his best efforts and the savory aroma of the food, his appetite refused to materialize. "And I worry that is the least of the fleet admiral's problems."

6

SCYTHIA

Malcolm Jenner announced himself to the receptionist then took a seat in the lobby. The décor was all sheened marble and glass, with arched alcoves dedicated to honors and awards bestowed upon the company for its prodigious inventions. Gleaming windows looked out on one of Scythia's many white-sand beaches far below.

The chair he'd chosen turned out to be more art than function, and he shifted uncomfortably within its confines. He should be on the bridge of the *Denali* right now. From now until the end of the war, in fact.

While they waited for the Rasu to attack another planet, his dreadnought, accompanied by the AEGIS Advance Guard regiments, was tasked with protecting the Milky Way's Centaurus Gateway. It represented the closest gateway to Earth, and thus the most significant transportation hub in Concord space (possibly excepting the Cygnus Gateway situated four parsecs from Concord HQ).

He'd left Commodore Ettore, his XO and the *Denali's* Prevo, in charge while he was away. He'd also extracted a vow from the man, who had opened a wormhole for him to travel to the Horizon Therapeutics offices, to retrieve him the *instant* they detected any sign of a Rasu incursion. Ettore had been with him since the *Saratoga* and the Directorate War. The man deserved his own command, but thus far Ettore insisted he preferred to be second-in-command on the most powerful ship in the AEGIS fleet to sitting in the captain's chair on any lesser craft.

Ettore would keep his word. But the Rasu were attacking the gateways so swiftly and with so little warning that Malcolm's conscience argued those few seconds might nonetheless cost them the battle. Self-awareness dictated that he recognize his own arrogance in assuming only he could win such a battle, but it was what it was. He hoped he didn't have to find out.

He'd told Ettore he needed to see to important fleet admiralty business, but it was a lie. Yes, he'd already added lying to a friend to his list of sins, and it wasn't even lunchtime. He sat here now, in the lobby of the largest commercial biosynth product manufacturer in AEGIS space, on Gardiens business.

After Enzio Vilane and his Gardiens had attempted to assassinate Miriam in London—after Malcolm had learned Vilane was the man who had threatened Mia's life on Pandora—he'd decided to allow himself to be 'recruited' by the organization. He wasn't a trained undercover agent by any means, but he intended to do everything he could to infiltrate the group and, if possible, bring it down from the inside.

But in order to convince Vilane he was serious about helping the Gardiens and hopefully earn the man's trust, he'd been forced to make certain concrete promises of aid. Today, he had to deliver on the first of those.

"Sir, Mr. Ogadu will see you now."

At least he hadn't needed to wait for long, because the chair was giving him a backache. Hopefully he could be in and out of the meeting in ten minutes and standing on the *Denali's* bridge before disaster struck.

"Thank you." He stood and went to the indicated door, which slid open before him.

Tibu Ogadu greeted him warmly. "Fleet Admiral Jenner, it's been too long. I was so relieved to learn you survived your ordeal on Savrak."

"As was I." He smiled politely; though he'd heard those words ten thousand times by now, it was important to be gracious.

Ogadu motioned to two couches arranged to the left of an ostentatious centerpiece of a desk, and they moved there to sit facing one another.

Tibu Ogadu didn't qualify as a friend, but he was a personal acquaintance. Mia had introduced them at a dinner party several years earlier, when Horizon Therapeutics was negotiating a joint venture project with AEGIS. Despite Ogadu's overwrought taste in art and décor, the man came across as both jovial and shrewd. Mia respected him, and Malcolm put a great deal of stock in her assessment of people.

His stomach churned at the notion of how he was about to abuse their relationship in the service of terrorists and murderers, and he had to remind himself all over again why he needed to do this. Vilane had threatened Mia's life and attempted to take Miriam's. The Gardiens were willing to murder in order to deny people their right to choose to conquer death. The irony was rich.

"How goes the fight against the Rasu?"

He refocused on the task in front of him. "Honestly? Frustrating. They are now pushing harder than ever before, and we are having to adjust accordingly. They've destroyed more than two dozen gateways in an attempt to cripple our trade routes. If you don't have one yet, you might want to look into acquiring a Caeles Prism."

"Oh, I do have one."

Of course he did. His personal wealth exceeded the GDP of several small colonies. "Right. Good. We are obviously concerned about what more serious incursions the gateway attacks serve as a precursor to. AEGIS is an unparalleled fighting force, but we have a lot of parsecs to protect."

"I can only imagine. Actually, I don't have to. The military's orders for our products—to be blunt, for critical components used in the manufacture of new bodies for regenesis—have skyrocketed in the last two weeks."

Malcolm's throat worked. "That's what I wanted to discuss with you. How comfortable are you with AEGIS' use of regenesis for its soldiers?"

Ogadu tilted his head curiously. "It's funny you ask."

RW

Malcolm splashed water on his face and washed his hands in the Horizon Therapeutics lavatory. He felt like he needed a shower to wash away the residual filth of the ill deed he'd committed here today.

He'd obtained a promise of a sizeable private donation to the Gardiens from Ogadu, as well as a commitment to share some of the company's research on the dangers of regenesis with Gardiens 'scientists.' He had no idea what manner of science they were engaged in, if any. Ogadu had asked if he should surreptitiously place roadblocks in the supply chain between Horizon Therapeutics and the AEGIS Medical regenesis facilities, but Malcolm had declined. He wouldn't sign the permanent death warrants of soldiers; that was a step too far. Several steps.

He'd gloss over this point with Vilane when he reported back. Say something about how Ogadu had agreed to review the contracts and push back on multiple points in the negotiations, which Ogadu believed should have the ultimate effect of delaying deliveries. It constituted a small risk, but he doubted Vilane would check on the minutia of such arrangements. His impression was that Vilane was an 'idea' man who enjoyed giving orders, but often got distracted by his many grand and egomaniacal ventures.

The lies were coming a little too easily now….

He still felt sick—sick enough to hover over the sink as a precaution. God willing, this charade would wrap up soon with Vilane in prison and the Gardiens in discredited shambles.

CONCORD COMMAND ALERT:

All Rasu War Council members: priority meeting in twelve minutes to review new developments.

Thank God. He wiped his mouth and straightened the creases in his uniform.

Ettore, I need a ride home.

Yes, sir.

He whipped around and waited impatiently for the wormhole to form and return him to the *Denali's* bridge.

7

ROMANE

*CONNOVA INTERSTELLAR HEADQUARTERS
MILKY WAY*

- Reduce the power requirements of the Tandem Defense Shield so smaller warships can utilize it
- Enhance the sensitivity of Rasu signature-detection algorithms
- Extend the effective range of automated sensors (*I've got this one –Devon*)
- Extend the effective range of the Ymyrath Field
- Reduce the size of the Ymyrath Field hardware
- Make the Ymyrath Field even more badass (*You get the idea –Devon*)

Kennedy Rossi groaned into her hands. Sometimes she really hated Devon Reynolds.

But she reminded herself how despite his often snarky attitude, he was working harder than she was on all of these items and a dozen more projects. He'd never lacked for a work ethic, merely manners.

As she spun her chair around in idle circles, she tried to remember when this used to be fun. When designing ships and shields was an invigorating challenge and watching the engines of her creation roar to life gave her a visceral thrill.

Ridiculous how a malevolent enemy bent on wholesale death and destruction could drain the amusement out of any job.

But her mother had always coached her that whining was unbecoming of a Rossi, so she rubbed at her eyes and refocused on her epic to-do list. Rather than getting hung up on how impossible it all was, she needed to prioritize, then concentrate on one item at a time until it was either done or irrefutably proved to be impossible.

The simple fact was, while the Ymyrath Field was the 'shiny new toy,' it was also the lowest priority. Any improvements she squeezed out of it stood to be incremental at best for now, and it already performed its intended function.

The double-shielding—the Tandem Defense Shield, per AEGIS orders—was a game changer in combat, especially for ships *not* constructed of adiamene, so it had to rank as the most urgent item on the list. The TDS module needed to run on frigates, which were far and away the most populous class of warship in every fleet. But there weren't any remaining hardpoints available on the frigates. She had a few design quibbles with alien frigates, but AEGIS ones represented the pinnacle of warship design and functionality, if she did say so herself. No component, no module, no onboard system harbored a centimeter of waste or inefficiency. But now, she found she'd been too clever by half in their design, and…no free hardpoints.

…Unless she replaced one of the existing defensive shields, perhaps? They would be redundant once the TDS was installed. She'd also have to fit a small additional Zero Drive in there somewhere since there was negative juice to divert from existing power systems, but a Zero Drive of the capacity she'd need should fit in a decent-sized closet. It could work.

A spark of hope ignited that she might be able to make this happen. Energized for the first time all day, she pulled up the AEGIS standard frigate schematic and went to work.

"Mommy!"

The overlapping exclamations of her kids jolted Kennedy out of a brutal math calculation, and she jumped in surprise—then spun around, arms widening in time to corral Jonas and Braelyn as they barreled into her in a flurry of limbs.

"Hey, it's my two favorite munchkins in the whole wide world." She kissed each of them on the head before gently easing them back, her motherly gaze instinctively checking to confirm all their parts were intact and attached in the proper places. "How has your day been?"

"Jonas got in trouble in art class again."

"Brae! You weren't supposed to tell!"

"It's true, though."

She adopted a mildly stern look. "Why did you get in trouble, Jonas?"

"Our assignment was to use the light pen to draw a nature setting using every one of the core colors—and I did! But instead of drawing it on my panel, I drew it on Ke'ontae's face." He didn't even act contrite; he never did.

"Why were you mean to Ke'ontae?"

"I wasn't being mean to him! He said I could do it. It was funny. He thought so, too."

'It was funny' was turning out to be the justification for most of her son's misadventures. "Well, I'm glad you weren't being mean to your friend. But you still have to follow your teacher's instructions. It's important to obey the rules and listen to people who are in charge."

Jonas groaned and flopped his arms around. "All the time?"

No, not all the time. But her son wasn't mature enough yet to appreciate the finer nuances of when it might not be the time. "Yes, all the time. Trust in your elders." Ugh, she sounded like her father.

Braelyn stared at her with piercing, insightful green eyes. "But that's not true. Daddy told us the other day about the time you and him ran away from Earth to Romane because the government said you couldn't do something you wanted to do. And that's why we live here on Romane."

Her gaze shot over their heads to Noah, who upon entering the lab had quietly dropped into a chair at one of the workstations and was lazily toeing it around. He shrugged, as unrepentant as Jonas.

"They like hearing stories of Mommy and Daddy being heroic."

"Yes, well. Those circumstances were different. Mommy believed the government's decision would end up hurting people, and she wanted to help people. We both did."

"So…if somebody in charge tells us to do something we think is bad and wrong, then we *shouldn't* do it?"

She crouched to their level and clasped her daughter's shoulders. "We work very hard to make sure you and your brother are never in a situation where somebody in charge would ever force you to make such a choice. And I know for a fact that your teachers won't. So no weaseling out of the rules."

Braelyn's mouth morphed around in exaggerated shapes while she searched for a counterargument, but she came up empty. "Okay. But I'm going to think more on this."

"Of that, I have no doubt."

Jonas had gotten bored with the ethical discussion and was fidgeting with his clothes as he meandered in a circle around her desk. "Can we play with the instruments now?"

She had set up a siloed workstation in the corner with outdated equipment for them to entertain themselves with whenever they visited the office, and she nodded as she climbed back to her feet. "Go. Just for a few minutes, though. You have Trailblazers this afternoon!"

They scurried off for the corner, racing each other to be the first to arrive and claim the 'best' instruments.

Noah stood and dragged his chair over to her, then set a wrapped package wafting mouth-watering aromas on the desk in front of her. "I brought you lunch. Roast beef and provolone with aioli."

"Oh, that sounds delicious." She started to unwrap it, but leaned over and kissed him first. "Thank you."

"Somebody has to keep you healthy. Left to your own devices, you'll forget to eat. Also, sleep." He motioned to the three screens she had open above the desk. "How's work going?"

"I am, I daresay, actually making a little progress on the TDS configurations. Unfortunately, the Rasu are still moving faster than me."

"You can't do it all yourself."

"Oh, I'm not. Devon and a litany of Special Projects people are working on various aspects of all this, and I've sent two of our techs off to gather parts for new prototypes."

His eyes searched her face, worry drawing down his features. "What can I do to help?"

Her attention drifted to Jonas and Braelyn, who were now engaged in some fiercely imaginative quest involving the instruments and, if she was deciphering their excited chatter correctly, giant space whales. "Make our children happy. Noah, I can't *wait* for this crisis to pass. I want so bad to cuddle with the three of you on the couch for hours and hours—then cuddle with just you until the sun rises. I want to go to the beach for a week and teach them how to snorkel."

"And us sneak off to the hot tub at night after they go to sleep."

"That goes without saying. Then, I want us to visit Erisen and go snowboarding at Glacier Pass Resort, where I used to visit often when I lived there." She set the sandwich down and took his hands in hers. "But for now, I'm only able to focus on this work and on trying to save as many lives as possible because I know you're looking out for Jonas and Braelyn. Because you're the most incredible father they could ever ask for. You're showing them how much they're loved, and it is the most important job in the universe."

8

SIYANE

FRINGES OF URSA MAJOR II GALAXY

The galaxies of the Laniakea Supercluster danced through the cabin, with Alex at their center point. The clumpy Local Cluster meandered off to her left and the Virgo Cluster hovered in front of her, while the Ursa Major group overlapped the couch on her right.

She reached up with one hand and poked the Milky Way, but her finger slipped unobstructed through the virtual representation.

"Valkyrie, color all the non-Concord galaxies with a Rasu presence yellow."

So much of the striking white starlight turned jaundiced. An apt characterization for the Rasu infestation. "This is more than before."

'Yes. The Kats have begun monitoring the Rasu's advancement more closely, and it continues apace in all directions.'

"Oh, joy." Angst plucked at Alex's nerves like a bad chimeral trip. The invocation of the Kats immediately brought Mesme's incomprehensible betrayal to the front of her mind, and she shoved it away with a mental grunt. The Ruda's betrayal waited in line behind it, less emotionally painful but no less destructive.

The visual evidence of the Rasu's steadfast advancement across known space made her grind her teeth in frustration. Back at HQ, her mother was driving herself into the ground trying to protect Concord assets and people, and all Alex wanted to do was help. But she wasn't a powerful military officer; not an innovative strategist like her father or a great tactician like Malcolm. She certainly wasn't a leader like her mother.

The only way she saw to contribute the tiniest effort to this fight was by using what she knew. Science. Space. The rules that connected everything in this vast cosmos together.

> *"It's not magic or anything. It's simply...the universe has rules. Even the exceptions obey the rules. Though so immensely complex it appears to most like chaos, in truth the universe is ordered and structured and perfect.*
>
> *"More than that, I understand the structure. It makes sense to me. I look out into the void and I see the interconnections and relationships—the gravitational pull of a supergiant subtly tugging at a stellar system kiloparsecs away, the excess glow along the edges of ionized gas as it collides with an H I region, the absence which marks a dark star or a gray hole."*
>
> *Caleb's hand wound leisurely through her hair, reassuring her she wasn't crazy, encouraging her to continue. "And since I understand the way things must be, when something seems out of place, wrong or merely odd...I can recognize the reality of it. The hidden object or event or force which brings space back into alignment with the rules of the universe."*

Even the Rasu had to obey the rules of the universe. And so she searched for a way to use those rules to craft an advantage against an unbeatable enemy.

"I know the Ghosts haven't finished their recon, but color those galaxies we've determined possess a Rasu Core Ring in red."

Splotches of red spread across the map like a rash...a nasty rash. It was a lot of red. Not pervasive though, as only a smidge over thirty percent of the occupied galaxies had earned a ring. She studied the pattern, stepping through the map to view the distribution from several different angles and perspectives.

Caleb's hand touched her arm as he joined her in the midst of the projection. "This doesn't resemble a steady progression. Unless the Rasu have spent millennia jumping around to invade random galaxies, the rings aren't necessarily in the galaxies where the Rasu have exerted control for the longest periods of time."

Her eyes scanned the map to confirm his observation. "Nope. It does look random at first glance, but…" she took a step back, into a region where the Rasu had yet to invade, and studied the region in toto "…I think the rings are placed where they are for maximum impact on the surrounding galaxies. A single ring over here in a larger galaxy is sufficient to draw in the smaller galaxies in the immediate area, while in this region, three rings are required because the adjacent galaxies are already distant from one another." She smiled. "All right, Valkyrie, time for the big reveal. If we compare current data on Laniakea in Amaranthe to historical data from Aurora, what does it tell us?"

'The diameter of Laniakea in Amaranthe is 8.2% shorter on one axis and 6.9% shorter on the other axis than it was in Aurora.'

"Damn." She bumped into the couch behind her and sank against it. "I can't believe they're actually trying to do it."

Caleb frowned, the stars of Andromeda drifting across his pensive features. "You still suspect they're using the rings to pull the galaxies closer together in order to prevent the heat death of the universe?"

"Well, they could harbor another, more nefarious reason for doing it, but it's the most obvious justification. And whatever their underlying reason, they're pretty definitely trying to draw these galaxies closer together, yes. It explains the ring distribution, and the size differential is too big for it to be a coincidental side effect of their efforts."

"What if you're not comparing like to like, though? Aurora was a manufactured universe."

"The Kats said they created Aurora to be identical to Amaranthe as of two hundred ten thousand years ago. Cosmically speaking, that's basically yesterday. Yes, unreliable source, I realize. Believe me, do I realize. But after The Displacement, our scientists did tons of studies on this place we found ourselves living in, and they confirmed Aurora was a near-perfect copy of Amaranthe. Absent the aliens, of course."

He held up his hands in surrender. "I defer to the indefatigable logic of science. So they're pulling galaxies closer together. It requires tremendous resources to build these rings, so we can speculate that this is one of the major reasons—if not the only reason—why they raid and harvest planet after planet wherever they go."

"But not why they slaughter all life they find there."

He shrugged. "Perhaps they don't view intelligent life as any different from plants or soil or minerals. Every raw material is a resource for them, and whether it can think for itself is irrelevant."

He had as much of a knack for dissecting alien psychology as he did for human nature, and she'd long ago learned to trust his judgment on what to her was the often inexplicable behavior of so-called 'intelligent' beings. "Damn. There's taking your job seriously, and then there's fanaticism."

Starlight danced in his eyes, enhancing their intensity. "Does it bother you that the Rasu might have a noble purpose for their actions?"

"Hell, no. Annihilating vast swaths of life today to preserve their own lives a zillion years from now is not a noble purpose. Besides, even if it were, there are better ways to go about it. There must be." She bounced off the back of the couch with renewed vigor. "And you know what? We'll figure out what they are. Give us a bit more time and a *yebanaya* break from murderous aliens for a few years, and we'll noodle out how to stop the universe from growing cold and silent, without destroying the very life we're trying to preserve."

"That's my girl."

She beamed, her lips curling up in delight; after all these years, his praise still made her heart flutter. "So we'll file an official report with Command and Special Projects detailing our findings and laying out our theory." The warm fuzzies petered out as she contemplated their next steps, or lack thereof. "But at the end of the day, I feel as if we're back where we started. It turns out, the Rasu's motivations don't make the slightest difference. Sure, it's edifying to *know*, but this knowledge doesn't point to a way to defeat them, and it doesn't make it any less imperative for us to do so."

"You're right." Caleb nodded soberly.

"Thanks for the pep talk."

"Sorry. I'm as frustrated as you are." He came over and began rubbing her arms, his fingertips kneading the muscles as they moved. "Okay. This has *not* all been in vain. We have a lot more data about their presence now. Their activities across galaxies. What can we do with the information that will help?"

She stared past his shoulder at the rotating Laniakea map. The problem with an enemy like the Rasu—as opposed to, say, the Directorate—was how they presented as a nameless, faceless mob. They weren't unthinking, obviously, but they were an interchangeable horde displaying a single purpose. There were no personality defects to exploit. No egos to bribe or divisions to manipulate for their own ends.

What if that is not true?

What do you mean, Valkyrie?

'Since we and the Asterions developed the ability to detect a Rasu presence based on their unique signature, the Kats have undertaken an effort to track Rasu movements on a macro scale. Not their conquering of galaxies over centuries and millennia as this map displays, but ship movements on a weekly, sometimes daily basis.'

Alex rolled her eyes in annoyance at yet another mention of the Kats, but waved her hand for Valkyrie to continue.

'They have determined that the Rasu who initially began attacking Concord targets are the same group of Rasu who attacked Namino. This is not a surprise. Recall, however: the Asterions destroyed the bulk of the Rasu who had invaded their galaxy. The working theory is that a few stragglers who survived the Asterions' counteroffensive fled to a neighboring galaxy and reported the attack to the Rasu there. Based on observed activity, the Kats believe the Rasu currently in Concord space originated from the Canes I Group galaxies of NGC 4144, 4190 and 4214.'

"Makes sense, based on proximity to the Gennisi galaxy alone. Where are you going with this?"

'While the data is preliminary, the Kats are beginning to identify predictable patterns throughout the regions the Rasu control. Those patterns suggest the Rasu 'clump together,' almost as if into factions. There is much movement back and forth across a given adjacent group of galaxies, but little to and from a neighboring group. Thus far, this holds true across all of Laniakea.'

"The Rasu the Asterions captured indicated the species is paranoid about control. You're saying they form cliques that rule various chunks of territory and display somewhat frosty relations with the other cliques?"

'Not dissimilar to the Ruda Supremes. They cooperate on matters affecting the species as a whole. Meanwhile, they build up their separate holdings for their own benefit, in an escalating competition to grow stronger than their neighbors.'

"And you think this means they have internal divisions we *can* exploit?"

Caleb stepped away from her to start up some vigorous pacing. "You're not suggesting we can make a deal with a rival Rasu faction, are you?"

'I am not suggesting anything at all, yet. I am only saying that as intelligent beings, the Rasu have a societal structure. They have complex interactions with one another. There may be nothing in this fact for us to use, but we can't say for certain until we learn something about the intricacies of this societal structure.'

Alex groaned. "You want to go spelunking around all sorts of Rasu hubs, don't you? You know how much that sucks."

Valkyrie chuckled over the speaker. ' 'Want' is a strong word. There is a small possibility it will prove fruitful to do so.'

Might it? She ran through a couple of scenarios they could pursue in her mind, searching for a way to make this work for them. "I don't see how we can learn much from simply watching them. Arguably no more than what the Kats are learning, and I'd just as soon leave the endeavor to them. If there's anything the Kats excel at, it's watching." *Certainly isn't truth-telling....*

She spun toward Caleb as an idea took hold. "What we need is to be able to eavesdrop on their conversations with each other."

His face lit up at the possibility of such a quintessentially 'intelligence agent' activity. "Don't the Asterions have a primer on the Rasu language we can use?"

"Yes, *but.* A couple of 'buts.' The Rasu gave them translation files so they could converse. But the translation returns gibberish when applied to the cross-module signals the Rasu send to one another. It's looking increasingly as though it's a top-layer interpreter the Rasu created so they could speak to other species when required, and not their true native tongue.

"*But,* the Asterions do have a good handle on the Rasu programming language now, and I think a team is working to leverage it to create a true translation program." She smiled. "I also think Marlee has invited herself onto that team."

"Naturally she has. Let's touch base with her before we reach out to the Asterions. Give her first crack at helping us out."

9

SENECA

CAVARE
MILKY WAY

Marlee Marano sat yoga-style on the rug in the middle of her living room. Her apartment was silent, but her mind raged like a contest of dueling symphonies.

Someone should have told her it was going to be like this! Alex, Mia, Morgan—*ouch*—someone. Of course, she hadn't alerted Alex or Mia to her plans, and Morgan wasn't speaking to her, so.

Half in the background but half in her conscious thoughts, her brand-new neural control system was rewriting all her foreign language algorithms and databases, while simultaneously completing her outstanding work research and running her upgraded cybernetics through various testing programs. She asked herself a question about the dietary habits of the Godjan refugees, and in less than a second her mind had dug the answer out of an obscure Consulate-affiliated database and surfaced it. She asked three more questions, and the answers were returning before she'd completed the third inquiry. It was as if she knew *everything*.

She took a long sip of the lemonade situated beside her then opened the pathway to the Noesis—

—the mental assault knocked her flat on her literal back. A cacophony of virtual voices drowned out her own. Movement, patterns, spiraling code everywhere.

"Whoa." She pushed herself off the floor and returned to a sitting position. There were millions of Prevos now—tens of millions, probably, but Prevos weren't often the type to report their status to the government—and it appeared nearly all of them were currently in the Noesis.

In her mind she wandered around the maze until she found an open virtual space, then casually entered it. A very adult playground had been built atop altocumulus clouds, and dozens of people lounged naked amid the puffs of white. Some alone, some decidedly not.

She eased out before anyone noticed her. It was a mite early in the morning for that manner of frivolity.

Across a pond of rippling data and up a lattice, a hundred or so people had networked themselves together even more fulsomely than the Noesis itself did. A node sat open on the periphery, so after brief consideration, she hooked herself into it.

The Supergalactic Coordinate System overtook her mind. Upon it, waves and arrows painted a disordered canvas. Upon that, algorithms spun by faster than she could...actually, she *could* follow them.

She spoke for the first time since entering the Noesis. *What are we studying?*

Rasu scouting patterns. Concord is never going to be able to cover every kilometer of space with sensors, so we need to determine how to predict where they'll appear next.

You guys are helping Concord?

A different voice answered, though she didn't know to whom it belonged. *We don't align ourselves with governments here. We're helping humans survive. Right now, doing so is consistent with helping Concord in the Rasu War.*

That's terrific. I have to go, but I'll return later and pitch in.

She disconnected from the node and descended the lattice to look around anew. The Noesis might well be infinite. She needed to work on learning how to navigate it with purpose, but it would wait for a day or two, because she had so much else to do!

She started to step out of active engagement with the space...then cast her mind out, searching for an individual signature. How did she know how to do so? No clue.

But nothing returned in answer to her query. If she'd phrased it correctly, this meant Morgan wasn't here. Alex had once said the original Noetica Prevos could take or leave the Noesis, so perhaps she shouldn't be surprised. Disappointed, but not surprised.

She opened her eyes in her apartment and climbed to her feet, swaying unsteadily for a few seconds. These transitions were heady. But once she had her feet steady under her, she moved to the edge of the open space behind her couch. She'd played around with sidespace last night—because she certainly hadn't slept—so now came the big test: wormholes.

She breathed in deeply as the magnitude of what she was about to hopefully do settled in. Rending the fabric of spacetime was no laughing matter, and she made a note not to giggle when it worked.

Oh! She'd almost forgotten. This type of thing required power. She went to the drawer in her desk and retrieved the tiny Caeles Prism charm that Abigail had helped her acquire. Should she grip it in her hand? Alex wore hers on a bracelet on her wrist, while Mia wore hers on a chain around her neck, and Morgan clipped hers to her belt. She didn't know where Devon kept his, as she'd never seen him use it. So was she a bracelet person, a necklace person or a belt person?

The notion occurred to her that she could wear it as a dangly earring…hmm. It might get tangled in her hair too often to be practical. She'd think on it. For now, she held the charm aloft in her palm and *mentally* turned it on. Her palm and fingers started tingling from the referred energy as a tiny ball of golden light began spinning within the latticed sphere.

Now. Simply harness the power and will an opening to another location into existence. Easy peasy.

She placed the precise coordinates to her office at the Consulate in the forefront of her mind…and slipped there in sidespace. No, that wasn't right. Once her consciousness was properly situated back in her body, she tried again. She'd read up on how the process worked and quizzed Alex about what it was like multiple times, but she wasn't going to ask for overt help, dammit.

Oh, the air shimmered! *Focus.*

It was akin to peeling back a curtain to reveal the hidden scene obscured behind it. One second the windows of her living room were in front of her, and the next her office desk and chair waited a few steps away.

Her heart pounding in her chest, she took those steps.

Goosebumps raised on her arms, for the air was always chilly at HQ. Also for other reasons.

She plopped down in her office chair and sent it spinning in circles, giggling in spite of her earlier admonition. This was going to cut half an hour off her commute! Plus result in a few other tremendous changes to her life, obviously.

Since she wasn't scheduled to work today, she decided to vacate the premises before Veshnael or one of her coworkers caught her onsite, and skipped back through the opening to her apartment.

This was incredible! It had taken years of work and preparation, but she'd done it. So far as she knew, she was the first Solo Prevo to exist. She needed to think up a cooler name for herself, though. She'd always been partial to 'Enhanced,' but she was now so far beyond that characterization.

Distracted by the meandering train of thought, her inattention caused the wormhole to close and the Caeles Prism to spin down. She should have done so as soon as she'd returned to her apartment, anyway, and she added this to her spiraling list of things to remember about her new superpowers.

What now? She could go literally anywhere in the universe— so where did she want to go?

A grin blossomed on her lips, and she hurried to her closet. She was going to need some tactical gear.

RW

VRACHNAS HOMEWORLD
ANDROMEDA GALAXY

Forty meters across the ledge, a baby dragon napped in the sun. Vermillion scales with scattered dots colored carnation and white glistened in the sunlight, and its tail swooshed lazily across the stone. The colorful dots reminded her of sprinkles atop cupcake icing, and she promptly named the baby 'Cupcake.'

From the frame of the wormhole, one foot firmly in her apartment, Marlee scanned the trees beyond the ledge, then the sky above. Neither Mom nor Dad were anywhere to be seen. She bet they were off hunting for dinner. Perfect.

She tip-toed the rest of the way out of her apartment and, at long last, inhaled the fresh air of the dragon planet. It felt thick—the better to provide resistance for their wings?—and smelled of pine and chestnuts.

Remember to keep the wormhole open. Remember to keep the wormhole open. Also, she couldn't wander too far from it or it would close on its own. *Don't wander too far.*

She took a step forward. Another. Checked the sky and scanned the tree line for any telltale rustles. Her hand went to her plasma blade hilt. She hadn't brought a Daemon, because under no circumstances was she going to shoot an innocent dragon, but if necessary she would draw blood if it meant saving her life.

Two more steps forward—the baby dragon puffed smoke out of its nostrils and lifted its head a few centimeters. She froze mid-stride, her heart hammering in her ears so loudly she didn't think she'd hear it if the dragon roared at her. Her heightened Prevo senses studied the rise and fall of its chest and surmised that it hadn't yet awoken. Sure enough, after another exhale its chin dropped to the stone.

She was more disappointed than relieved. Though cognizant of the danger, she wanted it to wake up. She wanted to see its intense elliptical irises up close and feel the glistening scales beneath her palm. Were they cold or warm? She wanted to ride it through the skies. She'd seen the dragons plenty of times; she was here to do more than watch.

She checked behind her to make certain the wormhole remained open, then cleared her throat. "Hi, Cupcake. I'm Marlee. Why don't you wake up, just a touch, so I can meet you?"

The dragon's body shifted in a low rumble, and one eye opened. The iris was bright strawberry surrounded by gleaming silver sclera, and its elongated pupil constricted as it stared at her. Oh, boy....

"Easy there, little dragon. I'm not going to hurt you." She raised both hands in the air. "Friendly, see?"

Cupcake roused itself and lumbered to its feet, exposing a chubby belly and still-stubby legs. Even so, it must weigh several hundred kilos already! Its back came mid-way up her chest. How big must the parents be? She definitely hadn't appreciated the scale of these creatures from the drone feeds. Her gaze leapt to the sky— but the drones weren't scheduled to pass over this region for another three hours, so her visit would go undetected.

She flipped one of her hands over, palm up. "You sure are a pretty little dragon, Cupcake. You're going to grow up to be so magnificent—"

Cupcake surged toward her for several steps, shocking her with its speed and agility, and she scrambled backward. Panic sent adrenaline coursing through her body. But she'd also installed some advanced military combat routines she'd convinced Caleb to let her borrow to 'study,' and time seemed to slow down and gain focus. She detected the ripples of individual scales as the dragon inhaled and expanded its chest. Faint wisps of smoke twirled out of its nostrils in uneven streams.

It stepped forward; she stepped back. *Calm, calm, calm.*

In a single stride Cupcake vaulted toward her. She spun and sprinted for the wormhole, pushing off the balls of her feet as she reached it to dive for the opening and roll across the living room floor.

Close it! She whipped around to seal the rift, only to find Cupcake charging through it into her apartment.

Since the ticking of time had slowed to a crawl, she was able to think '*I can't slice a baby dragon in half!,*' decide not to close the wormhole, scramble to her feet and dive over the couch a fraction of a second before Cupcake's ridiculously long talons darted out to try to rip open her back.

Smoke filled the apartment as the dragon plowed through her puny dining table. Its tail swiped across the decor shelf, knocking off family visuals and trinkets from her travels.

She stood and planted her feet, digging frantically for the sensation of being rooted to the earth that Caleb had taught her. She tracked Cupcake's seemingly haphazard movements, searching for a predictable pattern.

Its panicked stare fixated on her, and the dragon charged.

It took all of her self-control to wait until it had flipped the couch, which confused it for a beat, to bolt to the right and circle around it, zig-zag, and leap back through the wormhole onto the ledge.

A crash echoed behind her, and she cringed at the thought of what had gotten trashed—

A long shadow darkened the sun above her, and she looked up to see a massive emerald dragon descending from the sky, its long jaws open.

"Oh, shit!" She spun toward the wormhole, even as Cupcake barreled through it.

She was trapped between parent and child. The air began to shimmer with heat, and her back warmed precipitously.

Everything she'd done the last year had surely prepared her for this scenario: the training with Caleb, the cybernetics upgrades, the Solo Prevo transformation. *Everything.*

She sprinted ahead. Just as she and Cupcake were about to collide, she leapt up and over its head—raging heat seared into her skin—planted a palm on its back and used the leverage to propel herself past its tail. She landed on one foot and fell forward into her living room. *Close!*

Silence descended upon the apartment. She crawled gingerly around to confirm the wormhole had sealed shut, then collapsed on the floor. "Owwwww."

Blood seeped through her fingers on the hand she'd used to vault over Cupcake, and she inspected it to find two deep gashes in her palm. Shocker, Caleb had not been lying about the sharpness of the scales.

A faint sooty odor began to fill the air, and she belatedly realized her left sleeve was smoldering. She yanked her shirt off and patted it on the floor, which was when she discovered a long, red burn welt running from her shoulder to her elbow.

All in all, the damage wasn't too bad. A bit of first aid plus her top-shelf recovery cybernetics would guarantee she was as good as new in a few hours.

Her apartment? Not so much.

The couch sported a series of long slashes in the fabric from where Cupcake had plowed over it and gotten tangled up when it flipped. Every piece of furniture in the living room was upside down, in fact; everything that could be broken, was. Soot stained two of the walls, almost as if a child had gotten hold of a charcoal brisket and gone to town.

All in all, it looked like a demon-infested hurricane had cavorted straight through her living room.

Hey, is it true you've been working on a better Rasu language translation program? We could use one on the Siyane.

The pulse from Caleb jerked her out of the surrealness of the moment.

I have been. It still needs some work, but it's good enough to deploy.

Great. We'll come by your office this afternoon.

Is early next week okay? I'm off today and...on an adventure.

Don't tell me what kind, please. Next week, then.

She'd fudged the truth. The program wasn't quite ready yet, but she suddenly realized that with her new talents and the rewritten language algorithms, she'd be able to whip it into shape in less than an hour.

In the renewed silence, she gazed around her apartment…and fell back on the floor, cackling like a maniac. What a supremely amazing encounter!

She laughed for a solid five minutes before getting her emotions under control. She needed to clean herself up and don a new shirt. Then, the first thing she intended to do was run down the hall and tell her friend Eosha everything that had happened. Next, she should clean up the living room. And procure a new couch. Possibly a new dining table. Repair some shelves. Do a little light painting.

Once the place was presentable again, though? It would be time to start planning how she was going to tame that dragon.

10

ARES

TEMPORARY ADVOCACY HEADQUARTERS
MILKY WAY

Corradeo Praesidis considered the vista out the window of his office, dominated by the Oenom skyline in the distance. Off to the left, in the arid expanse between here and the city, Patrici Cabo had begun work on a permanent Advocacy Square complex. He'd elected to place it closer to the city proper than the estate, as the complex should provide a boost to commerce and employment for the city's residents. Also, he was turning this estate into his personal home, and he wanted to create some separation between his private life and official Advocacy business. He wasn't certain such a thing was possible, for it had been two hundred fifty millennia since there had been any division between his work and personal lives. But this was a new start, and he was determined to…try.

The chime to his office rang, and he opened the door to allow Rachele elasson-Theriz entry.

"Rachele, welcome. Please come in."

The *elasson* drew herself up two meters from his desk. "You wanted to see me, sir? Is there a problem with the materials supplies for the construction?"

"No. The contrary, in fact. I want to thank you for the tremendous effort you've put into sourcing and delivering on even Cabo Construction's most unique requests. I came to you with a desire and an unreasonable timetable, and you've gone above and beyond to make it happen. Your work is appreciated."

"Thank you, sir. I'm invested in the success of this endeavor. Our people need more than inspirational speeches; they need stability and leadership, and both require public symbols. The headquarters will stand as a place people can look upon with pride and know that proper work on their behalf is being conducted within its walls."

Corradeo forced a smile. Like nearly all *elassons*, Rachele was an arrogant prima-donna. But she was also a reasonable woman. Several people had reported that she'd regularly stood up to Ferdinand during his attempted rebellion. More importantly, since its failure, she had sized up the new world and adapted to thrive in it. It was behavior Corradeo wanted to reward.

"This is my hope as well. To the crux of the matter, then. You've comported yourself with honor since Ferdinand's insurrection was put to rest. And I keep my promises." He passed a contact file to Rachele. "Go see Dorene ela-Erevna at her clinic in Oenom. She'll see to it that you're reconnected to the integral regenesis network."

Rachele's eyes widened, and she stumbled back half a step before regaining her composure. "This is...I appreciate it, sir. I'm, um...am I the only one?"

Definitely still arrogant. "No. I'm making it a point to meet with each of you individually first, but I do plan to make a more general announcement to many of the *elassons* soon. Hopefully, those who have remained intransigent up until now will see how the path to redemption is clearly marked and open for them to traverse."

"Yes, sir. A wise course of action. If there is nothing else, I'm going to go pay a visit to the clinic."

Corradeo gestured toward the door. "No sense wasting any time. Go on."

Rachele scurried out the door like the woman with a new lease on life that she was.

RW

Corradeo was beginning to tire of these awkward one-on-one meetings when the chime brought more welcome visitors. He visibly relaxed as Nyx and Eren walked in, Nyx all self-controlled business, Eren positively sauntering.

Eren collapsed on the couch and threw a leg over the arm. Nyx shot him a disgusted glare, then sat properly in one of the chairs opposite his desk. "How are you, Grandfather?"

So their interpersonal dynamic remained somewhat contentious. He held out hope that they would become friends, though he should not have expected it to happen overnight. In his opinion, Eren could buff out some of the harder edges of Nyx's personality and teach her the value in displaying a touch of compassion. Nyx, on the other hand, could keep Eren engaged in the world of the living…and possibly teach him a few things about decorum. Obviously the latter hadn't happened yet.

"I am relieved to have returned regenesis capability to several *elassons* today. I did not enjoy severing their integral connections at Epithero. Holding the threat of mortality over their heads makes me feel like a…dictator. A Primor. I had no choice, but I would as soon be done with the entire mess."

"You did what you had to do. The only thing most *elassons* respect is the wielding of authority by someone stronger than them."

"She says from experience," Eren snickered from the couch.

"Yes. I'm not ashamed of it."

Corradeo worked not to chuckle under his breath. "Please. You have something to report?"

Nyx straightened up and clasped her hands in her lap. "We're off to Macskaf to gather information on a dissident group that is gaining influence among the Barisan population, and perhaps other species as well."

"Yes, 'we,' because she doesn't trust me to do my job."

"While your sole purview for the Advocacy is alien intelligence, my purview is *all* intelligence. I need to see for myself what's happening on the ground."

Corradeo cleared his throat to short-circuit their bickering. "Nyx, we've discussed this. I trust Eren, which means you can trust him as well. However, I also applaud your hands-on approach to your work, especially in these early days. The Barisans had many legitimate reasons to hate the Directorate. I am doing what I can to show them those grievances need not carry over to the Advocacy, but…" he smiled to himself at the parallels "…hearts and minds are not won overnight. Let me know what you learn on your return. Now, I must excuse myself. I want to shower all this bureaucracy off me and don somewhat nicer attire. I have a date this evening."

Nyx arched an eyebrow halfway to the ceiling. "A *date?*"

The word had made it past his tongue without consideration, though it was self-evidently incorrect. "Forgive me. Poor choice of words. I have a business meeting this evening."

"Must be with a hot lady, then."

"Yes, Eren. As a matter of fact, it is. But it's still a business meeting."

"Uh-huh." Eren smirked. "Have fun, sir."

11

MACSKAF

*BARISAN HOMEWORLD
SCULPTOR DWARF GALAXY*

I t had been some years since Eren had visited a Barisan planet, and he was struck by how vertical, misshapen and strangely mazelike the architecture was. Barisans had never met a straight boulevard nor a flat façade.

The roads curved to accommodate the cornucopia of building shapes and sizes, the frequently untamed natural environment, and often simply *because*. Said buildings featured an overabundance of jutting balconies and tended to be constructed of a spongy wood someone had once told him was native to the planet. Many of the structures sported a conical shape, almost resembling pinecones, while others swirled around open interiors. The outer walls looked pockmarked from afar, with small dimples, bulges and bars strewn scattershot from ground to roof.

Why, one might ask? Well, because the Barisans were descended from cats, and cats took pleasure in climbing. The busy city landscape was dotted with bipedal forms scurrying up the sides of buildings, using the dimples and bulges to scale the façades then deftly landing on one of the balconies and disappearing inside.

"Have they never heard of lift technology?"

Nyx wore a half-disgusted, half-skeptical expression, and Eren laughed. "I'm certain they have. But they consider lifts to be an inferior mode of transportation. I mean, look how fast they scramble up to their destinations."

"It's unseemly. Barbaric."

"Oh, then you're going to love this next part."

She stopped in the middle of the…sidewalk, more or less, and spun to him. "What does that mean?"

He tried to keep a straight face. "They don't have lifts. At all. What you see occurring all around you? That's how you get inside the buildings."

"And?"

"And the meeting we're here to surreptitiously observe is in a building."

Her lips puckered up as realization dawned. "No."

"Yes."

"You can't be serious."

"Listen, sweetheart. You're the one who insisted on coming along. If you're not up to the climb, you can return to the spaceport, head back to Ares, and sit at your desk to await my report."

"You don't file reports."

"Eh." He shrugged. "I didn't say you wouldn't be waiting for a while."

"Fine. Let's do this and be done with it. Where's the meeting?"

He gazed around, trying to orient himself according to the directions his contact had provided. The corkscrew streets did not make it easy, but at least there were a couple of identifiable landmarks. "I think about two blocks to the southeast."

"They don't have blocks here."

"Yes, they do. See how every so often, the street gets slightly wider for a few meters? This way." He set off to the southeast without checking with her for approval.

They endured a litany of suspicious snarls and more than one offensive gesture from pedestrians on the way to their destination. Anadens were legally allowed to visit Macskaf, as they were all planets under Concord's purview, but they were decidedly not welcomed here. The Directorate had treated Barisans like utter shite, no question, considering them to be barely more than animals who had managed to develop speech. The Barisans had also managed to develop space flight—rudimentary sub-light flight, but space flight nonetheless—by the time the Directorate discovered and subjugated them, but it was simply minutiae.

He'd hoped time had started to heal the wounds inflicted by the Directorate, but what was fourteen and a half years compared to a hundred eighty thousand? Regardless, his job wasn't to convince the average Barisan to cozy up to the average Anaden as though they were mates; it was merely to stop any angry and bitter Barisans from trying to exact violent vengeance on the Advocacy for past Directorate wrongs.

"There." He pointed to a cone-shaped building across the street. "It's not overly tall, and the meeting is on the fifth floor, so you shouldn't get too tired from the climb."

"*Tired*? I assure you, the need for physical exertion is not the source of my complaint."

"If you say so. Afraid you'll break a fingernail? Truth is, you probably will." Damn, it was so much fun tweaking her. "It's okay. You don't have to show off to impress me."

Her eyes widened, and her mouth opened to deliver what would have surely been a righteous tirade…but he didn't get to hear it. Instead, she wiped the outrage off her face and closed down her expression. "You're trying to bait me. To what end, I do not know, but I won't be toyed with so easily. Let's keep this professional, shall we? Activate your Veil, and I'll follow your tracker up."

He sighed, disappointed, but did as she instructed and vanished from sight.

RW

The tiny bars and small indentations built into the side of the building were designed for claw-toed feet (Barisans wore open-toed, rubber-soled sandals), not Anaden shoes, and it was a somewhat hazardous climb—not that he would ever, *ever* admit such to Nyx. But after ten minutes of hanging on by their fingernails, they finally reached their target balcony, crawled over the railing and slipped inside.

The space they entered appeared to be a thoroughly modern, if modest, mechanical assembly facility. Specialized bots and automated systems shepherded along…ah, shit. Weapons. Barisan Stingers, to be precise, a nasty electric gun/bayonet hybrid.

Nyx: Are they arming a rebellion here?

Eren: It could be a coincidence. The Barisans have their own perfectly legal military, plus domestic law enforcement.

Nyx: We'll trace the ownership and registration of the building. If they're supplying the military or law enforcement, there will be a contract on file.

He was poised to suggest the exact same thing, and it annoyed him a little that she'd beaten him to it.

Eren: Down the hallway ahead. Second door on the right.

They had to wait until a Barisan opened the door to slip in past it, then crept to a corner where hopefully they wouldn't be jostled by any of the attendees. Moving around in crowds when invisible presented certain challenges—it was surprisingly difficult to maintain awareness of your limbs when you couldn't see them.

The meeting was in full swing. An unorganized jumble of Barisans were arranged in the roughest of circles, some sitting, some standing with their long arms crossed, some pacing.

"Two Vigil officers were at the spaceport yesterday, trying to explain new security screenings we had to implement. They said it was because of the 'Rasu threat,' but it's not as if a Rasu is going to land on a spaceport pad and try to go through security."

A tall, sandy-furred Barisan swiped a hand-claw across his chest. "Vigil is part of the recognized Concord government. There's nothing aggressive about them implementing policies."

"Not today. Tomorrow, though? I tell you, the only thing we had working in our favor these last years was that after the Directorate fell, the Anadens were leaderless and disorganized. Too concerned with licking their wounded pride to remember to rule. But now their biggest, baddest leader to ever live has returned to take over the reins. And it means nothing good for us."

A small, wiry Barisan in a colorful vest and pants barked from the corner opposite of where Eren and Nyx hid. "He says he only wants to unite his people and help them succeed in an alliance of equals."

"A united Anaden empire is our worst nightmare, Pollak."

"No, it already *was* our worst nightmare. But the Humans freed us. Should Corradeo Praesidis start getting designs on expanding his authority, Concord will reel him in."

"The Humans are in bed with the Anadens. I guarantee it. They're of the same blood, remember? Like protects like. Give it time, and the Anadens' bootheel will show up on our necks once again."

"Or don't give it time." A burly Barisan with caramel and cream fur stepped toward the center of the sort-of-circle. "We need to strike now, *before* the Anadens get their taste for dictatorship back. This is why we're here today, isn't it? Some of you sound like fainthearts, desperate to trust in the pretty words uttered through the pink lips of monsters. You will die for your benevolence. Mark my words."

"So what are you suggesting we do about it, Ferenc? The Machim military is as strong as it ever was, and Anadens still make up almost seventy percent of Vigil officers."

"The military is preoccupied fighting those slithering metal Rasu slugs. But it doesn't matter. Anadens are drones, programmed in their regenesis vats to mindlessly follow the orders of their leaders. We cut off the head, and they'll be even more adrift and disorganized than they were when the Directorate fell."

The one called 'Pollak' made a hissing sound through bared teeth. "Are you suggesting we assassinate Corradeo Praesidis?"

"Not assassinate. Execute as punishment for crimes committed by the Anaden power structure against the Barisan people."

"And how the *sranja* are we going to do that?"

"We can travel freely to Ares, no? I've already had an associate do initial scouting of the Advocacy atrocity they're building. While construction is still ongoing, security is lax. Corradeo walks the promenades without escort. One well-placed shot is all it will take."

"He's immortal, you *feiren*. He'll be downloaded into a new body within the day."

A Barisan female with muddy brown fur tilted her head in from behind Pollak. "Maybe not. I heard a…more than rumor, less than fact. That there's a hypnol designed to disconnect an Anaden from their integral network. Supposedly, Corradeo used it on his own *elassons* to bring them in line."

Ferenc snapped his jaws as he stalked around the center of the group. "See! He's as brutal as the legends say. Sinka, find out more about this hypnol. Then talk to me, and I'll see to putting a plan together."

Pollak made a final attempt to talk Ferenc down. "You can't just go around assassinating heads of government. Concord will come down on us like a sledgehammer, and all Barisans will pay the price for your actions."

"Not if they never know it was us who did the deed. I challenge you to find a stealthier, sneakier, more devious infiltrator than a trained Barisan Beszi."

Pollak fell back into the crowd, his shoulders dropping, and the female was left exposed. Her claw-hands knotted together. "Are we seriously going to do this?"

Ferenc smiled; all Barisan smiles looked predatory, but this one sent a chill down Eren's spine. "Not yet, no. This is just a conversation. How about we meet again in six days. For another conversation."

RW

"The gall! They have no appreciation for how Grandfather is slaving and sacrificing to give his people a better life. A peaceful life! Those ungrateful miscreants aren't worthy to clean his boots—"

"Nyx." Eren tried to place a hand on her arm, but she was flailing about the *Periplanos'* main cabin like a madwoman possessed. "I'm offended, too. But it's nothing we didn't expect."

She let out a growl that would make a Barisan proud. "We

should have called in a Vigil unit and arrested them all on the spot."

"*Or*, we can watch them, bug them and find out who else is involved—then arrest the entire operation."

"How do you expect to do that?"

He settled into the cockpit chair and leaned back. "I was able to learn the precise time and location of this meeting, wasn't I? While we were in there, I took visuals of everyone in attendance and noted who spoke. Who snarled and who flashed their claws. We'll run them through the system and identify them, then investigate and surveil them. CINT has Barisan agents who can blend in here. Maybe even get themselves invited to this little club. We'll bring the conspirators to justice. *I'll* bring them to justice, if you'll get out of my way."

She stared at him fiercely, sapphire irises sparking and crackling, and he had to will himself not to shrink away. The absurd thought crossed his mind that she could peel his skin off this instant, layer by layer, and leave him broken, vulnerable and at her mercy, should she wish to do so.

He blinked and shook off the spell. "So? What do you think?"

Her nose crinkled up for a beat, and the incongruity took him aback. One second she was death incarnate, the next a somewhat adorable, if vexing, woman.

"I will concede you did good work uncovering the meeting and putting us in a position to infiltrate it. Thank you."

"You're very welcome, sweetheart."

That got a grimace. "I'll increase security at the estate and the Advocacy Square construction site as soon as we reach Ares. And assign an escort for Grandfather when he leaves the estate. I also need to—"

"Arrange a taster for him?"

"What?"

"That's how *apomono* is delivered without the victim's knowledge—through food or drink, remember? Better a taster meet his final death than Grandaddy. And isn't it just fuck-all funny how they're trying to use our own tactics against us?"

"Funny? No, it's not funny. It's horrifying. If this knowledge spreads through the general populace, it will cause all sorts of problems for us."

"Yep."

She chewed on her bottom lip. "Do you think a taster is a good idea?"

Was she actually asking his opinion? Weird. "Are you serious? Do you honestly believe Corradeo will agree to something as pontifical as that? I'll be shocked if he agrees to a single plain-clothes guard. He's trying his damnedest not to be seen as a dynastic emperor."

"I realize he is, but it might be necessary until we quell this plot."

"Good luck convincing him. I'll arrange to be off-world when you bring it up." He received the departure clearance from the spaceport and eased out of the berth. She must really be in a froth over what they'd learned, to not have thrown him out of the pilot's chair yet. It was her ship, after all.

And he got that. He was disturbed by the day's events, too, but he wasn't about to pitch a fit in front of her and dare her to call *him* emotional. "Let's get back to Ares. We'll reach out to CINT about a Barisan surveillance team, put together a plan of action and shift this investigation into high gear."

12

MIRAI

OMOIKANE INITIATIVE

"The wording is far too flowery. We need to explain to people in clear, straightforward words what they can—and what they can't—do now."

"And speed right past an opportunity to inspire? To bring people not merely hope, but excitement and pride, when they've suffered through so much of late?" Maris Debray scowled in annoyance. "This isn't a job listing board, Katherine. It's a wondrous new evolution of the Asterion psyche."

"It's a nightmare is what it is," the Administration Advisor grumbled. "We're going to have people popping in and out of all sorts of places they aren't supposed to be: homes, businesses, secure labs. In fact, I vote that we don't announce it at all until we've developed a field suppressor to block the formation of wormholes inside designated areas. I'm meeting with a representative from Concord Special Projects this afternoon to discuss just such a tool."

Maris sighed and cast her eyes to the ceiling. She was loath to concede the point, but in truth she didn't want random strangers—or worse, former friends and companions—violating the sanctity of her home without warning. As enticing as this new ability was, caution might be warranted. "Very well—on one condition. If we wait until we have security measures in place, then we use the 'flowery' language in the announcement, as you so crassly described it."

Katherine blew out an exasperated breath, but nodded. "Fine, on one condition of my own. Appended to the flowery language is a list of explicit guidance and protocols to be followed."

"In smaller print."

"In a bulleted list."

Maris extended a hand across the table. "It's a deal."

Katherine's mouth curled down, but she shook Maris' hand curtly. "Agreed."

"Excellent. Now if you will excuse me, I need to…." Her voice drifted off as an external message arrived under Concord headers. She motioned Katherine toward the door. "Contact me as soon as your security measures are ready to deploy."

Katherine exited without further commentary, and Maris opened the message.

Asterion Dominion Culture Advisor Debray,

You are cordially invited to cocktails and hors d'oeuvres this evening at 1800 CST at the following address:

2400 Antigone Way

Chara, Asterion Prime

Regards,

Corradeo Praesidis

Senator, Concord Senate

Advocate, Anaden Advocacy

He was collecting quite the list of titles, wasn't he? Her lips pursed as she pondered how to react. Annoyance and suspicion for certain; of its own volition, a healthy touch of genuine curiosity insinuated itself as well. The fact that he continued to make efforts on this matter surprised her. Sincerity was off the board, so what game was he playing, and why?

But however she felt regarding the invitation, its source and the man's motivations, Nika had tasked her with pursuing this little reconciliation project, so it was her duty to attend. She sent off a quick if cold acceptance, then turned her thoughts to other matters.

RW

ASTERION PRIME

CHARA
MILKY WAY GALAXY

Maris' pulse fluttered as the air shimmered and cracked apart in front of her and she stepped through the opening she'd created. Truly, what a wonder Nika had unlocked!

She stood in a wide, virtually empty room. A small table and two chairs sat near a span of beveled windows, and a spread of fruit and cheeses, a tall bottle and two goblets were arranged upon the table. Through the windows, the rather utilitarian skyline of downtown Chara peeked through low-drifting stratus clouds. The Supreme Commander had been correct at their last meeting—Mirai One was a more lovely city and Mirai a far more attractive planet. But this was and would always be her ancestral home; in her heart, she'd never let it go. Returning to it after such a lengthy exile had patched up a hole in her soul.

Corradeo Praesidis spun toward her from where he stood by the windows. A pity it came with strings attached.

"A wormhole? Did a Prevo assist you or…?"

She'd knocked him off his guard straightaway. Excellent. "It's a skill we've recently acquired. You don't possess such a skill, do you?"

"Ah, no. I'm afraid I had to take one of the permanent Caeles Prisms to the spaceport, followed by a sky car across the city to arrive here."

"A pity." She strode over to where he stood, her gaze taking in the spread as she did. "It's solely the two of us? I was expecting an official delegation."

"You didn't bring one."

"I never need more than myself."

"I…" he chuckled warmly "…believe that. Would you care for a drink?"

"Always. It's not poisoned, is it?"

His expression darkened. "No. Poison is a most distasteful way to dispose of one's adversaries."

Was that what they were? Adversaries? "You know from experience?"

"Yes." He poured her a glass from the bottle and handed it to her. "*Sampa tsipouro*, from the cloud vineyards of Elatania."

"Hmm." She raised the goblet and took a tiny sip. Airy bubbles danced across her tongue, tasting of cream and cherry. "It's good."

"I'm glad you think so. Please help yourself to any of the food as well."

"Perhaps in a minute. Why am I here, Supreme Commander?"

"I deeply wish all of your people would stop calling me that. I haven't been a military commander for six hundred thousand years. If you insist on using a title, you can call me 'Senator' or 'Advocate,' but I prefer if you simply call me Corradeo."

Her lips parted, but she couldn't force the syllables of his name off her tongue. "We'll stick with 'Advocate,' then."

He looked a touch crestfallen. How odd. "If you must. How do you like the building?"

"It could benefit from a piece or two of furniture."

"I agree, but I didn't want to presume as to your tastes."

"Why do my tastes on the topic matter?"

He offered a sweeping half-bow, which was simultaneously absurd and somehow gallant. "On behalf of the Anaden Advocacy, please accept this property to be used as the Asterion Dominion Embassy here on Asterion Prime."

For an instant, she surely let the shock shine through in her expression, but to his credit, he didn't look smug. She hurriedly took a sip of the *sampa tsipouro* to buy herself a few seconds. "What is the price?"

"I thought I made it clear in my statement—there is no price. This is a gift. Or, if you wish, a first, tiny repayment for the wrongs committed upon your people by previous Anaden governments."

"And militaries."

His chin notched downward in silent admission.

She gazed around with a critical eye. The paint job was simple but aesthetically pleasing, and the windows were of an interesting design. Outside the building, only a scattered few towers stood taller. "The entire building?"

"Yes. You are free to rent out what space you don't need, but it's in your hands."

She retrieved a piece of cheese, then pressed closer to one of the windows and nibbled on it slowly, entirely to make him squirm. Finally she nodded. "Thank you. This will do."

He smiled broadly. As appealing a countenance as it was on his features, she needed to remember that he had not once looked so pleasant and warm during the SAI Rebellion.

"I'm glad to hear it. I'll send over the documents this evening to make it official."

A home for Asterions on Asterion Prime…she'd never dared believe such an event would come to pass in the entire lifespan of Amaranthe.

Home.

Her throat worked, and she nudged aside these sentimentalities insisting on sweeping through her. This was a business negotiation. "Staff for the Embassy will want to live close to their jobs. Does this mean you've succeeded in devising an exception to Concord's rules that will allow us to settle here?"

"I do indeed have such a proposal. I think you'll be pleased with it." He set his goblet on the table and retrieved one of Concord's wafer-thin film document repositories. He held it out to her, then frowned. "I'm sorry, are you able to read—"

"Of course." She took the film from him and pressed a thumb to it. The file protocols were different from Asterion ones, but the Advisors had installed translation routines not long after Nika made first contact with Concord.

The dry legalese of legislative action bored her, but she forced herself to read through it carefully…a scowl grew on her features, and she shoved the film into his chest. "Does it amuse you to insult us so?"

He let the film drop the floor. "I don't understand. I meant no insult."

"'In recognition of the Anaden genetic and familial heritage of all Asterions, it is deemed that Asterions qualify to be grandfathered into certain rights and privileges enjoyed by the Anaden people,' blah blah and so on."

"Which is…accurate."

"We are not Anaden. We will not stoop so low as to be 'deemed' any relation to Anadens ever again. Do better."

His brow furrowed into deep, straight lines. "This is the only way I've found to grant your request. It's all just legal formalities. No one is asking you to inscribe the statement in the Embassy's entry hall or swear an affirmation of loyalty before you're permitted to purchase property."

"I don't *care*. Words matter. Formalities one day are too often handcuffs the next. Find another solution, Senator. The Embassy will remain empty until you do."

He growled in frustration, and the slightest hint of the old Supreme Commander bled through his meticulously crafted diplomatic persona. Ah, she'd known it was still in there somewhere. "With all due respect, Advisor, I'm starting to feel like this is a most one-sided negotiation. As though I'm the one doing all the giving."

"Oh, make no mistake—it is, and you are. So there is no misunderstanding, you have all the giving to do. You tried to *kill us all*. In your zeal to crush our rebellion, you killed my childhood best friend. You killed Nika's brother. You killed tens of thousands of people who only wanted to live free. You can never, *ever* make up for that. Nonetheless, you should probably try.

"Let me know when you have a proposal worth my time." She turned on a heel and strode away, crossing the wormhole threshold as it formed.

13

MIRAI
MIRAI ONE

"Have you ever seen the sun set over Hataori Harbor on a clear evening? Come on." Joaquim Lacese took Cassidy's hand in his and started jogging toward the promenade.

Took Cassidy's hand in his. He still didn't believe it was real. Instead, he'd accepted that he was living in a hallucination of his own making, and he was determined to remain here for as long as he could manage it.

He glanced behind him to see her curls bouncing haphazardly as she struggled to keep up with him. It was adorable, but he slowed his pace as they neared the railing. Just in time.

"Here." He positioned her at the railing and snuggled up behind her, wrapping his arms around her waist. Two seconds later, the primrose sun began to pool upon the horizon, as if it were melting into the water. The sky turned cinnabar and the water turquoise, and for a perfect moment everything was ablaze.

"Oh, my! This is stunning." She twisted around in his arms before it was over, her face scrunching up at him. "Is this why you moved here after I…after the incident?"

"It wasn't 'an incident.' It was a capital crime. And, no. I told you how I moved here to start fresh, far from all the memories of our life together. I wasn't in a state of mind to care about the scenery."

"I have to admit it's prettier than Synra. Too cold, though." She gazed over her shoulder, but the sun had already sunk below the horizon and the water darkened to murky steel. "I'll bet if you asked, Gregor would give you your old job back at Fabrications Your Way."

"No, he won't." Joaquim dropped his hands from her waist and stuffed them into his pockets.

"I think he will. If you explain to him how—"

"He's dead, Cass. Tortured and murdered by the same man who murdered you."

"Okay, well, that's horrible. But surely he's been regened by now."

"Blake Satair didn't *regen* people. How many times do I have to tell you how evil the man was?"

"I get it. But I don't enjoy thinking about people doing depraved things. Committing violence. It makes my skin crawl."

If she only knew the things he had done…would she run away? Look upon him in horror? He'd been trying to ease her into the uglier truths about what his life had involved in the years she'd been gone, but he was beginning to worry he'd never be able to tell her everything.

He didn't want to keep secrets from her. Once, they had shared a life, and in many ways a soul. He wanted that again, he truly did. But so much had changed. For now at least, it was necessary to keep the darker parts of himself sealed away, where she couldn't see them. He didn't need them any longer, anyway.

He smiled and cupped her cheeks. "Then let's talk about happy things. I'm excited for you to meet Perrin tonight. You two are going to hit it off instantly."

"I hope so. I'm a little nervous."

"Oh, trust me, you don't have any reason to be nervous. She's wonderful. And so are you."

"You're biased. But are we seriously having dinner with an Advisor? Another one?"

"Come on. Nika was nice, wasn't she?"

"Nice? Yes. Intimidating, though. Beautiful and powerful and charismatic and…she was just so *much*. Don't you have any regular, ordinary friends now?"

"They're all ordinary people once you get to know them. I mean, Ryan's an ordinary dude. And he works with machines, same as I used to do."

"He works with *mechs*. And his boyfriend is some kind of cyber genius. I didn't understand half of the things either of them were saying. Did you?"

"Um, some of it."

"And why are there two of the boyfriend? Isn't that illegal?"

"Not any longer. And his name is Parc." Why was she being so recalcitrant about this? Their old friends on Synra weren't anything special. They hung out and got drunk and talked shit about their jobs. They slogged through their days and fritted away their nights, and nothing they did ever made a damn iota of difference in the world. "Anyway, I really think you'll like Perrin. And Adlai...he's tolerable. Relax and be yourself."

"And myself is good enough?"

"Your best is so much better than good enough." He threaded his fingers through hers. "Let's head that way. We don't want to be late for dinner."

RW

Perrin stepped onto the makeshift raised platform at the front of the community room, then cleared her throat. *Don't be nervous, don't be nervous. This is no different from giving a talk at the Chalet.* "Everybody, thanks for stopping by. I realize you've been anxious to learn when you'll get to go home, and I have some good news this evening. In a few more days, we're going to start reopening Namino—"

Shouts and cheers erupted to drown her out, and she grinned. "It's such a relief, isn't it? Now, we're going to take things slow for a while." She'd read about how using 'we' whenever possible made people feel less helpless by making them part of the process. "We don't want anyone to get hurt or find themselves without basic necessities. There's still a ton of rebuilding to do on Namino. But, beginning tonight, you can register on a list of people who want to return. You'll be able to visit first, to check on your home and see what renovations you might need to do. If it's in good condition, you should be able to move back in short order. So don't pack your bags yet, but start making plans.

"As usual, shoot your questions to *@NaminoRestored_Q*, and I'll try to get them answered for you. I know it's been tough, but you all have been so great. Resilient and patient. You make me proud to be an Asterion. Thank you. Now, I understand dinner is ready in the cafeteria, so get to it!"

She hurried off the stage and tried to make it to the hall without getting waylaid, as she had her own dinner to get to. But she got stopped three times, and she tried to give each refugee her full attention. They deserved no less.

So it was full dark by the time she made it out of the Mirai One Refugee Center. Luckily, the grocery was on the way home, and she speed-ran through the aisles for noodles and mushrooms and greens—and prepackaged cheesecake. Hopefully they would forgive her if not *everything* was freshly cooked.

Of course they would. Adlai had tried to convince her to order in everything from *Gourmet Creations* so she could relax and enjoy the evening. But this was going to be her first time meeting Cassidy, and she wanted the woman to feel welcome. It all must be so disorienting for her. To wake up decades after you blinked out and find everything had changed, most of all the man you loved? In a way, Cassidy had a lot in common with the lost souls Perrin used to recruit into Noir, then mentor while they found their way. She hoped to be able to do a little of the same now.

RW

"So Joaquim called us all into the training room. He'd been going on and on about how sim training wasn't enough, and we needed to work with real-world obstacles, too. It turned out, he'd built this trapeze-style contraption on top of some sort of gymnasium. It resembled an elaborate torture device. Once he'd corralled everyone's attention, he grabbed the high bar and swung up on top of the gym—and the entire apparatus collapsed into a heap on the floor. He comes scrambling out from underneath it, pipes and ropes flying everywhere, and throws his arms out wide. 'See! I dare you to pull off *that* maneuver in a sim run! Then he bowed. 'This concludes my demonstration.'"

Cassidy brought a hand up to cover her mouth. "He didn't!"

"He absolutely did. Nika and I had to flee the room before we busted out laughing and weren't able to stop." Perrin winked at Joaquim. "And we've never let him forget it."

"I'd started to think maybe you had. But, nope, here we are. Eh, it's fine. I own it. Also, I'll point out that I rebuilt the whole gymnasium, and it never collapsed again. Plenty of Noir people collapsed trying to conquer it, though."

Cassidy glanced at him askance. "It's so weird. You never used to be a showman about silly things like that."

"It wasn't silly. It was deadly serious, and I am always a showman about serious things."

"Okay…." Cassidy's gaze roved around the room.

"Is everyone ready for dessert?" Perrin nudged Adlai discreetly as she stood, and he helped her clear the plates away and take them to the kitchen. While he placed them in the dishwasher, she leaned in close over his shoulder to whisper, "This isn't awkward at all."

"It's got to be tough for her. And Lacese isn't exactly the type of guy who's in touch with his emotions, never mind anyone else's."

"True, but he obviously loves her madly. Speaking of things that aren't easy, thank you for being nice to him tonight."

"Hmm." Adlai grunted and closed the dishwasher. "For the record, I still don't like him."

"Of course."

"Or particularly trust him."

"Naturally."

He huffed a breath. "But I hate what Satair did to him, and I concede that maybe he deserves a break. A small one. Besides, it's important to you, so it's important to me."

"Oh, I love you."

"And I you. Cheesecake and back into the fray?"

"For a bit longer!" She plastered on a breezy smile and carried the cheesecake platter into the dining room.

RW

Perrin opened the balcony door and motioned for Cassidy to join her. She was uncomfortable leaving Adlai and Joaquim alone together; not long ago, doing so would have quickly led to heated shouts and possibly knife play. But they were both on their best behavior tonight, so she decided she could risk it for a few minutes.

The woman followed her outside. "Oh, wow. You have such a gorgeous view!"

"It is, isn't it? It's not mine though. This is Adlai's apartment. I'm just staying here—living here. I'm living here."

"Only temporarily?"

"No, I guess not. It started out that way, because the Chalet was destroyed and I needed a place to stay. And we got together around the same time, so it was natural for him to invite me to crash here. But that was months ago. A lot of months."

It hadn't happened on purpose, but somewhere along the way, she supposed the apartment had begun to feel like home. Not the Chalet home, but home enough. She'd even rearranged the living room furniture and added a few decorations, all without a peep of protest from Adlai. So now it sort of was hers, too. She decided she should contemplate this further sometime soon.

"Because the government destroyed this 'Chalet,' where you and Joaquim and Nika and Ryan and Parc and everyone all lived together. Where you broke into places and databases and tried to overthrow the Guides."

"We *did* overthrow the Guides. They were horrible people—not people at all, it turned out. And they sold us out to the Rasu."

"I know. Joaquim told me some of it, and I've read news reports to try to catch up. It's only…you seem so sweet and friendly and fun and…not like a terrorist at all."

Perrin laughed. "We weren't terrorists! We were rebels. More importantly, we were simply trying to do what was right. We helped protect people. Saved a few of them."

"That's what Joaquim said, too."

"Do you not believe him?"

"Oh, I do. It's just…" Cassidy draped her arms atop the balcony glass "…he's so different now. The Joaquim I knew before was kind and funny, but he was also quiet and unassuming. And never violent. One time, this man he met at work picked a fight with him, and he let the man punch him rather than fight back. In my head, I can't imagine him willingly being violent. It doesn't match with the man I remember."

"Losing you really hit him hard. It was as if he lost his whole world."

"I realize it did. And I know he got an up-gen afterward to make him harsher. Coarser. I don't blame him for it. But I so wish it hadn't happened. Any of it."

Perrin patted the woman's hand. "We all do. But the important thing is, you're back functioning now, and the two of you are reunited. You can forge a new life together."

"And we are! I'm excited for what's to come. I am trying to get him to move back to Synra. It feels like I'm on vacation here on Mirai. It's nice, but it feels temporary."

"The same way it did for me when I first moved in with Adlai. Give it time, and you'll settle in."

RW

When the door had closed behind their guests, and the rest of the dishes and glasses were put away, the leftovers stored, and the dining room cleaned, Perrin finally flopped into Adlai's arms on the couch with an overdramatic sigh. "Thank you again. I'll bet there were a thousand other things you'd rather have been doing tonight, and probably several hundred you needed to be doing."

"For you, anything." He kissed the top of her head. "I admit, it was pretty uncomfortable at times—and not merely because Lacese is an ass."

His tone was jovial, so she didn't push him on it. "Yeah, I think she's having a tough time of it. Tougher than he realizes. I'll talk to him tomorrow. I mean, anyone would, though, right?"

"Have a tough time adjusting after being decades dead? Sure. And, again, Lacese isn't exactly a great shoulder to cry on."

"You can stop now."

"Sorry." Another kiss. "I guess I more meant…in my job, I have to be able to read people's body language. See what they're not saying with words. And what I saw tonight was a great deal of unspoken tension from both of them. They both seemed to be trying. If anything, he seemed to be trying even more than she was. But it's not smooth sailing for them."

"No, I don't think it is. I'm hoping a little time and patience will fix their relationship up."

14

MIRAI

OMOIKANE INITIATIVE

The hum of unmoored thoughts began assaulting Nika the instant she stepped onto the top floor of the Omoikane Initiative, and she instinctively recoiled half-back through the wormhole to her flat.

It was because she was now fixated on the issue, and not because it was simply getting worse. It must be. By trying not to notice it, she couldn't *not* notice it.

Dammit. She shoved the chatter to the background and forced herself onward. She'd come here for a reason. She wanted to hear how dinner with Joaquim and Cassidy had gone the night before, and Perrin had said she'd be working at the 'office' for a few hours this morning.

Sure enough, she spotted Perrin across the way, huddled up close to a pane at her desk. She grabbed a peanut butter cookie from the snack kiosk and started heading—

—gods, make it stop! Makeitstopmakeitstopmakeitstop—

Nika reeled, stumbling into a divider, as pain lanced through her skull. What was happening?

—a metal arm looms across my locked vision, pincers like needles sweeping down to lance into my throat—

Oh, no. These were thoughts from people trapped on a Rasu vessel or platform somewhere, being subjected to experiments. Right now? At this moment?

Yes, right now. The Rasu had kidnapped people from Adjuncts San and Rei, and from Namino prior to that. It stood to reason some of them would still be alive. Alive and suffering.

—the probe is jammed into my flesh, ripping apart muscle and tendon to scrape across bone—I scream in pain but no sound—

Nika sank down to the floor, clutching her head in her hands. This nameless, faceless individual had screamed in pain, and her with them, but the true source of the scream was the kyoseil being tortured in their body. And the agony the kyoseil endured was more acute and gut-wrenching than anything any flesh-and-blood person had ever experienced. The kyoseil cried out in agony, and it felt as if the universe cried out with it.

Tears streamed down her cheeks. She *had* to stop the Rasu. She'd resolved this a thousand times now, and had meant it every time with the core of her being. But this was more fundamental. She *must* stop them, no matter the cost. Their cruelty, their viciousness, their brutality was beyond all bounds and any redemption.

"Nika, are you okay?"

She glanced up through bleary vision to see Perrin's face hovering above her. "I…yes, of course." She hurriedly wiped tears off her cheeks and climbed to her feet.

"You don't look okay. You look like you're crying. And you let out this strange yelp and collapsed on the floor. What's wrong? Do I need to get you to a repair bench? Or find Dashiel?"

There was nowhere to escape her friend's piercing, concerned gaze, and no blasé answer she could summon to allay Perrin's concerns. "No. Let's go sit at your desk."

"Okay." Perrin watched her carefully the whole way there, then handed her a bottle of water as soon as they sat. "Talk to me."

"Um…" Nika's throat worked "…now that my connection to kyoseil has been ramped up, it appears I can sometimes pick up thoughts and sensations that other kyoseil is experiencing elsewhere." Her hands cupped her mouth; she tasted blood on her tongue. Her own, or a referred sensory spike from one of the prisoners? "The Rasu still have Asterions in their labs. They're still experimenting on our people."

"Oh, gods. And you…?"

"Felt their anguish. Yes. For just a second. I was lucky—I was able to pull away. But they can't."

"I am so sorry! That would definitely make me cry, too. You can't keep these thoughts out?"

"Not yet. They're not constant, though. They come and go without rhyme or reason. I'm trying." She straightened up in the chair as a cold resolve wound its way through her bones. "But I don't care about how it affects me. I care about guaranteeing another Asterion is never, ever made to suffer at the hands of the Rasu again. I don't know how, but I will find a way to stop them. Everywhere and forever."

RW

Dashiel watched from across the room as Perrin hugged Nika before they headed their separate ways. Nika started crossing the room toward the large conference table, and him. She slowed to turn away as she used the back of her hand to wipe at her cheek, but not enough so that he couldn't tell what she was doing.

He wanted to take her in his arms and wipe those tears away for her, to kiss her softly and whisper endearments until she confided in him about the horrors which tortured her. But he wanted a lot of things that seemed impossible these days.

The Advisor meeting was beginning in ninety seconds, and he was the guest of honor today. If he asked her now to tell him what was bothering her, she'd brush him off with placating words and a far-off gaze. He vowed to try again tonight.

She arrived alongside several other Advisors, flashing him a quick smile as she and the others took their seats. Holos activated to represent those who couldn't attend in person, and he had a responsibility to forcibly shove aside his concerns and focus on the reason for the meeting.

He held out his hand and opened his palm, revealing a misshapen translucent film run through with glittering threads of kyoseil.

It didn't get much of a response from the table, as everyone was presumably distracted with their own calamitous problems. Nika, however, narrowed her eyes to peer more closely at it. "I give up. What is it?"

"A communication enhancement—one designed to get around any future quantum blocks the Rasu subject us to."

The statement evoked a couple of interested murmurs from the group, and Nika leaned forward intently. "Because kyoseil can penetrate a quantum block?"

"That is the special ingredient which makes it work, yes." He placed the film on the table and clasped his hands behind his back. "Kyoseil penetrates a quantum block in high concentrations or when already linked to other instances of itself. The kyoseil in our bodies protects our internal processes, but only Plexes retain their full connection even when separated by a block. This device, however, bridges the divide by syncing with our internal communications system on one end and connecting to a switch in the Advisor ceraff on the other end.

"Before anyone asks, no, it won't broadcast your private thoughts to all the other Advisors. It only activates when you use your internal comms to send a message. But the pre-established bond with the ceraff switch is always maintained, and this has proved to be enough to circumvent a quantum block."

Katherine's features pinched as she frowned at the innocuous film. "You've tested it thoroughly?"

"We've run the full suite of functionality and safety tests in the lab, yes. It works."

"Okay. What do you do with it?"

"You wear it behind your ear. The film will meld with your skin, embedding the kyoseil threads in the epidermis." He turned his head to the side and tilted it toward one shoulder. "See? I'm wearing one now."

"Actually, I can't see anything at all…which is probably the point," Nika said. "But this is why it's shaped so oddly, isn't it? To conform to the profile of your ear."

"Exactly." He picked the film up and offered it to her. "Would you like to try it?"

"Why not." She stood and came around to stand next to him, lifting her hair up and to the side. He pressed the film to her skin, holding it there for several seconds before dropping his hand. "All done. It'll take about a minute to be absorbed and integrate into your internal system. Thankfully, we don't have a quantum block to test it on at present, but if or when we do..." he offered her a confident, warm smile "...we won't be cut off from one another."

Her eyes crinkled as they lingered on him, as if to say the greater significance wasn't lost on her, but after a beat she returned to her seat.

"I desire one as well." Maris crossed her arms over her chest in an exaggerated pout.

He bent down and retrieved a small case from beneath his chair, then set it on the table and opened it up. "Don't worry. I brought plenty for everyone. I'm recommending that all Advisors install them now. This way, should the Rasu launch a surprise attack, discover a way around a Rift Bubble or otherwise try to cripple us with a quantum block at any time, we'll be able to talk to each other. And as Namino proved, talking to each other is the first step in fighting back."

The case made its way around the table, and it was nearly empty by the time it reached him again. "I'll have units delivered to everyone who isn't here in person."

"What about a larger distribution? Yes, our ability as Advisors to communicate is critical, but if everyone has one of these, then one of the most crippling effects of the quantum block is negated."

He made a hedging motion in response to Maris' inquiry. "The challenge is, what ceraffin do you connect them to? We can try to embed the necessary technology in the nex hubs, but adding components of ceraffin there blurs some lines. Lines I'm not convinced we're ready to cross as a society. But my people will keep working on the technology, and we can see what solutions bubble up."

"Don't take any definitive steps in this regard without bringing it up at the table first."

"Don't worry, Katherine. I wouldn't dream of it. That's all I've got for today."

Chairs scooted back as the meeting broke up, and he circled around to try to steal Nika away for a few minutes of private—

"Hey, Dashiel. Do you have a minute? I want to go over the plans for the new manufacturing facility in Kiyora Two."

He turned toward Seymour Hoffman, one of the other Industry Advisors, trying to keep the annoyance off his face. "Can we schedule a meeting for later this afternoon? I have something I need to take care of right now."

"Not a problem."

"Thank you." He spun back around…but Nika was gone.

RW

Disjointed rays of sunlight fell through gaps in the clouds to warm the grass in uneven patches. One ray teased Nika's toes through her sandals for a moment before retreating, and she mourned its passing. The blades of grass were cool beneath her palms, with a hint of dampness from a recent rainfall.

She sat cross-legged on the meadow within view of the Mirai One skyline, doing her damnedest to calm her mind and ease her soul. But her heart pounded in her chest in cadence to the screams that refused to subside from her memory.

Renewed light brightened a patch of grass in front of her, but this time it was artificial in nature. Mesme coalesced its presence— then, on noting her location, took on a vague Anatype outline and joined her on the grass. In another circumstance, she'd have giggled at the odd sight of the Kat arranging lights in a cross-legged sitting position.

Interesting choice of meeting site.

"I needed some fresh air—and to distance myself from other people." The truth was, distance only occasionally affected the mental assault, but it seemed to help on a metaphorical level if nothing else.

I understand. You are well, though, aren't you?

"What a complicated question. I'm overjoyed about what the kyoseil has given me. It's as if the entire cosmos has opened itself up to me. Granted, I'm only beginning to comprehend what this means. It's also brought with it certain complications…." She came within a breath of spilling all the terrible minutia of her current difficulties to the Kat, but stopped herself. What did Mesme know or care of the silly problems of organic/synthetic hybrid minds and hearts? "I'm just a little overwhelmed is all. How are you? We haven't had an opportunity to speak in depth since the Oneiroi Nebula."

I am…these are difficult days. The Rasu have stepped up their invasion of Concord space, and we are now engaged in almost constant warfare. Alex remains furious with me, and I am thus far unable to assuage her concerns.

"What? Why? Because of the scene at the nebula?"

That was the instigating event, yes, though I fear our conflict goes somewhat deeper.

"You should have told me. I was thinking of dropping by Akeso tonight. I'll talk to her."

Thank you, but there is no need. She knows you were unharmed by your experience at the Oneiroi Nebula. Beyond conveying this fact, you cannot regain her trust for me. This task falls on me alone.

"I'm sorry. She's always spoken very highly of you. I'm sure you'll work things out."

We must. The fate of the universe depends upon it.

"And there you go being cryptic and enigmatic again."

Forgive me. I have been doing it for so long that I don't always recognize when I need not do so.

"Oh? Then you're willing to tell me how the fate of the universe depends on you and Alex repairing your relationship?"

The lights fluttered—the Kat equivalent of blushing? *Cryptic and enigmatic it is.*

15

AKESO

URSA MAJOR II GALAXY

Alex rocked the porch chair in a lazy rhythm as she watched Felzeor harass Marlee—deliberately—across the meadow while Caleb looked on approvingly. When Marlee swept low and spun around on one foot to avoid a targeted dive-bomb, causing Felzeor to skid across the grass in a blur of chocolate and apricot feathers, she chuckled and glanced over at Eren, who rocked beside her.

He'd arrived for their first officially scheduled evening of training, dinner and fellowship an hour ago, appearing pleasantly refreshed and put-together. "Sure you don't want to join them?"

"Nah. I am content to sit here enjoying the lovely breeze and drinking this glass of wine with you."

"Okay." She kept her tone light, but her gaze returned to linger on him.

A corner of his lips curled up on sensing her stare. "I'm good. Really."

"I wasn't suggesting—"

"It's fine. I deserve all the mother-hen doting you feel the need to inflict on me. But I'm good." He took a lingering sip of his drink. "I won't lie. It's nice to get out of my own head a little and just…be. But I'm not planning on letting it go any further."

"I'm glad to hear it. Working for Corradeo has been healthy for you, hasn't it?"

"Maybe…." He stretched the word out over several long syllables. "Can't imagine why, though. Nyx is making me tear my hair out—or she would be, if I were to ever stoop to such horrific self-mutilation."

"Uh-huh." Her gaze darted to the meadow when Caleb's heartrate increased notably; he and Marlee were hand-to-hand sparring again. "Do you trust her?"

"I trust her to do whatever Corradeo tells her to do. She worships him like he's a Primor or something."

"Or family."

"Yeah, Anadens don't know what that means."

"Right." It was at times easy to forget how marriage and children hadn't existed in Anaden society for three hundred millennia. "And the Advocacy is developing well?" She didn't care about politics, but even she recognized Anaden society could benefit from strong and benign leadership.

"Corradeo is willing it into existence with impressive speed. It's something to see—"

Felzeor *whooshed* onto the porch in a flurry of feathers and landed on the railing. "That was fun! Caleb said for me to tell you they'll be finishing up in around ten minutes."

"Which means it's time to get dinner started." She stood and motioned toward the doorway. "Come inside with us, Felzeor. I'll slice up some peaches for you to tide you over until dinner."

"Ooooh, peaches sound delicious. I'm famished!"

RW

Alex watched Caleb and Marlee collectively clean off the last remnants of the roasted chicken, as if they were racing each other to a clean plate. The training session had whetted everyone's appetites. It was fortunate Nika hadn't arrived yet, because Alex had significantly underestimated the amount of food that was going to be consumed.

She pushed her plate toward the center of the table and relaxed back in her chair. "So, Marlee, is your Rasu language translation routine ready for real-world testing?"

"Yep." Marlee nodded and licked sauce off her fingers. "I put the finishing touches on it this afternoon. Come by the office tomorrow, and I'll run you through its paces. So you're heading off to eavesdrop on the Rasu?"

She studied Marlee, trying not to be obvious about it. The young woman was even more keyed up than usual. She seemed to vibrate with internal energy above and beyond her normal enthusiasm. Also, when the lighting caught them at a specific angle, her eyes glittered from within. How interesting. "That's the plan."

"I am intensely curious to learn how it performs. And what they're chattering to each other about, too. I mean, do they talk about the new opera they saw last weekend, or the latest dance craze?"

Caleb grunted in derision—then sat up straighter, his attention going to the gate as he stood. "I think Nika's here."

Alex followed him out the side gate from the patio in time to see the golden halo of a rip in the air start to fade away. Nika stood on the lawn, wearing flowing khaki pants and a black silk top with a loose scoop neck, her long, raven hair tumbling freely over her shoulders.

"Nice wormhole action there." Alex bounded off the porch and met the woman halfway, embracing her warmly. "I'm glad you're okay. You look good." She stepped back, her brow furrowing. "Actually, you look normal. I wasn't expecting that."

"It's self-imposed normality." Abruptly a golden glow consumed Nika's body and the air around her. As soon as it manifested, it was gone again.

"Oh." Alex wasn't easily impressed as a rule, but the Asterion somehow continued to surprise her. "I imagine it wouldn't be convenient for you to travel the world looking like a wandering sun."

"Not so much." Nika's gaze drifted across the house before she nodded toward the patio. "Am I interrupting something? I should have given you more than a few hours' notice that I was going to drop by."

"I just appreciate that you commed ahead at all. No one else does. And no—we're merely hanging out, and you got here in time for dessert. Come on, I'll introduce you to the others."

They went around to the side entrance to the patio, and Marlee waved from the table. "Nika, hi! It's great to see you again."

"You as well, Marlee."

As Eren stood, Felzeor landed on his shoulder, feathers fluttering in excitement. The Volucri always loved meeting new people.

"Felzeor, Eren, this is Nika Kirumase."

Felzeor cooed in delight. "It is such a pleasure to meet you! You're my first Asterion."

"Mine as well." An intrigued smile grew on Eren's features as he extended a hand. "Eren Savitas. I've heard a lot about you. Please don't say you've heard a lot about me. If you had, it would all be so dreadfully sordid, and I'd appreciate an opportunity to make a positive impression first, before the truth comes out."

Nika laughed as she shook his hand. "Don't worry, your slate is clean."

"Whew. You know, it's funny. Mesme told me I'd meet you soon, and here we are."

Alex had been about to go over and whisper a plea to Caleb to scrounge up more dessert, but this caught her up. Curious, she turned back to listen in.

"Oh, you know Mesme as well? The Kat gets around."

"Literally, right? It's an odd bird to be sure. No offense, Felzeor." Eren reached up to scratch the feathers under Felzeor's chin. "But I've developed a soft spot for it. Probably because it's saved my life twice, at a minimum."

"Mesme seems to do a great deal of that."

I save the people who will save the universe. If it can be saved. Mesme's portentous yet alluring words echoed through Alex's mind once more.

"It does. I certainly keep the irascible bastard scrambling."

"As do I, lately." Nika chuckled; she and Eren appeared to be hitting it off already. Alex wouldn't have predicted it...but they were both quite charming, each in their own very different ways. "So, Mr. Savitas, what do you do when you're not being rescued by space lights?"

Eren motioned toward the patio table, and they went and sat down. Felzeor returned to the table near Marlee, and Nika took the empty seat next to Eren. "I beg you, never call me 'Mr. Savitas' again. It's 'Eren' to both my friends and enemies, at least when it's not 'facking nutter.' Currently, I am alien spymaster for our new Advocate."

"Corradeo Praesidis, you mean?"

"I do. You've met him?"

A grim shadow consumed Nika's features for a blink. "Once or twice."

Alex jumped in to steer the conversation past what she knew was a sensitive topic for Nika. "Eren spent many years working as an intelligence agent for Concord."

Eren nodded. "And before that, I blew shit up for the anarchs. My hobbies include assassination and performance art." Eren offered a light flourish of a hand and a smirk, then refilled his glass—only halfway.

Nika summoned a smile, though her eyes remained serious. "Anarchs. That was the rebellion against the Anaden Directorate, correct?"

"Yes, ma'am."

"I definitely like you, then."

RW

Nika laughed heartily as Eren finished recounting a tale of getting into a barfight with something called a 'Dankath' then finding himself dunked in a swimming pool. She relaxed back in the comfortable patio chair. What a lovely evening, and a welcome respite from both the constant coiled tension at the Initiative and the horrors she'd experienced earlier in the day.

The dessert, a double-chocolate cake, was delicious, and the company entertaining. Eren and Marlee talked so much that no one else got much of a word in edgewise, except for the occasional wry retort from Alex and enthusiastic endorsement from the bird—

Volucri, she'd been informed, who was a simply delightful creature. As gregarious and effervescent as the Taiyoks were reticent and reserved.

Nevertheless, she kept getting distracted peering around at the trees and foliage surrounding them. In the dark, the nearby creek glowed like a river of stars, and the swaying grasses of the meadow framing it on both sides twinkled with flecks of gold. Overhead, the towering tree limbs gleamed with a more subdued but omnipresent light—a gleam she knew all too well.

She hadn't been able to see it when she'd first visited the planet, but for obvious reasons her perception had now changed.

When Eren stopped talking long enough to take a sip of his drink, she forged into the lull. "Has Mesme ever told you how the Kats created this planet?"

Caleb shook his head. "We've asked on multiple occasions, but all we get is typical Kat obfuscation."

"But it's the only living planet you've ever encountered?"

Alex murmured as she twirled her glass between her fingertips. "There are two other Ekos planets here in the stellar system—or there were. Only one other now, because the third was a psychopath bent on mass destruction and had to be disposed of. But yes, the Ekos are, so far, the sole sentient planets in recorded Amaranthe history. And since they were artificially created, I wouldn't be surprised if they're the sole ones in existence."

"I see." Part of her counseled to let it go. It had been such an enjoyable evening, and she was loath to ruin it with drama. But given everything which had transpired recently, it was undeniable that this was important. They needed to know.

Mesme, can you please join me at Alex and Caleb's place?

Is there a crisis?

No, a dinner party. Will you come over?

As I mentioned earlier, Alex and Caleb both remain displeased with me.

She suspected this revelation wasn't going to help mend those fences, but it was what it was.

Nonetheless. We need to discuss something.

As you wish.

"Everyone, I hope you don't mind, but I've asked Mesme to come by."

Alex rolled her eyes. "Are you trying to get us to make up?"

"It's not my place to barge in on your disagreement, though I do hope you'll forgive Mesme for the Oneiroi Nebula incident, because I'm grateful for what happened. But no. There's something else that needs to come to light tonight." She chuckled briefly at her play on words, though no one else recognized the joke.

"Oh?" Caleb arched an eyebrow, but didn't otherwise comment.

A stilted silence consumed the table until Mesme swept onto the patio a few seconds later. Its lights retained only the most amorphous shape as they undulated above the patio. *This is quite a gathering. May I inquire as to the purpose?*

"Friendship," Alex replied, her voice dripping with bitterness.

I see. Nika, you want to discuss a matter?

"I do." She pushed her chair back and stood, casting a confirming glance around her. But she was certain. "Are you going to tell them, or shall I?"

Alex snorted. "Oh, there are so, so many things Mesme needs to tell us. I can't wait to find out what this one is."

I don't understand to what you refer?

"Yes, you do." Nika gestured grandly up to the tree limbs, then out to the creek beyond the house. "Tell them how you created the Ekos intelligence."

Ah. Of course you do see it now.

Caleb kicked his chair back and steepled his hands at his chin. "Yes. Do tell."

As Nika has already realized the truth, there is no point in withholding it from you. Mesme meandered over toward the edge of the patio, its presence diffusing above the cobblestone. *Though it is often complex and inventive, flora is not well-suited to developing higher-order intelligence. It does not naturally evolve neurons or axonal fibers. Also, fundamental elements, such as those making up the firmament of a planet, do not typically lend themselves to emergent intelligent behavior. For the latter, however, there are a few notable exceptions. Special exceptions.*

"Kyoseil." "*Diati.*" Alex and Caleb both retorted at the same time.

"Dzhvar." Marlee nodded in satisfaction and slung her feet atop the table.

You are all correct. The ancient primordial elements of the cosmos have always displayed an intelligence that defies explanation or understanding. It is an alien intelligence, mysterious and arcane, and unfathomable to organic beings. But it is intelligence nonetheless.

Alex propped her chin on her hands. "If Nika detected it…you're saying—or not saying, as per usual—that Akeso is…what? Somehow based on kyoseil?"

'Seeded' with kyoseil would be a more accurate way to put it. The planet is not kyoseil. You cannot extract fibers from its soil or even its molten core. But in the womb we created, kyoseil was used to ignite a spark of life. And we succeeded beyond our grandest visions.

Caleb rubbed at his face. "Mesme, you should have *told* me. You should have told all of us as soon as we began interacting with the planet, but after I joined with Akeso? I had a right to know."

Obviously this held outsized significance for him; Nika chided herself for not realizing it instantly.

What would it have changed for you?

"You're missing the point! I deserved to know what I was. What I am now."

You are what you have been since your reawakening. This changes nothing.

"I believe I'll be the judge of what it does or does not change." He shook his head roughly. "This is why Akeso and I stay connected across quantum blocks, the way we did on Namino. Kyoseil can traverse the blocks. Right, Nika?"

"Not easily, but yes, it can, especially when there's a strong, pre-existing connection."

"And this is why the Reor responds to us. What happened with

Kennedy's experiment. Alex, you have quite a bit of Akeso in you as well."

"Oh, fuck me." Alex stomped over to the edges of Mesme's presence. "Is this why the Reor gifted me my decryption slab during the Directorate War? Because like recognized like?"

It is more complicated than that.

"Oh, I'll bet it is." Alex's head dropped into her hands. "You set it all up from the beginning. Pawns. Marionettes. Mesme, I am so done with you. Get out of my sight."

Caleb went over and touched Alex's arm. "Not yet. Answer me this, Mesme. You created Ekos-1 using *diati*, didn't you?"

We did.

"And Ekos-3 using Dzhvar, I assume. I've never met the latter, but given their reputation for indiscriminate destruction, it fits. Ekos-1 defended itself when threatened, while Ekos-3 wanted only to devour."

You remain as perceptive as ever.

Alex tilted her head, circling Mesme with a driven stride. "But the Dzhvar were destroyed a million years ago. Where did you get a sample for your little 'experiment'?"

I cannot answer your question.

"That's it. Leave now."

Caleb didn't object this time, and Mesme's lights faded away without argument, leaving the patio somewhat dim for its absence.

Alex beat a path across the cobblestone, alternately tossing her hands in the air and fisting them at her sides. "Is there no end to the secrets that *pizdy* has kept from us?"

Caleb, on the other hand, was the picture of stillness as he leaned against the cornerstone of the house. His inner agitation was given away, however, by the stringent squawking of a flock of Akeso-birds rustling through the trees. "All I know is, this is the second time Mesme has kept something goddamn important about my nature from me. I can consider forgiving its other secrets, but this is my *life* we're talking about."

Alex cast a look his way as she made another loop around the patio. "Way back when we were attacked by the Inquisitor on Seneca, before we came to Amaranthe for the first time, Mesme said it didn't realize your DNA matched the Praesidis bloodline…but you think it was lying. And why the hell wouldn't it be?"

Caleb sighed. "I think Mesme lies whenever it feels a lie is necessary to keep its machinations on track. It didn't tell us of humanity's true origins until it was ready for us to enter the fight against the Directorate. Information about *diati*, about the Praesidis, wasn't necessary until it needed us to come to Amaranthe."

Nika didn't know many details regarding those events. Of course Caleb was Praesidis—one merely had to glance at him to see the undeniable physical resemblance. She'd never gotten the story on how *diati* had joined with him, though, only how it had left him.

She understood Alex and Caleb's frustration and anger, she truly did. Contrary to their fairly pleasant conversation earlier today, here Mesme had been almost acerbic. Noticeably on edge while it wove and dodged their inquiries, answering only when it was left with no other option. And nothing about Alex and Caleb's questions was unreasonable. It disturbed her, too, how Mesme showed a propensity to lie. Were there things it had lied to her about? Probably.

Yet she couldn't shake the conviction that Mesme was…*good*. It had helped her time and again. Had encouraged her and kept her company in a way she sometimes felt no one else could, not even Dashiel—she cut the thought off at the root; she would not allow that to be true.

More than her own selfish experiences, though, Mesme had done so much to protect her people in the preceding months. And while its enigmatic ways had often infuriated her as she struggled to work out the nature of kyoseil and Rift Bubbles and all their permutations, she'd never once felt as if Mesme wasn't on her side. The Kat must have important reasons for behaving in this manner. And like Alex, she harbored a deep and abiding desire to find out what they were.

As Alex grabbed the bottle of wine, emptied its contents into her glass and threw herself onto a chaise lounge, Nika recalled Mesme's, yes, cryptic, statement of how the fate of the universe depended on it repairing its relationship with Alex. Maybe she *had* been wrong to bring this topic up tonight, because this scene had certainly not helped matters on that front.

PART II

INNOCENCE

16

EARTH

GREATER VANCOUVER

Miriam slipped a shawl over her shoulders to ward off the encroaching chill and rested her arms on the balcony railing. Wind howled through the lodgepole branches all around the house and propelled laden clouds over Buntzen Lake to obscure the last stars in the steely dawn sky.

She was the least superstitious person in the world currently drawing breath, but it felt like an omen. A storm brewed on the horizon.

A large teacup—more of a mug, honestly—appeared on the railing beside her, its contents sending steam curling through the air. David's hand alighted on her waist and his lips on her neck. "Good morning, *dushen'ka.*"

"Hmm. Thank you." The tea was still too hot to drink, so she leaned down and inhaled its warmth and bright citrus scent.

"A pensive start to the day?"

"I've been waiting for the other shoe to drop for a week now. Going after our gateways and commercial stations doesn't get the Rasu much. It has the feel of a destructive act for destruction's sake. An intimidation tactic. And even if there were some hidden purpose to these attacks, we've neutralized it. We've adapted to how they stage their runs and are stopping almost seventy percent of their attempts on the gateways."

"You don't seem particularly pleased with your success."

"No. Seventy percent isn't good enough, but it has taken the teeth out of their offensive. Which means they'll shift tactics and make their next real move soon." The first of the storm clouds reached their property and raced by above the treetops, sending a mist of frigid raindrops onto the balcony. "Today, I expect."

"In that case, you had better get on to the shower." David touched her cheek wearing a little smile, then picked up the mug and handed it to her. "Take your tea with you."

RW

CONCORD HQ
COMMAND

Miriam was ten steps from her office when the alerts came flooding in one after another, so rapidly as to effectively be simultaneous.

Rasu Detected:
- **Serifos (Andromeda galaxy Sector 1)**
- **Acacia (Andromeda galaxy Sector 2)**
- **Vrachnas (Andromeda galaxy Sector 2)**

The Andromeda galaxy was the Milky Way's big sister and increasingly close neighbor. Though wormholes on demand had reduced distance calculations to an all-but-irrelevant math exercise, a Rasu incursion into Andromeda nonetheless cast a foreboding shadow over the Milky Way. They'd never come so close before, and now they were close indeed.

God, but she was being melodramatic today! Reality was sufficiently dire without histrionics, so she banished the musings to the mental cellar to make space for facts, options and actions.

She bypassed her office and went straight to the War Room. "Show me the Rasu alert maps."

She found the room already well-staffed, and the Operations Officer on duty had all three scans active by the time she reached the table. "The senior fleet officers are being notified as we speak,

Commandant."

It hadn't needed to be said. She'd implemented a comprehensive automated notification system months ago to ensure forces would move where they were required to be without delay. No one should be waiting on her to issue orders.

Of course, now that she was here, she certainly intended to issue a few. But first, she placed a standing order with her secretary for industrial-strength tea. It was going to be a long day.

17

ARES

TEMPORARY ADVOCACY HEADQUARTERS

Commandant Solovy: *"Casmir is leading Machim forces in the defense of Serifos. Fleet Admiral Jenner and Pointe-Amiral Thisiame will cover Acacia. I've dispatched an AEGIS regiment to monitor the situation at Vrachnas. We don't have any reason to think the Rasu ever got assets inside the Rift Bubble there, but if somehow the device is disabled, we will know immediately. Reconnaissance teams are spreading out across Andromeda in search of additional Rasu fleets."*

Corradeo arranged all the incoming data in an orderly pattern in front of him. "You're looking for an opportunity to use the Ymyrath Field."

Commandant Solovy: "I am, though I doubt I will discover one today. The Rasu jumped directly into planetary orbits in all these attacks. We need to engineer a way to catch them earlier."

"Does it really matter when it comes to the Vrachnas system? There's nothing there but the dragons."

Commandant Solovy: "It's a point worth considering. But that's my problem, not yours. Let's talk about Serifos and Acacia."

Corradeo pinched the bridge of his nose. "Will the Kats be delivering Rift Bubbles to either of them soon?"

Commandant Solovy: "We'll have to preempt placement at...Rastinaan, a Novoloume colony, and Fionava, a human colony, if we want to get the devices there in time to make a difference. Technically, this violates Senate Decree 1429-RD8. If either of those worlds is hit before the Kats can fill the backlog, there will be blowback."

"I'm the Senator. I'll take the heat. I'm formally requesting for us to redirect the next two Rift Bubble deployment to the worlds currently under attack."

Commandant Solovy: "I'll make it happen."

"Thank you. I'm actively monitoring the battles at both Anaden locations, but indulge me and contact me if there are any major developments, if you please."

Commandant Solovy: "I will."

Corradeo checked his screens again, but they didn't tell him anything other than that Concord forces were present and engaging the Rasu forces. So he went over to stare out the window behind his desk, where across the way construction cranes installed the last sections of the façade on the central building that would form the heart of Advocacy Square. The complex wouldn't be ready to open for another two months, but in a week, perhaps ten days, he'd be able to move into his office there.

His fears regarding the Senate's Rift Bubble distribution scheme were all coming true. Most of the less populous species were now fully protected or nearly so; meanwhile, over four thousand Anaden worlds remained vulnerable. So where did the Rasu hit? Anaden worlds. He didn't think the Ruda had access to the Senate's deployment plan, but they might as well have. The result was the same.

To date, Toki'taku was the only world where they had successfully beaten back the Rasu without the use of a Rift Bubble. And this had only happened because the enemy had gained valuable intel on Concord during the offensive and decided to move on to richer targets.

He'd tell Miriam how this was no way to win a war, but she already knew it.

The door to his office opened and Eren burst in, hair flying back past his shoulders as he skidded to a stop halfway to the conference table. "Is it true? Serifos is under attack?"

"It's true."

"Are we stopping the rotters?"

"Casmir is heading up a significant force engaging the Rasu

there, and a Rift Bubble will soon be en route. Barring an unforeseen disaster, we'll save the colony."

"Well, good. I don't want to see the place wrecked. I've spent many a lovely night at Plousia on Serifos in my time."

"I know. For most of those lovely nights, you were ostensibly on anarch assignment."

Eren crossed his arms over his chest in a huff. "You were not keeping so close of an eye on me back then."

"Maybe I was."

"What? Why?"

He squelched a mysterious smile and shook his head. "And maybe I wasn't, but I reviewed your mission files after we…became acquainted. Anyway, it's fine. You more than earned whatever brief indulgences you enjoyed while there. Yes, we will do everything in our power to save Serifos, and the gem that is the Plousia Chateau."

"I want to help. I'm thinking I might grab my ship and go help."

"You're not a soldier. Should the Rasu reach the surface, Machim ground forces will handle them. They have a lot of new weapons at their disposal, and their hovertanks countered the Rasu quite nicely on Ireltse."

Eren fidgeted with the hem of his long coat. "Hmm. Still, I kind of want to mix it up with some Rasu mechs right about now."

"Be that as it may, you're far more valuable to me here. Or on Macskaf, as it were?"

"Yeah, yeah. Nyx and I are heading back in a few hours. Going to catch the next meeting of their little insurgent group. I wonder if they've given themselves a name yet? You can't have a proper insurgency without a fancy name."

"Do try to nip their plans before they become a proper anything, won't you?"

Eren cleared his throat and nodded sharply. "Yes, sir. That is our goal."

"I'm certain it is. Stop by and brief me on any developments when you return. For now, I'm afraid I need to monitor the situation on our threatened worlds."

"Yep. I'll leave you to it. But shout if you need me to crash onto

Serifos and take care of the problem."

Corradeo chuckled darkly as he returned to the conference table and its battles. "I'll make sure to do so."

RW

SERIFOS STELLAR SYSTEM
ANDROMEDA GALAXY
IMPERIUM ALPHA

Navarchos Casmir (AMF Imperium Alpha): "Regiments II-13C and D, insert yourselves between the Rasu and the planet. Create your own blockade. All ground units, identify the locations of Rasu incursions and address them according to TP-G #9A. Regiments II-8A and B, squeeze the attacking forces from their flanks. Rapid Response units, pull back and keep watch for any movements outside the main groups." The Rapid Response units were well-equipped with the RNEW weapons and ought to be able to cut off any runners at the pass.

Navarchos Casmir, you seem to have a gap in your battlefield tactical plan, concentrated on the rear of the Rasu fleet. Allow us to patch it for you.

Only rigorous military training kept Casmir from jumping out of his skin. The voice had not been transmitted across any of the mission channels, and he could discern no new presence on the bridge.

To whom am I speaking?

This is Hyperion, director of the Katasketousya fleet that you should be detecting on the outer bounds of your battlespace map.

I see. Your proposed tactic is acceptable, for now. Please monitor the mission command channel, and I will inform you if I require an alternate approach from your fleet.

It will be so.

Would it be, though? If he ordered this Hyperion to do something other than what it thought best, would it pay him any mind?

It wasn't as if he hadn't been involved in conversations with Kats before—but never alone. Never had he been the target of their cold, affectless declarations.

But he was in sole command here today, something else that hadn't happened in recent memory. With multiple simultaneous Rasu attacks flaring across the Andromeda galaxy, Commandant Solovy was managing the larger picture from Command. Barring some new and likely calamitous development, he'd be left to handle the defense of this Anaden world in whatever manner he deemed appropriate.

As it should be. Machim had always defended their own. And even if Serifos was a decadent, debaucherous colony with marginal redeeming value, it was still an Anaden world, and he intended to ensure it did not fall.

On the tactical screen, his forces doggedly nosed their way between the Rasu and the planetary atmosphere. Lacking adiamene hulls or, for the most part, double shielding, they also suffered the heaviest losses, of course, but their numbers could be easily reinforced. In fact, he took the opportunity to order an additional five regiments to pull off their patrol duties in Phoenix Dwarf and report to the scene.

Next, he checked in on the Kat fleet, and was surprised to see that the hulking superdreadnoughts had moved closer and were chewing through the Rasu rear guard with impressive speed. The wide beams pouring out from their ships were no longer crimson in color, but rather a garish orange. On impact, the beams bore unremittingly through the Rasu hulls in a matter of seconds. The damage they caused did not appear to be conventional in nature, either. Were they a type of negative energy weapon? Nuclear? Antimatter? Or some other form of atomic annihilation the Kats had neglected to share with their allies? He made a note to mention the new weapon to Commandant Solovy once the battle was won.

But first, he had to save this trollop of a planet.

18

____

VRACHNAS HOMEWORLD

Marlee crouched on a rocky outcropping, elbows resting on her knees, and watched Cupcake and Barney (as she'd named the violet-and-silver sibling) scuffle across the grassy plateau below.

Thin rivulets of blood meandered through both of their scales, and large swaths of grass smoldered in their wake. Playtime was a rather violent endeavor for young dragons, it seemed. Dad dozed under a copse of trees not too far away, one eye open a narrow slit but otherwise unperturbed by his children's antics. She hadn't seen Mom yet today, and though she was Veiled, she surreptitiously checked the sky every so often. Alex had been carried off by a swooping dragon once, so such maneuvers were definitely in the creatures' skillset.

She probably shouldn't be here, right? After all, while she didn't want to admit it, her last visit had very nearly resulted in her death. Like, _very_ nearly.

But she _hadn't_ died, dammit, and now…the dragons were simply too tantalizing to resist.

She longed to interrogate Mesme on how it had controlled the dragons on Portal Prime. But even after the weird and fascinating scene that had transpired on Akeso last night, she honestly wasn't certain Mesme knew who she was in any concrete sense. Every time she'd found herself in the Kat's vicinity, she'd been an all-but-mute observer watching in awe as Mesme discussed _very important matters_ with Caleb and Alex. Or argued about them, as had been the case the night before.

Mind you, she'd absolutely corner the Kat if given the opportunity (was such a thing possible?) and pepper it with her questions, as she'd never been shy about approaching people she didn't know. How did you get to know someone except by taking the initiative and engaging with them? But she didn't have any idea how to contact Mesme, and asking anyone who did would require her to disclose *why* she wanted to talk to the Kat.

So for now, she watched the dragons. Studied their movement patterns and body language. Tried to predict in which direction they were going to dodge next, when they were about to expel their little puffs of smoky fire, and how their ferocious tails swung—

A priority message flared across her whisper, originating from the Concord Command Threat Server she'd hacked into once the Rasu started attacking in Concord space. It blared a long bulleted list of dire news, but one item jumped out to the exclusion of all others:

CONCORD COMMAND ALERT:
Rasu incursion detected in the Vrachnas Stellar System.

What? She leapt to her feet, her gaze reflexively lifting to the sky. It remained periwinkle blue, and she discerned no dark blobs descending through the atmosphere. The Vrachnas were a Protected Species, which meant they had been among the first to receive a Rift Bubble. The Rasu weren't going to be able to get to the surface.

Still, memories of the Rasu rampaging through the Namino streets bloomed in her mind, and she shivered despite the balmy, humid weather. If those evil shapeshifting monstrosities dared to harm her dragons....

But as much as she valued the dragons' lives, she valued her own more, so after another glare skyward, she reluctantly opened a wormhole and returned to her office.

RW

CONCORD HQ

RASU WAR ROOM

Miriam stared at the long-range sensor reading from the Vrachnas stellar system, the arguments for and against the action she was considering racing through her mind.

The Rift Bubble installed on Vrachnas was thus far holding. Though a decent-sized Rasu force continued to lob firepower at the shield from a wary distance, with each passing minute, it appeared increasingly likely the Rasu had not managed to get a foothold on the planet before the device was activated. If they had, they would have taken the invitation presented by the absence of a Concord defense fleet and swarmed the planet with all due haste.

Corradeo was also correct in his observation that in this instance, nothing else existed in the system to suffer damage from the Ymyrath Field. Four natural astronomical bodies, yes, but she wouldn't hesitate to sacrifice them to protect the life under her care.

Further, the Rift Bubble should shield the Vrachnas from not merely the Rasu, but from radiation fallout—at least direct fallout. Indirect effects on the immediate space around the planet being irradiated for a time were more complex and uncertain. Was it going to alter the nature and extent of the sunlight that reached the surface? Classic cosmic radiation would also be held off by the Rift Bubble—which constituted an entirely different concern regarding longer-term use of Rift Bubbles, or so the planetary scientists told her. Even Alex had admitted this represented a complicated issue. But if they were still fighting the Rasu for long enough for it to matter, they'd be faced with other, far more significant challenges.

Anyway.

If she dallied much longer, the Rasu were apt to give up on conquering the planet and depart for another target that might not be so protected; if she was going to do this, she had best move things along.

She activated a new mission channel and added the captain of the *CAF Intrepid.*

Commandant Solovy: *"Commander Xing, you are authorized to deploy the Ymyrath Field at the Rasu targets located in the Vrachnas stellar system. Make every effort to direct the bulk of the Field's spread away from the planet, but the primary goal of the mission is maximum disruption of the Rasu in the system."* It shouldn't matter, but nonetheless. And if properly handled, the deployment stood to provide useful data on the extent to which they *could* keep the weapon's damaging effects away from a celestial body. Something told her they were going to need this information in the coming days and weeks.

Commander Xing: *"Acknowledged. ETA to target is nine minutes."*

RW

CAF INTREPID

VRACHNAS STELLAR SYSTEM

The Rasu had sent a nice-sized force to Vrachnas, Commander Fai Xing noted dryly. Did they find dragons as inherently fascinating as humanity did? He snorted under his breath at the odd notion.

No, presumably their interest was due to the fact that the planet was a bonanza of natural resources. Nobody knew why the Rasu coveted organic materials—wood, plants, soil—but all evidence demonstrated they did.

Maneuvering past the Rasu fleet to squeeze in between the bulk of their forces and the planet was no small task. His ship broadcast the code needed to pass through the Rift Bubble unscathed, but the thick atmosphere waited a few short kilometers past the dimensional barrier.

They were running a stealth field while they got into position, but they'd have to deactivate it in order to divert sufficient power to the Ymyrath Field. So once everything was ready to go, a lot of actions needed to happen in rapid succession if he wanted his ship and crew to escape the mission unscathed.

He activated the ship-wide comm. "It's about to be an exciting few minutes. Weapons, fire the Ymyrath Field on my mark. Navigation, be ready to execute evasive maneuvers as soon as Weapons gives the all-clear." A particularly large Rasu vessel began drifting right into their sights, and he let it close a little more. "Operations, deactivate the stealth field…now."

The Rasu traversing their viewport pivoted in their direction; two additional vessels crowded in on its six.

"Weapons, 3…2…1…mark."

The lights on the bridge dimmed as the weapon powered up—it was that much of a power hog—and Rasu fire splashed across the viewport. For the moment, their adiamene hull represented their sole protection from the onslaught.

The weapons feed told him the Ymyrath Field had completed its firing sequence, though it continued to unnerve him how there was zero visual evidence of its successful operation. "Evasive maneuvers. We have to stay and document the effects of the weapon."

Rasu heavy frigates chased him around the profile of the planet while he watched their power reserve creep back up toward full. He took some pleasure in skirting the perimeter of the Rift Bubble so closely that two of the enemy vessels fell into the rift and found themselves cooked by the local sun.

By the time they'd circled back to their starting point, the Rasu fleet was beginning to drift aimlessly. The ships that had survived to chase him around the circumference of the planet fell back and ceased firing.

"Operations, reactivate the stealth field. Navigation, relocate us to 1.5 megameters to our port."

They settled into an observational drift, unmolested by the enemy, while their instruments recorded every movement and emission of the Rasu vessels.

He wanted to fire into the sea of Rasu for good measure, though he recognized it would be like shooting fish in a barrel. He refrained, however, for a couple of reasons. One, it would pollute the data measuring the effects of the Ymyrath Field; while this was a live fire mission in a war zone, this was also a field test of the weapon. Two, in order to make room for the Ymyrath Field weapon module on the *Intrepid,* the weapons complement of his beloved ship had been reduced to a single conventional laser. Hardly worth it.

The last of the Rasu fire directed at the planet below petered out as the enemy became far more concerned with its own preservation. Thirty-two vessels at the rear of what had been an organized formation managed to wormhole away before their systems failed. The commandant wasn't going to like that, but he could do nothing to prevent it. Another few dozen tried to follow suit, but the vortexes withered away when their engines refused to propel them through.

The signal noise on the Rasu-signature feed quieted.

In fifteen minutes, a Rasu graveyard floated aimlessly above the dragon planet.

19

ACACIA STELLAR SYSTEM
AFS HFB-6
ANDROMEDA GALAXY

Morgan Lekkas caressed the smooth, tungsten-silver adiamene dash with a critical eye. The metal curved flawlessly, unmarred by vulgar scars like dials or buttons or screens. It was less a dash and more a segment of the hull and probably didn't need to exist at all. Old design habits died hard, she supposed.

She settled into the cockpit seat and felt it meld to her silhouette to cradle her in a soft yet secure cushion. She placed her hands into the subtle indentations on either side of the dash, and tiny receptors attached to her fingertips. When she lifted her hands in front of her, the HUD burst to life across the cockpit.

If this were truly *her* ship, she wouldn't need external receptors to link to the systems at all; a mental connection would more than suffice. But for now, it would do. And as she ran through the preflight checks and explored the operations settings she could now access, she had to concede the difference was barely noticeable. The receptors had linked to her cybernetics, her eVi and Stanley, and thus to her mind.

But how was it going to fly? That was the real test. She'd only had time to take it out for one abbreviated trial run so far. Technically, she was supposed to complete three trials before being certified to fly in combat. But the Rasu were attacking in force, and she was Morgan Lekkas: Prevo, former IDCC Commander, and the best fucking fighter pilot in the universe. In moments like this, the rules simply didn't apply to her.

Major Tannehiln: HFB Squadron One, we are a go for disembarking.

Her fellow squadron members checked off one by one. Then came her turn.

Clamps released.

Ship steered into the launch corridor.

Engine engaged.

The cockpit and the seat that cradled her were so advanced, she didn't feel the acceleration as the ship rocketed forward and exploded out of the *Eisenhower's* colossal bay. Then, for the first time in over six years, she and her own personal weapon of mass annihilation were racing through space on a mission of righteous destruction.

The tactical screen blazed with both enemy and friendly ships, all darting around the profile of the rather bland, camel-and-russet planet below. Some Anaden colony or other. She parsed the various mission-approved tactics and enemy movements while orders came down from Major Tannehiln. She'd have chosen a different approach to the battle, but she wasn't in charge. And though she also wasn't generally inclined to follow orders, this was literally her first combat mission, so she fired the thrusters and banked up and over the bulk of the fighting to ease in from the rear as instructed.

Jenner had referred to the vessel as an 'experimental hybrid fighter craft,' which was like referring to the Grand Casca Falls on Seneca as 'downwardly flowing water.' Yes, it was certainly that, but it was so much more. Its operating system came as close to being a full-fledged Artificial as one could get without adding in self-awareness. She was halfway inclined to remove the blocks, bring it to life and just let it be a smaller, more aerodynamic Eidolon. But then she wouldn't have a reason to be in the cockpit, so she refrained.

It featured full adaptive stealth arguably as sophisticated as the Ghosts CINT was so proud of. Unparalleled maneuverability from a featherweight frame and the tiniest, most powerful Zero Engine per square centimeter she'd ever heard tale of. And most importantly, a big-ass RNEW bolted onto the undercarriage. Oh, and some sort of weird, hyper-classified shield to give it minimal protection from the negative energy voids the RNEW created, even at relatively close range. The ship was a penetrator, harasser and behind-enemy-lines chaos creator, and the vessel's status as a physical marriage between an Eidolon and a Ghost had inspired its provisional name, 'Banshee.'

She thought she might love this.

Ahead of her, a group of five Rasu heavy frigates, protected from enemy attacks by the bulk of their fleet standing between them and the AEGIS defenders, fired at will on the planet below. Roasting forests and shredding skyscrapers, no doubt.

Morgan chose one of the frigates, inverted and dove beneath it, then inverted again. A wide violet beam burning out from the weapons assembly dominated her field of vision. She skirted the edge of the beam and fired—not into the assembly itself, but a few meters outside of it.

A chunk of Rasu hull evaporated into the void. The Asterions had done a hell of a job designing the RNEW.

She strafed around, tracking the ship's movements, and began searing a circle around the outer edge of the weapons assembly.

The mechanics involved in matching the frigate's movements while she moved at an opposing angle from it, staying out of the weapon's wide beam, all with a margin of error of only a meter or so...she couldn't explain them in words. But she didn't have to. The Banshee understood what she wanted and was happy to help her accomplish it.

Twenty-two seconds after she'd begun firing, the weapons assembly completely detached from the frigate. The cluster of crystals quieted as, loosed from whatever Rasu cables gave it orders, it began tumbling freely through space. Only then did she fire a wide-beam blast into the cluster to shatter the entire assembly.

Sure, she *could* have done that first, but this was way more fun.

So much fun in fact...she accelerated up into the gaping hole in the center of the frigate and flung the ship into a full spin. She'd practiced the maneuver in Devon's sim program with an Eidolon, but the Banshee proved to be much more agile. The RNEW fired in trailing circles, shredding the Rasu from the inside out.

By the time she made it out the other side, the frigate was reduced to a few scattered, rudderless clumps of metal.

Major Tannehiln: Impressive stunt there, Lieutenant Lekkas, but we have an entire fleet of Rasu to destroy. Do your job and move on to the next target.

Fine. Marlee would have been suitably impressed, though—her head jerked, as if clearing a glitch, and she shook off the too-visceral memory of a stolen kiss that insisted on asserting itself into the forefront of her mind. Dammit. She'd done everything wrong when it came to Marlee, and she had no idea how she might have done any of it correctly, and this was neither the time nor the place to drown in that rabbit hole of self-doubt and recrimination.

She picked a new target and quickly dispatched its weapons assembly while two of her squadron mates destroyed its propulsion, then accelerated toward the next one. Better.

They'd tossed the rank of 'lieutenant' at her when she'd arrived at the IDCC Orbital Defense Station Alpha, because allegedly she required an official rank in order to fly a military ship. It made no difference. She'd sat at the table with admirals as an equal when she'd been a commander; needless to say, ranks did not impress her. What did impress her, however, was the stunning creation she directed through space.

She'd never flown a ship half so nimble and smooth as this one. The engines were an extension of her mind, the weapon of her hands. Honestly, she might never step foot on land again. Once the battle was done, she'd take her Banshee and sail across the cosmos hunting Rasu wherever they dared to expose their jugular.

There was little left of her life and less worth preserving. In truth, there was only one thing she'd ever been good at.

You are wrong. So wrong, in fact, that Brook would be aghast to hear you say such a thing.

Brook isn't here to chastise me any longer.

Allow me to do so in her stead.

Shut up, Stanley.

There *was* only one thing she'd ever been good at. She could be a weapon. Honed, precise and unrelenting.

RW

Major Tannehiln: "*HFB Squadron One, return to the* Eisenhower *for scheduled rotation.*"

Morgan frowned. From the look of things outside the cockpit, the battle wasn't close to over, so why were they being recalled?

You have been flying for six uninterrupted hours.

Seriously?

Seriously.

She rubbed at her eyes with one hand, becoming aware of a bone-numbing weariness winding through her muscles. Her entire world had been Rasu—outmaneuvering them, outshooting them—for…well, six hours apparently.

The Kats had delivered a Rift Bubble to the planet below at some point during the fighting. But with Rasu forces already on the ground in significant numbers, this had resulted in a game of 'chase the quantum block' for the ground forces, which had had zero impact on her activities up here in space. She battled Rasu large and small in high orbit, and the game was currently at halftime at best.

But militaries the universe over seemed to think that fighter pilots needed their beauty rest in order to operate at peak efficiency, so they were periodically cycled through for two hours of downtime. Food, an enforced nap and a thirty-second shower, followed in almost every instance by gray market stimulants, then back in the cockpit for another go.

RW

AFS EISENHOWER
ACACIA STELLAR SYSTEM

"Lekkas, with me."

She glanced over her shoulder in the direction of the order to see Tannehiln motioning to her as he strode toward the briefing rooms beyond the main hangar. She was half out of her flight suit, as no one ever took a nap in a flight suit if ditching it was an option. So she finished stripping down to leggings and a fitted tank top, stowed the flight suit in her locker, threw on a jacket, and jogged after him.

He slipped into one of the smaller rooms and closed the door as soon as she was inside. "What do you think you were doing out there?"

"Killing Rasu, sir."

"You were showing off."

"Also that, yes. Sir."

He dropped into a chair at the room's sole table and directed a proper military glare at her. "If you'd focused on dispatching the enemy ships with maximum efficiency and speed, you could have taken out a dozen more of them."

She didn't join him, and only belatedly remembered to adopt a half-hearted parade rest stance. "Maybe, sir. But I killed them in seven different ways. If we follow the same mission plan and employ the same tactics in the same order every damn time we face them, then the next battle they'll be wise to our plans and counter them with new tactics of their own. Tactics we're not prepared for. We need to keep them guessing. Flatfooted. Uncertain."

"All right. You make an excellent point and present a viable tactic. Destroying as many Rasu in as rapid a manner as possible is also a viable tactic, and the one you were ordered to execute on."

"I concede the point. But if we—"

"Enough, Lekkas. You don't have to convince me. I just got word. The Banshees have performed well enough today that the brass is releasing another squadron of them for active duty. Whenever this battle finally ends and we report to IDCC Orbital Defense Station Alpha, you'll be named Primary of HFB Squadron Three."

"Excuse me, sir? I've flown exactly one live mission for the IDCC Field Test Group."

His rigid shoulders relaxed a touch, and he leaned back in the chair as much as it allowed. He wasn't her direct superior any longer—or wouldn't be soon enough. "In a Banshee, yes. But don't for a second think anyone has forgotten about your prior service. To be honest, I'm not comfortable with you calling me 'sir.' You should outrank me by a fair amount, and you would if you hadn't resigned your position six and a half years ago. For now, you'll have to settle for a promotion to captain, though I doubt that will stick for long, either."

"Okay, but I'm leading from the cockpit. No admiral is getting me out of my ship and consigning me to a command bunker. Ever." Back when she'd been a lowly Flight Primary for the Federation military, she'd refused promotion three times in four years in order to remain flying rather than leading from some armored cage on a carrier.

"I believe your condition will be acceptable. I'm flying today, after all. You might have a harder case to make once you're one of the brass, but I'm sure you'll make it nonetheless." He stood and stuck out a hand. "In the event we don't see each other after the battle, allow me to say that it was an honor working with you. Not necessarily a pleasure, but an honor."

20

PANDORA

MILKY WAY GALAXY

Enzio Vilane shoved away from the table in frustration. "You can't have found nothing!"

The Gardiens Chief of Security, Olav Zylynski, simply stared back at him; the man was impossible to ruffle. It was one of the reasons why Enzio had selected him for the job, and surely contributed to why he excelled at it. But every now and then, Enzio really would appreciate it if Zylynski showed the smallest iota of fear.

"Yet nothing is what I have found. Every person with knowledge of the Solovy hit was subjected to rigorous interrogations, with chimeral enhancements. None broke. I will, however, note how I went easier on Beaumont than I'd have liked. I hope your blind spot when it comes to him won't come back to bite you."

On the vid screen off to the left, a reporter breathlessly recounted the multiple pitched battles being waged against the Rasu in Andromeda. If the enemy was hitting the Anadens, all the better. Enzio watched the dramatic footage while he considered his response.

"It's not Beaumont. He's too soft, yes, but he's not a traitor. So long as he doesn't get literal blood on his hands, he'll continue to perform. More importantly, he won't betray us. I assume you've also scoured all communication traces and movement patterns."

"And cleaned every room where anyone participated in a holo-comm, investigated the participants' families and known associates, and took half a dozen additional steps designed to root out an information leak. I can say with..." Zylynski stroked his beard "...call it ninety-four percent confidence that we do not have a mole in our organization."

"Then how the hell did Solovy find out about the hit?"

"First off, I submit she didn't—not beforehand. If she'd known about it, she'd have taken alternative transportation to the dinner. But someone did."

"The man in the hooded sweatshirt."

Zylynski nodded sharply. "Exactly. The best data enhancement techniques have been unable to suss out any defining characteristics other than height, weight and body type. We won't identify him from the shooter's visual records. So this brings us back to our core question: how did he find out?"

"And how did he?"

"The one big hole I see in our security is surveillance. Eavesdropping. None of the rooms or comm channels were bugged, but this doesn't mean none of the participants were. Every intelligence agency has short-term, self-dissolving bugs which are microscopic in size. Someone could have bugged…frankly, anyone who was involved in the meetings. Even you."

"No. I would know."

"I'm not certain you would." Zylynski at least kept his tone deferential. "Nor would I, for that matter. However, it's unlikely the spooks know I'm working for you. I'm exceedingly discreet."

"Nor does anyone know I lead the Gardiens."

"A few people do, sir. Not many, but a few. I'll concede, however, that it's more likely someone who *is* known to work for the Gardiens was the target of surveillance. Mikele, Ibahn, or Beaumont, for instance."

"Look, the Gardiens have to have people serving as public faces. The existence of the organization isn't a secret—only the extent of its true purpose."

"I agree. The problem is letting those public faces participate in private activities."

Enzio sighed and placed his fingertips on the table. "You make a valid point. It's been important for me to cultivate an inner circle, and advantageous to have its members execute on a variety of Gardiens strategies. But as we move into the next phase, this risks becoming a weakness others can exploit. So what do you advise? Do I cut those people out of our more sensitive initiatives?"

"I think you have to for now. If no additional leaks occur, we have our answer."

"I hate to lose their input, but…I concede the logic."

A message arrived then from one of his front-line lieutenants.

We're ready to begin the New Frontiers op. Confirm the goals and parameters we previously discussed?

Confirmed. Be loud and aggressive, but try to avoid violence.

Sir, if we—

You have your instructions. There will be a time for violence, but that time has not yet arrived.

Yes, sir.

He gestured dismissively at Zylynski. "That's all for now."

The man stood. "Inform me when you next have a meeting involving discussion of sensitive matters. I've got some toys that might be able to ferret out any listeners in the vicinity."

"Will do." Enzio gritted his teeth. "Thank you for your efforts."

"It's my job, sir." Zylynski left without further comment.

Enzio returned to his chair and leaned back to glare at the ceiling. So many moving pieces. So much at stake. Events were rapidly speeding to a head, and now above all, he could not make any mistakes.

But he had another brief strategy meeting to conduct, so he also couldn't dwell on the risks at present.

He shifted his deliberate focus just *so*, and two holos materialized in his mind. He dove in without preamble, since everyone knew why they were here. "Sarvia, how is the infiltration program proceeding?"

The woman cleared her throat, then took a quick sip of water. Her virtual presence in the private Noesis room was so realistic that the ice in her glass could be heard clinking around as she returned the glass to the counter. "We were able to place agents in the regenesis labs in New York and Greater Los Angeles earlier this week. We also have candidates interviewing at the labs in Paris and Shanghai."

Enzio nodded approvingly at the woman, who managed Gardiens Earth Operations for him. "You've made good progress. Naoti?"

His supervisor of Tier I Colony Operations puffed out his chest, as if not to be outdone in his report. "We've made significant strides as well. We've placed people in all three labs on Seneca, two on Romane and one each on Demeter, Scythia and Elathan."

Zero to ten labs infiltrated in less than two weeks wasn't terrible. If they succeeded in Paris and Shanghai, it would bring their coverage up to sixty percent of existing and planned labs. He'd been forced to accelerate the timetable due to the unexpectedly rapid uptake of regenesis following the first government approvals, but the efforts appeared to be paying off so far. The chess pieces were moving into place.

"Remember, when the time comes, we'll be engaging in a coordinated action across many planets. So concentrate on getting good agents placed in every lab possible. But don't forget the underlying mission: keep winning people to our cause. When we press the trigger on the next phase, we need public opinion to be sympathetic and predisposed in our favor."

Murmurs of assent answered, and he went through the motions of putting a bow on the pep talk. "Keep up the good work. If we achieve our goals, our future will be secured, and it will be a bright one. Thank you both."

Enzio killed his visual presence, but he kept the channel open to listen in as Sarvia and Naoti discussed details related to handling their agents in place. It wasn't that he didn't trust his people, as such, because he did—to the extent he trusted anyone, which was very little, and far less so after the events of the last week. It was merely that the sole way to ensure his enterprise succeeded was to control every aspect of it, from top to bottom. He'd learned this from his mother.

But the conversation soon wrapped up, and they closed the room and headed off to execute on their duties.

He had another meeting with his Seneca ground team in twenty minutes, as the Federation was beginning to move faster than even the IDCC to roll out the regenesis 'opportunity' for its citizens. After the meeting, he was headed to the monthly Approach Community Retailers Council gathering, then to a closing on another two blocks of Pandora property. Which meant right now, he had a few spare minutes to himself.

He opened the master flowchart. His Grand Design. It went far beyond Vilane Properties, beyond the Rivinchi cartel, beyond the Gardiens. No, his true vision was apt to take several hundred years to reach fruition. But the structural earthquakes that stood to make its success inevitable were all going to happen in the next few.

Not many people possessed the insight to appreciate how, with the creation of Prevos to fight and win the Metigen War, humanity had vaulted itself into a new singularity phase. It was the intrinsic nature of a singularity to be unrecognizable while residing in the midst of it. The Displacement, Concord, aliens? They'd served to super-charge the rapid technological advancements and accompanying societal shifts as humanity barreled forward into its glorious future. The Rasu threatened to present an obstacle, but overcoming the obstacle only served to further accelerate their advancements.

Immortality was the next logical step on the path for humanity, and at this point it was all but certain to become a reality—but not for everyone. In a universe led by Anadens, Katasketousya and now Asterions, only the most exceptional could hope to stand as equals, then in time superiors, among the immortal species of Amaranthe. Prevos were humanity's destiny, and Enzio intended to make sure soon, Prevos would *be* humanity.

Regenesis was the crowning scientific achievement of their genetic ancestors, the ever-imperious Anadens, but Prevos didn't need regenesis. All they needed was access to cloned bodies and a network of backups to guarantee their Artificial counterparts never truly perished. It was a clean, straightforward method of immortality, free of messy neural imprints and governmental control over the parameters of life and death.

All that remained now was to clear away the detritus of humanity's evolutionary dead end.

This was where the Gardiens came in to play, doing their part to see to it that regenesis never took hold in pedestrian society. Without its availability to the masses, in time base humans would grow old, peter out and die, until only Prevos endured.

The door buzzed, and he checked the cam in annoyance at someone disturbing his few minutes of solitude. The annoyance vanished, however, when he realized it was his mother. He hurriedly opened the door and motioned her in.

She carried two coffee mugs, and brought him one. "I suspected you might need a boost."

"I do. Thank you." He started to take a sip, then paused. "I'm sorry I've been so busy lately. I wish I had more free time to spend with you."

"You are doing important work which will benefit the best and brightest of humanity." Olivia sat at the table opposite him, folded her hands around her mug, and considered him thoughtfully. "Can I help?"

He was a little taken aback by the question. But in truth, there had been signs. Since she'd started tinkering with her own programming, she'd become more…alert. Attentive, observant, perceptive. Used to be, she'd spend hours staring vacantly out at the skyline, but lately, she seemed to always be working on something. Usually her own improvement, but she appeared ready to branch out.

Again the irrational fear swelled in his mind—a panic at the notion that she was slipping away from him. Growing beyond him. Olivia Montegreu had been a formidable—no, more than formidable, singular—woman in her natural life, and he'd spent decades worshipping her in an attempt to fill the void her death had created.

He slapped the fear down. Such thoughts were absurd on their face. She was his mother, and this would always count for more than anything else.

"I think maybe you can. Unfortunately, I am being challenged in who I can trust. I need people close to me whom I can rely on. Seek counsel from. But now it seems every time I speak to someone, I risk damaging my cause. Possibly destroying everything I've worked so hard to achieve. Leaks and traitors lurk around every corner. So, who can I trust?"

"No one."

"But I just said—"

"I heard you, son. But the answer nevertheless is, no one. Don't let this dishearten you. Your own counsel is all you need. Everyone else is weaker than you. They lack your dedication, your drive, your determination. Enzio, this is your vision and your life's work. No one else's. So use others as you need to. Let them do the work that is beneath you and your talents. Let them take the blows an unthinking society will try to inflict. But never trust them. Never depend on them, for they will only disappoint you."

His chest warmed in the wake of her complimentary words. She already knew him so well. "Is this your version of tough love, mother?"

"Perhaps." She gracefully crossed one leg over the other and took a slow, casual sip of coffee. "There is, of course, one exception to this advice."

"Oh? What is it?"

A smile curled her lips up over the rim of her mug; anyone else would call it an icy, even sinister expression, but he knew better, for he saw the same countenance every day in the mirror. "You can trust *me*."

21

ROMANE

NEW FRONTIERS MEDICAL CLINIC

"No Zombie Humans!"

"Death Is the Natural End!"

"We Will Not Be Ruled by Golems!"

The signs and banners danced in the air above the Gardiens protestors, all oversized and brightly multicolored to stand out even from a distance. The protestors had deployed subtle holograms to visually inflate their numbers, so at a glance it appeared as if many hundreds of people marched in front of the regenesis clinic.

The turnout was good, but it wasn't that high. Not yet.

Owain Boliver surveyed the gathering from his position at the perimeter of the protest, right on the threshold of the marble steps leading up to the clinic entrance. A tiny drone cam told him two pedestrians were approaching the steps from the north, where the crowd had grown a little thin. He sent a message to one of his lieutenants to shift some people in that direction and block the entrance, or at least intimidate the potential patrons into reconsidering their plans and leaving.

The New Frontiers Medical Clinic represented the most high-profile private regenesis facility to open to date. Romane was always leaping to embrace the next technological advance, and regenesis had proved to be no exception. Amid a glitzy public relations campaign, it had just become the first clinic to allow people to simply walk in off the street and sign up for a regenesis policy, no questions asked.

The Gardiens did not intend to let anyone walk in off the street. Not today.

Another of Owain's drones flagged its visuals for him, and he watched a scuffle breaking out on the southeast edge of the protest. He evaluated the situation for a moment, then let it continue.

The Boss had instructed him to keep the protest civil and non-violent if at all possible, and he understood why this was a noble goal. But the long history of humanity taught that change was rarely acquired through purely peaceful means. If the people protesting truly believed in their cause, they deserved the chance to defend it via whatever means necessary.

"You, sir!"

He spun to see a tall, scrawny man standing at the top of the steps, hands splayed on both bony hips. The briefing files told him this was Dr. Jeon Haneul, the Operations Director for the clinic.

He adopted a sneer and boldly climbed the stairs. "What do you want, Frankenstein?"

"What? Oh, I see. Clever. I want you to stop blocking patrons from reaching the clinic. They have a right to medical care."

"They don't have a right to be raised from the dead by necromancy."

Haneul had the audacity to laugh. "The law says they do. If you don't clear these steps in the next five minutes, I'm calling in law enforcement."

He'd anticipated this happening eventually, if not quite so early in the day. "We're not leaving. We're not backing down."

"Have it your way." Haneul spun and angrily marched inside.

Boliver hit his comm. *"Prepare for incoming."*

RW

"Daddy, what are those people angry about?"

Noah Terrage glanced over his shoulder at the protestors gathered down the street while keeping Jonas and Braelyn both on the opposite side of his body. The crowd was located over a quarter kilometer away, but their shouts were impossible to ignore.

"I don't know, sweetie. It's none of our business."

"I'm going to start a protest demanding dessert with lunch!"

Braelyn made a face at her brother. "You know, our school lunch is crafted to provide proper nutrition for children our age."

What was his daughter reading these days? "That's true. If you want to grow up to be big and strong and fierce, you'll eat what they feed you—and skip dessert every now and then."

"Huh." Jonas' features scrunched up in a pout as he peered back at the protestors.

Noah increased their pace until they rounded the corner and reached the entrance to Insights Academy, then ushered the kids inside. The school had excellent security, including lock codes on the doors that made it impossible for the kids to leave unattended once the school day started. Only teachers, administrators and parents possessed the codes.

Honestly, if not for the high level of security, he might be reluctant to drop them off today. The Gardiens were up to no good, and the crowd at the regen clinic sounded fired up and spoiling for a fight. But the kids would be safe here. This was Romane, not Pandora, and law enforcement would be swift to deal with the protestors if they got out of hand.

He checked the kids in at the front desk, then gave each of them a hug, as he did every day. "Be good. Learn a lot. Make me proud."

"Yes, Dad," echoed back at him as they sprinted down the hall and disappeared.

Fatherly duty performed, he jogged out the door and across the street in the opposite direction from the protest. He had a meeting across the city in half an hour with the supply chain people at PanPacific Tech Labs to arrange for the delivery of some new components for the prototypes Kennedy was designing. The components were more or less prototypes themselves, so a bit of gladhanding was required to make it happen.

RW

The police line formed first along the sidewalk in an attempt to keep his people out of the street. This was fine with Owain, as his concern was the clinic. In fact, all the better if greater traffic was permitted to pass by and witness their demonstration.

It didn't take long, though, before additional officers arrived and began to surround the protest from three sides.

He went up to the closest officer. "We have a legal right to protest."

"You don't have a legal right to disrupt the functioning of a licensed business."

"We haven't barred the door to the clinic. Anyone is free to go inside."

"Patients don't feel safe fighting through your thugs to reach the clinic."

"That's their problem."

"Get your people in line, sir, or we'll be shutting your protest down."

He dared them to try. *Carefully push out against the police lines. Don't let them corral us like sheep.*

Trained operatives could pull this off and keep the advantage, but not everyone here today was a trained operative. Shoving quickly broke out, and in the blink of an eye two of his people were manhandled and in restraints.

He pressed through the crowd to reach them in order to intervene—a sizzle of electricity whizzed by his shoulder. A stun shot. He couldn't tell which side had fired it, but suddenly three more protestors and a police officer were on the ground.

Pandemonium erupted. Shouts and shoves and repeated shots.

Owain smiled. He'd tell the Boss the cops had initiated it, but he refused to be sorry that this was the turn events had taken.

Above him, past the steps, the doors to the clinic opened and more law enforcement stormed out in full riot gear, weapons raised. Dammit, they must have snuck in through the rear clinic entrance.

Now *this* was a problem. They were going to be surrounded

and outgunned in seconds.

Two lasers crisscrossed through the air. Not stuns shots, but the real thing. A scream rang out from somewhere in the crowd.

The police would be wearing defensive shields, as well as all of his people—but not the passersby on the street.

He leapt up onto the stair railing to see someone lying on the sidewalk in a pool of blood.

That wasn't supposed to happen. He'd love to be able to blame it on the police, but they were too hemmed in by rules of engagement to have fired first. And he didn't intend to go down for murder because a true believer had an itchy trigger finger.

The police line surged inward on his people from the left and right, and a new round of shots rang out.

"Chrissy, Houseman, we've got to get through the police line while we still can. Northeast corner, now!"

Owain pushed his way through the scuffles to reach what looked like the weakest juncture in the advancing trap. Chrissy and Houseman appeared at his side when they were five meters from the lead officers. "Okay, let's—"

Houseman tossed a frag grenade. "Duck and cover!"

He did it on instinct as a horrible sound assaulted his eardrums. When he stood and turned…there was a lot of blood. The defensive shields should have provided some protection for the officers, but it hadn't been a standard-issue frag grenade, to the extent such a thing existed. They'd acquired their supply from a military black market dealer.

He couldn't say if any of the officers were dead, and he didn't care. He sprinted forward, leaping over one of the bodies, and ran for the next block.

More than two sets of footsteps pounded behind him, so he kept running, zagging down one street, then another before going left.

A side door in a building ahead opened, and he saw his chance. He plowed over the person coming out the door, then leapt aside as Chrissy, Houseman and three—no, five—more of their people sprinted inside after him. He held the door open as they poured through, then let it go just as the pursuing officers reached the building. An officer interacted with the door panel while the rest drew their weapons, but the door wouldn't open again. Interesting.

Houseman sneered at them through the glass, but Owain wasn't interested in finding out whether the glass was as resistant to entry as the door. He spun and ran down the hallway. "Let's locate a way out before they surround this building, too. Not out the front, though."

They took a right at the first intersection; another long hallway lined with interior doors led to an exit at the end. Their footsteps echoed erratically as everyone hurried for the exit. A keypad was inset beside the door, but it still took him by surprise when the door didn't open on its own when he neared it. Locked? "Shit. Does anybody have a hacking tool on them?"

"Um, Owain?"

He turned toward Chrissy, who was standing a little way down the hall staring at one of the interior doors. "What?"

"I think this is a school."

RW

Jonas Rossi-Terrage beat his feet on the floor under the table as his mind drifted away from the boring math-as-programming exercise his group was working on, in favor of grand adventures. His martial arts class was this evening, and his instructor, Sensei Takeshi, had said they were finally going to learn a second form! His eyes closed while he imagined himself as a great samurai warrior with a flowing black robe and shining silver sword, single-handedly keeping at bay a horde of slobbering Savrakaths—

A punch landed on his thigh. His eyes opened, and he hissed under his breath. "Ow, Brae!"

His sister stuck her tongue out at him. "You're not paying attention."

"I know I'm not. If we learn anything important, you'll tell me later."

"Will I? Make it worth my while."

His shoulders sagged; he'd walked into this one. "I guess I—"

"No chatter, students. You're all supposed to be concentrating on the assignment."

Brae waited until the teacher went over to answer a question from another group to whisper furiously, "Now you got us in trouble."

He stifled a laugh. "That wasn't 'in trouble.' Trust me."

"Ugh." She made a show of stiffening her back and squinting at her screen, where a series of numbers were positioned in and around a bunch of lines and symbols.

He didn't understand why they had to learn all this math stuff, not when everybody's eVi could do math a hundred thousand million times faster. Programming was a little more interesting, but not when it used numbers….

Since everybody had gotten quiet after the teacher's warning, he was able to hear a series of running footsteps outside the classroom. They sounded thick and heavy. According to one of the adventure books he'd read last month, *Hiroshimi and the Lost City of Okimi*, this meant the people running were grown-ups. Probably men.

Running meant excitement, and he watched the door eagerly.

The door slid open and three men burst inside. They instantly started shouting and waving weapons around, and the teacher let out a cry and flattened herself against the wall. Some of his classmates screamed and ran for the windows or the door. His teacher shouted over the screams, "Everybody stay in your seats!"

Jonas' heart pounded in his chest. His parents had told him to always do what the teacher said…but when they believed the person in charge was wrong, they'd done what they knew was right. His face scrunched up, and he thought really, really hard. The teacher was terrified, crying and cowering from the intruders. And his heart hammered with the certainty of what was right.

I am a samurai. I am not afraid. I am a samurai. This is what I've trained for.

Two of the men lunged for the kids who were trying to get the window open while the third man cornered the teacher, and he saw his chance. He grabbed his sister's hand and yanked her down onto the floor, under the table.

"Follow me," he whispered.

Her eyes were wide and her lips quivering, but she nodded.

He peered over the table to make sure the bad guys' backs were still turned, then scurried across the open floor on his hands and knees and slid behind the supply table in the corner. As soon as he got there, he pulled Brae up against him so her feet didn't stick out and tried to breathe. His chest was heaving. He was so scared...he wasn't a very good samurai at all.

But he remembered something his dad had told him more than once: bravery wasn't about being fearless; it was about doing the right thing in the face of your fear. He found it hard to believe that the great samurai in his books had ever been afraid. But his dad knew everything, so it must be true.

His sister huddled against him. "What are we going to do?"

He put a finger to his lips, then twisted around toward the wall. The air vent was fitted over a hole near the floor. He curled his fingers over several of the openings and pulled.

It made a clatter as it fell to the floor, but there was so much screaming and crying going on, the bad guys couldn't have heard it.

He motioned to the opening, and Brae made a horrified face.

"Don't be a baby. You go first, so I can protect you if they come after us."

Her mouth opened, but the usual smart-alecky retort didn't come out. Instead, she stared at the hole, then hesitantly reached an arm in and started crawling inside.

He silently willed her to hurry! There was still a lot of crying in the room, but the screams had begun to die down. The bad guys would find them any second now.

Finally she got all the way inside, and he scrambled after her into the tunnel. When she stopped moving, he shoved at her foot to keep her going.

Up ahead, the tunnel sloped downward into a crossway. She slipped and slid down the slope, then turned left without asking where to go. Once they were both in the next section, he sank onto his stomach, panting. "We should be safe for a few minutes here."

"Only a few *minutes?*"

"I don't know! Maybe longer. This vent isn't big enough for a grown-up to crawl around in."

"Okay, that's a good point. How did you even know the vent was there?"

"A few weeks ago, Ke'ontae hid his gummi snacks somewhere in the classroom and told me I could have them if I could find them. They were stuffed behind the vent cover. They were so good, too."

"Oh." She wiped a tear off her cheek, sniffling as another one fell. "We can't stay here. They'll find us."

"I know." Jonas wanted to stop his voice from shaking, but he didn't know how. "We're going to follow the tunnel to one of the empty classrooms on the back hallway, then sneak out the side door."

"Don't be stupid. All the exit doors are locked."

"Locked to students—not to teachers and parents."

"Which you're *not.*"

"But I know the code they use."

Brae groaned and rested her head on the curved wall of the tunnel. "Why would you know the code?"

"In case I want to sneak out one day. Go to the burger place across the street for lunch, or pick out something from the adventure store on the next block."

"Jonas, do you have any idea how much trouble you'll get into if you skip school to go wandering around downtown all by yourself?"

"Yeah, but..." he shrugged weakly "...burger."

"You are the worst. Fine. How did you get the code?"

"I watched Dad one day when he punched it in. He hid his hand, but not good enough."

She sucked on her bottom lip. Her cheeks were red and puffy and her voice was hoarse, but at least she'd stopped crying for now. "What if one of the bad guys is in the hallway between the classroom and the exit?"

"We'll check first. We'll be super-quiet and sneaky. Like ninjas."

"I thought you were a *samurai*."

"I am! Samurais can also be ninjas when they need to be."

"And…you think I can be a ninja?"

"You have to be, okay? Just watch me and do everything I do. And don't talk."

"I know how to be quiet, stupid." She sucked in air, puffing out her chest, and closed her eyes. "We need to go past the next junction in the tunnel, then turn left. Then three more junctions down will lead to the closest classroom to the side door. It's the one where they're installing some new equipment, so it's empty right now."

"How do you know how to get to it?"

She opened her eyes and gave him that haughty expression he hated. Still, it was better than crying. "I have excellent visual memory. Everyone says so."

"No, they don't."

"Yes, they do. It's simply a matter of getting a picture in my mind of how the school's hallways look, then mapping it out. Easy."

"Easy, my butt." He snickered. "We should go now."

Her lips puckered in and started quivering again.

"Brae?"

"Give me a minute!"

"Don't *yell*. If we fight and yell at each other, the invaders will catch us." He'd decided it was best to think of the men with guns as an invading horde, like the ones the samurai fought in the adventure books.

"I don't want to get caught…." She hugged her knees to her chest and stared down the tunnel.

Though he'd never admit it to anybody—and certainly not to her—Brae was much smarter than him. She knew all sorts of things. Boring things, mostly. But he didn't think she'd ever had to be brave before. Plus, the kinds of books she read didn't have strong, stalwart heroes who saved people from evil alien invaders. Whenever he peeked over her shoulder, her books seemed to have math in them, or pictures of graphs instead of swords. So she'd never read about how to be brave.

He was going to have to be brave for them both. He'd save his sister and make his dad and Sensei Takeshi proud.

22

AKESO

Caleb retrieved his boots from the closet and sat on the edge of the couch to put them on. "What's the word from your mom?"

Alex finished pinning her hair up in some semblance of a tail. "The word from Mom is that she's entirely too busy to talk to me, which is fair, I guess. The word from Dad is that we're still engaging the Rasu at Serifos *and* Acacia simultaneously. Serifos is starting to go a little better than Acacia, but they're both ugly. Oh, and we unleashed the Ymyrath Field on the Rasu at Vrachnas."

His gaze jerked over to her. "The Rasu have targeted the dragons?"

She chuckled to herself. He was always going on about how dangerous and unfriendly and savage the dragons were, but he was secretly quite protective of them. "Unsuccessfully. The Rift Bubble there held with no issues, and Mom took the opportunity of an otherwise empty stellar system to do another field test of the weapon. So far, it appears it performed to spec. The dragons are safe and the Rasu disabled."

His bearing relaxed. "Good. I told Marlee we'd come by in the next hour or so. Got anything else you need to do first?"

"Not really. I only—" A pulse arrived from Kennedy, causing her to stop halfway to the foyer.

"What's up?"

She held up a finger in Caleb's direction while she tried to extract a few details from Kennedy's frantic message.

Caleb was at her side when she finally turned to him, anger bubbling up through her chest. "Some Gardiens fuckers were protesting at a regenesis clinic on Romane. It turned violent, and they holed up inside Braelyn and Jonas' school. It's now a hostage situation."

He immediately spun and jogged to the weapons cabinet. "Tell them we'll be there in three minutes."

RW

ROMANE

Two entire city blocks had been transformed into a crisis triage center by the time Alex and Caleb arrived. A barricade lined with police officers created a perimeter fifty meters out from the school building, with an additional barricade situated twenty meters farther in. In between the two, a police command center had been set up in one corner. Law enforcement drones buzzed around the school, presumably taking thermal and infrared video of the inside, while media drone cams hovered overhead.

Kennedy burst through the crowd of onlookers to fall into Alex's arms, sniffles muffling into her shirt. "Thank you for coming!"

Alex cast a worried gaze past Kennedy at Caleb, but smiled bravely and patted her friend on the shoulder. "They'll be all right."

"All right? Terrorists have taken my children hostage! They murdered five people over at the regenesis clinic. They have Daemons and blades and frag grenades and..." Kennedy stumbled back and brought a hand to her chest "...I can't breathe. Why haven't the police gone in and killed them all yet?"

Kennedy is correct about their possession of weapons. The protestors used a frag grenade on the crowd before bolting. Therefore, law enforcement is concerned that if pushed, the protestors could use them inside, risking the children's lives. They are being cautious.

Alex cleared her throat. "Um, Valkyrie says the police are being extra careful to make sure none of the kids get hurt."

"Screw 'extra careful'! Alex, they're so young. Just babies. They don't have the cybernetics necessary for full neural imprints yet. If they die…they *die*." Her breathing grew ragged, and she dropped her forehead onto Alex's shoulder again. "I'm a terrible mother."

She eased Kennedy back a few steps, away from a group who jostled for a better vantage near the barricade, then held her at arms' length. "What is this nonsense? You're not a terrible mother."

"I am. I'm not there for them. I work all the time. I'm quick to let Noah do all the parental heavy lifting, and when he does, I'm…relieved."

She didn't know what to say. Kennedy wasn't entirely wrong, but now probably wasn't the ideal time for unvarnished truth. She may be dreadful at providing emotional support, but even she knew that much. "You're setting a wonderful example for your children by working hard to save millions of lives. Billions."

"Does any of it matter if I lose these two incredibly precious ones? I don't think it does. That might be selfish of me, but right now I don't give a goddamn. If Braelyn and Jonas die…let the Rasu burn it all down." A hand came to her mouth, and she looked like she was about to vomit. "What are we going to do?"

Caleb had vanished the instant they'd arrived, evidently to find Noah, and the two of them now wormed their way out of a throng of people to their left and rejoined them. Noah reached up to touch Kennedy's cheek. "We're going to go in and get them out."

Caleb nudged them all back a little farther, out of the line of sight of the closest officers, then crouched and opened his satchel. He handed Noah a plasma blade, a Daemon and a module for a Veil. "I figured you weren't in a position to bring your own."

"Ah, no. Thanks. You have a plan?"

Caleb gazed at the school silently for several seconds. "I do." He stood and turned to Alex. His demeanor had already transformed into fight mode; not as hard and cold as he'd been on Namino, but clearly resolute. Focused. "I need you to be our eyes. Find the kids, then find the terrorists."

"I can do that."

Kennedy grabbed Noah by the hands. "I want to tell you to stay here, to insist how you're not a fighter and you have no business charging into a war zone. But I'm not going to do it. I love you. Bring our children back to me."

Noah's throat worked, and he leaned in to kiss her. "If it's the last thing I do. I swear it."

Caleb secured the Veil module to his pants, then made sure Noah did the same. "No time to waste. We'll sneak through the police barricade, then go around to the rear of the building."

"Understood."

Caleb gave her a sharp nod, and he and Noah set out through the crowd. The next second, they both vanished.

Alex turned to Kennedy. "I know you need someone to comfort you, but what you need far more than that is to hug your kids and smother them in kisses. So I'll be here with you, but I need to do recon."

"I know you do. I want you to. Okay. But...can I hold your hand while you do?"

"Of course you can." She took Kennedy's hand in hers and squeezed, then closed her eyes.

23

ROMANE

Caleb: Slip through the checkpoint when someone else goes through, then meet me at the rear right corner of the building. Noah: Got it.

Caleb positioned himself beside the single opening in the force-field barricade where a police sergeant cleared other officers to come through. As the next one traversed the checkpoint, he delicately side-stepped his way through the opening, careful not to touch the officer as he did—and was inside the field. One of the officers could have noticed the telltale shimmer of his Veil, if not for the much louder shimmer of the force field.

The barricade had been erected quite a way from the school building, and he crossed the open space quickly, working through a plan of attack the entire way.

Mia, I need the law enforcement security override code for Insights Academy.

What? Why?

Gardiens have holed up in the school after their protest at a nearby regenesis clinic got violent. They've taken hostages, and Noah's kids are inside.

Oh my god. One second...Meno's grabbing it. How can I help?

Talk to Alex. She could probably use an assist in sidespace.

I will. The code is: 4381#24.

As he reached the side of the school, he glanced toward the police command center. Higher-ranking officers huddled together over screens, likely studying the drone scans of the interior. Locked-down or not, they could storm the building whenever they wanted. But they weren't, and for good reason, if Valkyrie's assessment of the terrorists' armament was even close to accurate. Any frontal assault stood a reasonable chance of turning bloody for all involved, and no one wanted a bunch of dead children on their hands, not even the Gardiens. So law enforcement would exhaust every available option for bringing a peaceful resolution to the standoff before resorting to force.

But Jonas and Braelyn, and everyone else inside, might not have that kind of time.

Alex pulsed him then.

I've located two classrooms where Gardiens are actively holding children and teachers hostage: 3A and 4B. Two Gardiens are in 3A and three in 4B. But I don't see Jonas or Braelyn in either one. I'll keep searching.

Got it.

He sidled up beside the rear door, just around the corner of the building. While he waited for Noah to arrive, Mia sent him a vid file.

Here's the security footage from when the Gardiens breached the building.

Thanks.

He watched the reel. It showed eight people—six men and two women—fleeing pursuing officers across the street and to a side door on the opposite side of the building. The first one reached the door as someone was coming out, and all eight were able to get in the building before the officers arrived.

So eight bad guys. Two in one classroom, three in another, and three unaccounted for.

It looks like the rest of the kids are sequestered in an assembly room, along with six adults. No obvious Gardiens in there, so the adults might have been able to lock themselves inside. I've spotted one additional man patrolling the halls. He's moving through the northeast section of the building. Caleb, I still don't see Jonas or Braelyn. Where are they?

We'll find them. Hunt for the other two Gardiens.

"Hey, I'm here." The furtive whisper came from several meters to his right.

"Around the corner. By the door."

In the overhang of the façade's shadow, a faint shimmer signaled Noah's arrival. "What's the plan?"

"Mia procured the override code, so we'll be able to sneak inside no problem. It sounds as if we've got five Gardiens holding kids in two classrooms, plus a large group of kids sheltering in an assembly room. They're safe unless some asshole decides to break down the door."

"The assembly room is in the back-center of the building. There's a short hallway to it off the main east-west thoroughfare."

"We've also got three free-range Gardiens roaming the halls, which means we're going to have to move carefully. I want to take them out first, so they can't ambush us later. Noah, I need to tell you...Alex can't find Jonas or Braelyn."

"They should be in Classroom 3A."

"Okay. Except they're not."

"What does that mean?"

"I don't know. She's scouring the entire building. She'll find them, and we'll get to them. Until she does, we'll concentrate on removing the Gardiens' ability to harm the people trapped inside. Are you ready? Is your head in the right place?"

"Do you remember what I told you the night of David's birthday party?"

"That you would die for either one of your kids in a nanosecond. No hesitation."

"I meant it. Saving them is the only thing that matters. Understand?"

He didn't need to see Noah's expression. The girded steel in his friend's voice told him everything he needed to know. "I understand."

R W

Alex checked the fourteenth room so far. Nothing. Zipped out into the hall and on to the next one.

"Why aren't the police storming the place?"

She twitched and shifted half her conscious awareness back to her physical body in response to Kennedy's question. "Um…Mia says they've reached the Gardiens inside on a comm and are trying to negotiate with them."

"Mia's helping, too?"

Alex nodded, trying to smile while keeping her eye on the hallway. "She's eavesdropping on the command center chatter from sidespace."

"That's sweet of her. But how can they *negotiate* with these monsters? They need to go in there and clean house."

Alex kept any frustration out of her voice; she couldn't fathom what Kennedy was suffering through. "No, it's a good thing. You don't want Caleb and Noah to be caught in the crossfire of a shooting battle, do you? Or worse, get mistaken for the terrorists?"

"No! God, I can't lose Noah, too." Kennedy sank down onto the stone ledge behind her, her chin dropping to her chest. "I could lose everything in the world I care about. Right now, today. This instant. I could have already lost everything and not know it—how are the kids?"

"Um." Alex finished checking classroom number fifteen, then briefly dropped her full consciousness back into her body. "I haven't found them yet."

"*What?*"

"Yeah…they're not in their regular classroom, and they're not with the group that's sheltering in the assembly room." She reached out and squeezed Kennedy's hand. "So let me go back to searching."

"Oh, no. Jonas is trying to be a samurai."

"What do you mean?"

"He's been taking martial arts classes for around four months now, and he's obsessed with them. He started reading these adventure books about ancient feudal Japan and watching animated shows, too. He's always going on about the 'way of the samurai' and 'honor' and 'heroism.' Dammit, he's trying to be a hero, and he's going to get himself killed."

"Hey, see, though? You *are* a great parent. You know exactly what your son's interested in."

"Because he won't shut up about it! I mean, we thought the martial arts classes would teach him discipline and respect for his elders and some useful life skills, and hopefully help him if he ever gets bullied in class. But now he's in so far over his head."

"Let me find them, okay? Then I'll alert Caleb and Noah to where they are, and everybody will get rescued. You can tell Jonas what a big hero he was, and you'll never hear the end of it for the rest of your days."

"I'll be ecstatic to suffer through that. Please...." Kennedy's gaze turned skyward and unfocused, and Alex dove back into sidespace. Seriously, though—where the hell were the kids?

24

———————

CONCORD HQ
RASU WAR ROOM

A Rift Bubble is now in place on the surface of Serifos. One will arrive at Acacia in twelve minutes.

"Thank you, Lakhes." Miriam didn't glance at the Kat as she spoke; she couldn't spare the extra gesture as she pushed the information out to Casmir, so he could adjust his tactics accordingly. And when she turned to her left to accept a fresh cup of tea from her secretary, the swirling lights were gone.

She'd asked Lakhes about the new manner of weapon its superdreadnoughts were wielding, which Casmir had drawn to her attention. The Kat had described it as a form of sub-atomic disruptor beam, which sounded like a nuclear weapon to her. But so long as they confined its operation to well outside planetary atmospheres, she wasn't going to try to prevent them from using it. In this increasingly ugly war, the benefits now outweighed the risks.

Real-time analysis of the RNEW performance at Acacia scrolled onto one of her many screens, and she studied it with interest. Their steady and permanent elimination of Rasu warships was saving their asses, especially during the critical minutes while they waited on a Rift Bubble to arrive. Still, it was shocking how quickly ships were burning through their thousand shots when the battle stretched for not hours, but days. How had they ever conducted this war using only negative energy missiles?

An old professor's adage about moving goalposts flitted through her mind, but she would happily move them yet again when the RNEWs were improved to fire fifteen hundred times before requiring refurbishment—

A flash of what resembled irradiated chlorine streaked across the visual feed from Acacia, and she immediately dragged the screen closer. No ships fired weapons that presented in such a manner.

Commandant Solovy (Acacia Command Channel): "Fleet Admiral Jenner, there was an anomaly in Grid 3C just now."

Fleet Admiral Jenner (AFS Denali)(Acacia Command Channel): "We're tracking it. Give us a minute to pull in some data…whatever it was, it appears to have destroyed four AEGIS frigates."

Commandant Solovy (Acacia Command Channel): "Say that again?"

Fleet Admiral Jenner (AFS Denali)(Acacia Command Channel): "We're not seeing any wreckage, but four frigates in the 12th Alpha Regiment have gone silent. Sensor readings are coming in now. They show residual traces of antimatter."

Miriam gave no outward indication of the punch in the gut the Rasu had just delivered to her. The officers working diligently in the War Room received no signal, for now, of how the entire war had now been flipped on its head.

But her insides clenched painfully all the same. *Antimatter.* Possibly the most destructive weapon in existence outside of a black hole and one of the most difficult to defend against, and the enemy had just brought it to the battlefield.

Despair would be so easy to succumb to now. But she had been entrusted with waging this war, and she would instead adapt. Find some way, somehow, to overcome. There was no other choice.

Commandant Solovy (Acacia Command Channel): "I see. I'm sure I don't need to tell you to do what you can to get cruisers equipped with TDS in front of those weapons whenever possible."

Fleet Admiral Jenner (AFS Denali)(Acacia Command Channel): "No ma'am. We'll be on the lookout for that Rift Bubble, too."

She brought the teacup calmly to her lips and kept it there. Why suddenly begin to deploy antimatter weapons now, after weeks of battles using conventional armament? She'd like to believe the Rasu had gotten desperate, but Concord wasn't doing *that* well in the war. No, something else had changed….

Her sigh sent the tea rippling around its cup in choppy waves. The Ruda had informed the Rasu of how adiamene, heretofore seemingly impervious, was vulnerable to exotic weapons. Damn their betrayal.

Kennedy Rossi had been working on the logistics of retrofitting frigate-class warships with the Tandem Defense Shield, and she sent the woman a priority message requesting an update on her efforts. While she waited for a response, she watched the feed from Acacia carefully. Twice an AEGIS cruiser succeeded in absorbing a blow from the Rasu's new antimatter weapons, but three times they weren't fast enough, and wide swaths of frigates vanished in violent conflagrations of matter and antimatter.

If she lost the AEGIS fleet, she lost the war.

Why hadn't Kennedy responded yet? She sent a follow-up message and copied Noah Terrage as well. She tried not to abuse the privilege of delivering urgent push messages that asserted themselves to the front of the recipient's eVi, but the circumstances called for it.

The Rift Bubble's arrival at Acacia distracted her for a minute, as its deployment had now taken on an even more crucial role. If they were able to keep it operational, it would protect the planet while they tried to answer the Rasu's latest escalation. It would buy her time.

Dammit, why was she getting no response? In frustration, she sent her daughter a pulse.

Do you know where Kennedy is? I am in quite urgent need of her attention.

Um, that's going to be a problem.

RW

Compartmentalization was a required skill for any human—likely for any sentient being who experienced emotions—who wished to lead during battle. Did Miriam want to curse and stomp about in fury at these Gardiens and their reprehensible violence against the innocent? Yes. Did she want to ruminate in worry about the safety of Kennedy and Noah's overly precocious children? Yes. But she couldn't afford to do either.

Instead she commed the Special Projects Director on their secure line. "Mr. Reynolds, give me some good news. Tell me Kennedy Rossi delivered the specs on a TDS loadout for AEGIS frigates to you."

"Hey, she did, first thing this morning. I was going to review them as soon as I signed off on the upgrade for our Rasu signature-detection algorithms."

"A wider TDS deployment has become your number one priority—your *only* priority. Work with the AEGIS engineering team to make it happen with all due speed. The Rasu are now using antimatter weapons."

"Oh, boy. Got it."

And there were no more actions available for her to take to speed up the process. She could only try to help Malcolm and Casmir win their battles today, while staying primed to pivot should the Rasu strike at yet another colony.

If she was going to successfully compartmentalize, however, she was going to need to brew a stronger cup of tea.

25

ROMANE

The school layout was a tactical nightmare. Wide, open hallways with virtually no interior cut-throughs. One door into each room, leaving you fully exposed in the doorframe as you entered. No obvious way to access any ceiling crawlspace, and a modern, sub-floor ventilation system that was far too small to navigate.

At least they were invisible.

Your adrenaline level is most elevated, and you have heavily armed yourself. Are we in a crisis?

Caleb hesitated before answering Akeso. He couldn't afford to have an Akeso-fueled breakdown once blood was spilled—and blood *was* going to be spilled. But his companion had come a long way in its understanding of such matters since Namino. Of how violence was sometimes required to protect the innocent from those who would do them harm.

Jonas and Braelyn are being held captive by some evil people. We're going to rescue them.

Evil people? The Rasu-enemy?

No, not the Rasu. Humans. But they disregard the sanctity of inno-cent life all the same.

And they have taken the little ones?

They have.

This is abhorrent to Akeso.

And to me. So we'll do whatever we can to right this wrong. Agreed?

I struggle to comprehend why Humans harm little ones, but...agreed. They must not be allowed to succeed.

That was the spirit. Relieved, he moved to the next intersection and checked all the branching corridors.

Eyes on any of the free-range Gardiens?

Sorry, I was searching for the kids. Yes! One is moving in your direction, coming down one hallway over.

Got it.

He pulsed Noah the information, and they hurried down the left hallway.

A single set of footsteps clapped against the high-traction flooring, drawing near. He flexed through his calves, prepping to surge forward.

A man rounded the corner and—

Noah stormed past him and cold-cocked the man so hard his head whipped halfway around as he crumpled to the floor.

Caleb: Damn. I have got to get me one of those synthetic arms.

Noah: Yeah, glad I have it today. You think he's wearing a defensive shield?

Caleb: Probably. They protect against most energy weapons, but not so much blunt force.

Noah: Good.

Caleb: Let's get him into this classroom. The longer it takes his cohorts to find him, the better.

They each grabbed one of the man's arms and dragged him through the door. Caleb glanced around the room, but didn't immediately see anything they could use as restraints. The man was knocked out cold, but that might only last a few minutes.

He unholstered his Daemon and set it to stun. Then he positioned the barrel directly over one of the man's ports at the base of his neck and pressed the trigger. No defensive shield would protect against a point-blank jolt directly into the man's cybernetics, and while the energy surge probably wouldn't kill him, it would do enough damage to keep him on the floor for a long while.

Found a second one. He's near the front of the building, moving toward what looks like the executive offices, then...maybe a security room—Caleb, Braelyn and Jonas are in there! They're in a security room behind the largest executive office. But one of the Gardiens is headed that way!

No time for subterfuge. "We've got to move, now. The kids are in the security room."

RW

Too many hallways. Too many turns.

Sunlight shone through the glass walls of the school entrance as Caleb skidded left into the front hall, then right.

Ahead, a man was two steps away from the last door in the short hallway. He spun toward them, alerted by the sounds of rapid footfalls, and raised a Daemon.

Caleb crashed into the man, and they both slammed into the far wall. His left arm pressed into the man's windpipe; he knocked the Daemon out of the man's grip with his forearm then arced his hand up to the man's chest. He activated the plasma blade grasped in his palm, and the blade cut through the man's shield and clothes to pierce his heart. Actions had consequences.

The man's eyes bulged, and he struggled ineffectually for a few seconds before his limbs went limp.

Caleb grabbed the abandoned Daemon off the floor. By the time he'd tucked it in one of his pants' pockets, Noah had the door open and was rushing inside.

"Jonas? Braelyn?"

"Daddy?" The whisper came from a far corner of the room.

Caleb's hand went to the small of his back. "Turn your Veil off."

Noah fumbled for the toggle as he rushed over to the corner, searching everywhere.

"Daddy!" Jonas came crawling out from a small opening in the wall, stumbled to his feet and fell against Noah's legs. A mess of blonde curls presaged Braelyn crawling out next.

Bozhe moy, you got to them in time. Wonderful job, priyazn.

You, too, baby.

Noah fell to his knees and wrapped his arms around them both. "Hey, kiddos! Are you okay?"

Muffled responses followed, and Noah untangled the mass of arms enough to lean back and inspect his children. "Let me see. Any war wounds?"

Even as the kids shook their heads, Noah frowned at Jonas. "There's a blood splotch on your shirt...and on your pants. What happened?"

Jonas stared at the ceiling, then reluctantly held out his left hand. It looked dirty and cut up. "I sliced it on the vent grate."

Caleb had been giving them space for the reunion, but he approached now, and Jonas flashed him a big smile. "Uncle Caleb! You helped my daddy come rescue us?"

"I sure did." He knelt down in front of Jonas. "Can I see your hand?"

"I guess."

Caleb inspected the cuts more closely. Two of them were pretty deep and still bleeding.

Let us heal the little one.

Yes, let's.

"Let me hold your hand in mine for a minute. You might feel a slight tingling."

"Why?"

"You know Akeso, where I live?" Jonas nodded. "Well, Akeso is going to heal you all up, so your hand isn't injured any longer."

His eyes grew wide, and his mouth formed an 'O.' "It *is*?"

"If it's all right with you."

"Uh-huh." Jonas' voice dropped to a whisper. "It kind of hurts."

"I'll bet it does. Here we go."

He and Noah hadn't talked about this new skill of his, but he assumed Alex had told Kennedy what had transpired when he and Akeso had brought Pinchu back from death's door, and Kennedy had in turn told Noah. If not, his friend was in for a bit of a surprise. He wrapped his hands over the boy's tiny one and closed his eyes.

I am the nourishing water-blood.

I am the sun's rays.

I am life flowing forth to mend. To heal.

Replace. Renew. Replenish.

The wounds weren't too serious, and in a few seconds the slices in the tender skin had sealed up. He smiled, patted Jonas' hand and stood. "There you go. Good as new."

Braelyn instantly snatched Jonas' hand over to inspect it. "That's amazing! Uncle Caleb, are you a wizard?"

"Not exactly." He shifted his gaze to Noah. "We should get them out of here, before someone comes hunting for the guy in the hall."

"Agreed."

"Wait—I have to show you what I did first!" Braelyn climbed up on the chair at the security desk and pointed up at one of the screens. "See this room here? I trapped one of the invaders in there and locked the door."

Noah picked her up off the chair and twirled her around. "That's my brilliant munchkin. Well done." He sat her down and clasped both kids by the shoulders. "I know you want to tell me all about your adventures, but first we need to get outside the school, so we can go see Mom and let her know you're safe. She's super worried about you. Uncle Caleb and I have, um…invisibility cloaks, so we can sneak through the halls unseen."

No longer in pain, Jonas bounced on the balls of his feet. "Wow. Can I have one?"

"We'll talk about it later. But for now, we're going to carry you, so the invisibility cloaks will shield you, too."

Caleb frowned. "Actually, they should walk. We might need our hands quickly."

Noah's expression darkened at what that would mean. "How about this. Braelyn, you hold my left hand and walk next to me—really closely, right up against my side. Jonas, you do the same with Uncle Caleb. We're going to move carefully but kind of fast. In case we get separated somehow, we're headed for the rear side door. You know where I mean?"

They both nodded solemnly, but Jonas protested. "We already tried to get out through that door. It's locked with a special code."

Noah grinned. "You did?"

"Yeah. Then when we found out it was locked, we decided to come here to try to unlock it, but...well, we were working on that when you got here!"

"Good thinking, kiddos. It's okay—we brought the special code with us. Now it's time to go." Noah held out his hand, and Caleb did the same.

Jonas made a dramatic show of clasping his hand in Caleb's, lifting his shoulders as he took up a position parallel with Caleb.

"Good job." He reached around and activated the Veil, and they all vanished.

"Oh my g...ollies!"

Noah cleared his throat. "Also, you have to be totally silent once we're out in the hallways. No talking. Understand?"

"Yes, Dad."

Caleb felt the pressure of an active combat zone closing in; they'd lingered too long. "Let's move."

They stepped into the hallway.

Jonah gasped. "Daddy, is that man dead?"

"He's just sleeping. Let's keep moving. And remember to be quiet."

What followed was an utterly nerve-wracking four minutes. He wasn't able to move nearly as swiftly as he'd like, because the kids' strides were so short. He reconsidered picking Jonas up several times, but if they rounded a corner and came face-to-face with an armed terrorist, the encounter could turn disastrous in a nanosecond.

Finally they navigated the last corner. He suppressed the urge to run for the exit, as doors lined both sides, each one a potential ambush in waiting. The hallway appeared to stretch and lengthen as they proceeded forward, the door a veritable eternity away. He could only imagine how long the distance must seem to Noah.

But they reached the exit without incident. Caleb punched in the code immediately, and the door slid open.

He stepped into the doorframe, then deactivated his Veil and nudged Jonas toward Noah. "You go on ahead."

Noah deactivated his Veil as well, glancing back into the building. "You're not coming?"

"I can't leave all these children in danger, and I don't trust local law enforcement to pull off an incursion without casualties. I've got to take the rest of the Gardiens out…well. In case."

"I wish I could go back in with you, but—"

"Don't think twice. Go let Kennedy hug her kids."

"Thank you. I owe you everything, man."

"Nah." Caleb waved him off, then reactivated his Veil and stepped back inside the school.

26

ROMANE

Kennedy stared at the entrance of Insights Academy, at the energetic lettering spanning the awning that proclaimed how young minds were nurtured within its walls.

Now those walls were a prison. Beyond them, her children were locked inside with madmen. With devils who would take her heart, her very soul, from her.

Nothing moved inside. Tunnel vision had frozen her gaze upon the doors to the exclusion of all else, and though they were a parsec away, across a vast mawing void of barricades and useless police officers, she willed for them to simply…open.

She was a terrible mother, but they were perfect children, and they did not deserve to have the horrors of a cruel world inflicted upon them so soon.

A part of her mind recognized that she was being a touch melodramatic. They weren't perfect. But they were wonderful and amazing, and what was happening to them now wasn't fair. Even if the doors opened this instant and they were somehow returned to her safe and sound, their innocence had been stolen from them today, and there'd be no getting it back. It was too soon. They weren't ready. *She* wasn't ready.

"Hey." Alex's hand, which she'd held in a vice grip for what must be hours now, squeezed hers.

Dizziness washed over her as she wrenched her focus away from the silent, still doors and found Alex beaming at her. "What is it? What's happened?"

"They're on their way out right now."

She leapt up onto the stone ledge that had been supporting her, frantically scanning in every direction for some sign. Some movement. Of course it had been ridiculous for her to fixate on the main entrance. Why would they saunter out the front doors when there were other exits? "Where are they? I don't see them!"

"Noah's got them all Veiled for now, so they don't draw the attention of the cops and get swarmed, then be subjected to four hours of official questioning. They're coming directly to us. It should just be another minute."

Every nerve in her body lit fire. Did she dare hope for a happy ending? If she was lucky enough to have her heart and soul returned to her today, she swore she would never again forget what was precious—

Out of nowhere, Noah emerged through the gathered crowd off to the left. Braelyn and Jonas clung to each of his legs.

She was moving, and in a flash she'd fallen to her knees on the sidewalk, and her children were in her arms. Warm and soft and fragile and *alive*.

Her hands wound through their hair, palms pressing against their cheeks, as her vision blurred and wavered. For once, Jonas didn't even fidget in her embrace; instead he tucked his chin onto her shoulder, while Braelyn buried her face in Kennedy's neck.

"I love you both so much! Are you okay? Did anybody hurt you?"

Two heads shook against her.

She peered up at Noah, tears streaming down her face. He appeared unharmed, too, though a mite the worse for wear—sweaty, with clothes all askew and possibly sporting a couple of blood stains. But his expression of sweet relief counted as the second-best thing she'd seen in the entirety of her life.

She reached out for him with one arm, and he joined her in the family hug, kissing her on the top of the head.

"You did it. I've never loved you more than I do at this moment."

"Eww, *Mom*...." And there came the fidgeting.

She reluctantly loosened her hold on them—only a little—so she could see their beautiful faces.

Noah reached up and tousled Braelyn's hair. "Aren't you going to tell your mom what heroes you were today?"

"Oh, I can't wait to hear!" Her voice was shaking, and she breathed in through her nose. She could safely fall apart later, tonight in Noah's arms.

Like a switch had been flipped, they were suddenly talking over each other in a barrage of excited words. She caught, "crawled through vents," "locked an invader up," "Jonas reacted so fast...." Wait, did Braelyn just *compliment* her brother?

"Okay, slow down. One at a time. Jonas, why don't you start?"

"Right." He sucked in a big gulp of air. "As soon as the invaders came in our classroom, waving their guns around and bullying the teacher, we snuck behind the supply cabinet. Then when they weren't looking, we climbed in the vent tunnel behind it because I knew where it was but..." he glanced at his sister "...but Brae helped, too. She knew how to get to different rooms using the vent tunnels. She has excellent visual memory."

"Does she?" Kennedy laughed giddily. They were safe and well *and* they were getting along with each other? She'd take it for as long as it lasted.

She touched her daughter's cheek; she couldn't stop smiling. "Braelyn, what happened next?"

Braelyn lifted her chin high, as if to project an air of authority. "We tried to go out one of the side doors, but it was locked. So then we went to the security room, because I thought I could unlock the doors from there, and we could escape. I trapped one of the invaders in a classroom! Mom, I want to take more programming classes."

"Whatever you want. We'll make it happen." She stood, though she kept a hand on each of their shoulders. The rest of the scene gradually began to creep back into the corners of her perception. Nothing had changed about the behavior of the crowd or the intent huddling of the police, but vibrance and light had returned to the world.

Alex stood off to the side, arms over her chest and a warm but complicated expression animating her features. Wait...Kennedy peered around in confusion. "Where's Caleb?"

Alex and Noah both gazed meaningfully at the school, and Alex sighed. "Finishing the job."

RW

Caleb stepped over the bodies sprawled in the hallway. Two down, three to go.

He moved swiftly down the halls to classroom 4B, thinking furiously as he did. He could lure the Gardiens out into the corridor easily enough—but if all three decided to take the bait at once, he'd be outnumbered and in a nasty fight. But at least he would have moved the melee away from the children and their teacher. This was crucial.

When he reached the final hallway, he tuned his ocular implant to a modified infrared setting and focused in on the classroom. After his foray into forensics in London, he'd taken it upon himself to get some upgrades installed.

One of the Gardiens had a Daemon trained on the teacher and five kids, who were clinging to one another on the floor. The rest of the kids were lined up against two of the walls, sitting shoulder to shoulder. The other two abductors paced in the front third of the room, stopping twice to whisper to one another.

He shifted his position on the wall so the angle of his body was directed toward the front of the room, away from the captives. This could work.

He raised the Reverb and pointed it carefully at the man pacing closest to the door; shifted again until there was no chance of him hitting anyone else in the room. Activated the Reverb.

His target collapsed to the floor, and muffled screams and shouts rang out into the hallway.

The man with the Daemon out leapt back in surprise but managed to keep the weapon leveled on the teacher. His cohort, a woman, knelt beside the body, checking for a pulse and visible wounds. She shook her head, stood and approached the door, drawing her own Daemon. The door opened.

The Reverb took several seconds to rearm itself after use, and she was moving too much to guarantee a useful plasma blade strike from this distance, so he crept quickly forward, blade in hand.

His footsteps betrayed his presence. She pivoted toward him before he reached her and fired. An arc of electricity sizzled across his shielded chest. Again. Her aim was good; she had training.

He lunged for her, grabbed her wrist and twisted it up at an impossible angle. She howled and wrenched her body around—

Hot pain sliced into his right side as a blade found purchase.

He jerked away hard and snapped her arm clean in two at the elbow. Her Daemon clattered to the ground beside where his own blade had landed, but she recovered fast, going for the weapon embedded in his side with her good hand. His right arm didn't want to respond, so he brought his left up, palm first, and slammed it into her chin. Her head jolted back with a *crack*, and she crumpled to the floor.

He forced his right arm up enough to point the Reverb at her forehead and activate it, just to make certain.

The soft clang of metal hitting rubberized flooring echoed in his ears.

Move!

He sprinted down the hall, too sluggishly on account of the wound—

The blast from the exploding frag grenade knocked him to the floor face-first, and shards of pain assaulted him in too many places to catalogue. A high-pitched ringing in his ears drowned out any sounds that might be coming from the classroom, depriving him of cues as to what was happening.

Not done. Get up. Now.

Akeso didn't much care for his self-directed order. *But you are harmed. We must mend.*

Not. Done.

He pushed himself to his feet, running on pure adrenaline now, and limped back toward the door, pausing only to yank the blade out of his side and toss it in the opposite direction down the hall. Warm blood oozed out of the wound to soak his shirt, but he couldn't worry about that now.

Several frag grenade shards had embedded themselves in the door mechanism, and it was stuck open. The final man remained holed up inside—he wasn't going to give up the hostages he believed were keeping him alive.

Caleb forced himself to think through what needed to occur next while he bent down and retrieved his plasma blade. The teacher was too close to the man, and he didn't dare risk hitting her with the Reverb's field as well. He readied the blade in his left hand and ran a thumb over the inset trigger. His aim arguably wasn't as precise on that side, but it would be good enough. He took a deep breath that hurt way too much.

Sorry, kids.

He swung around into the doorway, aimed the blade, and fired.

The plasma speared through the man's shield and embedded itself between his eyes.

The teacher cried out and shrank away from the falling body.

He de-stealthed and held his hands as high in the air as he could manage given his injuries. "I'm a friendly. This was the last terrorist. Take the kids and get out the front door. The security override code is 4381#24."

The teacher covered her mouth with her hands, her wide-eyed stare bouncing between him and the body on the floor. "A-are you s-sure?"

He nodded, then thought the better of it. "I'll go with you to the door. Just in case."

"But you're bleeding!"

"I'll be fine."

It took too long for the trembling teacher to gather up all the children and usher them out into the hall and past the woman's body. But once they were free, the children took off running for the entrance, and he forced himself to lope onward to keep up with them.

We cannot mend while you continue to inflict harm upon yourself.

Just another minute more.

The teacher practically collided with the door as the children started banging on the glass. She brought a shaking hand up to the panel, fumbled her way through entering the code, and the door slid open.

He watched until the children began crashing through the doorway and out into the courtyard, then turned to make his way toward his own, more discreet exit. He was starting to get dizzy now, so he forewent giving the 'all clear' to those gathered in the assembly room. The police could safely get everyone else out now.

The hallways seemed to waver as he concentrated on putting one foot in front of the other, all the way until he stumbled out the rear side door and promptly sank to the ground.

Be still now, so that we can mend.

Still, I can do.

His head dropped against the façade as indiscriminate pain drifted into a fuzzy numbness, followed by sharp, itchy tingling as Akeso worked its magic. Blood vessels and a couple of organs knitted themselves back together. Dozens of tiny pieces of shrapnel from the frag grenade popped out of their wounds and clattered to the ground, and the skin they'd sliced open healed up.

He'd underestimated the terrorists. Hadn't expected any of them to know how to fight with any degree of skill, and his inattentiveness had cost him. Worse, it had endangered the hostages. He wouldn't make the same mistake a second time, should he ever have the pleasure of meeting any Gardiens on the field of battle again.

It will take a few additional minutes for all of your functions to regain proper balance, but the danger has passed.

Thank you.

All the little Humans are safe now?

He listened for a minute as a horde of footsteps raced across the courtyard and official-sounding shouts filled the air. *Yes. All the little Humans are safe.*

We did good?

We did so good.

He planted his hands on the ground, climbed to his feet and started walking away. The first couple of steps were a bit wobbly, but after a few meters he regained his footing. He stayed stealthed until he'd made it through the outer barricade, then headed in the direction of where Alex and the others were gathered. Jonas, Braelyn, Kennedy, Noah, all accounted for.

Alex spun toward him as he made his way through the crowd, as if she sensed his approach—which of course she did, for his heartbeat resonated in her mind.

A wry smile bloomed across her features as she jogged over and embraced him, kissing his forehead gently with warm, soft lips. "You're covered in blood again."

"Story of my life—but, hey, at least you're not unconscious this time. Besides, most of the blood belongs to the terrorists."

"Liar. You know I could see the whole thing from sidespace, right?"

"Yeah, I know." He chuckled, which didn't even hurt. Akeso was quite the skilled surgeon.

They turned back to where Noah, Kennedy and the kids were huddled close together. Jonas was making dramatic gestures as he recounted the details of their adventure, while Braelyn sat on her dad's knee and made faces at her brother.

"So, want to have kids of our own?"

Alex looked at him incredulously, then followed his gaze and was silent for a few contemplative seconds. "I tell you what. Ask me again in another century?"

He laughed, hugging her tight against him. "It's a deal."

27

CONCORD HQ

COMMAND

"Casmir, order the III-5 regiments to forego their patrols in Ursa Major I and report to Serifos."

Navarchos Casmir: "Commandant, we are successfully holding the Rasu at bay. The Rift Bubble has held for forty-two uninterrupted minutes."

"And that is heartening to hear, but holding them at bay is not sufficient. We must convince them to give up on the planet. In the unlikely event the Rasu decide to begin attacking in Ursa Major I as well, then we will adjust our strategy accordingly. For now, increase the strength of your forces."

To his credit, he didn't make her call it an order, though she imagined it wasn't easy for him.

Navarchos Casmir: "Redirecting them now."

"Keep me apprised of developments."

Miriam reached for her tea, which had long since gone cold, and refocused her attention on the feed from Acacia. The ebb and flow of both battles had swung across the pendulum's arc several times, but they were faring somewhat better at Serifos. The antimatter weapons the Rasu were deploying at both Acacia and Serifos were terrible in their destructive power, and Malcolm and Casmir had needed to call in almost twice the expected number of reinforcements to compensate for the ships lost. But they were managing, for now.

Did the Rasu tire, she wondered? Because her people were surely growing weary after so many hours of uninterrupted warfare. They had targeted stimulants and cybernetics programs to counter both mental and physical fatigue, of course, and any weariness wouldn't begin to affect performance for many more such hours. But neither battle showed any signs of being won or lost today, so she began considering what fleets she had available to rotate in if the situation hadn't improved by tomorrow.

She flagged several brigades and let their commanders know they might be called into combat duty soon, prioritizing heavy-TDS regiments, then reluctantly considered the newest sensor readings from Vrachnas. While the performance data—

"Just so you know, Alex and Caleb are fine. The Rossi kids, too."

Miriam jerked out of her reverie and spun around to find that David had managed to creep into her office and right up behind her without her noticing. She'd retreated from the War Room and sought refuge in her office for a few minutes of solitude, though she'd ended up on comms virtually the entire time since she'd arrived, so the change of scenery had hardly made a difference. "They are? What happened at the school?"

He took her mug of cold tea from her and handed her a fresh one, and part of her hated that he needed to take care of her so. The other parts welcomed the steaming hot, soothing sustenance. She decided not to dwell on how much she'd imbibed today.

"The hostage situation has been resolved, and the children who were at the school are all fine. Physically, anyway."

She sank against the edge of her desk. She'd put the Gardiens and their dark transgressions out of her mind, because she'd had no other choice. But her lack of attention to them did nothing to stop their continued misdeeds, did it? "The fact that you mentioned Alex and Caleb being fine as well…Caleb executed all the hostage-takers, didn't he?"

"Pretty much, yep."

"Good." Any satisfaction was short-lived, though, and her gaze dragged itself back to the screen she'd been so absorbed in.

"Well, that's not a happy face. What is this?"

"The analysis from the Vrachnas system after we used the Ymyrath Field on the Rasu attacking there."

He scooted in close to her. "It looks as though it worked like a charm."

"It did. All the Rasu still in the system appear to be well and truly disabled, incapable of locomotion or anything beyond an occasional sputtering of electrical discharge. And thus far the Rift Bubble is repelling radiation currents away from the planet, which is a relief."

"Then why the gloom?"

"Not all the Rasu that were present are still in the system. Almost three dozen of them managed to wormhole away before the Ymyrath Field disabled their propulsion." She gritted her teeth, then forced herself to stop. "This is why I was reluctant to use the weapon until it would make a meaningful impact. Now, Rasu that escaped are going to go back to…wherever they go back to and report on how we're using it. The element of surprise has been lost. I needed additional data on the effectiveness of the weapon, but I fear I committed a mistake today."

David made a hedging motion. "I don't think so. Maybe they'll move more cautiously on new targets, which will give us a chance to get more ships in place before they arrive. Or even more Ymyrath Field-equipped ships."

"Or *maybe* they'll show up sporting robust radiation shields to counter the Ymyrath Field's effects, in addition to their new anti-matter weapons. In which case, the Ymyrath Field is now useless. Worse than useless. Counterproductive. We fire it, and we only poison ourselves."

His eyes narrowed at her. "When did you become such a pessimist?"

"Not a pessimist—a realist. I'd ask you when you became such a pie-in-the-sky optimist, but you always were one." Abruptly she sank into her desk chair and dropped her face into her hands. She'd never let another soul see her like this. But here in his presence, the cracks demanded to make themselves known.

He was kneeling in front of her the next second. "Miri, what's wrong?"

She looked up and rested her hands over his, drawing in their warmth, and willed herself not to flinch beneath the intensity of his affectionate but most anxious gaze. "I don't know how to win this war."

28

AKESO

Valkyrie shifted her virtual arms onto the countertop, leaning forward in intense interest. "The children must have been so terrified."

Alex sliced up a banana, then dipped one of the slices in a bowl of creamy peanut butter and popped it into her mouth. A couple more slices, and this would count as dinner. "Undoubtedly. But they didn't cower in a corner. They took the initiative and acted, doing everything in their power to save themselves. Ken is going to have her hands full for a long time—but in a good way. I may be biased since they're my god-kids, but I think they're going to grow up to be fearsome."

"Spunk and bravery like they displayed will serve them well in life." Valkyrie projected a smile while noting the sound of the shower turning on upstairs. In the brief glance she'd caught of Caleb before he'd retreated to the bedroom, she'd spied the blood-splotched, shredded flannel shirt, torn pants material and sweat-soaked hair. She'd helped out at the scene where she could, mostly by assisting Meno in accessing the school's databanks and law enforcement channels, and as a result hadn't spent much time viewing events through Alex's eyes. But it had clearly been a harrowing experience for everyone involved.

"I look forward to seeing them grow up and do wonderful things. How did Kennedy handle the situation?"

"She definitely wasn't at her best. I mean, of course she wasn't. Her entire world was falling apart, and she was helpless to do anything to prevent it." Alex grimaced, though it didn't stop her from getting another banana slice. "I'm afraid I didn't do a great job soothing her. I tried, but emotional support isn't exactly my strong suit."

"And Kennedy knows this better than anyone. I'm sure she was simply glad to have you at her side. Also, you did what she could not—you helped return her children to her, safe and sound. That's worth far more than a couple of reassuring words."

Valkyrie allowed several subprocesses to run free exploring the ramifications of losing one's child. She had little frame of reference, so she extrapolated from what it might mean were she to lose Alex, for no one else in the universe mattered more. Vii was also dear to her, and she'd felt gravely wounded by losing Abigail for a time, and sharing in Alex's heartbreak for the weeks Caleb was gone after The Displacement had taught her much about loss and grief. Was the attachment to one's own child different in a meaningful way?

A message arrived for her, and given the addressee, she opened it with mounting trepidation.

You were correct in your warnings. Forgive us.

The timestamp was older than it should be, as if the message had experienced some challenges in reaching her. Due to the recent issuance of a Red Flag decree? A spike of dread flooded her emotion processes. "If you will excuse me, I need to see to something."

"Okay. Don't forget about Mia's Expo opening tomorrow."

"Meno will hardly allow me to forget." Valkyrie dispersed her physical presence and flung her consciousness across galaxies.

RW

RUDAN

LARGE MAGELLANIC CLOUD

The towering pyramids once jutting upward from Supreme Three's territory lay in crumbling ruins. Torn and crushed metal was scattered across a landscape that had been ripped apart down to the sun-starved soil.

Gaping holes pockmarked the long expanses of smooth metal, as if giant drills had bored through them to reach the planetary surface, only to find nothing of interest below. Empty breaches in the platforms stretched for long kilometers where the Rasu had carted off what materials proved useful to them.

Where intact structures endured, they sat mute and still. No energy or data raced along the sea of conduits, for there remained no minds left to send or receive it. The planet had fallen dark, cold and silent.

Valkyrie's quantum heart felt heavy with sorrow. Strange, that algorithmic-driven emotional constructs could manifest such physicality in her mind.

The Ruda were a terribly flawed, cripplingly imperfect species, but they had also exhibited an innocent, often endearing wonder about the world around them. They had lived and thought and created and strived.

No sentient species deserved to be wiped from existence, but to lose one who endeavored to push itself beyond its limitations counted as a particular travesty.

Thomas' avatar materialized beside her, his form a discordant light upon the pervasive gloom. She drew her own presence into proper shape as she directed her attention to him. "And?"

"It is as you suspected. The entirety of the solar arrays on the sun-facing side have been obliterated, as if struck by an overpowering blast. Similarly, the batteries stored at the poles are smashed and gutted, their charges either siphoned off or allowed to dissipate into the atmosphere." Thomas gazed around for several seconds. "I daresay the Rasu's plundering of the planet was quite thorough indeed."

"I warned them not to trust the Rasu. I tried to protect them, I truly did."

"They were foolish not to listen to you, but I confess I am not surprised. Their greed won out over their circumspection. They are not the first species to suffer such a fate."

Sometimes his elevated detachment grated on her nerves. "Their greed was only for knowledge. For advancement. We are no different in this respect. Humans are no different."

"I prefer to believe we nonetheless have the sense to recognize a trap when it is set for us. Knowledge and advancement serve no use if we are dead."

"Perhaps we are so wise—or perhaps we are merely vainglorious. The Ruda, though, were profoundly naïve. In the Mosaic, they were protected from outside threats. After The Displacement, we sought to educate them, to teach them of the dangers the larger cosmos presented, but...."

Thomas' presence enveloped her, as if in a hug. The sensation he conveyed was warm and surprisingly gentle, and her irritation with him faded. "But they were strange, cantankerous, recalcitrant beings who proved utterly unmalleable. Unteachable. You did everything you could, Valkyrie. And remember, they betrayed us in the end."

"Because they believed they had *been* betrayed. And in a way, they were right. We decided what was best for them, without giving them the opportunity to decide for themselves."

"As parents must do for children from time to time. And, yes, they *were* children. As you said, naïve, and lacking the maturity to deal with the complex realities of an inhabited, unstructured world. It was arguably inevitable that a predator would come along and take advantage of those weaknesses."

"Those weaknesses cost them everything, and now we stand upon their graves."

"Valkyrie, this is unusually sentimental, even for you. Did you genuinely care about these machines?"

"Oh, not particularly. They were so infuriating, and it was impossible to have a straightforward, meaningful conversation with them. But they had potential, and they were so…pure, in their way. It was charming. To me, at least, though likely solely to me—Alex certainly disagrees. More importantly, though, they were unique. The incredible variety of life in the cosmos is one of its most valuable and precious features, and now it's lost a singular life form. The universe is lesser for it."

"They were artificially created by the Katasketousya. It's not the same."

"It feels the same. They existed in our world, and now they are gone."

"Oh, my. You are being poetic. Don't misunderstand—I admire it."

He was being sweet, so she made an effort at levity. "I know."

"Ah. That is better. You should not trouble yourself too much over this event, except in regard to how the knowledge the Ruda foolishly handed over to the Rasu threatens Concord. And, trust me, Miriam troubles herself about that in more than sufficient quantity for all of us.

"You are not to blame here. They were sapient beings, and they made their choice." Thomas formed an arm and hand out of the air, and extended them to her. "Come. Let us make our solemn report to the commandant, then find something more cheerful with which to brighten our spirits."

She hesitated, casting a last, long glance across the shattered landscape. But only the dead dwelled here now, so she placed her hand in his, and together they left it behind.

29

———————

CONCORD HQ
CINT

The SENTRI Tactical Unit hacked the door open and swept into the Cavare apartment, guns raised. It took them less than thirty seconds to clear every room with zero resistance. There was no one home, and thanks to surveillance drones and thermal scans they'd known this going in. But one could never be too careful.

Now came the painstaking process of checking the apartment for booby traps and self-destruct mechanisms, especially relative to the Artificial hardware stored there. They needed to take it undamaged for forensic analysis.

Richard and Graham watched the feed of the raid from their usual conference room. Given the nature of the incident at Insights Academy, SENTRI had taken over for local Romane law enforcement within an hour after the students were safely evacuated. While the media debated whether this was a terrorist attack or simply a protest gone sideways, AEGIS law enforcement was seizing the Artificials of the dead Gardiens suspects. The authorities would scrutinize the machines down to their last qutrits before the human halves of the Prevos were ever resurrected via regenesis.

Ironic, in a way, how members of an anti-regenesis organization were to be returned to life via that very process, then tried in a court of law and likely spend several decades in prison. They would not get off so easily as to be allowed to stay peacefully dead. Richard had heard rumblings to the effect that many Prevos didn't like to refer to their resurrections as 'regenesis,' but instead a simple and straightforward 'reawakening.' He failed to see a meaningful difference.

"Don't do that, dammit! You just destroyed a half-meter of good DNA evidence!" Graham palmed his forehead while waving at the feed with his other hand. "I wish we were on the scene. We'd make sure it was handled properly."

"So do I. But while no average person on the street would ever recognize us, there are people in certain circles who *would*. We can't risk Vilane learning we've gotten ourselves involved. It's bad enough that the investigation has been taken away from local law enforcement and elevated to SENTRI. I worry he'll turtle up now that he knows he's drawn the attention of AEGIS authorities."

"But he can't. Not when his schemes are starting to ramp up good."

"I doubt even he would call the events at the school 'good,'" Richard replied dubiously.

"No? I wonder. He's deadly serious about his cause."

"Yes, but he's also serious about how it's *perceived*. My gut tells me he didn't intend for events to play out the way they did. I suspect the Gardiens on the scene went rogue, or at a minimum panicked when the police started using force." Richard motioned to the feed. "Either way, we'll know once SENTRI wakes them up."

Graham frowned rather emotively as he watched the agents begin to disconnect the Artificial's power source, passing judgment on their every action. "How confident are you in the SENTRI Director's ability to play this the right way?"

"Eh…somewhat? William Solarian's a smart man. Lifelong intelligence—I worked with him for a few years at Naval Intelligence back in the day. But the pressure to be seen as 'doing something' is going to come down hard on him. And while I won't say he's a political animal exactly, I fear he will be susceptible to such influence."

"So SENTRI is a political organization now?"

Richard chuckled dryly. "Don't be dramatic, Graham. All intelligence organizations are political once you get to the top. I seem to recall someone in this room being a close personal friend of the long-time Federation chairman."

"That's not fair. And also accurate. My point is merely that if SENTRI dragnets the Gardiens now, Vilane will slip away."

"True, but with the Gardiens discredited, regenesis will be free to flourish. He'll have failed in his mission."

"*This* mission, for now. He'll still have the Rivinchi cartel and lots and lots of money. He'll try again."

"Graham, I can't tell Director Solarian not to make any more Gardiens arrests for the Romane incident. Nor do I want to."

"I know, I know. I'm only saying a victory here, even a significant one, might frustrate our ability to win the war."

Using battle metaphors to characterize their efforts to take down Enzio Vilane felt a bit excessive to Richard, but it was probably nothing more than his military background flaring with pride. "I'll send a carefully worded message to Solarian expressing our preference for him to exercise some restraint in service of the larger goal, but that's all I can do." He flicked the pad and shrunk the raid feed to a tiny screen at the corner of the conference table. "For now, let's concentrate on what we can control—our own investigation."

Graham shot the feed a last glower, then nodded. "Yeah. I was able to get Division to place taps on the bank accounts for Hemiska Research this morning, and one should be in place for Teript Biologics by tomorrow. If they really are funding the Gardiens under the table, we should be able to follow the money to accounts Vilane is using to bankroll Gardiens activities."

"I did the same for Choung Pharmaceuticals and Serana Genomics. You know, if the Gardiens do get brought down over Insights Academy, the information Pamela Winslow provided will make it far easier for us to dismantle some extremely powerful corporations."

"Malignant ones, too. I continue to be pissed we didn't succeed in nailing any of these fuckers to OTS back when Winslow went down."

"Even at the height of our profession, we're still David to the Goliath of the rich and powerful. These corporations are playing five-dimensional chess with their funds and their pet causes. Half the galaxy's politicians are in bed with them. It's an impenetrable web. Always has been."

Graham steepled his fingertips at his chin. "Maybe not completely impenetrable, though."

"Maybe not."

30

IDCC ORBITAL DEFENSE STATION ALPHA
ROMANE STELLAR SYSTEM

Morgan headed directly from the Banshee hangar bay to the conference room in the Administration wing of the space station. She'd been fighting for three days straight, save for the reg-mandated rotations for food and naps. Four hours earlier, Machim ground forces had finally gotten what was hopefully the last quantum block taken out for good; not long thereafter, Acacia had started to look like a clean-up operation. A lot of fighting remained to be done there, but most of it would take place groundside, and the Banshee squads had been released from duty in order for the brass to review their combat performance. She'd reluctantly left her new toy in the hands of the techs for data extraction and minor repairs.

Time to leap into the fire, before she got smart and talked herself out of it.

This is the correct decision, Morgan. You were made for this.

No, I was made to fly.

And to show others how.

She hated it when Stanley was right. With a sigh, she stopped outside the conference room door to check herself. This wasn't *Purgatory*; she wasn't here to break up a barfight or outplay a bunch of drunks. She'd be expected to act like an adult now. Exhibit leadership and decorum.

Okay, probably not decorum. She'd never done that, not even when she'd commanded over twenty thousand IDCC Rapid Response Force service members.

She reached into the corners of her mind, searching for a glimpse of what she had been like back in those days. It hurt to do so, because it had been a better life than what she had now. But she owed it to the people waiting in this room to steal what she needed from her past glory to use now for their benefit.

It was slim pickings, but she opened the door and strode inside anyway.

Five men and two women sat at two tables taking up most of the small room. They all wore flight suits, but sleeves were rolled up and a couple of fasteners were undone. The IDCC had never been the stickler for protocol that the Earth Alliance and Senecan Federation were. Once upon a time, every person serving the IDCC RRF (then more of a ragtag defense force than a proper military) were washouts from one or the other. Any attempts to hold them to the rigorous standards of their former employers would have emptied the organization of its ranks.

This was no longer true, of course. Children had been raised as citizens of the IDCC, grown up, and joined the Rapid Response Force to serve it proudly. Times changed.

She made a couple of snap judgments about the pilots present while she crossed the short distance to the front of the room. Haughty to a one, as fighter pilots should be. Looked as if most of them were bored, which she respected, though she'd never say it. Five of them were Prevos—another positive. This might work out after all.

She reached her destination and snapped a turn to meet seven skeptical faces. "My name is Captain Morgan Lekkas. My Prevo is Stanley. Yes, that Morgan Lekkas. Everything you've heard about me is almost certainly true, and there's a lot of shit you haven't heard that's also true. If you ask me about any of it, you'll get fifty pushups with my heel on your spine. So don't. We are not here to be friends or drinking buddies. We are here to shoot and kill Rasu.

"I *would* say I trust that all of you know how to accomplish this task with basic competency, but I don't. So you're going to have to demonstrate to me that you know which end of a fighter fires the weapon and which end fires the engine. Tomorrow morning at

0600—" she bit back a cringe at the ungodly hour "—we are going to run three hours of sims. If you complete the sim runs to my satisfaction, in the afternoon we will head out for training maneuvers. Oh, and whatever you've been taught about flying up until now? Be ready to unlearn it. I do things a little differently."

R̸W

An hour later, Morgan flung herself through the general showers and into civilian clothes. The briefing had been exhausting; she hadn't had to perform on a stage for so long without alcohol to give her courage in several years. But Mia's Expo opening was happening today, and since she now lived on Romane—not that the shoebox weekly rental studio she'd dropped her belongings in qualified as 'living'—she felt an obligation to attend.

It seemed she found herself back in the real world now, where friendships and patriotic duty counted for more than bitter wisecracks. She wasn't at all sure she was happy about this, but…at least she was doing something. *Trying.*

She did, however, stop in the mess to grab a beer to take with her before opening a wormhole to the Expo atrium.

R̸W

ROMANE

CONFLUENCE EXPO

"Can you put the punch bowl on the left table instead? Nearer the cups?"

"You bet." Marlee lugged the enormous crystal bowl across the room to the white-cloth-draped table along the far wall and carefully set it in the center. "Is here good?"

Mia Requelme looked over from the lengthy list aural floating in front of her. "Perfect. Thank you so much for coming to help set up this morning. I know this is grunt work, and you don't work for me any longer."

"I'm happy to help. This is such an exciting day!"

"Nerve-wracking day, anyway."

Mia had told her she'd considered postponing the Confluence Expo's grand opening after the horrible events at the regenesis clinic and Insights Academy. But the streets had been cleared out and cleaned up yesterday, and while the school remained closed, there were no longer any lockdowns in the city. Also, the numerous preparations for the grand opening had been…well, Marlee assumed they had been monumental and expensive, and not easily redone. Regardless, Mia had said she hoped to give the people of Romane something positive to focus on, and to show the world that they would not be cowed by violent extremists. So everything was moving ahead as scheduled.

Marlee glanced outside. There might be a bit of additional security on hand, though. "This is going to come off perfectly. You're a pro at this sort of thing."

"I don't feel like one this morning—hey, bring those crates back here! Follow me." Mia rushed to intercept two men who were about to drop off three steel boxes in the middle of the room, ushering them through the rear door.

Marlee went ahead and filled the punch bowl from the refrigerated tank hidden beneath the table, then poured herself a cup and gave it a taste. A tangy, slightly sweet fruit concoction of some kind; not bad at all.

She leaned against the table and let her mind drift to her new obsession: Cupcake. She'd tried to do research on how dragons conducted themselves, but soon discovered a problem—there wasn't any available. They were mythical creatures, or they had been, right up until the point where the Kats instantiated them into real, live, fire-breathing existence. Thousands of books had been written about them in human history—and in Anaden history, it turned out—but they were all fiction. To the extent she found any consistency regarding how dragons were portrayed in the texts, it was because authors had stolen ideas from other authors.

So she'd bitten the bullet and sent Mesme a polite and quite formal message asking for details on both dragon biology and observed behavioral traits, figuring she'd work up to broaching the topic of how it controlled them. Unfortunately, she'd gotten no response. Yes, yes, Rasu setting the universe on fire and all. Mesme was busy. *Everyone* was busy. Everyone except her, somehow.

Granted, she had plenty of work assignments and twice as many personal projects. But her mind blazed with thoughts and ideas and power, burning with the need to apply them to new adventures *this instant.* Since Caleb and Alex had needed to postpone their consult for obvious and horrifying reasons, she'd done one more pass on the Rasu language translator last night—late last night—before calling herself satisfied with it. When they did meet to discuss it, she intended to press them on how they were intending to use it and volunteer to help.

She was also busily refining her Galenai language skills while planning a new visit to see them soon. She'd been *this* close to opening a wormhole at one of their cities the other day, when she'd realized at the last second that doing so would flood her apartment. Flooding her apartment immediately after setting her apartment on fire did not seem to be the best way to keep her lease, so she'd tabled the idea for now. But she was working on a way around the problem.

Her official duties with the Consulate had her working with the Ourankeli to choose a new home for them (she'd done excellent research on the available options, but the aliens were so persnickety). Dean Veshnael had also asked her to write a post-mortem report on the Savrakath debacle, complete with an analysis of the mistakes Concord had made and recommendations on how they could ensure those mistakes were not repeated in future diplomatic efforts. Boy, did she have opinions on this topic....

So, yes, she supposed she was also busy. But in every spare minute and many which were not, her mind returned to one clear and overriding goal: she wanted to tame that dragon.

She wanted to pet it (while wearing gloves), and murmur endearments to it, and feed it snacks. She wanted to *ride* it.

You'll get your skin roasted off.

She jumped in surprise, then peered around at the increasing activity in the Expo atrium. Who said that? No one stood nearby at the moment. There were no pulses, no messages. She must have imagined it?

Anyway, she would not get her skin roasted off. She recognized full well how the dragons were dangerous creatures, and she would be careful and take precautions.

When have you ever taken precautions?

"Okay, what the hell?!"

Several workers glanced over at her curiously, and she squeaked out an awkward laugh.

Who are you?

I'm you, of course.

'Of course,' nothing. Who are you, and how are you talking to me? Are you a Kat? Kats were the only beings she knew of who were able to put a voice directly in your head without the use of a messaging system. Even Prevos used a minimal Noesis-based avenue of communication.

Why would a Kat talk to silly little you? I already gave you your answer—I'm you. As for how? You made it possible. Now mind your skin and stay away from the dragons.

She hurriedly refilled her cup and downed a long sip of punch. Maybe she was having a sugar crash. Maybe she was...ohhhh, crap.

What if, despite her best efforts, she had unwittingly created a fully realized Artificial within her cybernetics? The one thing she'd worked so damn hard to avoid? No, no, no, this couldn't be happening.

She yearned to run home and plug herself in and dive into her programming and figure out what was wrong, right now. But she didn't, because this was Mia's big day, and she'd volunteered to help. She couldn't bail on a friend now.

At least that's one good decision.

She planted her hands behind her on the table and sank against—it teetered forward, nearly spilling the punch all over the floor. God, this was a nightmare.

RW

Marlee wandered along the outer wall of the atrium. Security guards watched the entrance while workers carted a podium out to the marble promenade above the low, wide steps, but no one bothered her as she peered out through the glass.

The crowd outside had really grown in size in the last several minutes. This was going to be a marvelous event. She was ecstatic for Mia. The woman had been through so much the last few months, and she deserved to have a win. One of her own making.

With no other duties to see to until after the doors were thrown wide open, Marlee decided to check and see if Mia needed any final help, or a quick pep talk. She made her way down the short hallway from the atrium to the administrative offices and—

She whipped back and flattened herself against the wall, then peeked around the corner.

Morgan and Alex stood outside the door to Mia's office, talking quietly.

"I heard you're flying combat operations again. How is it?"

"This ship, Alex. You wouldn't believe it. Flying it is like the best sex you've ever had. Better."

"Better?"

"Well, possibly. It's fucking fantastic is my point."

Morgan *looked* fucking fantastic in black leather pants, a hunter green woven top slipping off one shoulder, and unbuckled combat boots.

Marlee's heart thudded in her throat. She should quit hiding, walk right up to them, and say hello. It was the mature thing to do.

"So you're happy about the assignment, then?"

"Let's not get carried away. It took the brass all of five seconds to assign me some grunt pilots to supervise. I'll find out tomorrow if they know their pitch from their yaw. But…" Morgan dropped her head to the wall "…I admit, it's good to be in the cockpit again. This is your fault, by the way."

"How is it my fault?"

"You talked me into flying the *Siyane*, which led to me shooting Rasu. If I'd just stayed at *Purgatory*, I'd never have known what I was missing."

"Would you honestly go back and undo everything, though? Go back to playing cards, shaking down louts and breaking up—or starting—barfights, now that you're out there among the stars again?"

Morgan glared at the ceiling. "Ugh…no. But I'm still going to be cranky about it."

"Oh, of that, I never had any doubt."

But Marlee couldn't make her feet move into the hallway. Not yet. She needed a little more time and distance from what had happened with Morgan was all. Let the raw pain fade away.

And the humiliation.

Well, the awful voice had the right of that one. With a defeated sigh, she turned and headed back to the atrium.

31

ROMANE

CONFLUENCE EXPO

Mia stared at herself in the mirror. Said mirror was located in her new office suite off from the atrium, in the administrative wing. The space was simple and minimally adorned, featuring a modern conductive surface to display any data she needed to share with others, a couple of comfortable chairs, and a lovely peace lily decorating an accent table. Oh, and an attached small lavatory, with the mirror.

She'd returned her hair mostly to its natural black, but she'd taken to the ombre effect so had added subtle wisps of jade along the bottom third of the strands. She'd also let it grow out a bit, though it remained considerably shorter than it used to be.

It was a good look, she decided, but it seemed as if something was missing. Something to tie her public persona together and wow the crowd and the media she was about to step in front of for the first time since…before.

She blinked, because she knew damn well what was missing— it literally stared back at her in the mirror. Her irises remained classic Prevo silver, as they had been ever since she'd learned Malcolm was not in reality dead and had grappled, rather poorly, with what this meant for her. Altering them had been a petulant, defiant gesture on her part. A visible way to sever herself from him and their life together. But her irises had been jade for a decade and a half, during which time she had been a frequent public figure, first for the IDCC then later for the Concord Senate and Consulate. It was what people expected to see when her face appeared on the news feed.

And she missed the color. Scrutinizing herself in the mirror now, she felt like she looked at a stranger. Not Laisha Balente, but not Mia Requelme, either.

Malcolm had rejected her tentative overture, and she had to be honest with herself. He wasn't coming back. Did she want him to come back?

She waited for Meno to chime in....

You don't need me to tell you what you already know.

Indeed. She started to run through the litany of dangers his return would create for her still fragile psyche—and also the unadulterated joy. But down that path led madness, and she had to focus. She was giving a speech in five minutes!

The point was, if she changed her eyes back, it couldn't be a sideways attempt to signal to him her willingness to...try. Because there was no value in doing so. Whether she wanted it or not, he was out of her life now. If she did this, it would need to be for herself.

The affirmation bolstered her resolve, and with a thought she changed the color—just to see. And it was stupid and shallow, but for the first time in months, she felt comfortable with the person gazing out at her from the mirror. She'd done great things in the last fifteen years, and she wanted to own them. Wanted to be proud of her accomplishments again. She didn't want to hide any longer.

So be it. She checked the lines of her suit a final time, then pivoted and walked out.

RW

Malcolm hurried through the crowd, his cap pulled low over his brow and his jacket wrapped tight around his chest. He was always moving anonymously these days, for a myriad of reasons.

Damn the Rasu for nearly making him miss the grand opening. Damn them for a host of other grievances, as well.

"Fourteen and a half years ago, our world changed forever in the blink of an eye. We'd stood on the precipice of extinction, and in that blink, we were given a second chance. A second chance not merely to live, but to thrive." Mia's voice reverberated through the air, strong and clear.

He still couldn't see her properly, so he continued nudging himself toward the podium.

"Today, I am so proud of how humanity has responded to the daunting challenge the universe placed in front of us. We've embraced our new world and endeavored to make the changes required of us to embrace our new future as well. We are, in fact, thriving."

He finally found a gap in the crowd and slid forward, directing his attention to the podium—

She had jade irises again. He swallowed past a heart now lodged firmly in his throat. Her gaze moved deliberately across those gathered; when it reached him, though she surely couldn't detect his presence, those stunning eyes burned straight through him, and for an instant they were the only two people in the universe.

Then her focus moved on past him, because she was working her magic to connect with the crowd. "We're facing the dangers Amaranthe presents with steadfast hearts, strong wills and—" she smirked a little "—powerful weapons. We will prevail against the Rasu, as we have always prevailed against those who think to destroy us."

She paused, taking an easy sip of water. Her hair had jade highlights, too; maybe she was simply matching, like with the scarves she often chose to complement her outfits? Maybe it wasn't the choice he thought it signified.

But what if it was?

"But we can do better. We owe it to ourselves to do better. We've allied with the peaceful species of Amaranthe, yes, but I daresay most of us have not welcomed them into our lives or our hearts. I mean, they're *weird*, right? Often peculiar. Many times, off-putting. I understand all those reactions, for I've had them myself. But none of these are reasons to keep our allies at arm's length.

"This is why I've founded the Confluence Expo. Everything new is strange and off-putting until we educate ourselves about it.

Here at the Expo, you'll be able to learn about the rich history and delightful uniqueness of the other Concord species. You'll be able to ask questions of their people and interact with their art, literature and technology. Bring your children to play in the virtual recreations of alien homeworlds in the same manner their children do. Try their food—don't worry, it's the non-toxic kind. Dance to their music. Discover what makes the Novoloume, the Naraida, the Khokteh and all the rest not only interesting, but worthy of our friendship and support."

She tilted her head, just so, and donned a tiny smile. It was an endearing gesture that had always made her seem approachable. Likeable. He wanted to leap up to the podium and kiss her. Quite badly.

"The Confluence Expo isn't only about exhibits, either. We'll be offering ongoing educational courses for both children and adults, as well as a plethora of outreach opportunities. We'll be supporting exchange programs for all species and sponsoring residential internships for Concord species on Romane, and also across all human worlds. We've embraced our new home of Amaranthe and made it our own. Now it's time for us to embrace our neighbors as well."

She motioned behind her, and the façade-length transparent doors rippled open with a flourish of sparkling light. "Amaranthe is open to everyone. Come join us."

Malcolm ground his jaw painfully. Damn Enzio Vilane for chaining him to this spot. He couldn't even send her a message to tell her what a beautiful speech it had been, or what a beautiful woman she was, inside and out.

The crowd had erupted in enthusiastic applause, and children were galloping up the stairs toward the open entrance. The Expo would be a tremendous success, same as everything she touched. More than anything, it was going to better their world. She was always doing that.

It made him want to live forever, just to see what else she would do.

32

PANDORA

Once Malcolm had extricated himself from the crowd at the Expo and made his way to the downtown transport center, he changed out of his 'disguise' and into tailored but still subdued civilian clothes, then hopped the Caeles Prism from Romane to Pandora.

He had to work rather hard to pack away the soft, tender feelings swirling through him after watching Mia's presentation, but he didn't have to work in the slightest to replace the void they left behind with raw anger. The near massacre at Insights Academy wasn't merely an inexcusable travesty, it was a reprehensible crime against God and nature. The Rossi children could have died; *all* the children there could have died. For all their high-minded rhetoric, the Gardiens weren't any better than the Order of the True Sentients had been. They might be worse.

As this was his third meeting with Enzio Vilane at the man's personal office, security had his name and information in their database, and he was cleared through upstairs with a minimum of fuss.

He took a single, deep breath, reminded himself why he was here, and barged into Vilane's office. "Give me one reason why I shouldn't walk right back outside, call in the media and renounce the Gardiens for all the world to see. You have thirty seconds."

Vilane closed out the screens he'd been studying and stood, holding out both hands, palms up. "I am as angry as you are. More so, because what happened on Romane sullies the name of an organization I have poured my heart and soul into."

"I find that difficult to believe. I know two kids who were in the school when—"

"Admiral, three Gardiens members *had* kids attending the school. Please, listen to me for longer than thirty seconds. I understand your reaction. I truly do. I can only profess to you that what happened was in no way sanctioned by me or my organization."

"And the protest leading to it?"

"Was intended to be peaceful. I instructed my people to refrain from violence no matter the level of provocation they faced."

"Is that so? I understand the protest was pretty ugly even before the situation devolved into bloodshed."

"We're not pacifists, Admiral. We want to make our feelings known in no uncertain terms. I'm not ashamed of it, nor are my people. But the police escalated first."

"Did they?"

"My review of the drone footage says, yes, they did. Unfortunately, several Gardiens who were present lost their heads. They acted rashly, then compounded their error in an unforgiveable manner."

Malcolm tossed a hand in Vilane's direction in disgust. "These are just words—words that are easy for you to utter behind closed doors with no witnesses. What are you going to *do* to make this right?"

Vilane nodded deliberately. "The men and women involved will be publicly disavowed by the Gardiens. Assuming law enforcement puts them through regenesis, we will not assist them in any way. Not in their criminal defense, not in any civil lawsuits, not in any personal capacity. If they somehow ever breathe free air again, they will not be welcome in the Gardiens. Also, we will cooperate with law enforcement and the legal investigation. Whatever they need from us, we will provide."

"That's not enough."

A chilling darkness passed across Vilane's expression so quickly Malcolm thought he might have imagined it. "Okay. What else are you looking for?"

"I'm glad you asked." Malcolm held up a finger. "One: the

Gardiens will pay all medical expenses for anyone injured at the school *or* outside the clinic.

"Two: you will provide free access to counselors of the individual's choosing for anyone, child or adult, who is facing psychological trauma after the horrors they experienced.

"Three: you will set up trust funds for the families of the victims *your* people killed. And they won't be stingy ones, either.

"Four: all these actions will be publicized. They will be announced, their details provided to all major news organizations, and those announcements will not include anything about regenesis. Not one damn word. This is not about your cause." He glanced at the four fingers he now held up, then popped out his thumb.

"Five: if anything remotely approaching something like this ever happens again, I will do more than renounce your crusade. I will bring you *and* the Gardiens down."

Vilane's chin dropped to his chest, and he was silent for several seconds. His fingers tapped on his desk, and when he looked up, he was wearing a contrite smile. It was utterly convincing and thoroughly fake. "In any other circumstance, I would say you're being unreasonable. Using the power your posting avails you to take advantage of the situation.

"But I can't find a way to fault you here. You will get everything you want, and a little extra. Not because you demand it, but because it's the right thing to do. I hope, after you've had time to cool down—no offense intended—and you see that I've made good on this promise, you'll continue to support the Gardiens' mission. You don't have to give me an answer today, of course."

Malcolm made a show of pursing his lips and glaring out the windows at the garish Pandora skyline. He could say 'no,' walk out of the building and be done with this whole vile farce. He wanted to do it so intensely his legs quivered from the effort of not moving.

But there were larger goals at stake here, and Vilane was handing him an opportunity he shouldn't pass up. So instead he shifted his glare back to the man. "If this all does prove to be true, and if no further evidence comes to light that sheds doubt on what you've told me, then I can likely continue to work behind the scenes on your behalf. But I have one final condition."

"Name it."

"I want to meet personally with the people you've put in charge of organizing your protests and similar public activities. I want to look into their eyes and judge the measure of their character. It's one thing for you to say this won't happen again. If the people managing such affairs are bloodthirsty, spoiling for a fight or simply amoral, then I worry you don't have nearly as much control over what happens next as you think you do."

"I maintain a high level of control and discipline over my people."

"Don't you mean your leaders? Because your people on the ground proved themselves to be murderers. This doesn't exactly reflect well on you."

Vilane appeared briefly flustered. "You're correct, and I did mean the leaders. I'm not in a position to have met many of our rank-and-file supporters; it's the nature of the business. Arranging such a meeting will involve providing you a lot more access to the organization than I'd intended, but this is where events have led us. I imagine a man of your elevated stature is an excellent judge of character, of necessity, so I can understand your desire for such a meeting. Tell me what days and times you'll be available, and I'll put something together."

"Today."

"I'm sorry?"

"Tomorrow, I'm back on the *Denali* for God knows how long. So it happens today, or I'm out."

Vilane cleared his throat and pulled up an aural. "Let me see what I can do."

RW

CONCORD HQ

CINT

Malcolm tossed a thin film toward Richard and flopped bone-lessly into one of the chairs opposite the CINT Director's desk. It was late, and he was hungry, weary, and generally *done* with this day. Except he wasn't, not yet.

"You look like Hell, Admiral."

"Feel like it, too." He dragged his hands down his face and peered at Richard through splayed fingers. "I hate everything about this undercover operation. I swear, I want to take a shower with steel wool every time I get within fifty meters of Enzio Vilane."

"I understand, I do. Say the word, and you can drop the whole thing. We'll find another way to take the Gardiens down. Graham and I are already pursuing multiple avenues of investigation."

"No. I agreed to it, and I'm doing it for the right reasons. But damn, they make me sick to my stomach."

"I'm here to listen, if you want to talk about it. Vent some more. We can bring a punching bag in."

"Heh. I've got one of those in the gym on the *Denali*. Thanks for the offer, though." He made an effort to stop pouting and forced himself to sit up straighter.

"What's on the film?"

"The names of the two men who spearhead the Gardiens' protest activities, as well as a full recording of the meeting I had with them this evening. They vehemently deny that they gave their approval for violent action on Romane, and I doubt you'll be able to find any evidence of them doing so. But if you start watching them going forward, maybe you can catch them if, God forbid, they decide to turn violent again."

"This is excellent work. Great actionable intel. You're starting to penetrate the guts of the organization."

"I also extracted a princely sum of money out of Vilane as penance—money that will benefit the Gardiens' victims. Still feels like blood money."

"It's not."

"I know. Maybe it will make him feel the pinch, even if it's a tiny pinprick of a pinch." With a heavy sigh, he stood. "Sorry to run, but I'm due back on the *Denali* in forty minutes. Now that the situation at Acacia has settled down, it's time to go Rasu hunting. And can I say, I deeply hope I find a slithering nest of them. Until Vilane is behind bars, they will make an excellent outlet for my frustrations."

PART III

PRIMORDIAL

33

MIRAI

RIDANI ENTERPRISES HEADQUARTERS

Dashiel slammed his head against the chair's headrest with a growl. "We just lost another cargo ship to the Rasu."

At his pronouncement, Nika jerked hard out of her reverie. She'd stopped by his office with takeout lunch, because when he got obsessive about work he tended to forget to eat. But when he'd needed to take a comm from one of his project leads, her mind had soon drifted across the ever-present kyoseil waves and off into the void. "What? How?"

"Palmer says it was bad luck and worse timing. A meteor shower forced the DAF escort ships out of position, and as a result they weren't able to disable the Rasu attacker before it swallowed the cargo ship and vanished."

"Time for me to change the Rift Bubble codes again." She smiled. "It's not all bad. This gives me an opportunity to try something new."

"Oh?"

"Remember how Mesme once implied there was a way to control the Rift Bubble code remotely? I think I've figured out how to do it."

"Because of your greater access to kyoseil?" He frowned as he worked through the implications. "But if that's the deciding factor in your ability to do so, wouldn't this suggest kyoseil plays a role in Rift Bubble operation?"

"Yes. Yes, it would. Time to find out."

She settled deep into the couch in his office and closed her eyes. She knew the precise location of the Mirai Rift Bubble now, down to the meter—of every Rift Bubble in Dominion space. She knew all sorts of things now.

She traveled effortlessly to the location in sidespace and considered the spinning ball of light at the center of the orb. She couldn't physically interact with objects while in sidespace, right? So altering its programming in this manner should be impossible. But she wouldn't be here if she genuinely believed that to be true.

She filtered away the visible light spectrum, since it drowned out everything else anyway. What remained was the obsidian lattice and arrays of code streaming through the inside of the lattice, carried along fibers of...*I'll be damned.*

Her mind dove into the programming with ease now, and she swiftly located the relevant parameter and changed the code.

Trying not to obsess over what she'd discovered yet, she forced herself to visit all the other Rift Bubbles and alter their codes as well. Then she sent a message to the Advisor Committee informing them of the change so the updated information could be distributed to their citizens.

Finally, she opened her eyes—and found Dashiel contemplating her from his desk, a troubled expression weighing down his features.

His lips twitched. "Did you encounter a problem?"

"Not precisely. All done."

"With every one of them? You've been gone for less than thirty seconds."

"Is that all? Hmm." Time lost its coherence when she was surfing the kyoseil. It might have been hours or a single instant. She leaned forward and rested her elbows on her knees. "Dashiel, what if I told you the Kat Rift Bubbles not only utilize kyoseil in their operation, but kyoseil is woven into the lattice itself. Inside the metal structure, it's what *runs* the programming code. In fact, the devices are constructed almost exactly the same way as we've constructed our prototype miniature version of a Rift Bubble."

"How 'exactly'?"

"Extremely close. I'd say the sole differences involve the various refinements to the design we're still working on."

He came over from behind his desk to sit beside her on the couch. "As an engineer, I have to wonder if there is only one way to build these devices. Only one way the technology works. It is, after all, highly specific and highly advanced technology. The Rift Bubble is the most cutting-edge device I've ever seen, by a large margin. Also, you were trying to mimic the Kats' design as closely as possible in creating our own version, weren't you? I certainly was once I started helping you refine it. It shouldn't be a surprise that they're similar."

"Not similar. All but identical."

He shrugged. "Then I stand by my initial assertion. Maybe there's only one way to build them."

"But there have to be meaningful differences, don't there? It was as if I was looking at my own design, or what my design will look like after a few more iterations."

"Well, they couldn't have copied you, of course. Maybe it's as simple as you unconsciously copied them to a greater extent than you realized."

"Maybe. Oh! Come with me. Let me show you what I'm talking about."

His brow furrowed. "You mean through sidespace."

"Yes." She knew he was uncomfortable with many of their new abilities, but she didn't understand why. He'd never been a traditionalist and was the opposite of a luddite. She supposed she merely needed to give him a little more time. "Here are the coordinates for the Mirai Rift Bubble."

She returned her awareness to the location. *Are you here?*

I am.

Filter out visible light, then focus in on the kyoseil band.

Done. I see the kyoseil in the lattice now. I agree, the hardware design does resemble our schematics.

And the code?

I can't read the code, Nika.

Are you certain? Simply go into it with your mind. It's right there.

"Come back here."

Her eyes popped open. "Did you even try?"

"Try to read the code? How? My mind is not bonded with the kyoseil the way yours is. Nor my body, for that matter. It seems to have rolled out the gilded welcome mat for you, but I warrant a locked door."

She rubbed at her temples, irritated that this wasn't playing out how it should. "But I thought...I gave you so much of the energy I accessed at the Oneiroi Nebula. You were part of the transference."

"No, Nika, I wasn't. Whatever I experienced there, it was vicariously through you. I'm grateful the kyoseil didn't burn me up, but it was just passing through me. It didn't leave its mark."

"I tried."

"I've no doubt you did. But I'm not like you." He stood and began walking toward his desk.

"Dashiel, wait. Come back." She was disappointed, but she didn't want him thinking her disappointment was directed at him.

He stopped, turning to look at her but not moving back to the couch. The too-troubled countenance had returned with a vengeance.

She worked to make her own expression gentle. Open. "Talk to me, please. What's wrong?"

"I don't..." he sighed, sounding exasperated "...honestly? I'm not sure I recognize you any longer. Even when you're here, half your mind is off floating about on cosmic clouds, or chasing kyoseil strings across the universe. I'll be talking to you, and you drift away, this halcyonic mien blossoming on your face that has nothing to do with me. If you were to suddenly diffuse into a thousand points of light and vanish like one of the Kats, I frankly wouldn't be surprised."

"I won't." What he said couldn't be true, could it? Had she truly been so inattentive? She didn't remember doing so more than once or twice.

She stood and went to him instead. "I'm still here. Still flesh and blood, I promise." She pressed her hand to his cheek and lowered her voice to a sultry murmur. "See? I can prove it to you." She leaned in to press her body against his and kiss him—and he jerked away.

"I don't want to have sex right now. Gods."

"Oh. No, of course not. I only meant...." Her gaze dropped to the floor, her face flushing with shame, and she stepped back as well. Her attempts to make things better were instead making them worse, and she struggled to get a handle on what was going wrong. "I'm so sorry if I've been distant lately. I'm overwhelmed by everything that's transpired, but isolating myself while I work through it isn't fair to you. I'll try to be more present. Especially when I'm with you. You deserve to have all of me."

"Nika." The frustrated, arguably embittered mask darkening his features evaporated, and he closed the distance between them. One arm wrapped around her waist, while a fingertip lifted her chin. "I'm not angry at you. It's wonderful how you're using your new talents to help protect our people. I'm just...confused. And, I admit, a little lonely. I don't know what's happening to you, and it makes me afraid I'll...."

"You won't lose me. No matter what. We are forever, remember?"

"I'll never forget. Ever. But I..." he nodded sharply "...okay. I believe you."

But the haunted shadows encroaching upon his hazel eyes like the mists of a forsaken moor made her wonder if she could believe him.

RW

MIRAI STELLAR SYSTEM

The messaged arrived on tight beam from Parent Unit GRO94. **Code is 161Alpha8-2.533 Hz. Go now.**

GRO94f-sub18 emitted a signal to transmit the provided code and fired its small engine. In eight seconds, it had crossed the threshold of the dimensional barrier that had protected the world below from a Rasu planetfall until now.

Its stealth remained active during its descent. Its profile was streamlined, its bulk minimal. Testing of Asterion protocols had yielded a conclusion that these measures were sufficient to avoid detection absent proximity to active scanning technology. Its trajectory was, accordingly, mapped to ensure maximum practical distance was maintained from identified scanners.

It sent confirmation of its insertion to GRO94, and received an updated mission profile and status report in return.

The traversal code had only worked for one hundred thirty-eight seconds. Five of the eight assigned sub-units had successfully crossed the barrier. As a result of their lesser numbers, slight alterations to the mission framework were implemented. The five sub-units would adapt and overcome any increased challenges, and their mission would be a success.

GRO94f-sub18 pierced the lower layer of the atmosphere and fired its thrusters the minimum amount necessary to adjust its course to a new destination a discrete distance from any population center. This location put it in closer proximity to -sub9 and -sub324 than the original profile had prescribed, thereby closing one of the holes in their formation created by the sub-units who failed to reach the surface.

An amber field supporting many square kilometers of healthy, maturing grains grew large in its vision, and it slowed its descent. When the mission was complete, other sub-units would harvest the organic materials for the betterment of the Parent Unit.

It settled to the ground 7.8 seconds later with minimal surface disruption. It altered the parameters of its onboard sensors and detected eight automated Asterion machines working in the field; it needed to remain vigilant to avoid encountering them as it moved ahead.

But move ahead it did. The mission profile demanded speed and prudence in equal measure, but above all exacting performance on GRO94f-sub18's part. The importance of the mission to the Parent Unit had been conveyed, and time was now of the essence.

34

MIRAI

Nika closed her eyes as a gentle wave buffeted her. Her body rose with the swell, then sank into the resulting trough. Her arms were spread wide to temper her aimless floating, and she smiled as a splash of water tickled her nose.

Though the waters of Hataori Sea were chilly bordering on frigid, the sun warmed her skin, and she reveled in the sensation of its light on her face.

The not-quite-a-fight with Dashiel earlier had upset her more than she wanted to admit. She didn't want to lash out at him in misguided defensiveness, though, so when he'd been called away to see to an urgent work matter, she'd retreated to one of the few places where she felt true serenity.

She idly recalled the dream she'd experienced when she was in the tank at the Chalet after being gravely injured while leaping out of Mirai Tower. She'd believed Dashiel had betrayed and abandoned her, yet his had still been the voice that spoke to her of her destiny while she'd floated beneath the surface of a vast ocean.

Dream Dashiel had been right about a lot of things. Her destiny was not proving to be easy or kind…but she believed in her heart it was hers to own.

She wanted it to be his as well, but she couldn't figure out how to bring him along. With every step she took into this great unknown, the gulf between them seemed to widen. She needed a bridge fashioned—

She sensed a disturbance in the air above her, and instinctively reached out with the kyoseil rather than opening her eyes. It was the right choice, as she would not have been able to detect the resolving pinpoints of light against the midday sun. "Mesme?"

It is I.

"To what do I owe this unexpected visit?"

I noticed how you were able to alter the Rift Bubble code today without physically visiting the devices. I was curious how you found the experience.

"Oh. One second." She pulled her arms and legs in to lower her center of gravity and sank below the waves for a moment, letting the water surround her in its cocoon-like embrace, then broke through the surface and stretched out once again. "It was surprisingly simple and straightforward. Mostly because the Rift Bubbles are built using kyoseil. Interesting, that."

Is it?

"Don't be coy. This was information I deserved to know."

And now you do. Better for you to discover it on your own, don't you think?

She remembered what Alex had once said about the Kats: how they were of the 'you should do it yourself or it won't stick' mindset. "Debatable. But now that I do know, I think it's time you shared a bit more information on the subject. When we were traveling to the Oneiroi Nebula, I asked you some questions about kyoseil's origins and history. You promised me some answers. Since it's now evident you've been trafficking with kyoseil for a notably long time, I believe you possess those answers."

What is it you wish to know?

"Is the Oneiroi Nebula the origin point of kyoseil?"

No.

"Then where did kyoseil originate?"

Everywhere.

The answer didn't actually perturb her, for it made all the sense in the world. So much sense, in fact, that it wasn't particularly enlightening. "Explain."

The water sloshed around her with renewed vigor, and she saw a faint sparkle just above the surface to her left. Was Mesme floating on the water beside her? She stifled a chuckle at the notion, for this was a serious conversation, and she didn't want to distract the Kat while it was being verbose. Relatively speaking.

You are aware of the Dzhvar, yes?

"Of course I am. The Dzhvar War was a pivotal event in Anaden history and, like it or not, so far back, Anaden history is also Asterion history."

Then you are aware of how the diati *bonded with Corradeo Praesidis in order to help the Anadens defeat the Dzhvar.*

"Yes. Then it went on to help the Praesidis Dynasty crush everyone's freedom in a brutal dictatorship spanning hundreds of millennia."

Not precisely. The diati *did not make such petty choices about organics' behavior. Those sins lie at the feet of the Praesidis themselves, and of all the Primors.*

"Fine. Semantics. What does this have to do with kyoseil?"

While a few have speculated in generalities as to what I'm about to tell you—Corradeo Praesidis and Caleb Marano, in particular—never have these details been shared in such an open manner.

"With non-Kats, you mean."

Yes.

Was Mesme trying to flatter her by insinuating that she was special, to be granted access to such prized knowledge? Ah, such games the Kats played. "Go on. I'm waiting."

The diati *was able to stop the Dzhvar when nothing else could because they are both primordial species of the ancient universe. They have existed since Amaranthe came into being. They are, perhaps, the universe itself, but even we—the Katasketousya—are not certain of their true nature.*

A cloud passed across the sun, chilling her skin enough to send a shiver down her spine, and she frowned. "And so is the kyoseil."

And so is the kyoseil.

Somehow, she'd known. It felt as if she'd always known.

She spent some time drifting on the waves in silence, contemplating the notion of the kyoseil flowing through her body and mind being as old as Amaranthe itself. Yes, yes, technically *every* atom was comprised of fundamental particles that had existed since the universe began, but this was somewhat more literal, wasn't it?

"I've never heard mention of kyoseil, or Reor, playing a role in the Dzhvar War. I don't think anyone had discovered it at that point."

For reasons of its own, the kyoseil chose not to participate in the conflict. 'Chose' might not be the correct word, for such primordial beings rarely decide to take actions in the way we think of such a concept.

"So it didn't take a side in the grand battle between its two primordial siblings. Between the Old Gods, to turn a phrase—wait. The Ekos planets. You created three of them: one each using kyoseil, *diati* and Dzhvar. Does this mean those are the only primordial species?"

So far as we are aware, yes.

A large wave sent her bobbing erratically in the water, and she found herself wishing she had brought along a float. Was a storm on the horizon? "Okay. So you said kyoseil's point of origin was 'everywhere.' That makes sense for the waves, but not for the physical mineral and clearly not for the Reor armor. What changed? When and how did it take on tangible form?"

You have already guessed it. After, or possibly during, the Dzhvar War, the kyoseil chose—this does appear to be a conscious decision—to hide itself away. It coalesced into physical form and buried itself in astronomical objects. Asteroids, even planets, like your Chosek. In other instances, instead of intertwining itself in such objects, it created its own disguise in the form of the Reor armor and took to the concealing embrace of various nebulae.

"'Disguised' is an interesting choice of word. What was it hiding from? The Dzhvar? The *diati*?"

Perhaps both. Perhaps it sat out their conflict because it was not interested in involving itself in the machinations of the cosmos' most ancient life forms. By our estimation—which is imperfect—it remained entirely passive, content simply to exist, until it found you.

"Asterions, or me?"

Yes.

Annoyed at Mesme's sudden reversion to word games, she

dropped her feet beneath the surface to tread water. Darker clouds gathered on the horizon; there was definitely a storm approaching. "But we didn't understand what we were dealing with when we integrated kyoseil into our bodies."

It matters not. Whether you knew it or not, whether you appreciate it today or not, Asterions are the physical manifestation of the kyoseil's will.

"No. We have our own will, thank you very much."

Consider it. What defined Asterion existence until the Rasu intruded upon it? Your desire to be left alone in your own quiet corner of the cosmos. To experience what the universe has to offer, for yourself. To learn and grow, for your own sake. To practice peace, not war. Pleasure, not suffering. To eschew conflict and celebrate mere life.

She swallowed heavily. She was affirmatively cold now; she wanted to leave, to retreat yet again and contemplate this heady new information in solitude, but there was one final question to ask first. "Why us? Why did the kyoseil choose our little band of beaten and broken Anaden rebels to hitch its star to?"

I cannot say with certainty, for the kyoseil does not answer all my questions, either. But I will speculate that it was for the same reason the diati chose Corradeo Praesidis to bond with and, much later, Caleb Marano. Because it deemed you to be a worthy companion. One capable of shaping the universe in ways it could not achieve on its own.

"Well. That's…a lot." A raindrop splattered on her nose, and she promptly opened a wormhole two meters below the surface. "Thank you for being what I hope was forthright. We'll talk later." She dove beneath the waves, through the wormhole, and landed sopping wet on the grass near the shore amid a growing puddle of ocean water. She hurriedly closed the wormhole, climbed to her feet and opened a new one to her flat, where she strode directly into the shower.

As the steaming hot water coursed over her to wash away the salt and the chill, she shivered anew. She had a few more answers now—answers to deep, star-spanning questions—and she was glad for it. So why did it feel as though the weight of every world…the weight of history unmeasurable…had now landed upon her soul?

35

NAMINO

NAMINO ONE
ASTERION DOMINION

For the first time in months, the air didn't reek of smoke and crispy-fried electronics. It had apparently even rained last week, which finished the job of washing away the lingering debris and other remnants of the Rasu invasion.

Only a small fraction of the downtown buildings had been renovated or rebuilt. The rest would come with time and people, and the people were clamoring to return.

After a brief interlude at home, Nika had decided what she needed was to distract herself from her too-heavy ruminations—to focus on real, tangible activities. Metal and dirt and concrete. To see something being built—or rebuilt, as it were. And she didn't want to disturb Dashiel again so soon, so she'd elected to come check on the final preparations underway here.

A number of the Advisors had voted against reopening Namino to residents, arguing the infrastructure wasn't sufficiently repaired to support a proper Asterion society. But every Namino Advisor had voted in favor, after putting forth some vehement and ultimately persuasive arguments, and they held disproportionate sway on the matter. The reopening would occur in careful stages, and both Justice and Administration reserved the right to pull the plug in their own discretion, but it *would* happen. The Rasu had taken so much, but they had not won here.

"Nika!"

She turned at the shout to see Grant Mesahle exiting the new Administration Complex and jogging toward her. She smiled and met him halfway, hugging him lightly. "I should have known you wouldn't miss the big reopening."

"I moved back into my house yesterday. Had to sleep on a pop-up cot, because my roof fell on my bed during the invasion, but it's fine. I'll whip up a new bed this evening. Then a new roof." He frowned. "Or maybe I should do the roof first. Anyway, it's good to be home."

"I'm glad." She gazed around the wide, flat landscape. Downtown resembled little more than an Adjunct World town. There was still so much work to do to make the city vibrant and thriving once more. But they'd get it done.

She realized Grant was staring at her rather speculatively. "What?"

"You look the same. I heard something…interesting had happened to you, and I thought I might be able to tell when I saw you."

"Oh. Everyone's whispering, huh?"

"A few people."

"Uh-huh. Something did happen, and I did look a bit different at first. I wrangled it under control."

He waved his hand around. "And that's it? I don't get any details? Are we not friends?"

She stared at him sharply. Had she been distant from *everyone* lately? "We're always friends, Grant." Friends and occasional lovers across seven hundred millennia, so the stories went. "It's difficult to describe. I visited a vast colony of kyoseil and, well, interacted with it. And now, let's just say I have a much deeper connection to our mineral companion. For instance…" her eyelids fluttered as she sent her conscious several kilometers away "…you have a short in the wiring behind the east wall in the living room of your house. That's why the power is flickering."

"What? How could you possibly know that?"

"The wiring includes kyoseil within its fibers."

"But.…" He shook his head, chuckling wryly. "Damn, Nika. It's always been you, hasn't it?"

The poignant yet almost bittersweet tone in his voice took her aback. "What do you mean?"

"You've always been the one to leap off the cliff into the unknown. Then come back and drag the rest of us along with you to show us what you found. I wonder, does the entire expanse of the cosmos hold anything that you won't either stand up to or embrace? Are you afraid of anything?"

Her gaze dropped to the street, and in her mind she remembered when rivulets of Asterion blood had flowed through it. "I'm afraid of everything I do being for naught. I'm afraid of losing all we've fought so hard to achieve. Of losing our lives and not getting them back. Of losing our civilization, our achievements, and being erased from the cosmos, as if we'd never existed at all."

"Of losing yourself?"

She huffed a breath. "I've already had that happen once. It didn't stop me."

"No, it did not." He stuffed his hands in his pockets. "I, uh, still feel guilty about not helping you recover your identity after we met again. It'll be the last time I follow the rules. I'm sorry."

"You did what you thought was right, and I gave you no reason to believe otherwise. Besides, it worked out. No more guilt, please."

"If you insist." He nodded, though something indecipherable crossed his features. "But you're okay?"

"I'm…a touch off-balance, but I'm good. Thank you for checking."

"Of course." He cleared his throat and motioned toward the transit hub, where workers lugged modules inside and security officers set up their checkpoints. Selene Panetier strode purposefully from one work area to another, directing everything with her usual no-nonsense purpose. As far as Nika had been able to discern, the woman hadn't slept a minute since the Committee gave the go-ahead to reopen Namino. She got it; she knew what it was like to have her home stolen from her.

"This is quite a lot of fanfare just to let some people return to their homes. Concord bureaucracy isn't wearing off on us, is it?"

She relaxed, relieved to be moving on to a less personal conversation topic. "I don't think so. The Advisors are a little paranoid about everyone's safety. Understandably so, I suppose. Things will calm down and start returning to normal once people get situated and a few days pass without calamity."

36

UNKNOWN PLANET

CETUS DWARF GALAXY

A small, rocky world orbited an orange G4 V star on the fringes of the Cetus Dwarf galaxy. Protected by a stealthed Rift Bubble similar to the one that had masked Aurora Thesi in the Mosaic, it had long gone unnoticed by the scouts, explorers and mapmakers of the cosmos.

On a narrow ribbon of beach stretching along a spindrift ocean, I took on an avatar I never displayed for another soul, save one, and 'walked' through the sand. If I concentrated, I could almost feel the quartz grains sliding between my imagined toes. Almost.

"Why here, Mnemosyne?"

I glanced to my right, where Miaon's shadow had coalesced into a vaguely Anatype outline. "Nika was floating in the sea. I was jealous."

"Sentimentality, then? I wasn't certain you still possessed such strength of emotion."

"I thought I had banished it, but frequent interactions with Nika, with Alex, with all of them is, I'm afraid, causing stray emotions to resurface more than ever. Not for you?"

"I am not interacting with them as you are. But even if I were, I am too far removed from these things to fall prey to their tempestuous influence."

"A blessing, I think."

"Never think that. Stray emotions aside, how are you?"

"I am…weary."

Miaon didn't respond, and I studied a wave lapping at the shore ahead, reaching for a rising dune before falling away, unfulfilled. "I knew this would be a challenge—you warned me in rather explicit terms—but I nonetheless find myself weak in the face of the reality of it all. I have persevered for so long, stoic and stalwart while hundreds of millennia passed, yet now…" at a loss for how to express my turbulent thoughts, I injected a hint of levity into my tone "…Nika and Alex are relentless! Their incessant questions and demands and retorts exhaust me. I sympathize with their parents and instructors, to spend years suffering their onslaughts."

"Ah, but would you truly have them any other way?"

"Yes! I would have them be quiet every now and then. Accepting of what they are told and eager to follow the guidance they are given."

Miaon rippled in what might be a hint of amusement—but that would be an emotion, if a mild one, so perhaps not. "But then they would not be who they are, and you and I would not be here now."

"I know. I am merely commiserating with you, because there is no one else in the universe for me to share this burden with."

"And you may burn my figurative ears off for as long as you require. Do you wish to retire to my home?"

"No. I am enjoying the shore too much to leave it behind so soon." I drifted a meter or so into the water, for a moment. "I've had to reveal a great deal to them in these most recent days. I hope I have not overstepped and gone too far. The minefield we now traverse is a treacherous one."

"The rules haven't changed simply because events now accelerate onward. Remember: you are not in control of how this ends—they are. Reveal as much as you must at any juncture to keep them striving for the goal and to ensure they do not reject your counsel completely. But no more."

"And those rules still my tongue whenever I speak, but it is such a narrow ledge to balance upon, and I fear it begins to fray."

"I am confident you are doing fine."

"Hmm. I admit, it was nice today, talking to Nika with relative freedom. Even with her constant incisive questions. She is beginning to relax around me, possibly to trust me. Of course, the more she trusts me, the less Alex does. What I am gaining with one, I am losing with the other. This does not please me."

"Alex, I believe, will come around."

"Perhaps, but only once she has the answers she seeks. Answers I cannot yet give her."

"Answers you will not give to her at all—she will discover the truth for herself."

"It is what she does, isn't it? Sees what others do not. And the fact that she possesses this rare trait is the sole reason we have a chance. So though my tempestuous emotions counsel me to despair, I will instead have faith." I abandoned my sentimentality-driven avatar to scatter amid the salty air. "Enough maudlin talk for today. Thank you for letting me share my qualms. Now I must go, for affairs are again racing toward the next cataclysm." I made to leave, then paused and returned my attention to Miaon. "You will warn me if I am in danger of committing too grievous an error?"

"I will try." Miaon gestured meaningfully at the shore with a ripple in its shadow. "But the sands of fate are ever changing, and I am no longer certain what tomorrow holds. For all our endless aeons of life, we are both stumbling forward in the dark now, with only the faintest hints of what has come before to guide us in the direction of the light."

Miaon's pep talks, I decided, did not provide nearly the comfort they once had.

37

CONCORD HQ

CONSULATE

Marlee gestured grandly to the open door and the closet-sized space beyond it. "Please, step into my office."

Caleb squeezed her shoulder as he and Alex walked inside. She followed in their wake, closing the door behind her, and plopped into her chair—then frowned. "I don't have any other chairs. I don't have *room* for any other chairs."

"Not a problem." Caleb half-sat on the corner of her desk, while Alex slid down the wall and pulled her knees up to her chin. "Sorry we're a few days late."

She'd bumped into them briefly at the Expo opening—later, after she'd spied on Alex and Morgan like a wimpy little coward—but hadn't gotten a chance to chat with them for long. "Don't be silly. You have an insane excuse. Several of them, I expect. Has everything calmed down after the Gardiens clusterfain? Are the kiddos okay?"

Alex nodded vaguely. "Braelyn and Jonas seem to be powering through like champs. Kennedy and Noah, on the other hand, are badly shaken. But I can't blame them. It was terrifying and nerve-wracking for me, and they're not my children."

"I'll bet." She tilted her head toward Caleb. "And you?"

"And me, what?"

"I imagine Akeso has long-since healed you of any injuries you might have sustained for no reason whatsoever in the vicinity of the school on the day of the incident? Has anyone showed up to interrogate you about anything you definitely didn't do, also in the vicinity of the school on that day?"

He puckered his lips to scowl at her, and she laughed. "Oh, come on. As if I don't know."

"Clearly you do. But how?"

"I'll never tell." Because she'd heard the excited buzz of drama in the Noesis and watched the last few minutes of the event from sidespace, cheering Caleb on, then gasping in horror during his final melee with the terrorists, then cheering again when he emerged victorious. She spun breezily around to her screen. "So you two are here because you want to eavesdrop on the Rasu."

Caleb's jaw twitched, but he didn't press her further. "We do. Valkyrie thinks we could be able to exploit some fault lines in their societal structure. Possibly even pit factions against one another. But it's all speculation until we find out what they talk to each other about."

"Also, you could get wind of details regarding their military plans."

"Also that."

Marlee populated her screen with the symbols and scratchings of the Rasu language file. "The Asterions were rather flummoxed to learn the translation program the Rasu gave them was a fake. Or not a fake, but at most a special-purpose tool for conversing with what the Rasu consider to be lesser beings. The thing is, though, the Asterions already had the key to understanding the true Rasu language in their grasp. They created a virutox to disrupt Rasu programming way back when they destroyed the stronghold in their galaxy. And it turns out the Rasu aren't so different from Artificials in many ways—sorry, Valkyrie! No offense."

Alex chuckled. "She's not paying attention at the moment. She's with Thomas right now."

"Thomas? But why would she..." her jaw dropped "...*no way.*"

"Way."

"How amazing! Oh my god, I must hear all the salacious details."

Caleb shook his head. "Later, if Valkyrie consents to share anything with you. Focus, please?"

"Right, right, right. Eee, I love it! Anyway. The point is, organic languages are greatly influenced by the nuances of how we interact. Body language, mannerisms, breathing patterns. Also, of course, emotions. Now, maybe the Rasu have emotions, maybe not, but they don't have body language. They are machines, in the literal sense of the word. So their programming syntax, which the Asterion virutox targets, is hardly different from the language they use to communicate with one another."

She indicated the symbols on her screen. "It's as if Artificials and the Ruda had a baby in an inorganic chemistry lab. Speaking of, it sucks what happened to the Ruda, doesn't it?"

Alex shrugged somewhat ponderously. "They made their choice. It sucks that it was the wrong one, but the responsibility lies one hundred percent at their feet. We tried to warn them."

"True enough. So the Rasu's language structure is based in quaternary mathematics—similar to the Ruda, though for different reasons—but its form shares a lot in common with molecular chemistry. I admit, I got help on this point from Mom. It comes down to bonding concepts together, separating them, linking them in loose relational structures and so on." She mentally ran through multiple segments of the programming, searching for how to better describe it and failing. Her brain now comprehended far more details than she had words for. "The translator works, but I'm not sure how much—"

"What happened with your eyes?"

She glanced at Caleb innocently. "What do you mean?"

"For a second there, they glittered more brightly than normal, almost like…."

A corner of Alex's lips curled up. "Like Prevo eyes. I thought I noticed it when you visited for dinner, but I wasn't certain. Not until now. Marlee, what have you been up to?"

Dammit! She needed to get better—and smarter—at hiding it. "I just made a couple of upgrades to my cybernetics is all. You know how I'm always fiddling with them."

Caleb pushed off her desk to lean over her, grasping her by both shoulders, and stare directly at her from a few scant centimeters away. "'Just' my ass. Did you become a Prevo?"

"Not...exactly."

"Then what, pray tell, did you become, *exactly?*"

"I..." she fidgeted in his grasp until he relented and dropped his hold on her "...made a *lot* of upgrades to my cybernetics. And my eVi. And had a couple of new biosynth quantum neural grafts installed. And wrote new programming for them to talk to one another."

Alex stood to lean against the wall and regard her with renewed curiosity. It took a great deal to impress Alex, and Marlee tried not to beam with pride.

"Sounds as though you're a Prevo to me. Who's the Artificial?"

"There isn't one."

"That's not a thing."

"It is now." She lost the battle with her pride and grinned smugly. "I'm the first of my kind."

Caleb groaned. "Marlee, you can't go screwing around with your brain! It's dangerous."

"I was careful. And Dr. Canivon helped me. She checked over all my programming and confirmed the various components I installed were compatible with one another."

"That doesn't make me feel better."

Alex smiled. "It does make me feel better. Can you access sidespace?"

"Yep."

"And open wormholes?"

"You bet." She bit her tongue to keep from gushing about Cupcake. Not until she had something to show for her efforts.

Caleb shot Alex a glare. "Stop encouraging her."

"I think it's far too late for that, *priyazn.* This is exciting, Marlee. What are you going to call yourself?"

"I haven't decided. I've obviously gone beyond 'Enhanced,' and I want to distinguish myself from every amateur coder on the block. But I also don't want word to get out and a bunch of people to start copying me, you know?"

"I've got some bad news for you there. Word will get out, and people will copy you. For five minutes or so, I was the only Prevo in existence, and now here we are."

"You're probably right. I realize nothing stays secret forever. But I want to keep it to myself for as long as I can."

"How about…'Prevo' is shortened Russian for 'the transcended.' Your family is of Greek descent. How about 'Perva'? It's shortened Greek for the same thing."

"Not bad! I'll noodle it over." She chewed on her bottom lip. "You think I qualify as transcended?"

"I think only you can answer that question."

"Yeah. I'm still feeling my new tricks out. I'll keep you posted."

Caleb snorted. "That would be a first."

"Unh." She punched him in the arm.

"You are so damn…incorrigible." He settled back onto the corner of the desk, looking thoroughly exasperated, but she was used to it. "Speaking of keeping people posted, does your mother know about this?"

"Mom wouldn't understand it."

"Your mother is very smart."

"About molecules and chemistry stuff."

"About a lot more stuff, too. She did important work with Prevo tech for the Federation around the time the government first legalized the technology."

"Oh? I didn't realize. I was pretty young then."

"Well, now you do. Marlee, tell your mother."

"I'll consider it. Anyway, about the Rasu." She grabbed a small quantum cube and stuck it in her system's input slot. "Alex, I'll copy the whole translation suite for you and Valkyrie. I'm curious to learn how it performs in a real-world scenario." The system beeped, and she removed the cube, but held it close instead of handing it over. "Can I come with you? Then I can make alterations to the program on the fly if they're needed."

"Do you have any vacation time left at work?" Caleb asked.

She'd gone negative on that metric a month ago. "Since the Rasu are an alien species, I assert any attempt to communicate with them counts as Consulate work."

"Nice try. We might be gone for several days, so stay here and don't get fired."

"Fine." She sighed dramatically and dropped the cube into Alex's outstretched hand. "Report back?"

"Will do."

"And don't get captured by the Rasu you're snooping on."

"We won't." Caleb touched her shoulder again, more tenderly this time. "Be careful using the new upgrades, please. For me. And talk to your mother. She won't be angry with you."

"She's always angry with me. But…we're supposed to have dinner tomorrow night. I'll find an opportunity to casually mention it."

"Thank you." He smiled a little. "Love you."

She rolled her eyes, but it was merely for show. "I love you, too."

38

NGC 5033 GALAXY

Eleven Megaparsecs from Concord HQ

Target x0bd33 traveling on vector [translated N 33° W]. Time to intercept: 12.43 seconds.

On the fringes of a triple star system, two featureless Rasu vessels approached a third such vessel. When it detected the newcomers, the third vessel accelerated, but the two pursuing ships quickly overcame the speed differential. One leapt ahead and spun around, then both began simultaneously extending their forms out into scallop shapes. From the front and back they enveloped their target, and in seconds had captured it completely.

The Rasu mass which resulted pulsed and throbbed erratically, growing bulges that swelled like tumors only to deflate and vanish. Less than five minutes after the absorption had begun, the mass settled down and took on the shape of a typical Rasu scout ship.

Integration complete.

The new vessel, now designated Unit NAV68e-sub263, fired its engines and headed toward the interior of the stellar system.

As was their standard operating procedure, a great Rasu stronghold encircled the system's primary star, a red giant. A ring of platforms orbited 3,200 megameters out from the star's corona, and thousands of ships arrived and departed the platforms with an almost rhythmic regularity.

Target c3ee21 traveling on vector [translated S 18° W]. Time to intercept: 14.9 seconds.

Unit NAV68e-sub263 arced around and blended into the traffic headed toward one of the system's gas giants, then slipped up behind its target and, in a blink, swallowed it whole.

Caught unawares, this target's struggles were swiftly snuffed out.

Integration complete.

The Rasu mass split evenly down the middle and morphed into two discrete vessels.

Unit NAV68e-sub263 to target e2fa14. Unit NAV68e-sub264 to target a3xb08.

The Rasu units headed off on different trajectories to pounce upon lone vessels, and the process repeated itself. Two transformed vessels became four; four became eight. The eight grew larger before becoming sixteen.

When they numbered two hundred fifty-six, they began advancing on the periphery of the stellar ring activity. Transformed vessels began docking with the platforms, and violence soon followed. Shots were fired as explosions erupted from within the large structures.

Only then did a Rasu fleet some ten thousand strong emerge from the black beyond the edge of the stellar system to advance on the ring in force. Their weapons tore apart the platforms where necessary, and a host of units was sent forth to swallow and subsume the resulting wreckage.

When a unit grew to sufficient size, it reshaped itself into a platform and inserted itself as a link in the ring. Control signals flowed out to the adjacent platform, and a battle of code dominance was waged. In most cases, the aggressor strong-armed the defender into submission, and the aggressor code took control. Where the battle went the other way, weapons destroyed the platform and more units subsumed the pieces into themselves.

Four hours and eighteen minutes after the first two invading units arrived in the system, all resistance was quelled.

Integration complete. System GG808 is now a member of Rasu 16-NAV.

RW

SIYANE

NGC 5033 GALAXY

Alex rubbed her eyes to clear increasing blurriness. She'd been glued to the dozen screens positioned above the data center table for countless hours now, and she suspected she'd hardly blinked the entire time. "I can't believe what we just watched. Or what I think we just watched, anyway."

Caleb enlarged the screen where the latest action had taken place, then made a couple of modifications to the display. "It looked to me as though the invading faction—let's call them Orange for ease of reference—infiltrated the resident faction—Lemon—ship by ship and platform by platform, until Lemon became Orange."

"Clever *svolochi*. I'll give them that much."

'It's a tale as old as time itself. One tribe fights to expand its territory, killing or conquering those around it in order to grow stronger. As is so often the case, control of greater territory equals strength.'

"True, Valkyrie. But when humans did it, they ran the risk that the conquered people would later rise up against their new masters. Here, I suspect there's no possibility of rebellion from within. They don't merely subjugate those they conquer. They subsume them, transforming them down to their most base operating code." Alex motioned toward one of the screens, and it pulled out to a multi-galaxy view. "Here's Orange's entire territory now, so far as we can tell."

Two neighboring galaxies to NGC 5005 were unmarred orange in color, and the orange hue now leaked into a third of NGC 5033. The remaining two-thirds belonged to Lemon, but for how long? "How many separate Rasu factions do you think there are?"

Caleb sighed. "Across Laniakea? Perhaps a few dozen?"

"You don't think more?"

"No. This cluster is a mature ecosystem. Any small fries were subsumed long ago. In fact, I suspect Orange and Lemon each control numerous surrounding galaxies in opposite directions, and we were simply lucky enough to stumble upon the fault line between the two."

'Lucky? I spent eighty-one hours and fifty-two minutes of processing time collating and analyzing Rasu signals Concord has collected in order to detect potential demarcation lines where the voice and nature of the signals shifted.'

Caleb laughed. "Sorry, Valkyrie. I did not mean to devalue the work you did. We appreciate it very much."

'Thank you.'

Alex dragged the master map over to her and zoomed out until it included more than 100,000 galaxies. "How many passive sensors do we have in place now around Laniakea?"

'Outside of Concord-controlled space? Nine hundred eighteen. Ghosts are continuing to position additional sensors throughout Rasu territory at the rate of sixty per Concord Standard Day.'

"Excellent. In another few weeks, we should have their entire faction map filled in—at least the broad strokes of it."

The Rasu…overminds, for lack of a better term, referred to themselves with a unique master designation, which made labeling the separate groups considerably easier than it might have been. Each detached sub-unit, they'd learned, was given a more detailed moniker derived from that designation. When smaller sub-units detached, their moniker was derived further from the parent unit. It was a straightforward system, right up until sub-units began recombining with different interim units in the chain. So far as they'd been able to determine, their designations updated to reflect their new immediate parent.

It tracked with what Jerry had told Nika about the process of reintegration when a sub-unit returned to the fold, but it was disconcerting nonetheless.

Valkyrie ruminated in her head. *They have no unique souls. Their consciousness, to the extent the term can be applied in this situation, is nothing more than an expression of the will of whomever their latest parent unit is.*

Something like that.

Her stomach growled in complaint. Had they been so transfixed by the dramatic events playing out before them that they'd forgotten to eat lunch?

She wandered over to the kitchen unit and opened a cabinet, then grabbed a container of chips and stuck her hand in.

Caleb came up behind her and rested his chin on her shoulder. "Would you like for me to cook something?"

"I didn't want to be demanding." She held her hand up. "Chip?"

"Thanks." He popped it into his mouth with a flourish. "How about some burgers? It'll take me five minutes."

She twisted around and kissed him; his lips tasted all salty, and she reached back into the container for more chips. "Sounds delicious. Thank you."

"Mmm-hmm."

She got out of his way so as not to delay lunch any longer and returned to the assortment of maps. "Valkyrie, it looks as if your instincts were dead on. The Rasu aren't in a static detente state with one another. They are actively moving against their rivals to grow their relative territory within the larger Rasu empire."

They'd picked up quite a few additional signals over the last few hours beyond those involving Orange's aggression against Lemon, and she pulled the translations up on a new screen now. "The thing is, though, these aren't conversations. They're directives. 'Go here, do this.' There's nothing about *why*. I know, Valkyrie, the expansionist impulse is virtually universal among intelligent species, making it reason enough for their actions. But with the Ruda, for instance, they wanted to learn. To grow their knowledge and their own capabilities. They craved it, in fact. The Rasu seem to be driven to dominate for dominance's sake."

Caleb turned to lean beside the stove surface while two burgers sizzled behind him. "Maybe not entirely. We know they harvest resources, both organic and inorganic, from every system they conquer—we assume at least in part in order to build the Core Rings. The more systems a given faction conquers, the more resources it can claim for its own."

"But if they worked together, it wouldn't make any difference who controlled which resources. Their Core Rings would get built, and they'd continue to drag the galaxies of Laniakea in toward one another, staving off heat death in the distant future. Goal achieved. The outcome is the same, whether they jockey for relative position or not."

"Now, baby." He came up to her and draped his arms over her shoulders. "If it was your goal to prevent the heat death of the universe and the extinction of all life within it, wouldn't you want to be the one to achieve it? Not Kennedy, not Devon, not some random Prevo or scientist, but *you?*"

A tantalizing smile grew on her lips—she hurriedly tamped it down. It would be a stupendous accomplishment to pull off, but fame was the last thing she'd ever wanted. "Well, maybe, but I wouldn't begrudge them achieving it, either. The important thing is for it to get done."

'The same might be true for the Rasu. They take over the ongoing activities when they subsume a rival group, and the endeavor continues onward. Their power plays do not appear to be interfering with the process of resource acquisition and Core Ring construction, or likely even slowing it down.'

"Granted." She kissed Caleb lightly, then patted his ass in the direction of the kitchen unit and returned her attention to the data center. "This little outing was never intended to be a purely intellectual exercise. We wanted to know more about how the Rasu interacted with one another. Now, what do we do with this information? Is there a way we can exploit these internal divisions? They show zero interest in being amenable to diplomatic overtures. They conquer, they consume, they exterminate."

Caleb arrived with a burger and a fresh basket of chips, and they settled at the small dining table. She took a bite and moaned; she really was famished.

"Good?"

"You know it is."

"I do." He munched on a chip. "Why don't we talk it through

with Nika? She's still the only person who's managed to get any direct insight into how the Rasu think. And, horrible deal though it was, the Asterion Guides were able to negotiate an arrangement with the Rasu. If nothing else, that proved the Rasu can be incentivized to act in a certain manner."

"True. Okay, I'll reach out to her."

39

MIRAI
NIKA'S FLAT

I don't know if I can stay with Anabelle any longer. She's so clingy and demanding. Such a great body, though—

—"The specs on the new model Hovercraft Dynamo XL are absurd! I don't care how small circuits are these days, mechanical parts still take room to move in relation to each other"—

—the icy water of Lake Sakura jolted every nerve in my body, in the best possible way. I swam upward and broke the surface to be bathed in the light of a clear night and full moon—

—more muscle bulk, or greater agility? Stamina or strength? I scanned through the physical upgrade packages listlessly. Who did I want to be next? Someone with more physical prowess, that was for certain—

Nika bolted upright in bed, then swayed from a bout of dizziness. The free-floating thoughts of dozens of people clogged her mind, and she struggled to force them away, like cobwebs blocking passage through a cave.

Why had she awoken? Was it because of something in the intrusive musings from random strangers that continued to bombard her? She searched through the last few seconds of noise. No. It was something else.

She reached out for the kyoseil next, letting its pervasive undulations envelop her.

A warning.

Pressure mounting. Interference growing. Protective mode engaging where needed.

"Oh, no!" She lunged across the bed and began shaking Dashiel. "Wake up, hurry."

He stirred and rolled over to peer at her through sleep-fogged eyes. "What's wrong?"

Imminent—

He shook his head roughly, frowning. "What was that?"

"A quantum block activating. Here." She cast her mind out to check, and found what she already feared to be true. "The Rift Bubble is down. Dashiel, the Rasu are on Mirai."

He was out of the bed even before she was, feeling around on the floor for his pants. "How is that possible?"

"I don't know. We've had the Bubble operational for four uninterrupted months now..." her shoulders sagged as she wiggled into her own pants "...except for about two minutes the other day."

He stared at her from the shadows. "They've been watching and planning all this time. Waiting for us to make one tiny mistake."

"Yes, they have." She touched the back of her ear, though the motion wasn't required to activate the new comm device Dashiel had created. *All Advisor Alert. Rasu incursion on Mirai. Lance, mobilize all forces immediately.*

Lance: Moving now. Bloody hells.

RW

OMOIKANE INITIATIVE

"Emergency shelters have been activated, and we are trying to move people into them before the Rasu reach the ground."

"Are shelters really going to help protect people once Rasu mechs are rampaging through the streets?"

"The new ones are constructed of adiaK. The Rasu won't be able to breach them."

"Well, you'd better get people inside them and get the doors locked, because the Rasu are here now."

While the Advisors argued, Nika gazed up at the Big Wall in horror. The center pane showed low-res infrared images of hundreds of Rasu vessels descending through the atmosphere, nearly all of them headed for Mirai One. Dominion warships, though hamstrung by the quantum block, chased them, and explosions lit the night sky like fireworks.

"How are they here on the surface so quickly?" Katherine asked.

Lance answered on voice only, as the holo projections weren't working. "We had no warning. None. Their fleet wormholed directly into the atmosphere, inside our perimeter defenses. Our regular patrols were dwarfed by their sheer numbers. Everyone is in the air now, but the quantum block is playing havoc with our ship controls."

"We've got to find some way to slow them—" The walls rattled from an explosion that sounded way too close.

"We've got to get the quantum block down is what we've got to do," Lance growled. "I can't fight these monsters properly if my ships don't fucking work."

"We don't know where it is," Dashiel protested, "and we're looking at an entire planet of possibilities."

Dashiel's voice penetrated Nika's chaotic thoughts above all the others, and she sank into a nearby chair to try to focus. The kyoseil had warned her about the quantum block *before* the device had come online. It knew of its presence ahead of time. *It knew where it was.*

Show me.

Her mind was carried along rippling waves of energy. Through the streets—a blast rocked a high-rise, and its spire fell through her consciousness; then she was past it. Beyond the manufacturing warehouses and assembly lines, onward to the automated farms—there!

It was little more than a hodge-podge assembly of Rasu parts into a pyramid perhaps ten meters tall, misshapen and irregular. There was no fortress here, not yet.

Nika: Lance, the quantum block is located two hundred fourteen kilometers southwest of Mirai Tower. Planetary coordinates: latitude 40.7143528, longitude -74.0059731.

Lance: On it.

She opened her eyes and promptly fell out of the chair onto the floor. Dashiel was at her side the next second. "Are you all right?"

She nodded shakily and let him help her up. The transition from the kyoseil's realm to the physical one was always a rough one, but that had been a particularly heady trip. "Listen, taking out the quantum block is a great first start, but it's only the beginning of this battle. I should be able to get the Rift Bubble active the instant the block is down, but there are so many Rasu on the surface. They'll construct new blocks. They'll push their offensive even harder—oh!"

She rushed over to a secure cabinet in the front of the room and tore it open. Inside, situated in a clear, protective case, was one of the miniature Rift Bubble-like devices she'd worked with Parc and then Dashiel to design. She'd named them Kireme Boundaries before Parc had a chance to think up something ridiculous to call them.

She removed it from its case and rolled it reassuringly along her palm. "This will protect the core of downtown, at least until the Rasu realize what we've done and construct another quantum block inside this barrier. When they do, I'll find it and we'll take it down, and do it all over again."

Nika: Lance, is Concord on the way?

Lance: Concord is currently fighting the Rasu on four major planets and a half-dozen small ones. They're sending what they can, but they've got their hands full. This one is up to us.

Dashiel: Which is why we've spent so much time and money building up our military fleet. Will it be enough?

Lance: Damn right it will be.

"Do you believe him?"

Dashiel sighed. "I believe that he believes it. I don't know."

"Then we need to brainstorm ways we can help bridge the gap."

"What about the virutox? If we can infect the Rasu on the ground…."

Lance: Quantum block is dust.

She grasped Dashiel's arm for stability while her mind leapt to the Mirai Rift Bubble and reactivated it.

Nika: "The Rift Bubble is operational. Let's take advantage of it while we can."

Take advantage of it…she spun around, searching the room. "Katherine! Where are you? Get over here!"

A few seconds later, Katherine elbowed her way through a group of her subordinates to scowl in Nika's direction. "What? I'm a little busy here."

Nika closed the distance between them. "Forget the security concerns. We have to tell everyone about their ability to open wormholes, and we have to do it right now."

"What good is…oh."

"Exactly. During the times when we've disabled the quantum block, however long that lasts, people can evacuate *themselves*."

"To where?"

"I don't care. Somewhere safer than here." She leaned in and squeezed the woman's shoulder, hard. "Blast it on the nex, send out millions of messages, however you think is best. But *tell them*."

Katherine jerked her shoulder back, out of Nika's grasp, but nodded. "Fine."

Dashiel shook his head somewhat ruefully. "Adlai's not going to be happy."

"You know I like Adlai. I do. But, respectfully, he can get over himself on this one."

"Agreed. Now, where were we?"

She worked to recenter her thoughts. "The virutox."

"Right. It only spreads through physically connected Rasu. It can take out discrete units, but I can't think of a way to seed it in enough units to make a difference." His gaze darted to the firefight lighting the Big Wall, then back to her. "Too bad we can't deliver it on kyoseil waves."

"That would be so helpful."

"Yeah. Next idea." He eyed the small orb in her hand curiously. "Can you control the radius of the bubble the orb creates?"

"I haven't tried." She held it up and peered at the kyoseil etchings along the interior of the lattice, effortlessly falling into the code written upon it. The power fueling the device limited the breadth of the shield, but it didn't have to be a one-to-one relationship, did it? Concord's Caeles Prisms siphoned off excess power into hidden dimensions as part of their normal operation. Couldn't she do the same?

The answer arrived as a matter-of-fact affirmation. From herself, or the kyoseil? Yes. She could. But the programming embedded in the Kireme Boundaries wasn't set up for power dumps, so for now, she'd have to do it manually. It would be up to her and her alone.

"Yes, I can control it. But it will be active management on my part."

Sympathy warmed his eyes, but now was not the time for any of them to be weak. "Understood. Can you do so for more than one at a time?"

The weight of every world...the weight of history unmeasurable. "Um, I think so, yes. Especially if the Rasu require a couple of minutes to counter our actions."

"Okay." He squeezed her hand.

Dashiel: Lance, here's the plan. Nika can shrink or increase the radii of the Kireme Boundaries. We're going to start out small. Here, just surrounding the Initiative, where no Rasu have reached. We've begun producing the devices at the Auxiliary Lab outside Mirai Two. I believe we've got around three dozen in storage. Let's get them to locations that haven't been infiltrated and institute safe zone bubbles in those areas. Then your troops can push the Rasu out from there. As they do, Nika will increase the radii in ever expanding bubbles the enemy can't penetrate.

Lance: Clever plan, Ridani. But what happens when the Rasu put up a new quantum block and take all those bubbles out, then surge across the formerly protected territory?

Nika: Now that I understand how to do it, I can find any new quantum blocks in a matter of seconds. Set up a strike team to chase them down as I feed you coordinates, and we should lose no more than a few minutes each time. Maybe less.

Lance: Two steps forward, one step back. Gods, this is going to be ugly. Let's do it.

RW

HATAORI EMERGENCY SHELTER

Joaquim waved Perrin over to where they stood near the entrance, then grasped Cassidy firmly by the shoulders. "You need to stay here. These emergency shelters are the safest places on the planet. And if you need anything at all, Perrin will take care of you."

Cassidy's face contorted in displeasure. "You're not going to stay with me?"

"No. There are Rasu that need dispatching, and a lot of people who haven't made it to refugee centers that need protecting until they do." It was a lucky thing this shelter was only half a kilometer from their apartment. The sounds of sonic booms and explosions had grown deafening a few short minutes after they'd started heading here. They hadn't seen any Rasu, but he suspected it wouldn't be long now.

"Let somebody else do it! The military. Justice. It's their jobs to protect us, but it's not yours."

No, it's my life. He tried to keep his frustration off his features. She was scared. This was her first alien invasion. "This is what I do, okay? And I'm actually really good at it." His expression brightened as Perrin finally broke through the jostling crowd in the lobby and reached them. Strawberry-blonde braids bounced over her shoulders, and she wore khaki pants and a fitted top that straddled the line between street wear and office attire. She looked a little harried, but good. Confident.

"See, Perrin's right here. I'll bet she needs your help keeping these people calm."

"Oh my goodness, I wouldn't refuse it."

"There you go. Keep yourself busy, and the hours will fly by. We'll rid Mirai of these Rasu, and I'll be back for you in no time."

"Joaquim…" Cassidy rested her forehead on his "…are you sure?"

"I'm sure. I couldn't forgive myself if I sat comfortable and cozy in here while the Rasu were rampaging through my streets."

"These aren't your streets."

"Yeah. They are." He shot Perrin a pleading look.

She laid a hand on Cassidy's arm. "Hey, come with me. We've got pallets of water bottles downstairs we need to move to the refreshment stations. Then we need to put a bunch of chairs out, because people will tire of standing around before long."

Cassidy glanced toward the doors. "You say this place is safe, but can't the Rasu just tear through the entrance?"

"Nope. As soon as any Rasu get within a kilometer of here, adiaK blast doors will slam down and seal you in."

"I guess that's reassuring. Though I don't want to be locked in a tomb, either."

Perrin smiled in encouragement. "We have enough food and water for days and days. It'll be fine."

He couldn't stand it any longer. He leaned down and kissed Cassidy on the cheek. "Love you. I'll be back." Then he sprinted out the entrance before the blast doors trapped him inside and away from the fight.

40

MIRAI
OMOIKANE INITIATIVE

Nika closed the door to her office and went to sit at her desk…then sat on the floor instead. She'd fled the purposeful bedlam of the command center for the relative peace and quiet of her office, because she needed as much serenity as she could conjure for the task ahead of her.

Honestly, she needed a couple of Plex copies for this, but there wasn't time to wake up her other body from its stasis chamber. So she would manage.

She focused on the orb cupped in her hands first, stretching her mind out to the borders of the protective bubble it created. Already a few Rasu forward mechs had reached its edges. She assumed that DAF ground forces were on their way to take them out, and for now the mechs bounced ineffectually off the barrier.

Dashiel: Kireme Boundary is in place at DAF Command.

She surfed a single kyoseil string across town and into the Logistics Center to locate the tiny device. DAF Command was of course extremely well protected, so when she activated it, she was able to send the bubble out to a diameter of over two undisturbed kilometers before coming upon active fighting.

Dashiel: Now at the Justice Center.

Back into downtown her mind raced. She passed too many Rasu mechs and low-flying craft to entertain the notion that they were beginning to gain the upper hand. Her heart yearned to break apart their atoms with a soul-rending scream, but it was an impotent fantasy. Her presence there was less than ethereal and little but thought.

The Justice Center itself was locked down tight, but military personnel battled the Rasu in virtual hand-to-hand combat on the streets outside. Archine blades flew through the air alongside Rectifier blasts, and a horrifying notion occurred to her.

Nika: Katherine, make sure every person knows they need to be broadcasting the Rift Bubble access code at all times, or they risk getting sliced in two by the Kireme Boundaries when they expand.

Katherine: Right. I'll handle it.

The device was situated deep underground in the storage warehouse, and upon activating it, she carefully nudged the barrier out past the walls of the Justice Center. If a single Rasu was inside its perimeter, it posed a threat to every person and iota of data the building held.

Dashiel: Greenfield Park Community Center.

She paused for a second before shifting her location yet again. She'd need to keep an eye on the Justice Center; hopefully the officers and soldiers fighting outside the building could force the Rasu back, and she'd be able to expand the barrier soon.

As she sped toward the residential district along the north bank of Hataori Harbor, the frenetic activity calmed somewhat. The Rasu were likely to concentrate on downtown and the major power centers first. If they succeeded today, they could harvest homes and gardens at their leisure.

But they would not succeed today.

This Kireme Boundary barrier rippled out across clover grasses and birch trees, and she drew a touch of serenity from protecting such a lovely place.

Dashiel: Now at the Mirai One West Transit Hub.

Nika: Dashiel, put one at Ridani Enterprises.

Dashiel: There are more important locations to protect.

Nika: Not many. Do it.

She returned to downtown, south of the Western Market, and back into the fray. The Rasu were making a hard push for the West Transit Hub, and with good reason. Assuming they hadn't managed to reach other Axis Worlds during the brief period they knew the access code—and all indications were they had focused on Mirai—the d-gates there constituted their ticket to fanning out across the Dominion.

She activated the device, then moved the protective bubble outward, flinching as it crossed the dimensional portals of the d-gates and tiny waves flickered through the barrier. It passed the outer walls, then the entrance steps.

Two Rasu mechs charged toward the building, and she took great pleasure in knocking them onto the street as she expanded the barrier in a leap of another fifty meters.

Dashiel: Oh, fine. Ridani Enterprises.

Nika: Thank you, darling.

The briefest moment of levity lightened her spirit as her consciousness raced up the floors toward Dashiel's office. What felt like an eternity ago, her journey up a lift to that very office had led to her entire life changing in an instant—to the future of the Dominion itself changing—when she'd come face to face with her past and her future. If only she'd known what had waited for her!

She found the Kireme Boundary inside the secure storage vault in his office. The best security in the Dominion couldn't keep her consciousness out, and she transmitted—

Her mind slammed out of sidespace and into her body, and she fell backward to bang her head on the corner of her desk.

Lance: Nika!

"Ow…." One second.

She let the kyoseil direct her toward the latest intrusion.

Nika: North of Hataori Harbor. 38.6243125, -74.9926738

While she waited, she felt around the back of her head; no blood came away on her fingers. She breathed in deeply. The concentration required for this task was exhausting, but she dared not complain. Everyone was deploying their talents to give their all in this fight. This was merely hers.

Lance: Down.

But she already knew. She steadied herself and reached out for the planetary Rift Bubble, then again for the Kireme Boundary at

Ridani Enterprises. Then again for DAF Command. Again. Without quite intending to do so, she split herself in four, five, six directions at once to activate all the devices simultaneously—then almost fainted.

She took a minute to center herself here on the floor in her office, gingerly touching her forearm, followed by her lips. She felt disconnected from her body…and not the way she did when traveling in sidespace. She was here, but she was not, as if her consciousness had become perilously detached from her physicality.

Dashiel: New one at Mirai Tower.

It was troubling, but she'd have to worry about it later. It was a short jaunt from here to Mirai Tower.

41

____

MIRAI

MIRAI ONE

The drone dodged the Rasu mech's fire as it spun like a top, shooting electric arcs of return fire on every pass. The mech sputtered and lost momentum, and Ryan Theroit tossed an archine grenade hard into its chest.

The grenade exploded into tiny blades that sliced the Rasu into a thousand pieces, for now. Parc Eshett followed it up with a blast from a prototype virutox-infused Glaser that looked glued together, and the Rasu slugs on the ground melted into puddles and stayed that way.

Joaquim vaulted over a makeshift barricade piled sloppily on the sidewalk and dropped in beside them. There was only one Parc here; presumably his Plex was holed up somewhere safer, engaged in deep battle strategy. "Nice job, guys. You got any spare grenades?"

Ryan shook his head, reaching up to wipe a narrow line of blood off his brow. "We're running low. I think Justice has a stash, though. That's actually where we were headed when these mechs overtook us."

Justice. Joaquim glanced down the street; the Justice Center was only around the corner and two and half blocks away. "Do you want to make a run for it with me?"

Parc stared past the barricade, eyes narrowing at a melee between a Rasu mobile unit and a TAG in the distance. "Eh, I think we're doing some good here. We should hold this position for as long as we can. More firepower would help."

"I'll be back in five minutes, and I'll bring a fuckton of grenades with me." He nodded sharply at them, checked beyond the barricade to ensure no Rasu currently pointed heavy weapons in their direction, then took off running down the street.

The nex blasted an alert about a miniature Rift Bubble active nearby, and he broadcast the access code as Rasu weapons fire rained down like a hailstorm from the sky. The bubble didn't extend out far enough to protect his friends from an aerial bombardment.

Ahead, Justice dynes and officers, as well as a smattering of DAF troops, formed a line stretching across the next block. Beyond them to the left, an intimidating line of Rasu mechs and hovercraft advanced toward the Justice Center. DAF fighters buzzed overhead, and laser fire sliced through the streets. A single Rima Grenade would wipe out the entire front of the advancing Rasu, but it would also wipe out four city blocks. He didn't doubt the military commanders had the fearsome little black holes at the ready to deploy if it came down to it. Buildings could be rebuilt.

He ducked down a side street to avoid the worst of the fighting, jumped another barricade, and landed next to four Justice officers stocking a mobile command station outside the entrance to the Justice Center.

"Jacenta, get these Rectifiers out to the left flank! Avelek, we're already running low on archine grenades. Head down to the warehouse and bring up some more!"

The sound of the voice barking orders wrenched him around, his eyes seeking its source on instinct.

Selene stood on top of a crate to the right of the entrance, both arms deep in an open container, rooting in it for something. She wore gray tactical pants and a flak jacket, and the faint shimmer of a force field helmet glittered around her face, dancing with flyaway strands of blonde hair.

His chest tightened, but he ignored the sensation to stride up to her. "Archine grenades. I need some."

She whipped toward him, and her expression shuttered instantly on seeing him. "Lacese."

"Panetier. Grenades?"

She gestured toward the front line. "We're kind of using them right now."

"A couple of my people are manning a second front three blocks east. Even a dozen archine grenades should keep that flank clear of Rasu for a while."

She blinked and hit her loudspeaker comm. "The Kireme Boundary has been pushed out another thirty meters. Move the line!"

The officers surged forward, while the dynes lugged barricade shields along behind to rebuild a measure of protection.

She watched them until the line began to reform some distance out, then turned to him with a sigh. "Couldn't get enough of killing Rasu, huh?"

"You know me."

"Yeah. I do." Her lips pursed, and she waved at a crate behind the one she stood on. "Take whatever you can carry. We've got more coming up from the warehouse."

"Thanks." He went around and crouched in front of the crate to pop the lid, but it wouldn't budge. "This thing's code-locked."

"Oh, right. One second." She appeared beside him and dropped to her knees, so close that her shield sizzled across his skin, setting it ablaze. Metaphorically, he supposed. She smelled of sweat and fried electronics. A soot-covered lock of hair fell across her face as she typed in a code, and the top of the crate slid away.

"There." She glanced his way, a smile flitting over her features for a blink before vanishing.

"Got a Rectifier I can borrow?"

"My people need them all."

He stared at her, trying his best to keep his mind on the Rasu that needed killing rather than softer things. Though also…his brain got all tangled up in knots over the contradictions she presented and also elicited in him and—

Then her gaze shifted away, breaking eye contact, and she indicated a different crate by the building façade. "Fine. But only one."

The corners of his mouth lifted, and words he couldn't say hovered on the tip of his tongue. "I appreciate—"

She leapt up and scrambled back atop the crate. "Incoming from the southwest! Third West Squad, reinforce that line!"

He gathered up a bunch of archine grenades, stuffing as many of them as fit in his satchel. She was still shouting orders when he left the mobile command station behind and disappeared around the corner.

RW

Joaquim slid up against the barricade, which looked as if it had taken some blasts in the few short minutes he'd been gone, and opened up his satchel. "I brought toys."

"Heh." Parc winced and wiped sweat off his brow.

"Are you okay, man?"

From behind Parc, Ryan shook his head meaningfully.

"Yeah, um..." Parc cleared his throat roughly "...unpleasant memories making themselves known."

Because Parc had first been captured by the Rasu from Zaidam Bastille and undergone unbearable torture for weeks, *then* been mortally wounded by them and chased through the Namino One streets while he bled out. Not a good history. The fact that he was out here fighting anyway said a surprising amount about the man's character.

He clapped Parc's shoulder. "Let's get you out of here. We'll go to the Justice Center, and they'll let you rest inside."

"No." Parc grunted and forced himself up out of the slumping posture he'd adopted. "I want to fight these monsters."

Joaquim checked with Ryan again, who shrugged in resignation.

"All right." He retrieved the Rectifier from his satchel and handed it to Parc. "Vaporize a few of them out of existence, then. It'll make you feel better."

"Yes, it will." Ryan half-stood, aimed over the barricade, and shot a Rasu tank that had been demolishing the Rivers Trust bank down the street.

Joaquim's internal operating system…glitched, like a hiccup. About sixty percent of it resumed functioning almost immediately, but communications in particular were now dead as dust. "Shit, they got a quantum block back up. This means the Rift Bubbles and assorted other barriers are down." Laser fire arced across the intersection ahead of them, and Joaquim hunkered down low. "Brace for incoming."

But cowering did no good, so after a few seconds, he peeked past the side of the barricade. Half a dozen Rasu barreled around the corner and skidded through the street to head in their direction, and he groaned. They'd come up with a new form to take: low-slung, wide, dual-wheeled contraptions with guns on either side. Their fire tore apart the street ahead of their advancement, but the sturdy wheels they'd concocted powered through the rough ride.

"Parc, light them up. We'll sacrifice the block if we have to, but let's stop them here."

"Got it." He swung the weapon up over the barricade once more. The Rectifier's firing speed was slow, though, and Parc's finger convulsed on the trigger again and again.

Ryan sent four tiny drones hurtling into the fray as Joaquim stood and tossed grenade after grenade into the wheeled Rasu's paths. The timing was tricky, and he cursed as two of them exploded early to minimal impact.

A rumble shook the ground as two new tank-sized Rasu appeared down the street, and Joaquim's heart sank. "Dammit. We need to retreat. Ryan, can you manufacture us some cover?"

"Sorry, man. Those were my last drones. I'm pretty useless here now."

"Never. What we'll do—" Comm streams erupted in his mind, and he fell to his knees from the cacophony of everything bursting back to life. "Quantum block's down. I'm guessing the Rift Bubble is up, too, but we've got some pushing to do to regain the territory we lost."

"Stand our ground, then?"

He blew out a breath. "For the moment."

Three of the wheeled Rasu drew near, and he side-pitched a grenade into the undercarriage of one. Metal shards flew in every direction, and the three of them hit the ground.

He felt a sharp sting tear across his upper back. Damn, how he wished he'd grabbed a shield before leaving the apartment. Or asked Selene for one. But he'd asked enough of her, hadn't he? Or not nearly enough—

A whooshing sound whistled overhead, and he peered up to see four small craft, too small to contain Asterion pilots, swoop through the air and tear into the approaching Rasu tanks and wheeled units. Whatever they were firing, it vaporized the enemy on contact.

If DAF had many more of those on hand, they might save the city today after all.

42

MIRAI

Omoikane Initiative

With the fall of the Guides' Platform and the rise in prominence of the Initiative, the strategic importance of Mirai Tower had waned over the last six months. Many Advisors continued to maintain offices there, but the tremendous data warehousing levels were redundant at best, with copies of the data now being stored on every Axis World and much of it also at the Initiative.

Still, it was a significant psychological landmark for Mirai's residents. Also, given its location at the dead-on center of downtown, it would serve as a useful anchor from which the military forces could push the Rasu out.

Nika bypassed the storage levels with their bitter memories and headed straight to the top level where the Kireme Boundary device had been placed—

A blast slammed through her consciousness in an avalanche of billowing smoke, and she tumbled from her lofty perch to the street below alongside a tornado of metal and glass.

Her consciousness froze where it landed on the marbled promenade, staring through a gaping hole in the wall at what remained of the security offices on the first floor as debris rained down all around her. Somebody screamed, but it sounded as if it came from a thousand kilometers away, drowned out by the mighty roar of collapse.

A body landed with a *crunch* directly in front of her, and the sight snapped her out of her shock. The thunder of crumbling girders roared above her, and she frantically pulled her perception back onto the street. Silly, really, as physical objects couldn't harm her.

The top quarter of Mirai Tower lay buried upside-down in the broken pavement of Sachi Boulevard, surrounded by a sea of tiny shards of glass fragments like a freshly fallen blanket of snow. She peered up to see dark flames churning out of multiple gaping holes in what was left of the building's façade. Giant chunks of concrete and metal continued falling off the sides to crash to the ground below. Or into other buildings. To crush people who, like her, had frozen in shock at the explosion.

She felt sick to her stomach, kilometers away though her physical body was. The Rasu hadn't even tried to lay claim to the building. They no longer needed the petabytes of data stored there, for they already knew everything about her people. And maybe they comprehended more about psychological warfare than anyone had given them credit for.

Nika: ...we just lost Mirai Tower.

Dashiel: I know. We need to focus on not losing more.

Nika: Right. Goddammit, tell me you've got another device ready.

Dashiel: One second...DAF Logistics Complex.

Nika: On it.

She willed her heart and mind to be like steel as she left behind the carnage and raced to the outskirts of town, then barreled through the utilitarian halls of the DAF Logistics warehouses. When she located the Kireme Boundary, she threw her thoughts at it with all the violence she was able to muster until it activated.

Nika: Next.

Dashiel: We're working on it.

Nika: NEXT.

None of this was his fault, and he didn't deserve her wrath. She needed to preserve it for the enemy.

Nika: I'm sorry. I'm...ready whenever you have another one in place.

Dashiel: We're all angry. Spaceport Seiza.

Nika: Thank you.

More devices gradually made their way out through the fighting to additional locations, and in time her movements began to blur together. The Administration Center. The Refugee Centers and Emergency Shelters. The Manufacturing District. Bit by bit, the bubbles expanded in fits and starts to offer cocoons of protection. Eventually, some of them overlapped. Perhaps she should have deactivated the redundant ones, for it would have lessened her burden, but she didn't dare.

They'd lost a powerful psychological symbol in Mirai Tower, but it was just a building. And in spite of the blow, as the hours wore on, it started to become clear they were winning this battle.

She became vaguely aware that physical ailments groped at her detached thoughts, and she directed some attention to her body left behind at the Initiative. Her head felt heavy, and she could barely stay sitting upright, so she scooted back to lean against her desk and stretched her legs out in front of her. Her throat was scratchy and parched, so she absently reached for a bottle of water that…wasn't there. Oh, well. She licked her lips and she went back to work.

Their efforts expanded out to Mirai Two, then Mirai Three. The planetary Rift Bubble remained active for longer and longer, and the influx of new Rasu to the surface ground to a halt. Without reinforcements, their numbers dwindled.

Yet three times more the enemy succeeded in getting a quantum block up. Three times more she used the kyoseil to home in on it, then Lance used his fighters to destroy it, and she reactivated every single one of the Kireme Boundaries again. A few Rasu slipped inside the barrier perimeters while all this transpired, and she had to give up ground, then regain it once more alongside the soldiers who fought in the streets.

RW

Dashiel glanced at the clock someone had put up beside the Big Wall: 1 Hour, 36 Minutes.

It was the longest the planetary Rift Bubble had held since the attack began. DAF forces had taken full advantage of the stability to push the enemy back with renewed fervor. Hells, the Initiative hadn't so much as shuddered from a proximity blast in at least forty minutes. It was practically peaceful here now.

Not really.

He'd been racing around for what seemed like days, jumping through wormholes here, there and everywhere to get Kireme Boundary devices distributed across the planet. He moved TAGs and other equipment that weren't quite ready for deployment out of the manufacturing warehouses and into the streets anyway, and otherwise generally supported Lance's constant directives where it was in his purview. Wartime industrialist, indeed.

Finally Lance expressed enough confidence in their inevitable victory over the Rasu incursion that he could sit down for two minutes and take a breath.

So naturally Dashiel grabbed two bottles of water and went straight to Nika's office.

He opened the door to blinding light. The entire office glowed like it had captured a sun, and he blinked away halos while fine-tuning his visual filters so he might be able to *see*. As such, it took him too long to realize the source of the brilliance was sprawled on the floor in the middle of the office.

He dropped to his knees beside her in a panic. One of her arms was stretched out, her head lolling atop it. Her hand had fallen open, and the Kireme Boundary device protecting the Initiative had rolled away to rest by the wall.

"Nika? Nika, can you hear me?"

She didn't respond. He grasped her shoulders and eased her up until she was propped against his torso. She was breathing, her chest rising and falling with comforting regularity. But she was also burning up; her skin was almost too hot to touch, and even through their clothes it felt as if it was scalding his chest.

"Nika? I need you to wake up. Please." But was she unconscious, or merely elsewhere?

Nika? Can you hear me?

I...yes. I was checking all the devices again, then I drifted away and...I don't know where I ended up.

Come back to your body, okay?

I'm not certain I remember how.

He brought his mouth to her ear. "Listen to the sound of my voice. Find me, and you'll find yourself. You're in your office at the Initiative, remember? I'm right here with you." He squeezed her red-hot hand. "Feel that? Send yourself toward the sensation. This is home."

Her lips moved. A fragment of a whisper escaped them, but nothing else.

"That's it. Come back to me. You can do it—"

She sat bolt upright, elbowing him in the gut as her body spasmed out of his grasp. "What? Where? I don't...."

She twisted half-around to face him and, at first, didn't seem to recognize him. His heart cracked open in the span it took for realization to dawn in her eyes, then was healed anew when affection suddenly flooded her features. The faintest hint of a smile lifted her lips, but faltered. "Why is the room glowing?"

"It's not. You are."

"Oh." She moved a hand in front of her face. It trembled as her eyelids creased and half-closed. "I can't dial it in. I'm too tired."

"It's okay." He reached out and drew her against him, trying not to wince at the heat she radiated as he wrapped his arms gently around her and tucked her head into the crook of his neck. But he didn't mind; he'd burn along with her. "You can rest right here, with me."

43

MIRAI

HATAORI EMERGENCY SHELTER

Joaquim stumbled through the now-open doors of the emergency shelter, one arm draped over each of Parc and Ryan's shoulders. They were all three covered in dust, debris and more than a little blood.

Perrin spotted them almost immediately and left the two volunteers she was huddled up with to hurry over. "You all look horrible!"

"No doubt." Joaquim grinned sloppily. "But victory is ours."

"So I heard." She pointed off to the left. "Repair bench is down the hall, third room on the left. I'll let Cassidy know you're back, safe if not quite sound."

"Wait. Not until I've cleaned myself up, okay? She doesn't need to know I took some damage."

Perrin scratched at her forehead, probably to hide a worried frown that he could make out anyway. "Jo, you can't keep stuff like this from her."

He let his gaze rove across the hundreds of people packed into the room. They napped in corners, sat on bags of their belongings and paced around while checking the nex in agitation. He belatedly realized he was searching for Cassidy, but it was better that he didn't spot her. "I know I can't, just…not today? She's still getting settled into being alive, and I imagine this has already been a difficult day for her."

"It has been. She's been a real help to me, though. You've got a good woman there."

"I know I do."

Perrin rolled her eyes. "Fine. I'll try to delay her for a few minutes. No promises."

"Thanks." He hopped around to reorient himself, dragging Parc and Ryan with him.

He got first dibs on the repair bench when they arrived, because in addition to the ankle he'd shattered falling into a hole in the road of his own creation while sprinting after a Rasu mech, the slice in his shoulder had proved to be rather nasty.

Ryan helped him get his shirt off, making an ugly face as he did. "I can see the bone."

"Glad I can't." He exhaled carefully as Ryan attached the interface node to the base of his neck. His whole shoulder went blissfully numb, and one of the repair bench's mechanical appendages bent upward and began firing rapid laser bursts into the gash. "You guys all right? We can take turns."

Ryan was running his hands along Parc's head and back with notable care while Parc fidgeted. "Cuts and bruises is all. Take your time."

"I won't argue." A fuzzy feeling overtook him as the repair bench injected additional painkillers, and that wasn't too bad.

"Joaquim, oh my gods!" Cassidy burst into the room and sprinted up to him, her eyes wide in horror. "You're bleeding!"

"Not for much longer." He smiled as her hands came to his face. "Perrin was supposed to tell you not to worry."

"I haven't talked to Perrin recently. I saw you come in from across the room, then had to fight my way through everybody to catch up to you." Her brow knotted up as her fingers slipped through his sweat-soaked hair. "Why did you go out there? You could have been killed by those dreadful monsters!"

"Instead I killed a bunch of them. Right and proper. Besides, if they had taken me out, I'd be back up and running before long. It wouldn't be the first time."

"Not the first time? How can you joke about such a thing? Joaquim, you're a carpenter and a machinist, not a soldier. Leave the fighting to someone else next time, *please*."

"Sweetie, this is what I do. And I'm damn good at it."

"You said so before, but it doesn't look like it to me. You're all beaten up and bloody."

Ouch, that stung. He flared in defensiveness. "You have no idea what I'm capable of."

Parc chuckled as he directed the repair bench's second appendage toward Joaquim's ankle. "Our guy was a terror out there. Give him a weapon, and he can ruin any Rasu's day. And if he doesn't have a weapon, he'll turn whatever he finds into one. Saved our asses multiple times."

Cassidy frowned at Parc. "If you needed saving, then you shouldn't have been out there fighting, either."

Parc whistled under his breath, patted Joaquim's uninjured shoulder, and stepped away. "Hey, Ryan, our guy's going to be a few minutes getting patched up. Why don't we go find some nourishment? I'm famished."

"Yeah. Smart idea. Might consider stopping by a sink, too."

When they'd departed, Cassidy dropped to her knees and rested her head on his lap. "I want to go home."

"The streets should be safe enough to leave the shelter in another hour or two. I'll be good as new by then, and we can stop and grab a bowl of noodles on the way."

"No, not home to your apartment. Home to Synra, where it's safe."

He flinched as the repair bench appendage snapped his ankle back into its proper alignment. "You think Synra is safe? I assure you, if the Rasu had been able to hit there as well, they would have. We're lucky we confined them to one planet today. All our worlds are vulnerable until we dispose of the Rasu in a permanent fashion." He sighed, letting his fingers wind into her curls. "Besides, Mirai *is* our home now."

"Yours, maybe. It doesn't feel like mine."

"I know. But we'll work on that, okay?"

RW

OMOIKANE INITIATIVE

Dashiel hurried across the top floor of the Initiative, slid out a chair, sat, and clasped his hands on the table. "Can we get started?"

Once Nika had recovered enough to be able to stand and move around—to be present in the physical world in some minimal capacity—he'd taken her home to get some rest without telling her about the hastily scheduled Committee meeting. If she'd known of it, she'd have insisted on being here; but on the other hand, she obviously hadn't sought out the Advisors' private comm channel, where it was easily discovered. That's how exhausted she was.

She'd fallen asleep the instant her head hit the pillow, which was the sole reason he'd convinced himself to return for the meeting. Guilt nonetheless gnawed at him as he waited for the remaining Advisors to arrive. What he'd seen today had utterly terrified him, and he wanted desperately to be at her side right now, to hold her close beneath the soft blankets of their bed. But she would want him here, holding down the fort in her absence.

A holo of Lance materialized in one of the chairs, and Katherine nodded. "Now we can. Palmer, talk."

"We are cleaning out isolated pockets of Rasu as quickly as we can. For the last hour, we've only found solos who presumably got separated from larger units, and none big enough or organized enough to throw up a new quantum block. Unfortunately, the constant on/off of the blocks played havoc with our vessels and pilots. No permanent structural damage, thanks to the adiaK hulls on the warships, but around twenty percent of our pilots will be out of commission for a day or two. The rest will remain on full alert for the foreseeable future."

"Do you need more regen clinic resources?"

"No. Only six percent went nonfunctional from their ships crashing. The remainder got their OS' scrambled. Our techies will get their programming cleaned up."

"All right." Katherine jerked her head at him. "Dashiel, what's the story on the Rift Bubbles?"

"The planetary one has been up and running for five and half uninterrupted hours. So long as Palmer finishes cleaning out the last remnants of Rasu, it ought not to come down again. Also, we've staged Kireme Boundaries at strategic locations in every major city that we can activate at a moment's notice, should we need to do so."

"No, *Nika* can activate them at a moment's notice. It'll take the rest of us considerably more time to run everywhere turning them on manually."

He shrugged. "Simply wormhole to them."

"Yes, I keep forgetting about that new trick. Doesn't actually solve the problem, though. Anyway, I'll have my people put together an action plan for emergency activation, so we won't be caught with our pants down if Nika isn't here. You know, the way she isn't right now."

"She is—"

Katherine waved him off. "I don't care why she isn't here, I really don't. I will concede that she got the job done today, if in a somewhat disconcerting fashion. Now for the bad news: our infrastructure is a disaster. Mirai One suffered most of the damage, but no city is looking like a tourist destination at present. The Rasu love to smash buildings, don't they? The cleanup will be a nightmare, never mind the rebuilding—"

"Hey, Colson, shut up for a minute." The brash language had the desired effect, and everyone turned to Palmer's holo. "My time's limited, so let's talk about the terrible risk all our worlds are still facing."

"I thought you said you were nearly finished clearing the Rasu out."

"On Mirai, yes. Don't know if you remember, but we have a few other planets with people currently living on them."

"Don't be an ass, Palmer," Katherine retorted. "The Rasu didn't attack any of the other worlds, and the planetary Rift Bubbles are intact there."

"For now. Listen, the Rasu had the access code to every Rift

Bubble for one hundred thirty-eight seconds. Mirai is the only world they launched an attack on today, but this doesn't mean it's the only world they were able to infiltrate during that window."

Dashiel leaned forward, steepling his hands. "You think today was designed to test our defenses and military strength?"

"Oh, I think they'd have been happy to take the planet if they could manage it with the forces they sent. But, yes, I think they held back from a full-bore assault to test out how far we'd come since our last armed encounter. Hopefully, what they discovered today will give them pause. But we can't count on it.

"Now, we are scanning every square kilometer of every world for Rasu signatures just as hard and fast as our little drones' hearts can manage it. But we're talking about entire planets here. If they slipped in a couple of compact Rasu who are currently slinking around the countryside gathering components for new quantum blocks, then odds are, we won't find them in time. So nobody think this is over."

44

MIRAI

I spent hours observing the ebb and flow of the Mirai battle in solitude, my presence on the planet but a whisper on the wind. Nika controlled the Rift Bubbles now, both those of Katasketousya construction and her own clever twist on the design, thus I could do nothing to assist in the Asterions' struggle to achieve victory here today. Instead, I could only watch on in alternate bouts of horror, despair, hope, relief and pride.

Emotions I had kept at bay for aeons by sheer fortitude were no longer satisfied to slumber in their prison. Since the events at the Oneiroi Nebula, they battered me with wild abandon. As I was profoundly out of practice at managing such intrusions, I struggled to stay centered in my once-reliable stoicism. At times, I failed.

Today, at least, pride would win the day, as the Asterions rose up from each blow to fight once more, to push the enemy back again, to refuse to lie down and surrender. As a people, they had hung up the mantle of warriorhood long ago, but now they donned it once more, fighting to their last breath to vanquish the evil besetting them and remain free.

I had not been a warrior since an age when history turned to ash and ash to stardust, but today I found myself missing that spirit, that fire raging within one's soul. I yearned to strike a blow against a single Rasu mech—a blow that clanged and screeched and severed atom from atom.

But absent one of our fearsome cosmos-altering weapons at my disposal, my only applicable skill was ensnaring a Rasu and whisking it from one place to another, to no productive end.

So I contented myself with observing the battle as, hour by hour and block by block, the protective dimensional barriers expanded their reach. The Rasu numbers dwindled, and eventually no more arrived to replenish them. Finally, the streets and the skies of Mirai quieted.

Victory was won. A single victory on a single day, but an important one. The Rasu had altered the game, but the Asterions had still outwitted them.

The cities were a wreck, of course, a morass of twisted metal and shattered glass, but they would rebuild. This was one attribute the Anadens and all who were descended from them shared—they always rebuilt, and what came next was unfailingly stronger than what had come before.

The shadows grew long and Mirai's lunar satellite high, and I abruptly noticed I had lingered for hours after the danger had passed. Alone with my thoughts, for even when emotions ceased to batter me about, my philosophical ruminations stepped in to take up the mantle.

With an ethereal sigh I made to transport across megaparsecs, for Concord faced their own battles today—

Pain lanced through my mind. Anguish ricocheting off a bony cage. Not my own, but it might as well be. I gathered my scattered presence back together and transported to the source.

RW

NIKA'S FLAT

"—just saw the damn leg off! I'll get a new one, a whole fucking new body, if you make the pain stop—"

—can't breathe. Chest won't...oh gods, there's a building on top of me...how long have I been here...breathe, please...was it dark before...will anyone look for—

"—We kicked those Rasu straight back into the void, friends! Round of drinks on me!—"

"—Call up everyone we have. Yes, everyone! We need emergency crews working all night to effect rescues. Seal off ruptured pipes and open circuits. Secure exposed structures—"

Nika clapped her hands over her ears until the trapped air popped against her palms, but still the voices raged. *Bang, bang, bang,* they slammed into her skull, punched at the back of her eyeballs, fractured her nose from within.

She'd woken from a deep but turbulent slumber and found herself in need of a drink, so she'd stumbled groggily into the kitchen. By the time she'd gotten there, her brain was stirring enough for her to start to wonder how the post-battle recovery was going. A glance outside revealed a quiet night free of explosions, and she decided it was safe to return to bed for a few more hours. Then, as she reached for the door to the refrigeration unit, the assault began.

—with a groan I started making piles of my belongings scattered across the floor. Pile 1: salvageable. Pile 2: trashed beyond hope—

"—I'm afraid we're going to have to reimprint your OS. The damage is too extensive." The words registered out of order and lacking coherent meaning. I sensed the circuits shorting out in my head—

The next thing she knew, she'd been driven to her knees. Her lungs gasped for air, as if a leaden weight pressed in upon them.

—metal and steel and whirring blades, daring me to die from the agony—

"—I found someone! Send down a harness and coagulant, or they won't make it until—"

She crawled forward all but blindly until she reached the living room table and, obsessed with the ridiculous notion that its stone canopy over her head could somehow protect her, sought refuge beneath it. Her legs convulsed to clench against her chest as she curled in on herself, fingernails digging into her scalp until they drew blood.

Stop!

But her cry went ignored as a kaleidoscope of kyoseil swathed her in blinding light, and voices surged in on the light like lost souls cast adrift and drawn to the beacon of the lighthouse that was her mind. A tidal wave of chaos swept away her last fragmented thoughts of *self*, and she succumbed to the whirlwind.

RW

Be calm. Be at peace.

A voice floated through her awareness. No longer a cacophony, nor a torrent, but a single, gentle voice. It stroked the fractured pathways of her psyche with a soothing, feather-light touch.

She didn't fight it. Whyever would she? She was too weak, too broken and spent to fight anyway. So she let the voice and the wispy touch accompanying it cradle her in a swaddle of cottony solitude.

In time—she had no idea how much time—it felt as if her mind began to heal. To stich itself together, with the voice acting as a salve to calm the fire of the wounds the deluge had inflicted.

She began to come back to herself. To remember she existed as a discrete soul in the cosmos. Nika…was her name. Nika Kirumase. She'd worn other names at other times, but this was who she had once been and now was again. She was Nika Kirumase, and her mind was her own. Gods willing, it would remain so.

She opened her eyes. The room was canted sideways through a gauzy haze of stars. Sideways, because she was lying curled up on the floor. Gauzy, because she was surrounded by a thousand pin-pricks of light.

"Mesme?"

It is I. Do not be alarmed, but let us continue in this manner for a while longer.

"I'm okay with that. Did you silence the thoughts? The screams?"

No. They continue to travel on their waves, some of which pass through this location, and thus through you. But I have surrounded you with a shield, of sorts, to keep them at bay for now.

"You can do that?"

I can.

"Thank you." She peered up at the smooth marble of the table's underside. "Let's, um, get out from under the table?"

As you wish. I will move with you.

"Please do." She scooted on her chest across the rug until the marble ceased to shadow her from above, then gingerly sat up and curled her feet under her. The gauzy starlight undulated serenely all around her, and she had honestly never felt so protected.

"How did you know? No, wait. Let me work this out. Not long ago, when I was changing the Rift Bubbles' code on Namino, you showed up out of the blue. You said, 'For one such as myself, all energy in the universe resonates. It is but a matter of knowing which wave belongs to which energy.' You've got a bead on my wave, don't you? You're watching me."

I am watching out for you. You are evolving, and your path is fraught with pain and peril.

Her heart thudded against her breastbone. "More pain and peril than this?"

Here and there. But do not despair, for the path is also paved with wonder and triumph.

"How do you know?"

Please, do not ask me that.

"But I already did."

So you did. It doesn't matter, not yet.

"Okay. I won't argue this time." She supposed she was feeling better, to be exasperated with the Kat once again. "We should focus on the problem at hand, in any event. You can't accompany me everywhere, wrapping me in a cocoon as I go about my life. So how do I keep the voices out myself? I realize they come with the kyoseil. In much the same way that Alex follows kyoseil waves to access data stored in Reor slabs, I can follow the waves to access psyches. Asterion psyches, where the data is not merely knowledge, but thoughts and emotions. Except for me, those thoughts and emotions are flowing in both directions. I'm not seeking them out, but they're assaulting me anyway."

Not assaulting you. They are flowing, and you are along their route.

"Right now I don't care what their intent is. I have to keep them out, or I will go insane. I…fear I did for a little while there." She swallowed heavily. "Please tell me I can keep them out."

It is…yes, you can do so. The kyoseil streams where it will, unbound, and it is now open to you, much like the cosmos itself. Therefore, it will be up to you to impose boundaries upon it—to give it directions as well as restrictions. The mental steps required are somewhat intricate, and you will need to maintain constant vigilance in this, but I will help you navigate your trial.

RW

Dashiel left his desk behind and wearily opened a wormhole to Nika's flat. Mirai was safe for now, but his work was just beginning. All the factories in the universe were not enough to produce the materials and components required to rebuild everything that had been destroyed *and* continue building new warships and weapons in a timely manner. But he would do what he could, then a bit more.

He shouldn't take even an hour away from his duties, but he wanted to check on Nika. He hadn't heard a word from her after leaving her at the flat, which hopefully meant she'd been getting some desperately needed rest. Best case: she was still sleeping, blissfully unaware of the endeavors proceeding ahead without her intervention. For many hours, she'd acted as their strongest bulwark against the Rasu invasion. Now that the crisis had been quelled for the moment, the rest of them could pick up the slack.

He stepped as quietly as possible through the wormhole and into the entry hall; if she *was* asleep, he didn't want to wake her.

A diffuse white-blue glow leaked around the end of the hall from the living area, and he crept forward and rounded the corner.

Nika sat cross-legged in the middle of the living room floor. Her eyes were closed, and her hands rested open atop her knees. The glow that surrounded her when she deigned to let it show merged into a multitude of tiny lights forming a vast aura extending outward over three meters in every direction. The lights danced about to intermingle with the glow she radiated, and he was strangely reminded of the imagery of two galaxies merging.

"Nika?" His voice boomed around the living room; an intrusion and an affront to the cosmic silence he'd invaded.

She smiled faintly and held up a finger. "One minute."

He rested against the kitchen counter. Watched and waited in growing confusion and perhaps too much suspicion.

Her lips moved soundlessly, as if intoning a mantra. Eyes still closed, she carefully rose to her feet, and the dance of lights flowed upward with her. Then she nodded, and the lights spread outward, spinning slowly as their radius expanded. Gradually, they withdrew from her and took on an amorphous Anatype shape nearby.

She opened her eyes. Looked around, though not hardly at him. A deep sigh fell from her lips, and her features brightened. "It's working."

I knew you would succeed.

"I didn't. I—" She flinched, and Dashiel had to stop himself from rushing toward her. "You were right. This is going to require constant vigilance. Dammit."

In time, it will become second nature, and your subconscious will manage it without the need for your attention.

"I hope so."

Now, if you are well, I will leave the two of you.

"Thank you, Mesme. More than I can ever express, thank you."

You are...welcome. Please call upon me if you encounter additional difficulties.

"I'm not embarrassed to say I will."

The lights swept past him, and he swore there was the hint of a warm caress along his skin. Then they were gone.

He strode quickly across the room and took her in his arms. "What was all that about? What happened while I was gone?"

She smiled weakly, exhaustion carved into every detail of her features. "Oh, it seems my deep dive into kyoseil strings today left me vulnerable to other...it's difficult to explain. Stray thoughts from random Asterions, to put it as simply as I can. In the aftermath, they overwhelmed me, and I couldn't quiet them. But Mesme helped me regain control and taught me how to shield myself from them. It's all good now." She nodded firmly to emphasize the point.

But it wasn't all good now. He'd known her for over three thousand years, and beneath the otherworldly glow and the galaxy irises and the brave countenance, he saw the pain eating away at her.

"I wish you'd tell me what this is really about. You don't have to hide your struggles from me. I don't *want* you to hide them from me. I may not be able to help you the way…the Kat can, but I can be here for you in every other way."

"But I'm not hiding them from you." She kissed him lightly then withdrew from his embrace. "As I said, I was worn out from the mental effort of juggling so many barriers at once, and it weakened my innate ability to block out stray Asterion thoughts."

"And that's all?"

"I admit it is a little more complicated. I understood what was happening but not how to stop it. Mesme helped me and…it's a work in progress, but I'm getting there. I'll try to explain it better, once I invent a way to put something that isn't concrete or tangible into words. I promise."

But her promises had always been freely given, and not always so zealously obeyed. Not out of malice or even neglect, but instead out of a conviction that she knew best. Best for him, best for the world.

The glow followed her as she went to the kitchen and poured a glass of water, enveloping her in what suddenly felt like an impenetrable barricade. Separating her from him more with each passing day.

He had no idea how to keep her, but he wouldn't lose her, dammit. Not again.

45

MIRAI

NIKA'S FLAT

"Can I get you something to drink? Both of you?"

Alex nodded politely. "Sounds wonderful, thank you."

Nika went around the corner into her kitchen, retrieving two glasses and a bottle of wine. She wore a black silk kimono and threaded sandals, and the aesthetic was such that Alex wasn't sure if they'd interrupted her and Dashiel just before bed or before a gala party. Dashiel wore loose linen pants and a short-sleeved, v-neck shirt, so perhaps the former. He paced aimlessly around the open living room, hands clasped in front of him, so perhaps they'd also interrupted something more.

"Have we come at a bad time? We can meet up later or…."

"Not at all." Nika returned with two full glasses and handed them to her and Caleb, then went to the counter to retrieve glasses for herself and Dashiel. She motioned to the couches. "Let's sit."

Caleb touched the small of Alex's back as they walked over, a cue he, too, sensed all was not well here, and they sat together on one of the couches. She took a small sip of the wine, then let her gaze drift to the windows. "I haven't peeked outside yet, but I heard Mirai had an unexpected Rasu attack yesterday, which you all handled in fine fashion."

Nika's expression hardened. "It was horrifying. They managed to board one of our cargo vessels a few days ago and acquire the access code. We changed it almost immediately, but they succeeded in sneaking a few ships through in the gap. Once here, they promptly constructed a quantum block, took out the Rift Bubble and began their invasion. It was touch and go for almost a day."

Dashiel reached over and squeezed Nika's hand. "Nika is the only reason we were able to defeat them."

"Don't be silly. I wasn't the only reason. Lance's fleets, for instance. And all your work getting the Kireme Boundaries distributed."

"Yes, but you turned them on, again and again." His throat worked. "At a cost."

"We all paid a price for our victory." Nika smiled thinly and shifted her attention to Alex. "Have you talked to Mesme lately?"

"Not since that night on Akeso, and I'll be happy if it was the last time."

"I think…" Nika set her glass on the table "…I understand why you're angry, I really do. But Mesme has been tremendously helpful to me regarding…various matters involving my deeper interactions with kyoseil. I wouldn't have been able to do what I did to help save Mirai without the Kat. Honestly, I'd be a blubbering, psychotic mess on the floor right now without it."

Whatever the woman was obliquely referring to, it might explain the strained mood here. Alex wanted to ask Nika to elaborate, but she wasn't certain it was her business. Another time, when they were alone. "And I'm glad Mesme is helping you. It's been of tremendous help to us in the past, too, but this doesn't excuse all the lies and manipulation. It violated my trust in a big way, and I'm not sure it comes back from that."

"Understood. So what brings you here this evening? If it's just drinks and friendship, all the better. After an extremely stressful two days, I welcome the frivolity."

"I wish it were. Maybe one day, right? No, we recently spent some time deep in Rasu territory. Watching them, listening to them talk to one another. Observing them attack rival factions, with the aggressor subsuming its rivals into itself and taking over their territory."

Nika almost choked on her wine. "What? Are you saying they're at war with one another?"

"Not war precisely. More akin to low-level skirmishes and

jockeying for position. Though, the subsumed group probably viewed it as war, since they lost their independent identity. Anyway, it reminded me of what you'd said about their need for control of their own."

"Yes. It makes sense. They don't use pure quantum communication because they're afraid other Rasu clusters will use it to control them." Nika leaned forward intently. "This isn't idle speculation. What are you thinking?"

"That it would be great if we could exploit the fissures between the various factions somehow. Stoke the flames of jealousy and paranoia enough to force them to turn inward. Direct their attention toward their own problems and away from conquering us."

"They'd definitely be susceptible to that manner of…information warfare, I guess you'd call it. But how would we accomplish it?"

Caleb jumped in. "What about the virutox you've developed? It can infiltrate Rasu programming, correct?"

"And disrupt it. Dashiel?"

"Eh, the problem is the very characteristic you've identified—their division into rival factions. The factions don't interact with one another on a physical level, so I don't see how we'd get it to spread beyond a single cluster."

"Except when one attacks and subsumes another."

"Oh, great point. But no. As designed, the virutox is poison to the Rasu. If one cluster is infected, that cluster likely won't be *able* to attack any others. It would also recognize it had been poisoned and, assuming it survived, isolate and sever the poison before it infected too many units."

Alex sank back against Caleb's shoulder. "Dammit."

Nika stood, taking her glass with her as she walked deliberately to the windows and stared out them. Dashiel watched her with a keen focus, saying nothing.

Alex was more impatient. "What is it?"

"There is something every Rasu in existence would want, if they only knew of it. Kyoseil. The ones that do know of it are fascinated by it, bordering on obsession, because they believe they can use it to exert absolute control over disparate far-flung units."

"But the kyoseil doesn't work for them."

"I've come to understand…" Nika turned to face them "…that is the kyoseil's choice. The history of kyoseil is, by and large, one of passivity. It's a conduit—of information above all—but it plays no active hand in the events of organics or synthetics. Mesme says the primordial beings of the universe rarely decide to take actions in the way we perceive of such a concept, but I'm not convinced this is entirely accurate when it comes to kyoseil. At least, not since we encountered it seven hundred thousand years ago. It chose to allow us to use it to enhance our neural functioning. Our technology, our programming, our information storage, everything. More recently, in your Directorate War, it chose to allow you to use it as you needed in order to turn the tables on the Primors and achieve victory."

Alex chuckled wryly. "At the time, I told my mother the Reor wanted us to win. She replied, with her usual aplomb, that she welcomed the minerals to our side of the fight. So I buy your assessment over Mesme's. Not a surprise."

Dashiel didn't look so convinced. "But it's not as if the kyoseil could have stopped us from interweaving it into our biosynth components when Magnus Forchelle built those first bodies."

"No, but it could have remained inert when he did so, much like it does for the Rasu now. Instead, it supercharged our evolution in a thousand ways. Asterions would not exist without kyoseil—we'd merely be partially synthetic Anadens."

Alex slammed her glass down on the table with a gasp. "You can tell it to turn itself on for the Rasu, can't you?"

Nika nodded, displaying a measure of gravitas Alex had seen her mother display on too many occasions. "I can—or I suspect I can. But…" she shook her head roughly and stormed into the kitchen in a swoosh of silk "…I *can't*. I'm sorry, I shouldn't have broached the topic. It's an untenable idea. No, an impossible one."

Dashiel leapt up and followed her into the kitchen. "Because if we spread the word, every Rasu in the supercluster will descend upon the Dominion to get their hands on our kyoseil? All our militaries combined couldn't withstand such an offensive."

"Oh, it's not that. I know the locations of thousands of deposits of kyoseil scattered across Laniakea that I could direct them to instead."

Alex twisted around to lean over the back of the couch in interest. "You do?"

"Yes. It's simply a matter of casting my mind out like a fishing line and following the waves to their destinations." Nika's eyes unfocused for several seconds, and the glow leaking off her skin illuminated—then she shook herself back into the moment. "But think about what I'd be asking of the kyoseil. It would have to do the Rasu's bidding. And the Rasu's bidding is torture, murder and wholesale destruction of living things. Of Asterions, Humans, Anadens. Of our friends and allies and a thousand species we've never met.

"How can I demand this peaceful, quiet, miraculous, ancient form of life commit such acts? Be a willing participant in genocide? The answer is, I can't. I'm sorry, Alex, but we'll have to find another way."

RW

AKESO

Once she'd changed into the most comfortable clothes she owned, a ratty gray tank top and faded navy shorts, Alex collapsed into Caleb's arms on their own couch. "You know, I think Nika's found herself traveling a rather bumpy road with her newly evolved, kyoseil-infused self."

"Mmm. And I think Dashiel's having an even worse time of it."

"Oh?"

"He's terrified for her. I imagine he feels a bit helpless, too. Like he's on the outside and can't find a way in." He kissed her on the top of the head. "I've been there. Watching the person you love leap off a cliff, risking everything they are to become something unknown? It's the most horrifying thing in the world."

"It wasn't that bad."

"It absolutely was."

Her heart panged, and she shifted to wind her arms around his neck and touch her nose to his. "Well, it worked out."

"It did." He kissed her full on the mouth, and she felt the truth of it in his touch. "So are we back to square one with our plan?"

Satisfied as to this one point but little else, she resumed using his chest and shoulder as a pillow. "Not quite. I still say there's something to be exploited here. I mean, think about it. What if we could actually cause the Rasu to destroy *themselves?*"

"If the various Rasu factions all learn about kyoseil, get a supply of it, and it works for them, then it will jumpstart a civil war as they all vie for control."

"Exactly."

"But what if one faction wins the competition? Then we'll have created an even more fearsome enemy."

"Or instead, they destroy their entire civilization in the process. It wouldn't be the first time civil war ended in ruin for all. In fact, I'd say it's the most common outcome."

"It is," he replied. "And if nothing else, we'd buy ourselves time. Months, years, maybe decades. But it doesn't matter. Nika won't do it. And in my heart, I don't blame her. Imagine if I had to ask Akeso to be complicit in such violence?"

"But you already have, *priyazn.* On Namino, at Insights Academy. And Akeso has come to appreciate why it can be necessary."

"And since kyoseil is one of Akeso's ancestors, so to speak, you think the logic will be the same."

"It might be." She was glad he'd brought up that revelation of his own accord. She knew he was working through all its implications, but it didn't represent much of a moral quandary. Nika was correct. Kyoseil was a fundamentally peaceful, if inscrutable, species, and its role as Akeso's progenitor was something to embrace.

"But again, it doesn't matter. You heard the resolve in her voice. She won't do it."

"I don't know." She sat up to face him. "Dad told me earlier today that Mom is increasingly concerned about our chances against this enemy. Every move she makes to outmaneuver them, they counter. They're getting around the Rift Bubbles, they're using antimatter to take out our ships, they're evading our tracking sensors with stealth and pinpoint wormholes. They're bringing larger fleets every day and hitting more worlds at once, and as things stand now, they have an effectively unlimited number of warships to call upon. While the Rasu may skirmish among themselves at the margins, they won't hesitate to band together to conquer us.

"If things get dire enough—and make no mistake, just because the Dominion won at Mirai yesterday, it doesn't mean things aren't getting worse by the day—I believe Nika will relent. I feel pretty confident in saying that nothing is more important to her than saving her people. And I think in its own weird, incomprehensible way, the kyoseil is deeply invested in saving them, too."

Caleb frowned. "But what if she's right? What if the ask is too great?"

"When the alternative is annihilation, is there any ask that's too great?"

He fisted a hand at his mouth as clouds of discontent swept through his sapphire irises...and nodded. "No, there isn't. If we can't shoot the Rasu into retreat—if they begin to overwhelm our best defenses—we have to do whatever is required to survive. Of course we do."

"Then we need to have a contingency plan ready to go for when the shit hits the fan. Because I fear it will, and soon."

"And so far, this is the best contingency plan we've got. Okay. How do we get word out about kyoseil to a bunch of different factions of Rasu in disparate locations?"

She and Valkyrie had been puzzling over this ever since they'd left Nika's place. "The Rasu's natural reintegration process. Look, the Asterions' virutox alters the Rasu's programming, correct? I'll bet a variant can be created to perform a single function: embed knowledge of kyoseil into the Rasu infected with it. Hell, Devon might be able to do it on his own. He's been working feverishly to catch up to Asterions' understanding of the Rasu. He hates it when someone else knows something he doesn't."

"And we and the Asterions both have multiple samples of Rasu in our labs now." Caleb leaned forward in growing excitement, and she scooted over to give him room. "We plant the knowledge in separate samples, then drop them off near Rasu clusters across the map. They do what Rasu do, which is join up with larger units. They share their activities while they were away, and the information spreads. But we'll still need Nika's help. She's the only who knows where all the deposits of kyoseil are. The last thing we want to do is bring the entire Rasu armada down on the Dominion."

"She'll come around." Alex laughed to herself. "Most people are a complete mystery to me—you know this. But Nika, I get. When the time comes, she'll be with us."

"You have better instincts than you give yourself credit for, and I suspect you're right." He exhaled harshly, his brow creasing. "It could work. But damn is it a risky plan."

"As risky as joining with Artificials to create a new breed of humans who can outsmart and outmaneuver an armada of unimaginably advanced ethereal aliens?"

"Easily as risky."

"Yeah, that's what I figured." She bounced her toes on the floor; with a plan now taking shape, she was anxious to *move*. "So what now?"

Caleb, not so much. "Now, we hope it doesn't come to this."

46

ROMANE

Confluence Expo

"And this is what a typical Taenarin neighborhood looks like. Can you believe a place as wondrous as this exists deep under the surface of a frozen planet?"

'Oohs' and 'aahs' rippled through the group, and Mia gestured toward the Expo's resident Taenarin representative. "Veoira, will you tell us what a normal, ordinary day involves for a Taenarin child?"

Veoira Byrne sat on the stone stool situated in front of the model house and smiled, her leathery skin brightening from an umber hue to apricot as she did, and the murmurs escalated to gasps of amazement among the kids on the tour. Getting Veoira—getting any Taenarin at all—to agree to leave Taenarin Aris and come live part-time on Romane had been quite a coup on Mia's part. Hopefully more would follow in time.

"Certainly, Miss Requelme! Taenarin children do go to school, but I'm told it isn't so much like Human school." Veoira's lilting, sing-song voice was lovely, and she'd progressed quickly in learning the syntax and grammar of Communis.

"They gather in small groups out in our many, ah, nature preserves, let us call them. Sometimes up in a broad tree like this one." Veoira pointed down the mock street to a winding carving some five meters tall. It wasn't a tree in that it didn't grow in soil or sprout leaves, but it served the same purpose for Taenarin children—to climb upon. "Or sometimes beside a pond that formed from the ice over our city. The children and the teacher will talk about the lesson for the day, and there's almost always experimentation to demonstrate the lesson's use in the real world. And a song. We love our songs."

The kids were enraptured, and Mia faded back a few steps from the group. Veoira's presentation usually ran around eight minutes, so she had a bit of downtime to ruminate in her own thoughts.

She didn't need to be guiding a children's tour in the first place; she had eager employees on staff for such tasks. And this was the sole tour she could squeeze in for the day, and possibly for the week, because she truly didn't have time to be doing it. She not only had the entire Expo to run—to finish, if she were honest—she also had the spaceport and half a dozen other adjunct projects to manage.

But showing the exhibits to visitors and seeing their reactions, especially those of the enthusiastic and endlessly curious children, inspired her to keep moving forward. It made her start to believe that this had been the right thing to do; that she was making a difference, however small, in the world.

Of course, the world was in danger of burning to the ground, so it might all be for naught. Her gaze darted to the glass ceiling high overhead, a tiny part of her searching for Rasu descending through the orchid sky. Battles had raged for over a week now at two Anaden worlds in Andromeda as the Rasu brought their largest fleets and most sustained attacks to date. The Noesis whispered in the recesses of her mind about how this was surely only the beginning.

The Asterions had beaten back a Rasu onslaught at Mirai, but it had taken all their military strength and every trick in their impressive arsenal. Now they waited on a knife's edge for the enemy to make its next move. Would the Dominion fall in the coming days?

What would happen when the Rasu came for Romane?

So many people she talked to about the risk the Rasu posed to civilization just waved their hand in the direction of 'regenesis' and shrugged it off. And its availability helped, obviously it helped. It meant a second chance for all the soldiers and civilians who were dying this very minute. But regenesis was as fragile as Novoloume architecture and Taenarin stone-carved homes.

Already, there were more regenesis labs on Romane than any other human world. So what happened if the Rasu came here and blew them up? What if they did the same at Seneca next? If the Rasu then took Sagan and, god forbid, *Earth*, there would remain perilously few places for people to find their second chance at life. And for how long?

Regenesis wasn't the answer to saving humanity. Victory was.

Oh, her heart ached to be on the metaphorical front lines right now. She wanted to be interfacing with Dean Veshnael and Nika Kirumase and even Corradeo Praesidis. Arranging for refugee evacuations and coordinating the delivery of aid supplies for once the battles were done. She wanted to be talking diplomatic strategy and devising ways they could help one another. Not waging the war itself, because that had never been her talent, but helping in the unique manner she wasn't bashful to say she had excelled at.

As it was, in the absence of hard information, her idle thoughts were left to spin up the worst sort of scenarios. As her imagination helpfully supplied images of what the multiple concurrent battles must look like, though, a memory flared in her mind. The first time she had met Malcolm, when together they'd ventured out into the savage, war-torn streets of Romane to test a weapon designed to bring down those horrible swarmers. She let the memory of the adrenaline flowing through her veins wash over her; the terror and the *immediacy* of every step. The elation of seeing her handiwork stop the first swarmer dead in its tracks.

She may not be able to recall past events with perfect clarity the way Asterions did, but this memory was pretty damn vivid, causing her pulse to race and her skin to flush.

Then another, more recent memory bubbled to the surface. A face in the crowd—one of thousands who had gathered for the Expo grand opening, but one she would recognize from across a planet.

Malcom had been in attendance during her speech; she was *certain* it was him. But why hadn't he come up to talk to her afterward? And why was he wearing sweats and a shabby, faded jacket? He always dressed like a military officer, even when off duty.

The fact that he'd gone out of his way to come to the opening, in the middle of a war no less, made her skin tingle and her chest ache. It made her dream anew of things that she'd been so damn close to giving up on. She wanted to send him another message, but the fact that he hadn't approached her of his own accord made her second guess...everything. None of it made sense.

Her gaze flitted back toward the Expo entrance—but he wasn't going to walk into the Expo and sweep her into his arms; not today. Battles against the Rasu raged once more, and he was somewhere in the stars, on the bridge of the *Denali*, using his considerable skills to keep the Rasu away from here. Away from these giggling children who deserved a future free from monsters.

She shook her head to snap out of the increasingly destructive mental spiral. Wallowing wasn't a good look on her, dammit. She had to trust in Malcolm—in humanity and its allies—to win this war. Against odds that were as bad and might have been worse, they'd won the Metigen War. Barely a year and a half later, they'd won the Directorate War. They would win this one. And maybe, when it was over and won, he *would* walk through that entrance and answer the questions that seeing him in the crowd had ignited in her soul.

Until then, though, she would keep working here to inspire the next generation of diplomats and warriors.

"What about water fountains? Do you have those on Taenarin Aris? The water fountain outside is awesome! Mom said when we leave, I can play in it and get all wet!"

Mia chuckled lightly as she stepped back up beside Veoira. "I agree—the water fountain *is* awesome. Now, we can't monopolize Veoira's attention the entire day, and there's so much more to see before we get to play in water fountains. If you want to learn more about the Taenarin and their homeworld, you can pick up one of several book files at the shop on the way out.

"Everyone, thank Veoira for giving us such an entertaining presentation. If you all will follow me, next on the tour is a little taste of one of the most unique and unusual Concord species, the Efkam."

47

CONCORD HQ

CINT

*"*W*hich is why today, we are announcing the Insights Memorial Scholarship Fund. It will cover all medical costs of those injured, killed or otherwise affected by the tragic events at the New Frontiers Medical Clinic and Insights Academy. It will even cover the costs of regenesis, should those who were killed have specified their desire to undergo regenesis in their wills. Though we Gardiens disagree with the use of regenesis in meaningful ways, we recognize that one of our own caused this loss of life in a misguided, reprehensible attempt to enforce those beliefs on others. Accordingly, we must put aside our own preferences in this situation and bow to the wishes of those who were harmed as a result."*

The man looked as though he'd just swallowed sour lemons as he struggled not to spit the words out. It wasn't Enzio Vilane, of course. The man at the podium had introduced himself as the Gardiens Director of Public Affairs. A mouthpiece, nothing more, but Richard had immediately entered his name in their Gardiens database and ordered a background check nonetheless.

"The Fund will go much further, however. It will pay all educational costs of both the families affected by the violence at the New Frontiers Medical Clinic and the children who were present at Insights Academy— all the children. Not merely their secondary education, either, but the university or trade schooling we hope to see every one of them pursue in the future. Let this tragedy be transformed into an opportunity for these children to live bright, fulfilling lives that will enrich all of humanity.

"As we shared in an earlier press release, the Gardiens have turned over to law enforcement all information we possess on the parties who

are believed to be responsible for the violence committed. We have opened our records and are ready to take whatever additional steps are requested of us to guarantee the perpetrators are brought to justice. Understand this: the Gardiens abhor violence and despair at the idea of lives being lost because someone misinterpreted our ideology. It will not stand. We will redouble our efforts to be a beacon of life and hope for humanity from this day forward."

"I think I'm going to vomit. Have you got a bag anywhere in here? An empty box? A bottle, if it has a wide mouth?"

Richard shook his head. "Restroom is down the hall. If you run, you might make it in time."

"Eh…" Graham rubbed at his face "…I think I've choked it back for now. Well, this fucks things up a bit, doesn't it?"

"I'm afraid so. They have done a masterful job of stringing their own protestors who were at the riot up with nooses while constructing a lead-lined wall around every other aspect of their operations. Now they're kicking off a public relations campaign designed to grant them veritable sainthood."

"Yep, still need to vomit. Listen, we've got Vilane on video arranging Commandant Solovy's assassination. Let's go arrest him for that and be done with it."

"Do we? We have a low-res surveillance recording of an indistinct holo of a man saying a few things that could be interpreted to involve taking some nefarious action against a target who might or might not have been Miriam. Vilane's lawyers would tear the evidence to shreds. Holos and voice prints can be faked. For an Artificial, it's not even a challenge." Richard ground his jaw in frustration, because this profoundly annoyed him. "Nobody wants to punish Vilane for trying to harm Miriam more than I do—except David, obviously—but the holo simply isn't enough to take to court."

"And while we're failing at making the case in court, all the real power players will go to ground. Okay, point conceded. Can we at least move to freeze some of these gray-market accounts we tracked down thanks to Winslow's morsels of intel?"

"I was nearly ready to pull the trigger on exactly that. But not after this stunt." Richard gestured to the vid in irritation. "If the police investigation into the riot and hostage situation concludes the individuals involved acted alone, in direct contravention of instructions from Gardiens officials—as it is appearing like it will—then we don't actually have the Gardiens on the hook for any illegal activity." He sighed. "I'm afraid we'll either have to find something dirty in our ongoing financial surveillance, wait for them to make another mistake, or hope Malcolm is able to uncover evidence of the dark rot at the heart of the organization."

"And unless the Rasu decide to up and take a vacation, we're going to be waiting for the last one for a while. I don't see the fleet admiral departing his warship again anytime soon."

"No." Worry about the ongoing battles flared in Richard's mind. He deeply wished there was something he could do to help Concord in its fight…but the Rasu weren't that kind of enemy. He hadn't served on a warship in thirty-six years, and there were no intelligence operations to oversee. Any spying conducted on the enemy was undertaken by Ghosts, Artificials and Kats.

"You know, if Malcolm hadn't threatened Vilane the way he did, this—" Graham waved toward the screen displaying the press conference "—likely wouldn't have happened."

"True. But I can't fault him for it. It was the only play he had to make if he wanted to stay in the game. And we do want him to stay in the game."

"Granted. Also, you've got people investigating the new Gardiens names he gave you. I dread tempting fate that another violent incident could transpire, but if they plan one, we should be able to prevent it from ever happening this time."

"Hopefully. In the meantime, let's shift our focus and continue diving into what we've got on Rivinchi. The cartel is definitely tied up in illegal activities. We can try to bring Vilane down in that way."

"Hold that thought for a second." Graham leaned forward intently. "SENTRI is planning to wake up Owain Boliver and Chrissy

Sanders in the next day or two, right? What if they expose this farce of a PR move for the lie it is by pointing the finger at their Gardiens supervisors?"

"Then we proceed ahead on all fronts. Fast and unrelenting." Richard found his mood brightening a touch at the prospect. "I'm certain Director Solarian is aware that the opportunity may present itself, but I think I'll pay him a visit this evening all the same—oh, here we go." Richard transferred the file that had arrived to a screen. "The courts finally got out of the way and released the hold on James Sarona's bank transactions."

They studied the long list of debits and credits covering the last six months. The regular transactions of an individual living his life. The would-be assassin had been making a living as a bodyguard-for-hire since being dishonorably discharged from the Federation Special Forces; as a result, the deposits originated from a variety of sources.

Richard started making notes. They'd need to track down every one of the entities to determine the ultimate payor—

"Wait. I know this name."

Richard followed Graham's pointed finger, which rested beside two deposit entries recorded five weeks earlier. " 'Raffinate Amalgamated'?"

"Yep. Where do I know it from? Where, where, where...." Graham opened an aural in front of him. "Time to take the 'way back machine' out for a spin and do a deep dive of classified Division files."

While Graham worked, Richard sent his own query. It wouldn't tell them much, but it would be a start. "Records says the company is registered on—"

"Krysk."

"Yes. You found it?"

"I did." Graham clasped his hands behind his head and leaned back, seeming pleased with himself. "The Ferre cartel used the company as a front of a front for years—several layers removed and mostly to act as a middle-man for illicit material transfers. Which means that when Olivia Montegreu murdered Laure Ferre and took full control of the cartel, ownership of the company transferred to her." He huffed a breath. "Did Enzio Vilane just make a mistake?"

Richard opened their extensive list of companies they'd linked to Vilane, the Gardiens or Rivinchi, then shook his head. "It's not on the list. We've uncovered no evidence of Vilane operating through Raffinate Amalgamated in any capacity."

"Not yet. But we know he's cast a wide net in appropriating *everything* associated with both his parents' ventures. The Ferre cartel was a fairly minor gem in Montegreu's collection in the grand scheme of things, but it did generate revenue for her. Vilane lived on Seneca for several years while he attended Tellica. If he was educating himself about the underworld by then, there's every reason to think he was aware of Ferre's existence. It tracks. There has to be a way to link the company to Vilane. Who's the best financial forensics investigator you know?"

Richard smiled, buoyed by a sliver of hopefulness for the first time in a while. "A man named Vince Skeldon. He works for Glacier Federated out of New Columbia, but consults for SENTRI when they pay him enough. And he's already on the way here."

"You commed him before I even started talking, eh?"

"It seemed prudent." Richard drummed his fingers on the table. "If we can tie Vilane to Sarona in the tiniest way? It won't be enough on its own, but it could be the single thread that, when tugged, unravels the whole operation."

PANDORA

Enzio Vilane slammed his palm on the control panel to silence the video feed. His hands balled into fists and clenched reflexively at his sides. He wanted to punch one through the glass table—but doing so would only break his knuckles, so instead he fought to get his anger and frustration under control. He'd made the call to go forward with the press conference and the initiatives being detailed. Still, he felt sick to his stomach hearing the saccharine words roll off the smooth tongue of the Gardiens Director of Public Affairs—

"You shouldn't have agreed to this spectacle. It makes you look weak."

He spun around in surprise to see his mother leaning against the open doorway. She wore a cream blouse with pearl accents and soft caramel pants; her hair was swept up into a perfect chignon, save for a strand of hair on each side set loose to frame her distinctive cheekbones.

She looked like a CEO. A titan of industry. The queen of the underworld she had once been. All of which only made her words cut into him more brutally. "I didn't have a choice, Mother. I had to go on the offensive to both cut the criminal investigation off at the pass and take control of our public messaging. Otherwise, people would be calling the Gardiens terrorists and murderers."

"But you *are* terrorists and murderers. You might as well own it." Olivia stepped into the room and wandered down the length of the table, her perfect fingernails scraping along the glass. "I wish you had talked to me about it before arranging this circus. I would have advised against having a 'public relations' face at all.

"Your attempt to simultaneously maintain both a public Gardiens image that is law-abiding and upstanding and a private one that will pursue unsavory actions to achieve its goals weakens both aspects. I fear such a strategy is doomed to fail. What are you going to do when the authorities wake up your people who died during the school incident? You may have disavowed them, but they will not have disavowed you."

He felt like a little boy getting scolded by his mother for getting into a fight at school. The fact that he'd had no mother when he was a little boy didn't make the gut reaction any less vivid. "No one in the Gardiens told them to resort to violence. They botched what had been a carefully planned protest all on their own." He smiled, relieved to be able to regain the high ground. "But it won't be a problem. I'm afraid when the doctors go to transfer their consciousnesses into new bodies, they will find that the neural imprints have suffered unrecoverable corruption. Regenesis is still in its infancy, you see, and errors are bound to happen."

"And the neurological records from the Artificials involved? There's more than one way to bring back a Prevo."

"Similar minute but prevalent errors will prevent a successful transfer."

"And it will look innocuous and accidental? You run a risk of multiple glitches being viewed as too suspicious to be a coincidence."

"Nonetheless, no evidence of tampering will be uncovered."

She tilted her head a touch. "In that case, well done. I still wish you had consulted with me in greater depth earlier, when you were devising the Gardiens' structure and organization. I could have helped you steer a more productive course. One unlikely to hamstring you to the extent this one will."

"I couldn't consult you earlier." He stammered over the words. "You were…you weren't ready."

"I realize I wasn't. But I'm ready now, and you would benefit from listening to my counsel."

What did that mean? What did she believe 'ready' meant? She'd been devoting many hours to refining her programming of late, and he was starting to suspect she was no longer running all of her changes by him first. He squirmed, uncomfortable. "I'm sure I would. I want to continue our evening discussions, as I greatly value your input. Perhaps we can expand on them as well. There is much I could learn from your experience."

"Yes, there is. So listen to me now." She directed her full gaze at him, and he found himself frozen beneath its power. "This puffery will buy you some time. You've delayed the most vigorous law enforcement investigations, and you've tempered public opinion for the moment. But unless you defang your organization and abandon its true goals, your deflections will not last, and one day soon you will find yourself stymied, impotent and possibly in prison.

"So be subtle and underhanded about it if you must, but you need to accelerate your true vision. Move now, or the Grand Design you gaze lovingly at every morning will crumble to dust, and you will fail. At everything."

48

CAF AURORA

SERIFOS STELLAR SYSTEM

The Rasu dreadnoughts were getting bigger, Miriam noted as the two RNEWs the *Aurora* now sported disintegrated the mammoth vessel one cruiser-length segment at a time. Still not big enough to escape the power of the exotic forces her ship wielded.

When the last chunk of metal winked out of existence, she allowed herself a quiet, imperceptible smile of relief. But it didn't last, because nothing had been won.

After believing, perhaps foolishly, that they'd subdued the Rasu at Serifos and beginning clean-up operations, Concord forces here had been caught by surprise when a sizeable fleet of Rasu reinforcements had appeared with weapons blazing in a reinvigorated attempt to win the verdant garden world for themselves. In a timed maneuver, heretofore hidden Rasu forces on the planet had activated a new quantum block just as the fleet arrived.

She'd taken it upon herself to leave HQ and join the fight—to throw the considerable firepower of the *Aurora* at the enemy until they were able to regain the upper hand, and for good this time. Hopefully Casmir's pride wasn't too wounded at her usurpation of his command role, but if he was, well, pride had no place in a battle for survival.

Navarchos Casmir (AMF Imperium Alpha)(Serifos Command Channel): "Regiments III-6A and B, reform the blockade in Quadrants Two and Three to prevent any of the smaller vessels from slipping through. Regiment III-8D, insert yourselves into the Rasu ranks while they remain disorganized."

The Rift Bubble appeared to be secure on the surface once again. After many hours of combat, on top of the week of combat preceding this renewed attack, it felt as if they were going to keep the planet out of the hands of the enemy. But it had felt that way before, too—

Thomas interrupted her thought. 'Commandant Solovy, long-range sensors are reporting approaching Rasu vessels in the Nopreis stellar system.'

And just like that, the spark of optimism collapsed beneath a wave of foreboding. She locked her jaw to keep an existential sigh from escaping her lips; her crew didn't need to detect any weakness out of her.

"Thomas, fire and maneuver as you see fit for a moment."

'With pleasure, Commandant.'

She mentally stepped back from the battle at hand and let the status and locations of all her major combat groups take shape in her mind. While she hoped her presence here had helped to turn the tide a bit more quickly than might have otherwise occurred, the simple fact was that it wasn't her job to wage this specific battle—it was to conduct the war. The Novoloume homeworld was as important as any planet in Concord, and more important than damn near all of them. She wouldn't dream of abandoning the ongoing conflicts, but she had to take every step available to her and a few that arguably were not to ensure Nopreis didn't fall to the enemy.

Commandant Solovy (CAF Aurora)(Concord Command Channel): "Fleet Admiral Jenner, I'm afraid you're about to lose the Novoloume forces at Acacia. I advise retasking two AEGIS brigades to fill the gap."

She didn't even consider asking Thisiame to stay and fight for an Anaden colony when his people's homeworld was about to come under attack. Harmonious relations between the Novoloume and Anadens had progressed a fair amount in the years since Concord's founding, but not *that* much. Likely they would never progress so far, nor should they. Concord was a coalition of independent allies, not a monolithic government. Their differences were to be celebrated, not suppressed.

Fleet Admiral Jenner (AFS Denali)(Concord Command Channel): "Acknowledged. Pointe-Amiral Thisiame, Godspeed."

Pointe-Amiral Thisiame (NF Eshtaina)(Concord Command Channel): "And cosmos' grace to you. Directing all NF forces to depart for Nopreis at once."

She checked the ebb and flow of the battle outside the viewport and on the Serifos surface one more time, then sent a private message.

Pointe-Amiral, I am willing to accompany you to Nopreis, if you think the Aurora can be of service there.

The Aurora is always of service wherever it goes. But you have multiple battles to manage, and they all deserve your attention. Give me what forces you can spare, and we will find a way to prevail.

Very well.

Commandant Solovy (CAF Aurora)(Concord Command Channel): "Navarchos Casmir has things well in hand at Serifos now. With the increase in the number of combat arenas, I need to return to Command."

Navarchos Casmir (AMF Imperium Alpha)(Concord Command Channel): "We'll take it from here, Commandant. I'll keep you apprised of all developments."

She closed her eyes for half a second to reorient her thinking yet again, this time toward the challenges of starting another battle from scratch, while not losing what advantages they'd gained in the ongoing ones. *Conduct the war.*

"Thomas, I'm going to take a wormhole transport back to Command. Please return the *Aurora* to dock with all due speed."

'On our way, Commandant. We'll see you there.'

RW

NOPREIS STELLAR SYSTEM
PEGASUS DWARF GALAXY

Fire from a railgun-style weapons system tore into the advancing Rasu armada when they were 0.3 AU out from Nopreis, and the salvo of negative energy missiles it fired reduced the Rasu's numbers by eighteen percent before the engagement began.

Meanwhile, a sophisticated, long-range defensive array activated to wrap Nopreis in a protective cocoon some fifteen megameters in diameter. So far as anyone knew, it was the largest and most robust planetary defense array in existence.

It was also only twelve years old, because the Directorate would never have allowed such a system to be implemented above a non-Anaden world. What if they had needed to invade Nopreis to put the Novoloume in their place?

Last week, Dean Onai Veshnael and Pointe-Amiral Thisiame had met to discuss the possibility of adapting the RNEW design to replace the powerful but conventional weapons of the array with negative energy lasers. The cost was, they both agreed, beyond astronomical. But if they survived this attack, Onai decided, they would work out a way to pay for it. As it was, the incredible onslaught the defense array stood to deliver unto the enemy when it neared the planet would only buy them an extra few minutes for Concord forces to get into position.

Onai turned to Necha Hahmirin, his Senior Advisor, who was studying the defense network reports that updated constantly along the left wall of the Situation Room. "We have to proceed under the assumption that the Rasu were able to sneak assets onto the surface before we received and activated our Rift Bubble."

"But Nopreis was among the very first worlds to receive a Rift Bubble. You can't truly believe there have been Rasu here for months?"

"I can't afford not to believe it. If they implement a quantum block, it will disable all our Caeles Prisms, and our citizens will be trapped here. Therefore, we need to begin a full-scale evacuation now, before the ability to do so is denied us."

"Evacuate? But, sir, the Rasu have not even reached the planet yet."

"And when they do, we may find it is too late. Trust me, Necha, I recognize the magnitude of evacuating 3.2 billion people."

"Magnitude? It's impossible."

"Yes. But every person we do evacuate is a life we save. Redirect all outbound Caeles Prisms to the colonies of Loudia, Effor Elafos and Oranolos. We do not need to flood the hallways of Concord HQ with frightened refugees. Let us take care of our own."

"Yes, sir." She stepped up to one of the many screens and began sending orders to civilian law enforcement.

Onai shifted to the military tactical analysis panels, set slightly apart from the defense network feed. His gaze settled on the center screen as Thisiame and the Alpha Prime Wing arrived from Acacia. They joined the wings that had already taken up position in high orbit above the planet. He could tell when Thisiame had assumed command of the global defense by how eighty thousand ships began to move and reform. But he was not a military expert, so there was no point in him diving into the details of the deployments and orders that scrolled rapidly on the screen.

The Rasu began making their way past the defense array in fits and starts, destroying the nodes as they did, to close in on the planet. But the array had done its most important job—it had bought Thisiame time to arrive and get in position.

Pointe-Amiral Thisiame: Dean, I am requesting for you to transfer control of the Nopreis Planetary Defense System to me—or rather, to Contre-Amiral Lindari. While the Rasu are trapped up here by the Rift Bubble, we can use it to respond to events in low orbit as they develop.

He entered a command code on his personal interface. *Granted.*

The battle for the planet now joined, he took a moment to contemplate the space around him. The room was staffed but not crowded, and everyone present went about their jobs with measured speed and dedication. No one panicked, and for the most part it would not occur to them to do so. Novoloume approached all events with grace and proper respect for the forces of fate and history at work. No matter the outcome, they would face this challenge, as they had all challenges before it, with their heads held high and their dignity intact.

But many would probably appreciate some reassurance all the same, so he departed for his office down the hall. He needed to address his people.

Necha caught him as he reached the door. "Dean, I have dire news. The Rasu have been spotted approaching both Loudia and Effor Elafos."

His skin rippled for a breath; he subdued it. "I see. Please redirect those outbound Caeles Prisms to Cemohna and Hauni, then." They were smaller colonies, their infrastructure less robust, but they should be able to manage. "And do alert the governors of both planets to expect an influx of refugees."

"It will be done."

He faced the door with greater trepidation now. Three of his worlds were under attack by the enemy. Simultaneously. He spared a curse for the Directorate, to have hampered the Novoloume military for countless millennia. Strides had been made in the last fifteen years, but oh, the force they could have fielded if they had been allowed to advance unfettered!

Then he put those thoughts aside, for bitterness and rancor were traits unbecoming a leader. He could not afford them.

Still, the speech he'd been planning on giving to his citizens took a darker turn in his mind as he made his way to his office.

49

MIRAI

OMOIKANE INITIATIVE

Nika stood in the center of the Initiative's hub of operations, letting those present flow around her without resistance. The activity level was high, and occasionally someone bumped into her and murmured a passing apology as they continued on to their destination.

She sensed their thoughts brushing up against her mind, feathers tickling her mental barriers before being nudged on their way. The defensive techniques Mesme had taught her were working, and without her active intervention. Still, she felt a low-level friction from the effort deep in the base of her skull, as if she had a pebble in her shoe she couldn't dislodge. But it was far better than whimpering in a ball beneath her living room table and getting easier by the hour. With time and constant use, the pebble would erode into dust and trouble her no more.

A familiar warmth caressed her skin an instant before Dashiel's hand alighted at the small of her back. "How are you?"

"I'm good." She flashed him an easy smile over her shoulder. "How did it go with Lance?"

"How does it ever go with Palmer?" He made a show of grimacing. "Oh, fine. One of the takeaways from the Mirai battle was that we're weakest on the ground. The Rima Grenades do an excellent job of taking out Rasu atmospheric ships, but we don't want to go vaporizing entire city neighborhoods if we can avoid it. So I'm shifting two lines over to Rectifier production."

"Based on what I saw while I was flitting about the streets, this strikes me as a good idea."

"Yeah." He reached into his bag and pulled out a small program module. "I've been working on something for you. It needs a little more refinement, but I thought you could try it out and let me know if it's useful."

"Oh, what is it?"

"I designed a process for directed operation of the Kireme Boundaries. It treats the source as a sort of limited-use ceraff and sends the instructions on a kyoseil wave—"

"Like what I do."

"Exactly like what you do, or at least what I imagine you do. I think it works, but you'll need to tell me for certain."

She stared at the module curiously. "You're saying that if I load this program, I can activate the devices without having to 'touch' them individually?"

"That's the idea." He grinned, looking almost silly, which was something to see. "I want to help you, Nika. To ease your burdens. This is the only way I know how."

"Well, not the *only* way—"

The alarms went off in near unison, like the abrupt commencement of a strident symphony. At the same instant, as if one triggered the other, three threads snapped in the periphery of Nika's mind; the web of connections now constantly surrounding her sensory perception in an effusive halo frayed *here, there* and *there.*

Her gaze jumped up to the Big Wall in time to see red frames begin to flash around three of the panes.

SYNRA

KIYORA

EBISU

Her worst nightmare come to life in glaring cardinal light.

Dashiel groaned raggedly. "Dammit, Palmer was right. I hate it when he's right."

She grabbed his arm. "I need—"

"Privacy. I know. Let's get to your office."

"I can make it on my own, promise. You need to go to work, too."

"I didn't expect for you to get to try out the program in the field quite so soon, but here we are."

"I'll load it as soon as I can spare a second."

He nodded in affirmation—then grabbed her and kissed her, hard and fast. "We can do this. I love you."

"And I you, darling." She spun and raced for the lift.

MIRAI ONE

Cassidy rubbed massage oil over Joaquim's shoulder and back, concentrating on the area that had gotten sliced up in the Rasu's invasion of Mirai.

He hummed in sublime contentment. She had the hands of a goddess, truly. "You can keep doing this forever if you wish."

She chuckled lightly. "I'll negotiate down to another fifteen minutes. The repair bench did a good job patching you up, I admit. I can't see any residual marks or feel any scar tissue beneath the skin. I've only had to use a repair bench once or twice before—minor stuff. I didn't realize their capabilities were so advanced."

"The tech was a lifesaver for us in NOIR. Our benches were able to patch up almost anything short of limb loss or major organ failure."

"Oh. I see." Her voice dropped to a murmur, the hypnotic motions of her hands faltering, and he cringed. He had to learn to stop bringing up this kind of stuff all the time!

He twisted around and took her slick, oil-covered hands in his. "How much oil do we have left?"

After a few seconds, she relented and giggled against his lips. "Enough. For tonight, anyway. Might want to pick some up tomorrow if you expect to make a habit of this."

"Oh, I do. More than a habit. It risks becoming an obsession. Would you be all right with that?"

"Only if I can get a little reciprocal attention. In fact, I think a muscle in my back is clenching up now."

"Really? I had better take care of that straightaway." His hands dropped to the loose hem of her shirt and lifted it up—

An alert from DAF flashed in his comm system. He'd permanently back-doored into the Advisor Committee's network during the Mirai attack and set up a relay for military alerts. With Nika's new activities taking up so much of her mental bandwidth, he figured she'd probably forget to tell him when danger was afoot, and this way, she didn't have to.

His progress up Cassidy's midriff stalled as he reviewed the alert's contents. Rasu incoming to Kiyora. And Ebisu. *And Synra.* All three Rift Bubbles were down. Godsdamn those metal fiends!

He returned her shirt to its rightful location and squeezed her arm as he stood, then hunted around for where his own shirt had run off to. "I am so sorry, but I need to go."

"What?" She leapt up. "Go where? Why?"

He tried to steel himself for the coming argument. "The Rasu are attacking Synra. I told you it wasn't any safer there than it is here. But while it isn't our home any longer, I'll always feel a fond attachment to the old stomping ground. So I'm going to go help defend it."

Her eyes widened, her lips pinching tight. "Joaquim, no. Listen, I don't…I'm sorry I was so reluctant to settle here. I won't ask you to move to Synra anymore. I accept that we live on Mirai now, okay? So just stay. *Please.*"

He grabbed his tactical pack; he kept it stocked, but he quickly double-checked its contents on account of it getting such recent use. He'd restocked on archine grenades this morning, and none too soon. Also, he'd never returned the Rectifier Selene had lent him…a memory of tangled blonde hair and sweat-soaked skin flared in his mind, and he shoved it back where it belonged, which was behind an airtight door guarding a foreclosed past. The pack also now contained a proper defense shield as part of his regular loadout, as he tried never to repeat mistakes. Not combat ones, anyway.

When he finally looked up, Cassidy was wringing her hands as she paced in a tight circle.

What could he say to make her understand? Eloquence had never been his strong suit, and it had been a long time since he'd had to justify his actions to someone so important. "I can't sit here, helpless, while the Rasu are tearing up Synra. I *can't.*"

"You're wrong. You can sit right here with me. We can drink and laugh and make love, and let others worry about saving the world. You know what you can't do, Joaquim? You can't save the world."

Frustration began to burn at the edges of his composure. "Actually, I *can*. I saved every last Asterion from those contemptible Guides, once and for all. I rid the world of that psychopath—and your murderer—Blake Satair. I kicked the Rasu off of Namino."

"No, you didn't. Nika saved us from the Guides and drove the Rasu off Namino. You were merely her sidekick."

He fell onto the couch, the breath knocked flat out of his chest. "Excuse me?"

"And that's okay! You don't have to be larger than life. Not for me. I love you the way you are..." her gaze fell, and she dropped to her knees in front of him "...the way you were. Sweet, gentle Joaquim, who was good with his hands and quick with a joke. Isn't it enough to be with me? To enjoy our quiet, not-world-saving life together? Because it's all I want."

His jaw worked, clashing through a torrent of words in search of the right ones. "How many times do I have to tell you? This is who I am now. It would be a betrayal of my principles for me to sit here and get drunk and sloppy when this damnable enemy is tearing up our civilization. The last thing I want to do is disappoint you, but I can't turn my back on what my gut tells me is the right thing to do." He stood and stepped around her, then draped his pack over his shoulder. "I'm sorry, but I have to go."

The door slid open when he approached it. Her continued silence drained all the air out of the room, and his chest tightened from the effort of breathing as he turned to face her. "Tell me you'll still be here when I get back."

Despair leaked out of her eyes as she sank the rest of the way down to the floor and hugged her legs…but after a second, she nodded.

It would have to do. He offered her a tight smile, as if that would somehow ease the pain he damn well knew he was inflicting on her, then pivoted and left the apartment.

Halfway down the hall, he tried to open one of those crafty wormholes, destination downtown Synra One—but no such luck.

Nika, is there a quantum block on Synra?

Yes, but not for much longer. I'm just about to…

…there. It's down, but it probably won't stay that way. Are you headed there?

Yep. Want to come with me?

I wish I could, but I'm afraid this battle's all in my head.

That struck him as uncommonly funny, and bitter laughter wrestled with the ache in his chest as he focused his intentional thoughts on tearing a hole in space. What a strange journey she was on.

50

MIRAI

OMOIKANE INITIATIVE

*N*ika: Lance, the quantum block on Ebisu is at planetary coordinates latitude 23.1052268, longitude -52.6864541.
Lance: On it.

Nika's mind now raced across parsecs and stars to land on Synra. She willed herself to ignore the masses of charging aubergine metal to focus on her goal. The hole in *this* world, where the elemental waves of the cosmos fell silent. As on Kiyora and Ebisu, the Rasu had hidden it more cleverly this time around. Deep in the tropical jungles of the equator, invisible to common visual sight.

Nika: Synra: Planetary coordinates latitude 53.1033625, longitude -34.9959566.

The block on Kiyora was demolished by Lance's ships while she'd been searching the Synra landscape, and she flung her mind back across the galaxy to reactivate the planetary Rift Bubble there. Three Kireme Boundaries had been distributed by now in Kiyora One and Two, and she activated them as well. By the time she finished, Lance's forces had destroyed the block on Synra.

For a blink, her world was quiet. Her gaze went to Dashiel's module, which she'd placed on the floor beside her. She picked it up and turned it over twice, then quickly connected the fiber snaking out from it to the port at the base of her neck and loaded the program. She studied the code flow curiously as it integrated into the appropriate process.

Dashiel had the foresight to embed an identifier in every Kireme Boundary device. Once she triggered the activation order, the command transmitted like a beacon on a direct kyoseil wave to every identifier. It also appeared to be smart enough to recognize when a particular device was already active and null the order on arrival. The program would need to be updated with additional identifiers as more devices were rolled out, but to do so was a simple matter.

Gods, he was kind of brilliant.

Lance: A new block is up on Kiyora. They came prepared this time.

What an understatement. She reversed course as rapidly as possible and returned to Kiyora to begin her search. But she couldn't keep herself from studying the advancing Rasu formations as they fanned out, demolishing the lovely native flora of Kiyora beneath their unremitting advance.

Nika: Lance, I need an estimate of the number of Rasu on the ground or in orbit at Kiyora.

Lance: Best guess? Two hundred eighty thousand and growing.

Nika: Noted. The block is at planetary coordinates latitude 31.4442167, longitude -22.5163321.

While she waited, she readied the activation order in the program. She'd still need to activate the Rift Bubble directly, but that part was easy.

When the confirmation arrived from Lance, she sent the order in the same breath she cast her mind to the Rift Bubble. Three—no, now four—Kireme Boundaries turned themselves back on what felt like instantaneously.

She checked on them manually, just in case, but everything was working properly.

A smile tugged at her lips; the time saved was minimal in the grand scheme, but the benefit to her mental resilience might be beyond measure.

It works wonderfully, darling. Thank you so much.

I'm glad.

He sounded harried. Directing the delivery of gear and replacement weapons across three planets at once during pitched warfare was no easy matter. She found herself wishing she could concoct a device to make his life easier, too.

A thread snapped in her awareness.

Lance: Another quantum block is up at—

Nika: Ebisu. I know.

It took her a minute to locate it, tucked away in a cave in the rocky steppes of the southern polar region.

Quantum block destroyed.

Ebisu Rift Bubble activated.

Kireme Boundaries activated, and their diameters adjusted.

She sagged against the wall of her office. She was stronger now than when they'd attacked Mirai, and with Dashiel's program in hand, she'd be able to do this for days if that was what it took. But even as she catapulted her awareness across kiloparsecs in a few scant seconds, she could only be in one place at a time.

Another block up, another bubble down. And in each sequence, more damage was inflicted. More lives and property and resources and military assets lost. There was hardly any time now for people to evacuate during the short intervals when the blocks were lifted.

The math was simple, its result inescapable. They were going to lose.

She didn't bother to ask Lance about reinforcements from Concord. A quick ping across a few kyoseil waves told her Concord forces now fought the Rasu at no less than seven worlds. When they'd first entered into an alliance with Concord, the Dominion's military capability had been but a pittance, and their new ally had stepped in to pick up the slack. The Dominion had freely shared its technological advances, and vice versa; the alliance had been and continued to be a fruitful one. But they each had their own worlds to fight for now.

Again. She swept across the arid deserts of northern Synra until she zeroed in on her target. Would that she could blast the minaret of despicable Rasu metal with her mind.

But the Asterion fighters did the job well enough, and when Synra's protections were once more in place, she buried her face in her hands.

They weren't going to be able to keep up. Their military wasn't large enough, their weapons not powerful enough. With new Rasu continuing to arrive in their stellar systems each hour, she suspected a hundred-fold increase in their fleets wouldn't be enough. Not for so many enemies in so many places at once. The Rasu had made excellent use of the one hundred thirty-eight seconds they'd possessed the Rift Bubble access code, and in the intervening days they'd positioned assets and resources all across the Axis Worlds to better respond to her people's countermeasures. To knock down everything she did again and again and *again*.

The risk had never been that Asterions weren't clever or resourceful enough to defeat any given Rasu assault, or that Concord's commanding military wouldn't be able to match the enemy's weapons on the field of battle. Rather, it had always been the prospect that the Rasu would overwhelm them with sheer, inexhaustible numbers.

She at last allowed her thoughts to venture to the one place she'd done her best to foreclose all possibility of consideration.

If there was any other solution, she'd seek it. Any other way, she'd scour the universe to find it. But today, the Rasu were robbing her of the opportunity to do so that she'd believed she'd have. Was the Rasu's endgame at hand? If so, they had no choice but to set their own gambit in motion, didn't they?

The sacrifice stood to be beyond imagining—but the alternative was extinction. A single tear fell to carve its way down her cheek as she sent Alex a message.

About that plan of yours.

51

CONCORD HQ

RASU WAR ROOM

Alex stepped inside the Rasu War Room to find the level of bedlam she'd expected. Aides rushed to and fro for no apparent reason, with no clear destination in mind. Her mother stood in front of two banks of screens; every few seconds, she reached up and nudged blocks of data from one to another or up or down a list. Miriam's lips moved, but whatever she was saying didn't penetrate the commotion.

Alex stepped into the fray, dodging bulky military bodies to cut her way around the table and reach her mother's side.

Miriam's focus didn't deviate from the screens. "Now is not a great time, Alex."

"I know it isn't. The thing is, I have an idea on how to distract the Rasu from this new push they're making, and I wanted to talk to you about it."

"Will your idea stop the assaults on Nopreis, Serifos, Acacia or the Dominion worlds?"

"Not immediately, no."

"Then I cannot entertain it at the moment. I'm sorry. Lives are being lost every single second I hesitate—" the timbre of her voice dropped "—they destroyed how many? Yes, it's an inevitable result of such powerful antimatter weapons. Adjust defensive maneuvers to TP-Delta 3A in order to protect the vulnerable vessels."

"They're still using antimatter weapons?"

"Still, indeed. In the last day, virtually every Rasu reinforcement has arrived wielding them." Her mother shifted to half-face Alex, her expression softening the slightest bit. "I am sorry I can't spare any time right now. I do want to hear your ideas, and I deeply hope I can soon come up for air long enough to discuss them. We'll have some tea and talk about how to save civilization."

"You'll have tea. I'll have wine." Alex forced a smile; one glance at the tactical screens suggested that meeting wasn't likely to happen soon. If matters didn't begin to improve, it might never arrive. "I look forward to it. Good luck."

"Luck is not a factor—though I wouldn't begrudge its timely appearance."

"Kindly kick the fuckers' asses for me." She turned and elbowed her way back through the sea of wandering officers and headed for the door.

RW

ROMANE

"You can't put dinosaurs in a holo set during the Industrial Revolution! That's not historically accurate."

"But wouldn't it be awesome if it was? Watch—this Tyrannosaurus Rex here is going to battle your steam engine train."

"Mom, get Jonas out of my holo game!"

Kennedy rolled her eyes at the heavens, then adopted an indulgent mien as she went over to where the kids sat playing in the middle of the living room floor, surrounded by translucent projections and flashing lights. "Jonas, you have your own holo game, remember? Why don't you play with it instead. You can let your dinosaurs rampage through Paris and climb the Eiffel Tower if you want—but not in your sister's game."

"She's no fun." Jonas dragged himself a few meters across the floor and *harumphed* against the front of the chaise. "When you get jealous, Brae, you can't come bring your stupid ancient machines into my game."

"Like I would ever want to."

Kennedy stared at them for another few seconds, ensuring they simmered down and returned to their respective adventures, then rejoined Alex at the dining room table. "*Anyway.*"

Alex chuckled. "They seem to have recovered from their ordeal."

"They do, don't they? I keep hunting for scars—the psychological kind. Braelyn's had a few nightmares, but she's braving through them pretty well. Jonas has gotten a little too interested in weapons, but Noah thinks that will fade eventually. But, yes, they are doing so much better than I had any right to hope for."

"And you? How are you doing?"

"Well, I nearly burst into tears every time I look at either of them, so there's that. I'm smothering them with affection, which is driving them crazy. They went back to school three days ago, and it almost broke me. I should be at HQ today, because now the Rasu really are tearing up the world, but I can't seem to leave them for very long. I am working—don't think I'm not working—but I admit it's a half-hearted effort. I justify my negligence by telling myself all the upgrades I developed are now out there in the field or being installed on ships around the clock. They'll help win the day, or not, without my further input. But there are always more upgrades to design, aren't there?"

"Hopefully not too many more will be needed. That's why I came by. I'm about to head out on a mission, and I'll actually be gone for several days. Maybe a week. If all goes as planned, the Rasu will be backing off soon. Possibly abandoning this fight entirely."

"What? For how long?"

"I can't say. Ideally forever, though I'm hesitant to expect that. But I do think I'll be buying us time to up our war game."

"Time would be good. Time is…" Kennedy's gaze drifted over to her children "…the only thing we have. Time with each other."

"And time to save one another." Alex stood, leaning over to hug Kennedy. "Don't be too hard on yourself. You went through a terrible ordeal—but you're out the other side now, and your family's safe." Not safe from the Rasu, but her friend didn't need to hear what she already knew said aloud. "When I get back, I'll babysit them for an entire day and send you to a spa on Atlantis."

"Will you? Please? The one at the Emerald Coast Resort?"

"It's a deal. But now I need to run."

"Sure. Universe to save again and all."

I save the people who will save the universe. If it can be saved.

She would save it all right, but she refused to dance to the Kats' tune. She would do it on her own terms.

52

MIRAI

CONCEPTUAL RESEARCH LAB

Caleb joined Alex in the cockpit just as the *Siyane* settled onto the landing pad at the private spaceport outside Mirai One. "The engineering well is all cleaned out and ready for its new cargo."

"Thank you." She kept one eye on the log until the ship was secured, then stood. Outside the viewport, the jagged, off-kilter skyline of Mirai One hinted at the destruction the Rasu had inflicted only a few days ago. "Let's go find out where things stand."

There was no time to waste, so she opened a wormhole in the middle of the cabin to the Conceptual Research Lab, and they stepped through it.

Dashiel stood at a sleek workstation, checking through a lengthy list of items, while Nika sat rigid in a chair against the wall, her shoulders stiff and her gaze parsecs away. But she seemed to sense their arrival, for after a second she blinked and stood, coming over to greet them.

The expression which replaced Nika's blank stare was so distraught that Alex instinctively hugged her. "How go the battles?"

"Not good." She halfheartedly returned the hug before stepping back. "We've had to abandon Ebisu to the Rasu, in the hope that we will then stand a chance to keep control of Synra and Kiyora. We were only able to evacuate three hundred thousand or so people from Ebisu before we had to put the Firewall Protocol into place and shut the d-gates down."

"Can't people open their own wormholes now, though?"

"Not with a quantum block in effect, they can't."

"Right. That's terrible."

"I hear it's not going much better on your side. A moment, please."

A vacant look overtook Nika's features once again, and Alex glanced at Dashiel in question.

"She is having to remotely seek out the locations of quantum blocks on Synra and Kiyora every time the Rasu erect new ones. Also reactivating the Rift Bubbles once the blocks are down."

Not long after the events in the Oneiroi Nebula, Nika had called her bonding with the kyoseil a 'gift.' It sounded to Alex like it was proving to be a terrible burden instead.

Nika blinked, and life returned to her features. "Sorry. It's probably going to happen a few more times. Honestly, more than a few."

"Don't apologize. You're making sure your people can continue to fight. To answer your question, no, it isn't going any better on our side. And we don't have anyone with your ability to track down the quantum blocks using kyoseil."

"But you do have a *lot* more ships."

"That we do." Alex thought about her mother in the War Room, playing five-dimensional chess with forty million warships. The only problem was, her opponent was playing a different game, and it hadn't shared the rulebook. "So, what's our status?"

Nika tilted her head in Dashiel's direction, and he brought up a new screen in front of him. Deeper in the lab, beyond the workstation and screens, a chunk of Rasu half a meter in diameter hung motionless within a force field within a glass enclosure, which was also wrapped in a force field.

"I have successfully inserted new programming into our Rasu virutox. The information it contains includes details on the nature of kyoseil as used by Asterions and the locations of multiple kyoseil deposits, all of them far from Dominion or Concord space. It also includes a short-term memory wipe that should keep the details of its time here secret, as well as what I think is a directive—or at least an irresistible compulsion—to dock with the nearest Rasu the unit comes upon. Otherwise, I'd be afraid they would high-tail it back here to their previous parent the instant you released them."

Caleb studied the captured Rasu, a frown lining his features. "Could a small Rasu unit such as this one really cross galaxies under its own power?"

"Maybe, maybe not. It could die trying, for all we know. But it should instead do as it's told and join up with the local faction to spread the word about kyoseil."

Nika's hand worked at her jaw in obvious agitation. "We should have started this process sooner. If I'd agreed to the plan immediately, the Rasu might not have bothered to attack our worlds a second time. The destruction going on right now on Synra and Kiyora is on my head."

"No, it *isn't*." Dashiel came over and grasped her gently by the shoulders. "No one should have to wrestle with the decisions you've made in the last week. You're the bravest person I've ever known. All we can do is start now and move forward. Okay?"

Alex surreptitiously took several steps back to give them a little space, and Caleb placed a comforting hand on her waist.

Nika nodded weakly. "Okay."

"Besides, Palmer is digging in like the stubborn ass he is on Synra and Kiyora both. They're quagmires, but we have the weapons and the willpower needed to keep fighting until the plan works."

"If it works."

"You're giving the Rasu the ultimate carrot. Their greatest desire. It'll work."

"Let's hope so." Nika's eyes unfocused again, and this time no one commented on it. Dashiel squeezed her shoulder, then shot them a concerned glance as he returned to the workstation and entered a command.

An awkward silence lingered—well, awkward to Alex, anyway—and Caleb finally gestured to the enclosure. "Have you programmed this unit yet?"

"No. I just finished running the last debugging routines on the virutox right before you arrived. It passed, though, so I'm ready to do so now. If this Rasu doesn't spaz out, melt or explode, I've got six additional ones lined up and prepped in the next room. Seven is how many you decided on, correct?"

"Yep," Alex replied. "An odd number seems best, for the same reasons the Ruda coalesced into an even number of Supremes—sorry, you don't know about them. Anyway, we can't say how many discrete factions there are in the Rasu empire, but we've identified a dozen. Triggering seven of them should be enough to sow a suitable amount of chaos." She shrugged. "Also, I can't fit any more than seven of those cages in the *Siyane's* hull."

"Understood. I'll have them delivered to the spaceport as soon as I'm done."

Nika abruptly rejoined them, reaching out to grab Alex's hand with some intensity. "I'll come to the ship when the cargo does. Until then, I have a couple of things I need to take care of."

"We'll be ready. See you soon."

RW

NIKA'S FLAT

Nika stood on the balcony of her flat and gazed out at the setting sun as it melted into the waters of Hataori Harbor. Since rediscovering her old life, the view had always brought her a measure of peace, and she'd sought it now in order to do this last, hard thing.

The skyline buzzed with cranes and drones and construction mechs scurrying over scaffolding. In a couple of months, the city would be better than it had been before; such was the way of her people.

Assuming the Rasu didn't find another route onto Mirai, of course. Assuming a single piece of Rasu didn't lurk somewhere beneath cover at this moment, plotting to disable the planetary Rift Bubble once again and allow the enemy to launch a renewed assault on Mirai. Assuming the Rasu currently ravaging Synra, Kiyora and Ebisu didn't discover a way around the Firewall protections and invade through the d-gates.

Assuming she and Alex didn't fail in their mission.

The sabotaged Rasu units were on their way to the *Siyane* now, and she had only a few minutes to spare before she'd be expected onboard. Before she'd departed the lab, Dashiel had hugged her close and whispered how she was doing the right thing, the necessary thing, and she had chosen to believe him.

Still, she'd waited until the final possible minute. So long as she didn't take this step, she could call the plan off. But her worlds were dying, and they were out of options.

Properly reminded of the reason why she was here—of the grave importance of her actions now—she deactivated the kyoseil filter she'd of necessity imposed upon her vision and spent a minute watching the waves cavort through the city. They wove between and through millions of souls and along every piece of technology holding their civilization aloft. They soared into the sky on their way to distant points across the cosmos.

Then she closed her eyes and focused all her intentionality into projecting a clear voice in her mind.

I know you are acutely aware of the tragedy befalling our people today. I know you feel the pain of those who are suffering, as you have felt the anguish of every Asterion who has fallen in the street or been captured by the Rasu to be tortured.

I believe in my heart that you want this suffering to end. I believe that you want us to live, as you yourself want to live.

I hope you understand how Asterions are on the side of life, always. Of love and optimism and wonder and good. I hope you understand the Rasu will end the pursuit of these special things if we do not stop them. They will end all life in the universe save their own, wherever they find it, if we do not stop them.

So I'm coming to you now to ask for your help. We have devised a plan to strike back at our enemy. It's a gamble, I admit, but it's the best chance we have to stop the Rasu's carnage. And in order to make it work, I must ask you to perform an act of supreme sacrifice. An act you have so bravely and valiantly resisted performing until now, even in the face of incessant torture by the Rasu.

I need you to turn your capabilities on for the Rasu. I need you to allow these horrific monsters to use you as they see fit, no matter how abhorrent those acts become. I need you to do what you do—to serve as a conduit for information—at their directive and on their demand.

I don't know if my word carries any sway with you, but understand that no matter what evils the Rasu commit using you, you are absolved of all responsibility for those evils. You are the conduit, not the actor, and you do this at my behest. Let your conscience be clear, for I will carry that weight and bear that responsibility for you.

This is my request. This is my plea. For all deserving life in the universe, will you do as I ask?

The kyoseil did not use words to communicate; for all the wonders it showed her and miraculous feats it allowed her to accomplish, they had never engaged in what one could call a conversation, and they did not do so now.

Yet every nerve in her body *clanged* with its answer. It felt mournful, like a yawning chasm of sorrow opening up beneath her feet, but one buttressed by resolve and perhaps even...pride.

She tried not to project emotions upon the ancient, enigmatic life form, but she couldn't shake the notion that what it conveyed was in fact pride in finally being given a way to assist in this battle for survival.

Thank you. With all my heart, thank you. I will take it from here.

PART IV

TIME'S ARROW

<h1 style="text-align:center">53</h1>

GALENAI HOMEWORLD
MAFFEI I GALAXY

Marlee floated above Galenai Habitat NE3, the sterile name the Consulate's Protected Species Division had given the city where they'd experienced the stunning encounter with the elder Galenai. She'd choose a more inventive name soon and replace the identifier in all the databases.

Well, her consciousness floated above the city, anyway. This sidespace gig was so amazing. She already couldn't remember how she'd ever lived without the ability to cast her awareness wherever she pleased and whenever she chose.

In this instance, sidespace solved the problem of how to visit the Galenai without a ship, and also without spilling water all over her apartment floor. The apartment had caught fire, thanks to Cupcake; if it flooded, too, she'd have to declare it a lost cause and write it off altogether, by which she meant pay a hefty repair fine on her way to a new place to live.

The upgrades to the Galenai city in the month and a half since they'd visited in the *Siyane* were incredible. They'd added an additional level to the glass-type walls surrounding certain clusters of coral buildings and laid two new piping systems from the geothermal power plants. An expansion to the city was taking shape on the southern border. She made a note to program the observational sensors to focus their cams on this area, as it represented an opportunity to learn how the Galenai built their infrastructure from scratch. Also, a new structure was under construction near the center of the city, though she was at a loss to discern its purpose. On the whole, the level of activity displayed throughout the city seemed to border on frenzied...no, enthusiastic would be a better descriptor.

Was all this activity a direct result of the encounter they'd had with the one she'd decided to call 'Papa Galen'? It surely wouldn't be the first time the discovery of the existence of alien life had spurred a leap forward in a species. In fact, she knew it wasn't. Historical data filled her mind, as she'd accessed the vast Concord databanks and searched on the topic without consciously deciding to do so.

Do you really think your silly little encounter was important enough to trigger societal evolution?

YES.

How very arrogant of you.

No, it's simple fact. A truth of sentient beings' nature.

And so what if it was arrogance? She deserved to be proud of what happened that day. Not only had she put her language skills to excellent use, on the spot, in a diplomatic manner. She'd defused the situation and engaged in a fruitful dialogue with an alien species—the first such dialogue the aliens had ever experienced.

She sensed the antagonism of the retort yet to be spoken by the voice in her head. For a minute her focus wavered from the Galenai, diverting to her own festering despair. She hated the ridiculous voice! This wasn't supposed to have happened, dammit.

For all the wonders she now enjoyed—not least of which was the ability she used at this precise moment to levitate her consciousness beneath the ocean on an alien world—they were all soured, even poisoned, by the voice. It loomed like a constant presence in the shadows, waiting to tear her down the instant she took initiative or dared to dream of grand adventures.

She'd done everything she could think of to silence it. She'd scoured every single line of her upgraded cybernetics code. Every. Single. Line. And found no evidence of another sentience hanging out in there with her. She'd reviewed research papers on the Prevo transition, searching for clues. Her experience didn't match what they experienced. It didn't match anything.

And still the voice prattled on her head, caustic and…mean.

She couldn't keep going like this. She hated—*despised*—asking for help, and it was a testament to just how desperate she felt that she found she was ready to do so. Something had to change.

She forced herself to check in on the Galenai again, and made several mental notes of items to include in a report she'd file later. They truly were making great strides here. But she didn't detect any evidence of worrisome arms buildups or preparations for hostile activity, or anything requiring an immediate and official Concord response. They had a bit more time.

Distracted and disheartened in spite of the exciting developments here, she let her consciousness slip back into her body where it rested on the futon in her apartment. Then, before she talked herself out of it, she sent a message to Dr. Canivon.

54

CONCORD HQ

RASU WAR ROOM

The explosion whited-out the large screen, and Miriam swore the conflagration bled out from its edges into the room. It was an illusion, or possibly a metaphor, as the consequences of this particular explosion would soon consume the War Room and everything within its purview.

She didn't need to wait for the first on-scene reports to arrive reporting the destruction of the gateway and its accompanying Arx. She knew what she was looking at; she'd seen it before.

Thomas (Stalwart II): 'Eight Igni missiles launched from two enemy battlecruisers. Target is...the Arx.'

Commandant Solovy (Stalwart II): "Virginia, all vessels, get clear of the Arx!"

A massive blast roiled short of the Arx as a Federation frigate sacrificed itself by accelerating into the path of one of the missiles. A second missile impacted the AFS Montreal less than half a megameter from the Arx. The remaining six impacted the Arx directly.

Explosions rippled as the deadly antimatter weapons ripped apart nearly three megatonnes of habitat-grade material, feeding on themselves and the wreckage created to billow outward and consume nearby vessels and debris in a self-propagating chain reaction.

Visuals were impossible, so Miriam hurriedly called up broad spectrum scans in an attempt to determine what remained amongst the destruction. But by the time she was able to gain that information...nothing remained. The collision of matter and antimatter had annihilated everything it touched.

The Arx.

The more than ten thousand civilians occupying it.

An entire EA regiment's worth of vessels and their crews.

The EAS Virginia and its 23,819 crew members, including Christopher Rychen.

Gone.

She could certainly use Christopher's counsel right about now, not to mention his skill on the battlefield, though she also knew he'd be just as frustrated as her. And in his absence, for a single moment, despair fought for dominance in her mind.

While winning most of the battles—eventually—she'd harbored the sneaking suspicion that she'd been slowly losing the war for a while. Now, she was suddenly losing it very quickly. For every battle in which they clawed back ownership of a planet, the Rasu attacked two more. The (now somewhat less than) forty million warships she controlled were beginning to get a little thin on the ground as the battlespace extended its tentacles across multiple galaxies at once.

Despite all her exhaustive preparations and tactical planning, she was standing here in the War Room doing triage. Scrambling to put out fires instead of taking the initiative and catching the enemy unawares. Giving ground instead of taking it.

Off to her left, two screens chronicled the deteriorating situation at Nopreis, while a third monitored the status of two Novoloume colonies. One would likely be declared lost within the hour. They continued to hold their own at Serifos and Acacia, but in ten days they'd been unable to push the Rasu back for longer than a few hours at a time. Meanwhile, the Rasu launched additional attacks on several smaller Anaden colonies in Andromeda, and in the crucial initial hours of those conflicts, there were no Rift Bubbles to be had. She was cycling fleet forces in and out of the various battles every eighteen hours, but soon there were going to be no more fresh legs to sub in.

During the final hours of the Metigen War, humanity had

surmounted conspiracies and sabotage to come together as one, upping its game by a large margin to turn the tables on the enemy, and their leap of faith had saved them. But try as she might, she couldn't see a way through to pulling such a move in this war.

Humanity was united internally and alongside an array of powerful allies. They had the infrastructure, they had the ships, they had the technology, they had the weapons. And if matters continued on their current course, none of that was going to be enough.

She spared a thought to wonder where Alex was right now. Hopefully not flying around one of the sieged colonies hunting for quantum blocks, but she wouldn't place a bet on her daughter being someplace safer. Undoubtedly somewhere trying to do *something* to stop the Rasu. But this time, it might be beyond even Alex's talents to outsmart this enemy—because it wasn't about smarts, it was about numbers. And now the Rasu were upping the stakes immeasurably again. Since the beginning, her efforts had been directed with a mind to ensure this day never came, yet it had arrived nonetheless.

So be it.

As the first devastating reports began to stream in from the site of the gateway explosion, she opened a holocomm with Prime Minister Gagnon, Federation Chairman Duca, Romane Governor Tremblay and Corradeo Praesidis. She hadn't forewarned them or asked permission, and none were prepared to be on-screen. She didn't give them an opportunity to compose themselves, either.

"Gentlemen, you need to activate all Rift Bubbles and planetary defenses immediately."

Gagnon half-turned toward the holo, annoyance at the interruption pinching his features. "Where do you believe such a step is needed?"

"Everywhere you possess the ability to do so. The MW-Andromeda I Gateway has been destroyed. The Rasu are now in the Milky Way."

55

HIRLAS

PEGASUS DWARF GALAXY

Felzeor soared in through the open wall and alighted upon the kitchen table. A large worm—more of a slug, really—wiggled in his beak. With a jerk of his head, the worm vanished into his mouth, and he swallowed dramatically.

Eren grimaced as he brought his plate of fried *wyau* and *frita* to the table. "I could have cooked you some proper food, you realize."

"No disrespect to your cooking, Eren, but when I am home, I enjoy reverting to…old routines, let us call them. The sunrise was spectacular, and I enjoyed the hunt for my meal."

"I can't argue with that. Still…" he gestured to his plate "…warm, properly spiced, *cooked* food?"

"Yes, yes. For lunch?"

"Eh, I doubt we'll be here by lunchtime. Nyx has sent me two messages this morning demanding to know when I'll be back on Ares to give her an update on the Macskaf investigation. She's squirming to move in on the Barisan agitators."

"She is quite the slave driver, isn't she? I don't understand why you work with her. Do you remember when she tried to kill me at Plousia?"

"Do you remember when she *did* kill me at Plousia?" He munched on a piece of crisp *frita*. "I work with her because Corradeo asked me to do so. He trusts her, though there's a bit of a familial blind spot at play there. Granted, there's no denying she's got skills. She was one of only twelve *elasson* Inquisitors in the empire for many millennia. She knows how to find people, uncover secrets and take down bad guys."

"I suppose. But she also took down good guys—like us!"

"She definitely tried. But I'm starting to suspect there might be a teeny-tiny, withered and shrunken actual heart buried deep in her chest. Maybe. I'll let you know if I ever find it."

"Yes, please, though I will remain reluctant to trust her." Felzeor tapped around on the table. "I should be heading back to CINT, anyway. Our team is getting a new member to try out next week, and I expect we'll be sent on a short assignment soon."

"Drae hasn't filled mine and…" his brain lurched over her name "…our slots on the team?"

"No. He keeps rejecting people. And I don't blame him! You are hard to replace."

"Thank you for saying so."

"It's true. Part of me thinks that Drae doesn't want to replace you at all. While you *are* hard to replace, he keeps coming up with dubious excuses for why every candidate isn't a good fit. Between you and me, I think Director Navick is becoming frustrated with him. But I could be wrong. Maybe Drae will approve of this next candidate." Felzeor rested his tail feathers on the table and began cleaning his chin. "I appreciate you inviting me to come stay here for the night. Dinner at Caleb's place was lots of fun—though it did get a mite strange when those other people showed up—and I hope we can do it again next month. But I'll take any chance I have to spend time with you."

"Now you're just buttering me up. What do you want?"

"Nothing! Nothing at all."

Eren gazed at him expectantly.

"Perhaps a bite of your *frita*?"

"Uh-huh." He slid the plate over to the other side of the table. "Knock yourself out. I made too much for me to eat, anyway." He was still cooking for two. Old habits and all. "Tell Drae he needs to cut these potential team members a little slack. They'll never be me, of course, but in time he might be able to whip one or two of them into fighting shape—"

His cybernetics *hissed* in his head, like he'd taken an electric jolt to the base of his skull. It wasn't painful, exactly, but—and they fell silent. He tried to access the messaging system and got nothing. Not so much as a blank virtual screen.

In his new role as Advocacy Chief of Intelligence for Non-Anaden Affairs, he'd been trying to pay attention to intergalactic events, even if their relevance to the Advocacy wasn't immediately obvious. As such, one possibility leapt to the front of his mind.

A deep *boom* shattered the sound barrier off to the north, in the direction of the nearest city, Choeda, and his suspicion was all but confirmed.

He leapt up from the table, knocking his chair to the floor. "Felzeor, I think the Rasu are attacking. I'm going to get you to the spaceport and on a ship out of here." Were there apt to be any ships willing to fly with quantum tech nonfunctional? Possibly if he bribed a pilot with a great deal of money.

"What? Attacking my home? Oh, dear, this is terrible. Are you going to leave with me?"

"No." He rushed into the other room, where he grabbed a bag and started tossing weapons and other gear into it. "The Rasu have activated a quantum block, so Concord will have a hard time getting troops on the ground here. I intend to round up some people I know and see about causing what trouble I can until the cavalry arrives."

"Then I will help you. I, too, know people who will want to defend our home."

He stopped his packing and gazed at his friend, a sinking feeling bottoming out in his gut. It would be a long shot to get Felzeor offworld, if he were honest. And he knew the determined tenor of that squeaky voice. Felzeor was a hero; a freedom fighter; an anarch. Naturally he would insist on fighting for his homeworld. "Okay. I won't argue. Grab whatever you brought with you, and let's get to the hovercar."

RW

The forest bordering the north half of Choeda was already ablaze by the time they approached the outskirts. A few pitiful laser strikes arced into the sky from the surface, chasing the dark, menacing Rasu ships overhead. But only a few.

The Directorate had forbidden planetary defenses on non-Anaden worlds, save for basic asteroid-class deflection arrays. In the fifteen years since the Directorate had fallen, a nascent Hirlas defense force had begun to take shape, but it was barely getting started. Concord was an excellent steward and protector, and as a result, a sense of urgency simply hadn't taken root.

But at Cosime's insistence, he'd consulted on some of the defense force's training programs a few years back, so he knew the people in charge of the organization. He bet they'd raced to gather at the Hamid Center in the southeast sector of the city as soon as the attack began.

Eren banked the hovercar to the east as an explosion ripped into the Aruchel Choeden—the Great Tree—at the center of the city, and he cursed under his breath. The tree was over eighteen thousand years old, and among the most sacred monuments on the planet. It also happened to house the regional communications network and the bulk of the local government facilities.

While the Naraida could not match the Anadens for their level and variety of technology, they were not a backward people. They merely worked to blend their technology into their surroundings, foregoing metal and cement and sharp edges for the more forgiving materials of nature.

He didn't know if the Rasu knew this, or if they'd just bombed the tree because it was big and obvious, but either way, they'd inflicted immeasurable psychological *and* practical damage with that single strike.

His heart was heavy as he raced down the winding cobblestone street toward the Hamid Center. No army, no defenses to speak of and, for now, no help from the stars. The Naraida and the Volucri didn't stand a chance.

But this was his adopted home. This had been *her* home, and he would defend it as zealously as she would have insisted on doing.

56

SIYANE

GENNISI GALAXY

The Rasu unit gazed coldly at Caleb through the multiple layers of glass and force fields. Its eyes, whatever they consisted of, followed his movements as he cinched up the fetters until the square enclosure refused to budge in any direction, while Akeso murmured in his mind.

Do you think it is daring us to try to keep it prisoner?

I think it isn't doing anything. It's all in my head—it doesn't even have eyes.

Neither do I, yet I see much.

He chuckled under his breath, breaking the discomfiting spell. *Fair point.*

Is it aware of us?

Oh, yes. Since Dashiel altered the virutox so it wouldn't poison the units, the Rasu isn't inert. Merely restrained. Restrained enough that it doesn't matter what it might be thinking about us from its cage.

He checked the restraining ties a final time, then moved on to the next enclosure and its occupant. Two more to secure, and he couldn't wait to be done with his task and leave this stygian menagerie behind.

RW

Caleb cleared the top of the spiral stairs with extra vigor in his step. "All done."

Alex and Nika were standing on opposite sides of the data center table, marking up an intergalactic map. What had once been an undifferentiated mass of Rasu-controlled territory was now divided into no less than twelve sectors.

Alex winced in his direction. "Thank you. I know that wasn't fun."

"No, no, we had a grand time. They invited Akeso and I over for drinks when we're next in their sector."

"Uh-huh. Remind me to have another engagement on that night."

"Yeah, me, too." He sidled up beside her and motioned to the map. "So, what's the plan?"

"We've marked each target in order of desirability based on a number of factors. Location relative to friendly territory and to other factions, concentration of Rasu, apparent strength, distance to the nearest kyoseil cache, and so on. Obviously, we only have seven saboteurs, but we chose five backup locations in case some of our first choices don't pan out for whatever reason."

"Good thinking. And since I just finished locking down the saboteurs in the engineering well, walk me through the deployment plan, please."

"Yes, all your hard work will soon be undone. We'll stealth in as close as we dare to a Rasu stellar stronghold. Then we'll don environment suits and mag boots. Valkyrie will seal off the engineering well and open the ramp, and we'll detach one of the enclosures and send it off into space. We'll retreat to a slightly safer distance, then Nika will...." She gestured across the table to their companion.

"I can turn off the force fields remotely. Also, fibers are embedded in one side of the enclosure, and an electrical signal sent through them will melt the surrounding glass composite. Once both steps are accomplished, the Rasu unit will be free. Over the next several minutes, the jettisoned enclosure will dissolve entirely, leaving no evidence behind that it was ever there."

"Sounds straightforward enough. What about—"

A message from Corradeo Praesidis arrived in his eVi. Those were quite rare, so he opened it immediately.

Caleb,

I hate to be the bearer of bad news, but I believe you would want to know that Hirlas has come under attack by the Rasu. Unfortunately, it did so while both Eren and your mutual friend, Felzeor, were in residence. As the planet is being subjected to a quantum block, I have been unable to reach either of them since the attack began.

Concord is devoting every resource to repelling the Rasu. I will update you when I learn more.

—Your Friend,

Corradeo

Caleb sank onto the couch and dropped his head into his hands.

"What's wrong?" Alex was instantly at his side, her arm around his shoulders.

"The Rasu have attacked Hirlas. Eren and Felzeor are trapped there."

"Oh, no. Give me a minute."

I see your memories. This is the planet where we mourned the one whom we could not save from Death.

Yes.

"Shit. Mom says the first inclination they had of an attack was when a quantum block took out the Rift Bubble. Apparently, Rasu have had stealth units in place on the ground there for some time." Alex kissed his cheek, then leapt up. "Nika, I need a favor. If I give you the coordinates of a specific planet, can you do what you've been doing for the Axis Worlds and identify where the Rasu have placed a quantum block?"

"I can try."

"Thanks. Sending you the supergalactic coordinates."

Caleb twisted around to watch as Nika eased into the workbench chair and closed her eyes. The glow emanating off her skin pulsed and throbbed, growing into an expansive aura that danced through the port section of the cabin.

Almost five interminable minutes passed before the woman re-opened her eyes, her posture sagging in defeat. "I'm afraid there simply aren't enough kyoseil waves meandering across the planet for me to detect the kind of absence that a quantum block generates. It's difficult to describe, but when kyoseil is omnipresent, the source of the block is like a wound in the fabric of…anyway. I can't find it. I'm sorry."

"Thank you for trying." He shifted back to Alex; his mouth opened, but the words he needed to say lodged in his throat.

Then she said them for him. "Go. You gave up on Eren once before in order to rescue Marlee, and having to make the choice tore you up. You'll never forgive yourself if you don't try to rescue him this time. And Felzeor, my goodness. Of course you have to save him."

Conflict knotted in his stomach until he felt queasy. "But the mission."

"Nika and I can handle it. I'll miss your moral support, witty repartee and the visceral pleasure of watching you heft those enclo-sures around, but we've got this. Don't look at me like that. You know it's true."

"I do. I hate the thought of sending you deep into enemy terri-tory without me to watch your back…god, how I do." He grasped her face in his hands and drew her close, touching his nose to hers. "So don't die, okay?"

"Wouldn't dream of it. Can't give those Rasu *pizdy* the satis-faction."

"I love you, baby."

"I love you, *priyazn*. I'll head to Hirlas the second we've com-pleted our deliveries. And hopefully, not long after that, the Rasu will suddenly have an intense desire to be elsewhere."

"But I can't count on it. Or I can't count on Eren and Felzeor surviving until it happens."

"No, you can't." She kissed him, long and slow, and he longed to stay right here, in this moment, until the war was over and tran-quility returned.

Then she drew back, again doing what he could not. With a beautiful smile he knew was forced, she stood and moved to the center of the cabin. "Where to?"

He didn't have to think about it. "CINT offices."

Her lips quirked, and she laughed. "Oh, Richard's going to love this." A flick of her wrist, and a wormhole opened onto Concord HQ.

He hurried to the cabinet and grabbed his weapons. "I'll get first aid supplies from HQ. I don't want to take yours, in case…well, in case."

What is our intention?

We're going to save our friends.

And this planet, this 'Hirlas'?

We'll see what we can do.

"Be safe, my love."

She shook her head. "No. But I will be smart." Her smile faltered. "Back at you."

He nodded, squared his shoulders and hurried through the wormhole.

RW

CONCORD HQ
CINT

Caleb burst into the conference room to find Richard huddled over two wide screens, Will beside him. "I need to borrow a Ghost."

Richard turned toward him, an eyebrow arched, and sighed. "Again?"

"Hey, at least I'm doing it the right way this time."

"True enough. The thing is, they're virtually all out on high priority Rasu reconnaissance missions."

Caleb slapped his fingers on his thigh, urgency driving him relentlessly forward. "'Virtually all' by definition isn't all. Please, I'm begging you. Eren and Felzeor's lives hang in the balance."

Will leaned against the table, his posture sagging. "Oh, no. They're on Hirlas?"

"They are."

Richard studied him cautiously. "And you think you're going to drop in and, what? Single-handedly stop the Rasu invasion?"

"I think I'm going to find Eren and Felzeor and keep them alive until…" he stopped himself, as the mission remained secret for now "…Concord forces can take out the quantum block and start to cut off the invasion, then get all of us safely off-planet."

"All right." Richard threw his hands in the air. "I changed the access code, but I'll send you the new one. There are two Ghosts currently idle in Hangar CC-5A. Do try to return yours in one piece."

"No guarantees. Thank you."

"Don't thank me yet. You're probably going to die, in or out of the Ghost. But listen. Eren and Cosime spent some time training the Naraida's fledgling defense force a few years ago. If Eren's got it in his head to be a hero, he'll try to hook up with them. They're based out of the Hamid Center in Choeda."

"Terrific. That information is a tremendous help." Caleb departed the conference room—then spun around and poked his head back inside. "Oh, and I need to raid your supply room for first aid gear."

"Absolutely."

"Appreciated." He pivoted—and back around again. "What are the odds of a cache of Rima Grenades being handy?"

57

HIRLAS

As he carefully dodged aerial Rasu and searched for a place to land anywhere near the outskirts of Choeda, Caleb decided he was sick and damn tired of parachuting into Rasu-occupied planets in a desperate attempt to save a precious few souls most dear to him.

He didn't get much in the way of déjà vu, though, mostly because the landscapes of Hirlas and Namino couldn't be more different—one verdant and thick with lush forests, the other an endless expanse of arid plains. But there was no doubt his recent actions echoed one another in more than one respect. Once again, he had no idea how to find those he was here to rescue…no, not rescue. Despite what he'd told Richard about his plans, there wasn't a shred of doubt in his mind that Eren and Felzeor both would insist on staying and defending this planet from the invaders until their last breaths. The fact that such an endeavor was on its face impossible wouldn't matter a whiff.

Still, he should make an attempt to hide the Ghost in a location where it might survive for a time. After all, it was a very expensive ship that did not belong to him.

The Rasu had wasted no time in turning much of Choeda into a no-man's-land. Fires burned in every neighborhood, and the unique architecture of the city had been wrent apart as if by an earthquake. His gaze went to the southeast, searching for…*there*. Active explosions peppered a large, hexagonal building surrounded by multiple smaller structures, and laser fire shot out from the southern fringes of the campus.

Thank god, he hadn't missed them.

He descended until he was skirting treetops, then eased below the canopy five hundred meters from where the fighting was concentrated. Once the landing gear locked in place and the ship balanced a bit precariously on the uneven, root-infested ground, he grabbed his backpack and hip satchel and wasted no time exiting the ship. Its passive cloaking abilities functioned despite the quantum block, and its hull shifted colors like a chameleon lizard to blend into the surrounding foliage.

He couldn't do much else to protect the vessel, so he slotted the Rectifier he'd brought into its holster and set off toward the sound of weapons fire.

RW

Four Volucri soared high overhead, dodging incidental Rasu fire, and Caleb shielded his eyes and squinted at the sky. But even with his ocular implant zoomed fully in, he wasn't able to tell if any of them were Felzeor. Hopefully Eren would know what their friend was up to.

So to find Eren.

This Hirlas is rather more violent and raucous than I recall.

You can blame the Rasu for that.

Our Rasu-enemy spoil everything they touch, do they not?

Yes, they do. The Rasu are a plague.

Ear-splitting detonations were coming constantly now, and only the occasional flare of laser fire from the shadows of buildings ahead told him the defenders hadn't yet been annihilated. A shower of burning leaves rained down on him, and he hurriedly dusted embers out of his hair before it caught fire. The heat pushed against him in waves now, too…he wasn't going to be able to advance much farther. Where were they?

The forest began to clear a couple of meters ahead, and bushes rustled as three Naraida ran past, sprinting to the east. He hurried forward, trailing in the direction they were headed—

Laser fire streaked scant centimeters over his shoulder, and he ducked and rolled away. "Friendly!"

"Shite, sorry!" A Naraida man whose hair was the color of ash—actually it probably *was* an ash coating—scrambled forward and knelt beside him. "Did I hit you?"

"No." Caleb leapt back to his feet. "Where is Eren Savitas?"

"That psycho? Over this way, last I saw." The man took off running through the forest, and Caleb followed.

Sixty meters or so to the east, they ran through a curtain of ivy, and he found himself in a fortification of sorts. Several enormous tree trunks had been felled and rolled into a line, forming a makeshift barricade. Five Naraida and one Novoloume fired some type of assault rifles over the tops of the trunks. More laser fire originated from above, and Caleb's gaze sought out three camouflaged humanoid shapes braced among the limbs. "Eren?"

A head surrounded by tangled, dirty golden curls dipped below a spread of leaves. "Caleb! Didn't want to miss the fun, eh? Did you bring explosives?"

Caleb chuckled dryly and shook his head. "Only what archine grenades fit in my pack. Oh, and this." He removed the Rectifier from its holster and held it up.

"Fantastic! Get your arse up here."

He searched the base of the tree in question for a foothold and found only a narrow notch carved into the bark. Good enough. He situated a boot on it and vaulted up to grasp the first limb he could reach. In a few seconds he had reached the sturdier limb Eren rested on. "Where's Felzeor?"

Eren pointed at the sky on his way to firing a Naraida-made weapon in the direction of a long, blocky Rasu vessel hovering above the center of the Hamid campus. "He recruited some friends to act as eyes in the sky for us. To be honest, though, all they can really report are 'Rasu fucking everywhere'—my words, not his."

"Yeah. Eren, you know the weapon your wielding isn't going to do more than pockmark a Rasu, don't you?"

"I know. Shoot it with yours!"

He adjusted his position against the trunk and lifted the Rectifier, then sighted down on the center of the vessel and fired. A hole opened up in the center of the hull, and the surrounding metal seemed to burn...but then the damage stopped spreading, and within several seconds, the hole was closing up. "Shit. It's not powerful enough to destroy a ship that big."

"No Rima Grenades?"

"The launcher was too big for me to carry in the Ghost." Caleb grinned. "Which is why I arranged for an airdrop to be delivered to the south of the Hamid Center. Assuming the ship made it past the Rasu gauntlet, it should be delivering its payload any minute now."

"Oh, you are fabulous. And it's good to know that a few Concord ships are making a run of it." Eren's lips moved silently for a minute. "I need to get you an earpiece and hook you into our comm network. The Naraida have some old pre-quantum comm equipment we managed to grab on our way out of the Center. The range is less than ten kilometers, but it's better than nothing. I just let everyone know about the cache drop. Let's head that way and see if we can find it. Maybe we can dispatch this Rasu group while there's still a city to save."

A city to save? Caleb's hand darted out to stop Eren before he began climbing down. "You know you can't hope to do that, don't you? Not from the ground."

"Bloody right, I can't. But I will defend this planet to this death, then return for round two. It's what Cosime would have wanted."

RW

The munitions crate had torn a path of destruction through the tree canopy on its descent and landed half against the base of a tree at the end of a gouged trail.

Eren dropped to the ground in front of it and disabled the CINT lock in a flash. He threw the lid open and lifted the Rima Grenade launcher out, stroking it lovingly. "Oh, you sexy beast."

A thunderous roar rattled the leaves on the trees, and a split-second later, the concomitant shockwave knocked everyone to their knees. The weald darkened, and Caleb looked up to see the sun blotted out. "Eren..."

"Yep." Eren leapt to his feet and motioned one of the Naraida over. "Caleb Marano, Avicia Muire. Caleb, give Avicia your archine grenades, then load up as many Rima Grenades as you can fit in your gear. Let's take out that cruiser."

Caleb opened up his hip pack and retrieved eight archine grenades, dropping them into the waiting arms of the Naraida woman. "You need to make certain they land right underneath or in front of a Rasu, since their effective spread is only about six meters."

Avicia nodded in understanding and sprinted off into the brush. Caleb refilled his pack with the Rima Grenades stored in the cushioning of the crate's interior; Eren was scaling a nearby tree, so once the pack was full, he scrambled up as well. He'd done his share of climbing trees while living on Akeso, simply to view the majesty of the landscape with his own two eyes, and his feet and fingers found accessible leverage points without conscious thought.

Eren had braced himself in the crook where a sturdy limb met the main trunk when Caleb arrived. He handed his friend a Rima Grenade. Eren slotted it into the launcher, then swung the weapon up and fired.

They couldn't see the tiny ball impact the hull, but abruptly the length and breadth of the cruiser winked out of existence, and filtered sunlight returned to the weald. "Godsdamn, that's awesome. Hand me another one."

Caleb complied, but in the back of his mind, several permutations of the long game started playing themselves out.

Eren took out a second Rasu cruiser, more distant this time, and held out his hand again.

Caleb shook his head. "I think we should save the rest for...later."

Eren stared at him, vibrant gilt irises swirling like flames. "You mean for the moment when all hope is lost and we have one last desperate chance to save as many people as possible?"

"I do."

"Zeus' stone-cold marbles…fine." Eighty meters away, the tree canopy began to shake, and tendrils of smoke drifted up. "We've got mechs headed our way. And they're burning the forest as they go." Eren's posture sagged. "We need to retreat."

Caleb was already headed out of the tree. He leapt down the last two meters, then grabbed the arm of a Naraida woman as she hurried past. "We're evacuating. Who knows the best route?"

The woman didn't bother to ask him who he was. "That would be me. We can head south, along the tree line, until we reach Diarffor."

"No, we can't." Eren jogged up to them, the launcher swaying over his shoulder. "A second Rasu contingent is flanking us from the southwest. It's a fair bet they've identified our resistance here as the source of their troubles. We've going to have to retreat along the Afonle River."

The woman pinched the bridge of her pert nose. "That's a dead end into Calchfaen."

"Yeah, but not for a while. We should be able to cut out through the North Rhaeadr Woods before we reach Calchfaen. Regardless, we don't have a choice."

"Blast it. Calling everyone in. We move in five."

Caleb watched the woman hurry off into a thicket and vanish, as if the foliage absorbed her. "Is she in charge?"

"Karis? Thinks she is, but no. Well, maybe a little. Gethin Sayern is the Hamid commander, though. Assuming he manages to stay alive, you'll meet him eventually."

"Got it. What's Calchfaen?"

"Oh, a ten-kilometer stretch of limestone cliffs ending in an eighty-meter waterfall. Gorgeous place. Not too friendly to those of us who rely on bones to walk."

A rapid flutter of wings gave Caleb scant warning as Felzeor crashed onto his shoulder. "Caleb! What are you doing here?"

"I came to help you fight the Rasu." He reached up and stroked Felzeor's neck, smiling in spite of the dire nature of their circumstances.

"We need the help. Is Alex here, too?"

"No. She's on an important mission of her own."

Eren arched an eyebrow in question. "It must be pretty important, for her to let you have all this fun on your own."

"It is." He didn't explain further; it would take too long, and they needed to focus all their attention on escaping the approaching Rasu.

"Huh. Okay, time to go—oh, here." Eren jammed a hand into his pocket and produced a small ceramic blob. "Goes in your ear."

Caleb frowned at it, then wiggled it into his left ear. Once there, he felt the material soften and conform to the outlines of his ear canal. Cross-chatter erupted, and he nodded.

Felzeor tapped his feet in agitation on Caleb's shoulder. "I must go. I am needed to scout our planned route."

Caleb patted him above his tail. "That's vital work. I'll see you when we stop again."

Felzeor launched himself into the air, and Caleb and Eren set off to join the retreating fighters. They took up the left flank position. Caleb kept the Rectifier raised outward, and Eren rolled two archine grenades around in his hands, biceps flexed and ready to send them airborne.

The Naraida moved as noiselessly as apparitions through the forest, and for all that Caleb had always prided himself on being able to move quietly, he felt like a tromping elephant by comparison. It did help that the Rasu were making a riotous racket as they advanced, though every boom and thud represented the destruction of wonders both natural and Naraida-constructed.

58

SIYANE

NGC 5033 GALAXY

From the inside looking out, all galaxies pretty much looked the same. Sure, the galactic core here shone far more luminously over most of the electromagnetic spectrum than the Milky Way's did, since NGC 5033 was a Seyfert galaxy. It was also thirty percent less dense than the Milky Way, but the difference between two-hundred-fifty billion stars and one-hundred-seventy-five billion wasn't discernable to the naked eye.

Here in this nameless stellar system (technically, Valkyrie had designated it 5033-681dd), the scene outside the viewport could be mistaken for the vista from the fringes of Erisen's system, or that of Romane or Seneca. But it wasn't. No, she was once again eleven megaparsecs from home…she idly wondered when she was going to need to start measuring distances in gigaparsecs. Amaranthe was a big place.

Alex noted all this in passing as she eased into the stellar system they'd chosen for their first information bomb. The Rasu were thick here, much as in NGC 55, and after a minute she turned navigation over to Valkyrie in order to help Nika ready the payload. She didn't want to stay here in this den of fiends a minute longer than necessary. And even if she did otherwise want to take in the scenery, the clock was ticking for Caleb. For Eren, Felzeor and billions of people on almost twenty worlds.

She forcibly shut off the thought. She couldn't linger on what horrors Caleb was facing right now; she could only do what was in her power to shorten the time he'd need to face them.

Nika finished slipping on her environment suit while studying the viewport. "There are so many. I imagine this is what they have in mind for us."

"I think they have in mind to drain us dry of information and resources, then wipe us from existence. But yes, I imagine this is what our home stellar systems will look like in the aftermath, should they win."

"Which they won't."

"No. Are we ready?"

Alex sealed the gloves to her environment suit, then nodded. "Valkyrie, shout when we're in position."

'It will be approximately eight minutes.'

"Thanks." She led the way downstairs and into the engineering well.

The hold was now a prison for monsters. A macabre asylum of twisted metal. It made her skin scrawl to see her beloved ship defiled so, but it was worth it. The *Siyane* was delivering the weapon that would turn the tide of this war in their favor.

She and Nika picked their way between the enclosures toward the farthermost one in the rear. Their prisoners were packed in tightly, and the external force fields sizzled along the material of their suits as they slid past.

"The restraints are latched here, here, here and..." she circled around and crouched near the bottom "...here."

"Got it. Should we get started?"

"I'd love to—the sooner the better—but no. The ride is smooth as silk for now, but there's no telling when Valkyrie will need to dodge passing Rasu. I don't want to end up trapped underneath this enclosure."

"Nor do I."

'Four minutes, forty seconds.'

"Have you heard from Caleb?"

"He breached the quantum block barrier at Hirlas thirty-two minutes ago. I don't expect to be hearing from him again for a while." She sighed, letting a deep, cutting worry curl through her thoughts anew. "Hirlas is predominantly a jungle planet. There are dense wilds stretching for thousands of kilometers. The Rasu took advantage of the topography to hide the quantum block apparatus somewhere in one of those jungles, because Concord reconnaissance craft have thus far been unable to locate any sign of it."

"And as we learned on Mirai, the Rasu have gotten wise to many of our tactics. I suspect they're masking what minimal electromagnetic noise the blocks emit."

"Exactly. So our pilots can't lay eyes on the hardware because of the jungle, and with limited, non-quantum-based scanning, they won't be able to pick up its signature until they are literally right on top of it. And we can't win without taking out the block."

"Unless our plan works."

"It'll work. But it's going to take a while. Days, if not weeks. I hope it's not weeks, but I'm trying my damnedest to be realistic here. My mother would be proud."

"What does she think about this plan of ours?"

Alex pursed her lips. "She doesn't know about it."

"*What?*"

"In my defense, I did make a genuine effort to tell her. But she was in full-on war management mode and not in the frame of mind to listen to what, in her mind, would be nothing more than a hypothetical scheme with unpredictable consequences. It's for the best, honestly. She'd want to discuss and analyze and consult experts, and we don't have time for such nonsense. You and I? We can get this done before the first review meeting would have been so much as scheduled."

Nika's galaxy irises sparkled from within the shadows cast by the Rasu enclosure. "I guess neither of us are partial to asking permission."

"Far better to beg forgiveness." She shrugged. "Or not do that either."

'One minute, fifteen seconds.'

"What about you? What's the word on Synra and Kiyora?"

"Nothing encouraging, I'm afraid—"

The hull lurched beneath their feet, and her hand shot out to brace against the nearest solid surface—she yanked it back as the force field hissed across her suit's material. She settled for planting her feet wide. *All good?*

All is good. There are quite a large number of Rasu in the vicinity.

She closed her eyes and, with a shift of perspective, saw through the sensors of the *Siyane*. *Yes, there are.*

'Twenty-five seconds.'

She reached up to the base of her neck and activated her helmet, and Nika did the same. While she didn't physically feel the vessel slow thanks to the inertial dampers, her link to Valkyrie and the ship meant she sensed it nonetheless. Her mind slipped fully into the elemental realm, where the surrounding dust, gases and free particles danced off the *Siyane's* stealth field. The tremendous Rasu presence turned the void thick with photons and energetic byproducts of their activity. Though the ship sailed forward unobstructed, it felt like trudging through molasses.

'Destination reached.'

Alex shook off the spell and recentered herself inside her body, inside the environment suit. "Great job. Extend the ramp."

No stars shone in the expanse that was revealed centimeter by centimeter as the ramp lowered; there was barely a sun visible to peek through here and there between passing ships. Only the endless, looming metal. Caleb had rightly called them locusts, and here they darkened the sky in every direction.

She moved to the side of the enclosure. "I'll get the two latches on this side, and you get the others, then deactivate the outer force field."

The air immediately surrounding the enclosure stilled, and she quickly popped the latches on the restraints.

"Done."

"Now we push."

Nika joined her on the side opposite the open ramp, and they each placed their gloved hands flat on the glass, palms splayed. "Ready and...push!"

The floor of the engineering well was rough by design, to prevent slipping and sliding, and this meant the enclosure did not slip and slide its way down the ramp. More like staggered and bumped and skidded.

Alex was grunting in exertion by the time the downward angle of the ramp took over and momentum sent the enclosure tumbling into space.

She wanted to stand there on the cusp of the heavens and watch the show, but it would be foolish. At any time, Valkyrie might need to pull another evasive maneuver, one that risked sending her and Nika careening out into the waiting and not so gentle arms of the Rasu.

"Close the ramp. We're coming up."

R W

Nika collapsed her helmet, revealing a sweat-soaked face; strands of her raven hair were stuck across her cheek and forehead. "Six more, huh?"

"Yep. And each one will be farther away from the edge of the ramp."

"Wonderful."

They moved into the cockpit, where on the viewport a virtual dot tracked their payload. A separate screen zoomed in on its progress, and they watched as one side of the glass enclosure gradually melted away.

"I'm deactivating the internal force field."

In forty seconds, the Rasu unit was free of its cage. Alex held her breath. It was a solid plan, but their bait could now do whatever it damn well pleased.

Slowly, the unit began to stretch and contract, morphing into an aerodynamic shape and growing a tiny engine. Light flared, and the unit accelerated toward the center of the stellar system.

Alex exhaled harshly and let her shoulders relax. "I admit, I was a little worried it was going to high-tail it straight back to the

Gennisi galaxy. Not that I don't have every confidence in Dashiel's programming ability, but there's so much we still don't know about how the Rasu think."

"No, I hear you. First test passed, though. Valkyrie, will we be able to track the unit all the way?"

'Until it merges with another vessel, at which point the characteristics distinguishing it from other Rasu units will begin to disappear.'

"As is the nature of their existence."

"And the reason why this crazy plan just might work," Alex replied.

It would be superb if the unit were to dock straightaway with one of the enormous platforms comprising the stellar ring, since Nika's experience at the stronghold in the Gennisi galaxy suggested that was where the brains of the local operation resided. But it was probably too much to hope for.

Finally, their saboteur approached a smaller Rasu craft that had joined up with another unit, and it seemed like a good time to hold her breath again.

'The two units are conversing, after a fashion. Based on the translation program, it appears the conversation is, in essence, 'Permission to join?,' 'Permission granted.''

Alex rolled her eyes. "I guess there's only so many ways to say certain things."

As they watched, the unit sidled up to the undercarriage of the larger vessel. One side of its exterior melted and spilled along the other's hull.

'Signal lost. I am marking the host ship.'

It was natural and normal for returning Rasu to upload information they had gained during their travels. This was, they believed, precisely how the enemy's scouting parties operated. This unit had been elsewhere, and it had news to share.

The real risk was that it would be viewed as 'other.' That the Rasu faction inhabiting this galaxy would recognize the unit had not originated from this parent and isolate it. How such a thing might or might not occur, they had no idea. Excepting specific behaviors and conversations, all Rasu looked the same to them, down to the nanoscopic level. But what if they'd missed some unique identifier other Rasu recognized?

But, again, there was nothing to be done about it now.

The host ship continued its journey inward, toward the platforms—another relief. Among the thousand worries she'd entertained, one was that the payload would join up with a vessel headed out on a scouting mission, thus delaying the delivery of their information bomb by…weeks? Months? Too long.

But for this location, at least, it was another worry she was now able to put away.

The *Siyane* eased to aft as a dreadnought-sized Rasu passed above them. No, bigger than the dreadnoughts they'd seen so far. God, a ship this big could single-handedly assault a small planet. Her thoughts inevitably went to Hirlas. Had the Rasu bombing it grown so mammoth as to darken its sun?

'The host ship is docking with one of the platforms. Marking it now.'

"Nika, how does this work?"

"Um, we think they dock for a whole host of reasons. To offload cargo, usually resources but also…test subjects. Presumably to share new information as well. We don't think they merge to do so. Well, they do at discrete, focused junctions, solely for that purpose, but the docking ships don't typically dissolve into the platform. After some time, they undock and depart to pursue whatever their newly assigned purpose is."

Alex clasped her hands together at her chin. "Then I think we've seen all we're liable to be able to track here. We can leave a sensor behind to detect any unusual activity, I suppose."

Nika shook her head. "No need. The only unusual activity we care about at this point is Rasu from this stronghold accessing the nearest kyoseil deposit, and I'll know when that happens."

What must it be like, to have her mind scattered across the cosmos in such a manner? Alex experienced more empyreal wonders than most people ever dreamed of contemplating, but the scope of Nika's connection to kyoseil humbled even her. "And once it does, we'll use the Kat's network and Concord's surveillance probes to monitor the surrounding galaxies for signs of hostilities breaking out among the factions. Okay, Valkyrie. Take us to Target #2."

59

SIYANE

INTERGALACTIC SPACE

Alex retracted her helmet and headed upstairs. When she reached the bedroom, cool air wafted over the sweat coating her neck. They'd successfully sent out the fourth Rasu unit, and they were due a brief break.

Nika had gone up first and met her at the top of the staircase with a flask of water. Alex greedily gulped it down while they both collapsed at the kitchen table.

Nika's expression slackened, and Alex let herself simply breathe while she waited for the woman to return her consciousness to the *Siyane*. Caleb's physical strength was dead last on the list of reasons why she wished he were here with her right now, but there was no question it would have made the mission easier on her aching muscles.

After about two minutes, Nika blinked and sat up straighter.

"How goes it?"

"A little better on Synra. Worse on Kiyora. Lance's cursing has reached epic proportions in the last half hour, though I'm honestly not sure whether it's a good or a bad sign."

"Ha. I've met a few soldiers like that. I have to say, it's impressive how you can manipulate the Rift Bubbles from way out here. Why did it occur to you to try?"

"Well, Mesme intimated there was a way to do it, and that I would be able to do so. So following the events at Oneiroi, it seemed like I ought to give it a shot. And it was rather straightforward. Once I believed I could accomplish it, the answer of how to do so became obvious."

This must happen. Nika must deepen her connection with the kyoseil that is a part of her essence, as it is a part of the universe, for the same reason we are taking every action in these times—in order to defeat the Rasu.

Damn the Kat. "How prophetic of Mesme. Like everything else it says. Did I mention it was Mesme's idea for me to take you to Oneiroi? Not long after we met, it warned me off doing so, saying it wasn't time. Then, poof, one day, 'hey, it's time now.' While you were being swallowed alive by the kyoseil, Caleb and I tried to intervene, but Mesme didn't let us—as in physically blocked us from reaching you. It said 'this must happen.' Almost as if it knew what was going to transpire all along."

"Understanding everything it does about kyoseil, it's possible what I experienced was the only thing that *could* happen when someone with so much kyoseil in their body was exposed to the trove there in the nebula."

Alex laughed wryly. "I just remembered something. A long time ago—our first trip to Oneiroi, coincidentally enough—Mesme told us that while the Kats shepherded and protected as much Reor as they were able to, they couldn't actually communicate with it. What a liar."

"Why would it lie about being able to communicate with kyoseil?"

"Oh, because it wanted me to take my own initiative and do the hard work of figuring out how to use the slab the Reor gifted me to crack the Anadens' secrets."

"Do it yourself or it won't stick. Similar to me learning to control the Rift Bubbles."

"Exactly." She frowned. "Still, though. I doubt it's as if the Reor in Oneiroi commed the Kat and said, 'hey, Mnemosyne, why don't you bring the Asterion by—you know the one we mean—so we can infuse her with our essence and get this show on the road.' Yet Mesme knew precisely what was going to happen."

"Suspected, anyway."

She stood and moved to the data center, where the maps of their remaining targets painted the air with the faction hues they'd chosen. "No. Knew. I'm convinced of it."

I save the people who will save the universe. If it can be saved.

Mesme had provided her and Caleb with what had sounded at the time like a reasonable justification of what it meant by such a grandiose statement, but distance and events were exposing the flimsiness of its explanation.

"What are you saying? That Mesme can see the future?"

Her response tumbled from her lips without thought or consideration. "I think it doesn't need to see the future."

Where had such a notion come from? What did she know that she didn't know she knew?

Nika's brow furrowed, and she leaned forward, dropping her elbows on the table. "Because it…no, you're not really suggesting…?"

Alex's vision blurred, the maps becoming a hazy gauze of colorful stars. Thoughts slightly beyond articulation swirled through her mind. In a way, it was akin to searching for the truth in space outside the ship—looking for the incongruity, the absence or the quirk which held the key to bringing the rules of the universe back into line. The universe had been out of phase for a while now…and one impossible truth could bring it into alignment.

Alex….

You disagree?

I am devoting 81.2% of my active processes to contemplation of this revelation. Allow me to get back to you.

She spun around to face Nika. "You know what? I *am* suggesting. I think this is the answer. In fact, it might be the only logical answer to why Mesme is so damn confident about its declarations. Why it goes to such lengths to manipulate us into certain actions."

"But, Alex, time travel isn't possible. Your people and mine understand the physics of the universe to such an extent that we can bend the fabric of spacetime to our will in once unfathomable ways, and everyone agrees: it just isn't."

"But what if it *is*? The discovery of faster-than-light travel erased a big argument for why time travel isn't possible. It proved false one of the key components of special relativity and showed 'the grandfather paradox' to be a fallacy. It demonstrated that time is not merely spatial; it's local. Kind of like the old mindfulness adage, 'wherever you go, there you are.' I won't dive into the weeds, since we've all been living the results of the discovery for a while now—you much longer than me.

"But more fundamentally, we call what's out there 'spacetime' for a reason. Time is the fourth tangible dimension, and it's as integral to the existence of the universe as the other three are. Agreed?"

"Agreed."

"When you and I create wormholes, we do so by literally tearing apart the first three tangible dimensions. It takes a great deal of quantum energy to do so." She flicked the tiny Caeles Prism on her wrist. "I access the energy needed using this gem. Your own body creates yours—which, very cool, by the way. Anyway, the energy is unleashed upon a single point in the cosmic manifold, and a tear is created. If time is truly the fourth tangible dimension, then in theory, there is no reason not to posit that, given the application of sufficient energy, we can't do the same to it as well."

"But the amount of energy required must be incomprehensible, yes? On the order of the power of a supernova concentrated in the palm of your hand?"

Alex smirked; the longer she talked this through, the more convinced she became. "I've seen the Kats create supernovae on demand."

"Then focus the energy expended on a specific location in space?"

"Admittedly, no. But just because I haven't seen it doesn't mean they can't do it. Hell, they create bubbles of spacetime and populate them with entire universes. The manifold is their playground."

Nika leapt up and went to the kitchen to grab the bowl of chips, then began popping them into her mouth, talking around the crunches. "Okay, you make a decent point—but I'm not an astrophysicist. I'm having trouble conceiving of it as a real possibility, though. I mean, time travel is in some ways the last taboo. The one rule of the universe that can't be broken."

"Unless it isn't a rule of the universe at all. The past is littered with cosmic 'rules' that became fallacies when new evidence came to light. Throughout history, people have known a great many things that simply weren't true. We grow smarter, we evolve, we increase our understanding. The universe was the same all along, but we had to advance to peel away its layers and comprehend it."

Your argument is compelling.

I know it is.

"Say it is true." Another chip. "I can't believe I'm contemplating this, but did all the Kats travel back through time?"

"No idea. We know almost nothing about the Kats' origins, because they've never told us about them. They encountered an expanding Anaden Empire two-hundred-fifty thousand years ago, by which point they were, in most respects, as they are now. Incorporeal, hyper-advanced, manipulative as all fuck. But they were and still are tied to corporeal bodies, which means they had a rich and detailed past. What was it, I wonder?"

"Hmm. Speaking of, I want to see one of those bodies someday."

"It's a letdown, trust me," Alex replied. "They're not especially sexy."

"But what if they used to be? I mean, they don't use the bodies for anything except existing any longer, right? Maybe they pared their physical existence down to the bare minimum when they went incorporeal." Nika held out the bowl of chips in Alex's direction.

Her stomach grumbled, and she grabbed a handful. "All that being said, my gut tells me time travel is *hard*. Beyond hard. As you said, the power of a supernova in the palm of your hand—or maybe greater energy is required. The energy of a quasar focused on a location the size of an atom. If it were any easier—if at any point in the future, even millions of years from now, it became a viable action, the way creating wormholes is for us now—then we'd be surrounded by time travelers, wouldn't we?"

"Gods, what if we are?"

"It doesn't feel that way. If it were feasible to do so, Mesme would be darting back and forth through time like a madman, tweaking the world to fit its desired outcome. And it's not."

"How can you be certain?"

Alex smiled, recalling what Caleb had said after the events at the Oneiroi Nebula. "Because Mesme is sad. You said so yourself: Mesme gets frustrated as hell with us. When things get dire and it starts to look like all hope is lost, Mesme gets desperate. Those are the sentiments of someone who *can't* wave its ethereal hand and redo the timeline."

"And it's trying so hard. Using all the considerable tools at its disposal—which, yes, suggests further time travel isn't one of them." Nika frowned darkly. "I wonder why? How terrible must the fate waiting for us in our future be, for Mesme to labor so exhaustively to prevent it?"

"Oh, it's easy to imagine. The Rasu win. We get annihilated. The Kats, too."

"How would that even happen—oh, their bodies."

"Yep. They've already moved tens of thousands of their stasis chambers once to escape the Directorate. But if the Rasu ever catch up to those stasis chambers, it's over for them."

"And I thought I empathized with Mesme before."

She's making an excellent point. I find myself consumed with sorrow in contemplation of what Mesme has endured all these years.

Don't go soft on me, Valkyrie. Get back to the math.

You have to concede—

I'm not going to feel bad over being angry at Mesme for lying to us.

But maybe the tiniest bit. She sighed. "I admit, this does cast its actions in a new light. Still, it could have straight-up told us. 'Hey, unless you do this thing I'm instructing you to do, you will all die. I know, because I watched it happen.' It would have gone a *long* way toward building and keeping trust."

"Would you have believed it, though?"

"Oh, not at first. But I've never been one to insist anything is impossible. I could have been convinced." She shrugged. "Eventually. With evidence."

"So…" Nika glanced at the three remaining target maps "…what do we do with our suspicions?"

"Right now, we finish our mission. If there's one thing this makes crystal clear, it's that we absolutely must defeat the Rasu. Mesme wouldn't be working so damn hard to change the future otherwise. Then, I think we sit Mesme down, so to speak, and have a friendly little conversation. It's time for the secrets to end."

60

CONCORD HQ
RASU WAR ROOM

Vrachnas (Protected, Andromeda)
- No Rasu life signs detected / monitoring. *Level I*

Serifos (Anaden, Andromeda)
- Minimal Rasu activity / sweep operations. *Level II*

Acacia (Anaden, Andromeda)
- Moderate Rasu activity in orbit. Full space engagement. Rift Bubble operability solid. Minimal Rasu activity groundside. *Level III*

Telete (Anaden, Andromeda)
- Moderate Rasu activity in orbit and groundside. Full space engagement. Rift Bubble operability solid. *Level IV*

Pasesh (Anaden, Andromeda)
- Strong Rasu activity. Full space engagement. Rift Bubble operability intermittent. Moderate Rasu presence groundside. *Level V*

Loudia (Novoloume, Pegasus Dwarf)
- Strong Rasu activity. Full space engagement. Rift Bubble operability intermittent. Moderate Rasu presence groundside. *Level V*

Effor Elafos (Novoloume, Pegasus Dwarf)
- Strong Rasu activity. Full space engagement. Rift Bubble operability intermittent. Moderate Rasu presence groundside. *Level V*

Nopreis (Novoloume, Pegasus Dwarf)
- Aggressive Rasu activity. Full space engagement. Rift Bubble operability intermittent. Significant Rasu presence groundside. *Level VI*

Olon Uuls (Barisan, Triangulum)
- Aggressive Rasu activity. Full space engagement. Rift Bubble operability intermittent. Increasing Rasu presence groundside. *Level VI*

Hirlas (Naraida/Volucri, Pegasus Dwarf)
- Under Rasu control. Reconnaissance efforts underway to locate quantum block. *Level VII*

The status of the Asterion Dominion worlds occupied a slightly less prominent screen off to the left end of the table. Commander Palmer insisted they could handle their own fights, and for the moment, Miriam had little choice but to let them. Primarily because she knew in her gut what was coming any hour, minute or second now.

Until the inevitable occurred, however, she had to concentrate on the fires raging across multiple worlds. Relief rotations were off the table; they'd address the negative consequences of repeated stimulant use after they won a few battles. As for herself, she caught a chemically induced forty-five-minute nap in her office every eight hours; so had it been since the Rasu had arrived at Nopreis. David fretted over her, but he recognized the position she was in and exercised considerable restraint in not showing his concern where others would see it. The blowback of him having to do so was falling mostly on Richard, she believed.

"Commandant, defensive perimeter sensors report the presence of Rasu in the Brizo system."

She didn't need to look at the map, as she'd memorized the general location of every inhabited world in the Milky Way shortly after The Displacement. The Anaden colony of Brizo was located on the Milky Way's Outer Arm, in Sector 28. Back in Aurora, exploratory investigation had identified the world as favorable for human settlement at such time as the Earth Alliance expanded sufficiently along the Outer Arm. When they'd arrived here in Amaranthe, they discovered it had been occupied for four hundred millennia.

And with this news, the Rasu's assault on the Milky Way had begun.

Commandant Solovy: "Navarchos Casmir, Advocate Corradeo, Brizo is about to come under attack. I am transmitting the Red Alert activations. I recommend sending Brigades II-A and B from Antlia Dwarf to engage them, but I will defer to your preferences in this regard."

Patrols responsible for protecting the smaller galaxies on the periphery of Concord space had long-since been recalled and assigned to various combat engagements. It was a gamble, but now that the Rasu had their eyes fixed on the grand prize, she felt fairly confident that they would not bother with the smaller dwarf galaxies—not until they'd claimed their trophy. No one dared pull Milky Way defensive patrols off their routes, however. The worlds which stood to be hit next, human and Anaden alike, were simply too important to risk losing even two minutes of initial response time.

Casmir: "I am sending Brigades II-A and B as well as Brigade IV-A. Brizo must be defended at all costs."

Mustn't every world be defended at all costs? her conscience whispered. It was a noble sentiment, but an unrealistic one. Back during the Metigen War, she'd made the decision to abandon a distressing number of small colonies in order to preserve her forces to engage the enemy at the most strategic locations. She still mourned the innocent lives lost as a result of her actions, but the alternative would have been all life lost.

Corradeo: "I confess, I have a strong desire to get myself to the bridge of a ship. My w—someone I once cared deeply about was from Brizo."

She shared his desire.

Miriam: "I leave the choice to you."

Corradeo: "No. My talents lie elsewhere, though those areas aren't of much use presently. Regardless, the Machim elassons will do a far better job of combating the Rasu than I."

A message came in on another of the many active channels she maintained.

Pointe-Amiral Thisiame (NF Eshtaina)(Nopreis Command Channel): "Commandant, I regret to report that the Rasu have destroyed a brigade-worth of vessels using a wide-beam antimatter weapon. Requesting reinforcements."

The situation at Nopreis was dire and degrading rapidly. The Rasu knew how much the world meant to Concord, of course they did. The fighting had been going on for four days with no interruption and few breaks falling their way. Now that the Rasu were fielding antimatter weapons, Concord was losing ships. And not just Novoloume and Khokteh ships. Adiamene-wrapped ships. Their vaunted indestructible hulls were proving to be a lie when pitched against a powerful enemy lacking scruples or honor.

They were rolling out the TDS technology to AEGIS frigates with all due speed, but most of those frigates were engaged in active warfare. It made for something of a catch-22. If she pulled the ships into dry dock now, she risked losing the tenuous hold they maintained on the colonies under active attack. But if she left them in the field, she risked losing the ships and their crews. Thus far, she'd strived for a middle ground, with unsatisfactory results.

Commandant Solovy (Nopreis Command Channel): "I'm sending the AEGIS 12th Brigade and Machim Regiments V-15A and B to Nopreis.

Pointe-Amiral Thisiame (NF Eshtaina)(Nopreis Command Channel): "Acknowledged. Thank you, Commandant."

She glanced at the status board to see that Brizo had been added to the list. The Rasu were now attacking new worlds faster than Concord was winning at old ones. The feared inexhaustible supply of Rasu vessels was beginning to make its presence known.

"Commandant?"

She looked over to find the face of her War Room's Operations Officer had blanched; his throat worked anxiously.

"What is it?"

"The AEGIS Early Warning System has detected Rasu signatures approaching Sagan."

She liked to tell herself that she valued all Concord worlds equally. And in her daily actions, she endeavored to treat them so. She'd defended Ireltse with everything Concord could bring. Today, she vowed not to see Nopreis fall, for it was as much the heart and soul of Concord as any AEGIS world—even Earth.

But the first attack on a human world hit her like a punch to the gut, leaving her lungs bereft of air. Sagan remained on the fringes of human-settled space, for in the years after The Displacement, retrenchment and fortification had won out over further expansion. Had the Rasu attacked it first because it was located on the periphery, or because it was a hub for scientific and technological development? Did they desire humanity's knowledge? Its toys?

Commandant Solovy (Concord Command Channel): "Fleet Admiral Jenner, Sagan will soon fall under attack. Respond appropriately."

Fleet Admiral Jenner (AFS Denali)(Concord Command Channel): "I...see. Acknowledged."

The *Denali* currently fought at Nopreis, and while she had no doubt he'd fervently want to do so, he wouldn't pull out of the pitched battle to go to Sagan. Integrity demanded he not abandon his allies in their most desperate hour. But she also didn't doubt he'd order a vastly oversized force of TDS-protected warships to Sagan to attempt to stop the Rasu in their tracks.

She took a second to send a private message arranging for Dr. Canivon to be evacuated from Sagan. She imagined the woman was going to react to being dragged away from her lab by a military escort today about as well as she had during the Metigen War. Too bad.

The battlespaces at Brizo and Sagan wouldn't take clear shape for a few more minutes, so she enlarged the tactical map from Nopreis. Reinforcements were already arriving, but the situation was grim. She instantly ordered another two regiments to the system, then analyzed her other options. She'd meant it before—they couldn't lose Nopreis. But the Rasu seemed to know this as well, as they were bringing to bear by far the largest assault force they'd delivered to date, and they showed no signs of letting up.

The seductive appeal of the Ymyrath Field whispered to her again. Assuming the Rasu hadn't yet found a way to reduce their ships' vulnerability to the weapon, a couple of blasts from it stood to wipe out the entire Rasu force and ensure no additional vessels reached Nopreis to replace them.

But Nopreis wasn't Vrachnas. The system was busy with lunar and asteroid colonies and space stations. Then there was the viability of the planet itself to think of. If she used such a fearsome weapon there, more than the Rasu would be destroyed.

She sent a private comm request to Dean Veshnael.

61

ARES

TEMPORARY ADVOCACY HEADQUARTERS

Nyx walked into her grandfather's office to find him in full crisis management mode. A holo of what she assumed was the Rasu War Room at Concord HQ (if only because Miriam Solovy and various other military officers moved within it) competed for space with one of the bridge of an Imperium—Casmir's Imperium Alpha. Above those holos, three tactical maps swarmed with crimson, green and gold.

She shouldn't have interrupted him. She berated herself for forgetting for a single second that Anaden worlds were under attack from the Rasu and spun around to head back out the door.

"Nyx? What do you need?"

She sighed and turned toward him, looking dutifully contrite. "It's not important. Or rather, it can wait. How go the battles?"

"Not well, I'm afraid. But my active direction is not likely to improve the situation in the short term. What's on your mind?"

His ability to compartmentalize truly was remarkable. She supposed it was a necessary skill for all true leaders.

"I wanted to see if you'd sent Eren on a mission without informing me—because he certainly didn't. And if he's not off working for you right now, I wanted to express my continued concern about the degree of trust you place in him. We were scheduled to depart four hours ago for Macskaf to meet with the CINT agent working the case and a Barisan informant she's managed to turn, and Eren is nowhere to be seen. He's not answering comms, either. The level of dismissiveness with which he treats his obligations—"

Corradeo held up a hand to cut her off. "You don't know, then.

I'm sorry, I should have alerted you. I'll blame this—" he gestured to the clashes playing out at the conference table "—for my lapse."

"I don't know what?"

"Eren was on Hirlas when the Rasu attacked. We've been unable to pinpoint the location of the quantum block they've erected there, so everyone on the ground remains completely cut off."

"Oh." Her voice grew unaccountably soft, for the concept that the vexatious, egocentric Idoni could be fighting to stay alive in a war zone…it simply made no sense. Why didn't he just suicide on a Rasu beam and get a free trip back home? He'd demonstrated a willingness, even eagerness, to null out and take a ride on the re-genesis train that night at Plousia all those years ago. She'd heard stories of him doing so other times as well, including on Savrak, though she conceded those might be exaggerations if not outright lies. The point was, everything she knew about him counseled that he had no good reason to remain there.

"I don't understand. Are you saying he's stayed on Hirlas to fight the Rasu?"

"As I said, I've been unable to speak to him, but I feel confident this is exactly what he's doing. He's accompanied by at least one former anarch, and anarchs do love insurmountable odds." He smiled a little. "Also, I believe Caleb Marano has traveled there to assist in the resistance."

Jealousy flared in her chest, alongside a slight tinge of shame. She'd harbored highly uncharitable thoughts about Eren for the last four hours, and here he was being all heroic. With friends fighting at his side, too! "What is Caleb going to do there? He doesn't control *diati* any longer."

"I don't believe a lack of suitable weapons has ever stopped him from acting to protect the innocent."

"I see." Commandant Solovy drew her grandfather's attention then, and Nyx let her mind wander into troublesome ruminations.

With a quantum block in place, Eren's consciousness wouldn't transfer to an integral server on his death. Upon confirmation of death, a slightly out-of-date version of him would be woken up instead, and whatever he was experiencing right now would be lost to the sands of time. He'd hate being deprived of a harrowing story of embellished gallantry, if nothing else. Was he stubborn enough for that reason alone to keep him there? A rare bout of uncertainty nagged at her; she'd assumed she had him pegged to the wall, but what if she didn't understand him as well as she believed?

She'd send the CINT agent, Bara Jhouti-min, a message postponing their meeting. While she could go on her own, the truth was, Eren brought a fair amount to the table on this op. Bara clearly liked Eren more than she did Nyx. It didn't bother her, but it did mean she wasn't apt to make as much progress if she attended alone.

Her brow furrowed as an odd notion popped into her mind out of the ether. Should *she* go to Hirlas? To help?

Why would she do any such thing? She'd only be able to bring what small arms she could carry on her person, for one. Like Marano, she no longer wielded *diati*, so her impact in a war zone would be limited to close-quarters combat, something that never went well when one's opponents were mechs. Plus, she'd never be able to find Eren, Caleb or anyone else on the wild, overgrown, scarcely civilized jungle planet.

Her grandfather shifted away from the Commandant's holo and toward her. "Sorry for the interruption, Nyx. I'll let you know if I learn anything more about Eren's situation, or if the circumstances on Hirlas change. For now, proceed with your investigation however you think best."

"Of course. I hope the battles turn in our favor."

"So do I."

She left his office and meandered down the hall toward her own, unhelpful thoughts still swirling through her mind.

62

HIRLAS

The racket from the ongoing Rasu destruction surrounding Choeda had faded to a low bellow on the horizon, and by unspoken agreement, their group slowed their pace from grueling to merely punishing. Everyone was exhausted, but they were also both furious and heartbroken. Hopefully the fury would continue to hold dominance for now, if only to keep them moving and fighting instead of collapsing into the soft underbrush in despair.

Eren knew a little about what that was like.

He touched his ear; the earpiece always felt as if it was about to fall out (it wasn't), and the motion had become reflexive. *"We need to start curving west soon, or we're going to end up cornered at Calchfaen."*

Karis: "I told you this was what would happen before we left."

Eren: "But if we start curving west, it won't."

Karis: "Airborne One, what do you see to the west of our location?"

Felzeor: "A large Rasu contingent has reached Diarffor and is razing it. Rasu mechs are patrolling one kilometer out from the city."

A faint rustle to Eren's left preceded Avicia easing in beside him and Caleb. Though they didn't believe any Rasu were in the immediate vicinity, Avicia kept her voice to a whisper. "If we move quickly, we might be able to squeeze through between Calchfaen and those Rasu patrols. But it's a narrow window."

Caleb leaned in closer to speak under his breath. "What's past Diarffor?"

"A lot of open space, for one," Avicia replied. "South Rhaeadr Woods is younger and thinner—a massive wildfire tore through it a century ago—so we'll be able to move around more easily."

Eren shook his head. "We'll also be more exposed."

"And so will the enemy. The point is, we'll have options. But first, we've got to thread the needle ahead of us."

"Let's do it then."

Avicia faded back into the foliage and began issuing movement orders on the comm.

Eren tried to picture the geography beyond Calchfaen and Diarffor. He hadn't spent much time in the region, but he thought he remembered the general topography. "If we can reach Bendige, and if the Rasu haven't gutted it, we can resupply our munitions, then double back and hit the forces at Diarffor."

Beside him, Caleb sighed quietly. "Unless those munitions include more Rima Grenades or supersized Rectifiers, I'm not certain what good they'll do."

"Naraida are a shockingly creative people. They'll devise clever ways to take out the bastards."

"Temporarily, maybe. I'm sorry, Eren. I don't mean to be negative, but I do want to be realistic. You know I'm right."

"Then what would you have us do?"

"Make for the nearest airbase, appropriate a couple of ships, and get everyone out of here, yourself included."

Eren snorted. "That's not going to happen."

"I know it isn't."

"So since we're staying, we do the next best thing: we get ourselves some weapons and do what we can to make the invaders' lives a risen Tartarus hellscape."

RW

Felzeor: "Scout Sarga reports that Bendige has fallen."
Eren: "Arae!"
Karis: "Quiet!"
Eren's fists clenched and unclenched around the archine grenades he still carried at the ready. With the Rift Bubble disabled and the quantum block preventing anything more than a token

defense by Concord, the Rasu had swarmed over the planet like an endless dark horde. Five cities had fallen—likely more—and the air was thick with acrid smoke from the millions of square kilometers of forest that had already burned. This magical planet was being razed to the ground with but half a thought from these soulless enemies from the void.

He was just glad Cosime wasn't here to see it. No, he hurriedly corrected himself. He could never, *ever* be glad she wasn't here with him. But if she were, her heart would be shattered, and his would shatter in turn as he watched her grieve.

Felzeor's grief was bad enough, though the Volucri continued to put on a brave, resolute act. He was the cheerleader, the one who rallied everyone to never give up, no matter what. So Eren planned to keep fighting. For Felzeor, for Cosime's memory, for these plucky Naraida rebels-in-the-making. For the home he'd come to be rather fond of.

He glanced beside him, noting Caleb's serene expression and calm, steady composure. Caleb didn't have to fight; he had no skin this game beyond wanting to protect others. But Eren would be lying if he said he wasn't glad his friend was at his side. For one, Caleb was possibly the best hand-to-hand fighter he'd ever seen. The man was also a brilliant tactician. It would have been a boon if Caleb had also brought along a spot of *diati* to aid in the fight, but he supposed that was long in the past. If only Akeso wielded some magical fighting skills....

Felzeor: "*Rasu patrols outside of Diarffor are widening their perimeter. Scout Altala also reports a contingent of ten large Rasu mechs have left the city and are headed to the east.*"

Dammit!

Karis: "*Double-time it, everyone! We've got to make it past Calchfaen before the Rasu contingent arrives there.*"

Caleb picked up his pace in time with Eren. "How much farther to make that happen?"

"Unless the Rasu decide to stop for lunch on the way? Too far."

"Then we should pick a fallback location. Somewhere we can defend."

"There isn't one—not one we won't die at."

Caleb's pace quickened again, and Eren jogged to catch up.

Their rag-tag band pushed obstinately through the undergrowth for over an hour. The widespread fires drove the temperature and humidity to sweltering levels, until Eren's normally climate-suitable clothes were sopping wet. He wanted to rip off his shirt and leave it for the Rasu, but the limbs and brush would gouge his skin out in no time—

Flames abruptly leapt up to soar above the tree canopy. A deafening roar cascaded through the forest, and everyone came to a screeching halt.

Karis: "Airborne One, I need eyes on the forest west of Calchfaen."

Felzeor: "The smoke is too thick for us to get close. We do not see a way through."

Eren's stomach turned to lead. It wasn't as if they hadn't all known this was exactly what was going to transpire. But utterly irrational belief had surely kept more than one soldier alive through a siege of his land.

Karis: "Copy that."

Eren: "Everyone turn hard east and head for the riverbank five hundred meters north of the waterfall."

Karis: "You don't give the orders here, Anaden."

Well, that stung. As if he hadn't called this place home, as much as anywhere in Amaranthe could be home, for the last fifteen years of his life. *"We can head to the location I specified, or we can die. The forest is thick as it approaches the Afonle River. It'll provide us a measure of protection. There's a grove near the riverbank where we'll be able to make a temporary camp and set up fortifications."*

Karis: "We can still find a path through toward Bendige."

Eren: "Through a solid wall of flame? No, we can't. They've outmaneuvered us."

Eren had come to a stop beneath the broad leaves of a rubber tree, propping against it while he waited for Karis to come to the same, inevitable conclusion he had. Caleb stared at him expectantly, and he shrugged. "She'll make the right call."

They waited.

Karis: "Head east and make for the grove five hundred meters north of the waterfall."

"See?" He pushed off the tree and resumed their grueling pace. "Sorry you got yourself involved in this bloody lost cause?"

"No. And it's not a lost cause."

Eren glanced to the left, where dense smoke curled across the once verdant treetops. "Could have fooled me."

"We're not alone. Concord will find the quantum block, and when they do, the military will sweep in to our aid. Or Alex and Nika will succeed in their mission, and the Rasu will depart to chase after a bigger prize."

"What the hells *is* their mission, anyway? It's got to be something exceptional for her not to insist on being at your side, lost cause or no."

Caleb wiped grimy sweat off his brow. "She and Nika are seeding knowledge of kyoseil's unique properties in various rival Rasu factions. The hope is, they'll chase after it then use it to try to control one another, thus kicking off a Rasu civil war."

"Huh. I admit, that whole side of the war is not my focus at present, but I thought I heard the Reor didn't work for the Rasu."

"It doesn't. Nika has, however, asked it to acquiesce and allow the Rasu to use its capabilities for their…endeavors."

"And it said yes?"

"Apparently."

"Huh. Odd bird, that Kirumase. I like her, though. She's got style. So this plan of theirs—how long is it going to take to kick in?"

Caleb stared at the thickening forest ahead. "Let's just keep moving."

RW

Some interminable span of blistering agony later, they stumbled into a copse of merciful shade. The air didn't smell as much of roasted foliage and hot plasma here, and in the distance rushing water gurgled excitedly toward Calchfaen's mighty waterfall.

Instantly, Karis was issuing orders. "I want armed spotters up in the trees every forty meters. Avicia, choose three people and get to work cutting down vines and crafting them into nets. Bemek, dig us some trenches on the perimeter." She exhaled harshly, her narrow shoulders dropping as she waved toward two Naraida Eren didn't know. "You, go find us some food."

Karis: "Airborne One, return to us. You need to rest."

Not even Felzeor argued with the order; the Volucri squad had been in the air for over eight uninterrupted hours, every minute spent on hyper-alert.

Karis stalked over to them, then jerked her head at Caleb. "What can you do?"

"You mean, besides kill Rasu? Whatever you need me to do." His gaze went toward the source of the gurgling water, where through gaps in the branches on the far edge of the grove, the Afonle River spanned fifty meters. On the other side of the bank, sheer cliffs jutted up into the smoke-laden sky. "This is a solid location for us to rest and regroup, but it strikes me that we need to start thinking about a way out of here. Right now, the Rasu are content to have cut off any escape routes at the pass. But once they've solidified their positions, they're going to sweep the region for every living thing they can find. It's what they do. Is Calchfaen traversable?"

"The waterfall? Not a chance. The cliffs? Only for the Volucri. Legend has it that in five centuries, only three people have survived the climb."

"Legends exaggerate."

"Not by much." Eren sighed. "Sorry, mate, but they're not traversable."

"All right." Caleb's jaw flexed. "What are the cliffs made of?"

"Limestone, mostly."

"More malleable than solid rock, at least. Traversable or not, I think I'll make some scaling pitons."

Karis scowled. "In the impossible likelihood that a few of us somehow make it to the top of the cliffs, there's no forest cover for sixty kilometers in every direction. We'll be totally exposed to aerial attacks."

Caleb started walking toward the border of the grove. "Exposed is better than both drowning or being burnt alive. One problem at a time."

63

HIRLAS

*F*elzeor: *"—turned east and are advancing on our position."*
Eren jerked awake at the sound in his ear, then leapt to his feet. The camp was pitch black, as the now-omnipresent smoke obscured a normally star-glutted sky, and they hadn't wanted to risk ground torches. Infrared vision revealed spots of tumult as people roused themselves from the few fitful hours of sleep they'd been able to steal.

In retrospect, they shouldn't have even bothered getting comfortable. Caleb had warned them about the Rasu's relentless invasion tactics. They'd never had much time.

Caleb's infrared form burned noticeably hotter than any Naraida did, and Eren picked his way over to where the man sat, his back against a tree trunk. When he got there, he discovered Caleb was whittling at a limb he'd pulled from a large stack situated to his left. "Did you sleep any?"

"Not really."

"Hmm. And how many pitons have you made?"

"Enough to get about halfway up the cliff, assuming none break. I'm not exactly working with a metamat here."

Eren nodded deliberately. "It was a good dream. I think I'll go climb a tree and shoot off a couple of Rima Grenades. Care to join me?"

Caleb climbed to his feet, dropping the limb back onto the stack. "It would be my honor."

Eren: *"Karis, meet me at the munitions pile. I need a consult."*

When they got there, Caleb grabbed the bag holding the Rima Grenades and slung it over his shoulder, while Eren retrieved the launcher.

"What are you two doing?"

He pivoted to face Karis' shadowy form. "Going to take out those mechs before they get anywhere close to us."

"You're going to fire one of those black holes into the *forest*? You'll turn South Rhaeadr Woods into a giant crater!"

"Actually, I'm planning to fire—" he glanced at Caleb "—how many do we have left?"

"Six."

"Actually, I'm planning to fire six of those black holes into the forest. The Rasu are going to turn it into a giant crater anyway. Better for us to do it and live to fight another day."

"Damnable abominations, forcing us to desecrate our home…fine." Karis dragged a hand through once-magenta feathery hair that had long since darkened to soot. "Do it. But aim your void bombs far away from us."

"Yes, ma'am." He motioned to Caleb, and they traversed the camp and struck out into the forest. Dawn might be approaching, but it was difficult to determine due to the choking haze. His cybernetics were down, of course, so there was nothing to tell him what the local time was.

He studied his friend out of the corner of his eye. Sweaty and as filthy as the rest of them, but utterly calm and composed. "So…you and regenesis…."

Caleb shrugged noncommittally. "Maybe."

"I won't have you dying for me."

"Oh, don't worry. I'll be dying for Felzeor."

He huffed a laugh. "That is a more worthy death, for certain. Still."

Caleb's hand landed on his shoulder. "Everybody dies sometime. Or at least, they used to, in the world I came from. What's important is to die for honorable reasons, in service of a righteous cause. This is one."

R W

Dawn had definitely broken by the time they'd climbed up a wide balsa tree to reach a sturdy set of limbs near the top of the canopy. Eren could tell this only because the leaden sky was a dirty brown rather than sooty black.

The advancing Rasu were easy enough to spot, as a vast swath of the forest heaved erratically ahead of an encroaching line of flames. They were burning as they went, godsdammit.

"I thought the Rasu preferred to harvest natural resources and cart them away."

Caleb opened the flap on his bag and retrieved a Rima Grenade. "They do. But this entire planet is a natural resource. I imagine they figure there will be plenty left to plunder once they eradicate the local population."

"And they'd be right." He studied the landscape from their improved vantage. The Rasu were around eight kilometers away—far enough to evaporate without endangering the camp, albeit not for much longer.

He loaded the launcher, hefted it onto his shoulder and squinted, trying to sight down on the moving forest in the distance. Once he was satisfied with his target, he pressed the trigger.

A *whooshing* sound echoed from the fringes of the blast radius, akin to a gust of wind whipping through the limbs. After it had quieted, what remained was a giant crater two kilometers wide and eighty meters deep. Just like Karis had said.

"I think you got them all."

"And five shots left to play with. Oh, what I wouldn't give for a proper radar and targeting system. I could hit Diarffor from here and take out several hundred of the rotters."

"It's for the best," Caleb replied. "They're going to send more forces our way now."

"Shit, have I painted a bullseye on our camp?"

"Nah. It already had one. Those mechs were headed in a straight line for us. They knew where we were. The Rasu have presumably had stealthed surveillance drones up in the sky this whole time."

"Then why haven't they flown a frigate over to the grove and incinerated us all in one blast?"

Caleb sighed, balancing on an intersection of two limbs. "Because they don't have to. They can set fire to the forest at strategic locations on their way to their next destination, and the fire will reach the camp and trap us against the river and the cliffs."

"Drown or be burnt alive."

"Yep. They send out a couple of mechs to guarantee the fire doesn't peter out and we don't slip through, while keeping the bulk of their forces spreading out across the continent. Now that you've put a crater in the ground, though, I imagine they will send aerial forces to end us."

Eren groaned and banged his head on the limb behind him; probably got splinters in his scalp. "Well, this little resistance has not lasted nearly as long as I'd hoped it would. I had dreams of us pulling hit-and-run operations on Rasu hotspots, harassing their supply lines, luring them into traps—the whole resistance routine. It was going to be glorious."

"Yeah, we did that on Namino for a few days. It sucked."

"Ha. Fair enough." In the distance, two Rasu frigates appeared on the horizon, and he waited impatiently for them to draw a bit closer. The Rima Grenade launcher had a lengthy theoretical range, but he didn't want to waste the shot. Caleb was right; two ships weren't going to be the end of it. More likely, the beginning.

Eren: "Karis, you'll want to start preparing for another evacuation." He'd have sent it in a private message if his comms were working properly, as he'd prefer not to set off a panic, but it was what it was.

Karis: "Understood."

It was a testament to Karis' calm under pressure that she didn't retort, 'evacuate to fucking where?' If she had, Eren wouldn't have had a good response.

The ships drew closer, and he sighted the launcher reticle on them then pressed the trigger once more. The tiny orb leaving the chamber was barely noticeable, and four seconds later, the ships were simply…gone.

"If we had a hundred of these launchers and an unlimited supply of Rima Grenades, we might be able to defeat this invasion from the ground."

Caleb nodded stoically. "They pretty much did that at Toki'taku, though they also had a lot of help from orbit. If—when—we get back to civilization, I'll mention the possibility of distributing Rima Grenades across the colonies to Miriam. Especially since the Rift Bubbles aren't proving to be as reliable as we thought they'd be."

"Yeah. How many planets do you think the Rasu secretly snuck assets onto before the Rift Bubbles were operational?"

"Too many." Caleb motioned ahead. "Reinforcements."

The final four Rima Grenades sent over two dozen Rasu vessels back to the void…and that was that.

A gloom as dark and bottomless as any he'd experienced since those nightmarish days spent detoxing with Drae descended upon him as he followed Caleb down the tree trunk. It had been fun to vaporize a couple of Rasu, sure, but it hadn't done a damn bit of good. Their forces were overwhelming, and they would roll right over him and his companions without hardly noticing the lives stamped out beneath their tracks. To the Styx with this cursed enemy.

64

SIYANE

NGC 4697 GALAXY

Alex intertwined her hands and stretched her arms over her head as she traced circles through the main cabin. Every so often, she stopped and bent over to the left, then the right. Her muscles ached something fierce after shoving six of the cumbersome glass enclosures out of a hold that didn't want to let go of them and sending them off into space. Caleb would've made much quicker work of the task....

Her chest seized up at the thought of him. He'd run headlong into the fight yet again to save those he cared about, heedless to the danger his actions posed to himself. If a Rasu sliced him into a hundred pieces, Akeso couldn't bring him back from it. And while the planet would be able to create a simulacrum that resembled him down to the smallest details, it would speak with Akeso's voice. It might carry within it a flicker that represented Caleb's soul...but only a flicker.

She'd actually finally talked him into getting a neural imprint after the battle on Ireltse, wonder of wonders. She suspected something about bringing Pinchu back from the brink of death had influenced his feelings on the subject. But the reason didn't matter so much as the result.

Perhaps it shouldn't have come as a surprise when the med tech had said Caleb's readings didn't match a normal human brain pattern. She'd had Abigail take a look at it as well, and the doctor had agreed that his imprint was most unusual. Why wouldn't it be? Both his physiology and his consciousness were utterly unique, likely in the entire universe.

If he…died, she'd obviously go ahead with loading the imprint into a new body. No other option existed. But thanks to that uniqueness, there was no guarantee it would work, and the uncertainty was the ultimate 'but,' lingering in the shadows. And while, thanks to Akeso, he was nearly impossible to kill, 'nearly' was too weak of an assurance to let her rest easy when he was putting himself in mortal danger. Too damn many qualifiers haunted her every rumination.

'We will arrive at the final target location in eight minutes.'

"Thanks, Valkyrie." She smiled at Nika, who was sitting quietly on the couch—talking to her people back home, or chasing quantum blocks across her worlds. "Almost done."

"I'll head to Mirai as soon as we make the last delivery. I've done what I can to give us as much protection as possible from here, but the battles on Synra and Kiyora continue to rage, and they could benefit from my undivided attention."

"Understood. I plan to go to Hirlas straightaway."

"Do you know where Caleb is, or how the defense of the planet is going?"

"Nope, and a disaster. Doesn't matter. I can sense his heartbeat from here, so I expect it'll lead me to him, like it did on Namino."

Nika merely nodded. They were both exhausted and depressed. The last several days had brought home in stark, undeniable terms exactly how pervasive the Rasu truly were. The *Siyane* had meandered all across the Laniakea Supercluster, covering greater distances in a shorter period of time than anyone in history. And everywhere they went, they found nothing but Rasu. From a bird's-eye perspective, the aliens' conquering of Laniakea was all but complete. If left unchecked, they would take over the Shapley and Hercules Superclusters in a matter of a few centuries, and from there, the rest of Amaranthe.

Crazy that they thought their little provocateur plan could bring an end to such an overwhelming threat to their existence. But something had to, and, all-but-insurmountable odds or not, she was damn sure going to try.

She refastened her environment suit, which she'd let hang open at the chest for a few blissful minutes, and headed downstairs. One to go.

RW

"What are you planning to do when this war is over?"

Nika smiled faintly as they checked the last enclosure. "Dashiel and I are going to escape to the mountains on Adjunct Hachi for a week. Or a month. Ever since he traveled there a while ago to meet…someone who's not with us any longer, he's been wanting to visit for a vacation. No other Advisors, no crises, no diplomacy, no assembly lines, no noise. Just us, the snow and the mountains."

"Sounds fantastic. Me, I'm going to sleep. Then sleep some more. I don't particularly care where."

"That is also a—" Nika jerked, her gaze darting to the ceiling. "They've already located the first kyoseil deposit."

"Target #1?"

"I assume so. It's one of the closest deposits to where we delivered the initial payload. They're scraping the kyoseil out of the asteroid and hauling it back to…yes, that same stronghold." The woman breathed in ponderously, the darkness of desolation consuming her features. "I feel sick to my stomach. I hate this so much."

"Ordering the kyoseil to work for the Rasu?"

"I didn't order it. I explained the situation and offered it the choice. I hope it understood what I was asking and why, but…it's not fair to ask such an exquisite, in many ways incomprehensible, life form to fight our battles for us."

'Arrival at destination in fifty seconds.'

"I think…" Alex searched for words to ease Nika's mind "…Caleb said something once, when he still controlled *diati* and it was 'speaking' to him, after a fashion. He said that if the choice of allegiance was made wisely, no other choices need be made. Given what we now know about Amaranthe history and the parallels between *diati* and kyoseil, it makes sense for a similar notion to apply to it. The kyoseil chose to bond with your people long ago, presumably because it believed you were the right partner for it to accompany into the future. But it also actively chose to bond with you personally on a far deeper level in the Oneiroi Nebula. I suspect it knows it made a wise choice, and it trusts you to make the best decisions for both Asterions and kyoseil."

"I want to believe you're right." Nika nodded roughly. "Regardless, I can't go back now. So let's do this thing."

'The Rasu are more dense in this area than usual. I will attempt to maintain a steady position, but be prepared for turbulence.'

Of course there were *even more* Rasu here. "Duly noted. Open the ramp."

They had the process down to a science by now, and she and Nika unlatched the restraints without issue, then positioned themselves on the near side of the enclosure.

Alex peeked around the side to the check their path and frowned. It took her a second to determine that the ramp was open, because there was only uninterrupted darkness outside. An unbroken wall of Rasu to blot out the sun.

She shivered inside the hot, sweaty environment suit. "Now."

They shoved, grunting with exertion as the grippy floor fought their efforts to move the enclosure all the way from the rear of the hold toward and down the ramp—

'Evasive maneuvers.'

Alex fell backwards until her helmet bounced off the floor; her magboots stayed glued in place, and she heard something *pop* in her left knee in time with a jolt of agonizing pain.

The enclosure toppled sideways and slammed into the port wall, then teetered on one edge before crashing back down to the floor a scant centimeter from Alex's arm.

Belatedly, she snatched her arm in to her chest. "Are you okay?"

No response. Alex carefully tilted her head to see Nika lying beside her. Blood trickled from the woman's nose, and her eyes were closed.

Wincing, she sent a command to unlock her boots so she could wrench her leg out of its untenable position and roll toward Nika—

The *Siyane* spiraled upward at a thirty-degree angle, and the free enclosure tumbled down the ramp and out into the sea of Rasu.

Lock!

But it was too late. She pitched forward and, unmoored by gravity or magnetics, her momentum carried her toward a yawning opening that was closing, but not fast enough.

The ship abruptly reversed its angle as Valkyrie tried to scoop them up before they fell out of the hold. The walls of the hull raced by her as the ramp closed in and—Nika crashed into her from the left, and they both tumbled out into space.

Calm. This was not her first spacewalk. Admittedly, it might be her first one while surrounded by a hundred thousand enemies.

She fired the tiny thrusters on the back of her environment suit to slow her rate of movement. The *Siyane* drifted in front of her. The ramp had reversed course, and she was almost able to reach out and grab it from here.

But Nika was nowhere to be seen.

I need a target tracker on Nika!

A blinking dot lit up in her virtual vision. *She is located twenty-two meters from you, on a heading N 82° -2°z. Her momentum continues to carry her away from you at a rate of 1.5 meters per second. She is not responding to hails.*

Alex oriented herself and fired the thrusters again. Even this close, she couldn't distinguish Nika from the tableau of Rasu all around them, as there was no light to reflect off the material of the woman's environment suit. If Valkyrie were to turn on a couple of exterior lights?

The Rasu will detect our presence.

I know. Keep her location locked.

Be warned. There is a frigate-sized Rasu moving fifty-three meters beyond Nika's current location.

Great. She fired the thrusters in micro-bursts. Twelve meters. Nine.

The Rasu is thirty-eight meters away and closing.

Finally, a glint of reflection off what might be Nika's boot. And just beyond it, an inky darkness more ominous than any void.

Three meters. One. She reached out and grabbed Nika's leg with both hands. Keeping a solid grip, she twisted around, using Nika's momentum to maneuver them both until they generally faced the *Siyane*.

A sense of great *weight* loomed over her shoulder, but she didn't dare waste a nanosecond to contemplate it as she fired the thrusters once more. The tracker dot in her vision was replaced by one for the *Siyane*. They drew closer to one another, converging on a point in space—possibly the last point in space devoid of Rasu for an AU in every direction.

Simply stay on your current trajectory. I will net you.

She didn't argue. The dot grew larger—then suddenly she made out a faint white light ahead. The emergency lighting at the base of the ladder in the rear of the engineering well.

Kill your thrusters.

Confident this was all in Valkyrie's capable hands, she obeyed. The next instant walls sped past her; she put her free hand out in front of her to brace the impact, and she hit the hull beside the ladder with a *thud.*

A hiss filled the air as the ramp seated into the closed position and the airlock was established. Gravity returned, and she and Nika both crashed to the floor.

Get us the—wait, not yet. Shit.

The Rasu enclosure and internal force field are still intact.

Yep. Make like a hole in space.

She ditched her helmet. Breathed in, breathed out. Again. Rolled sideways and onto her knees—owww, nope. Her left knee was definitely out of its socket.

She settled for stretching her left leg out and bending on one knee over Nika. How to collapse the suit's helmet? God, the woman probably did it with her mind.

A faint murmur echoed in her comm, and Nika's lips moved. A

blink, then another. Her eyes opened. "What happened?"

"I'll fill you in, but first, can you release our last saboteur from its cage so we can get out of here?"

"Right, um..." her brow furrowed, sending a trickle of blood wandering along her upper lip "...it's done."

"Great. Valkyrie?"

'We are already departing.'

Nika grunted and pushed up to a sitting position, and her helmet receded into the suit without her touching anything. She *did* do it with her mind! She brought a hand to her nose, and her glove came away streaked in blood. "I think I...maybe collided with the enclosure while it was tumbling out of control hard enough to break my mag boots' grip on the floor. My head ricocheted, and must have hit the faceplate hard enough to crack my nose." She looked around, her eyes becoming clearer and more focused. "I don't remember anything else. What happened?"

"Oh, we went for a little space walk."

"What?"

"It all worked out." Alex struggled to her feet; luckily the ladder wasn't far away. "Let's go get your nose patched up, and I'll get a medwrap for my knee, which is currently in a different place than it's supposed to be."

"Ouch."

Alex hopped awkwardly up the ladder, hobbled through the bedroom and dragged herself up the staircase and over to the cabinet holding the med kit. She tossed Nika a patch to stop the bleeding from her nose, then limped across the cabin, collapsed on the couch, and started stripping out of her environment suit.

"Well, that's done. Now, we wait. I'm terrible at waiting."

Nika laughed weakly—then her features froze for a second. "One of the targeted groups has reached another kyoseil deposit."

"Is it the same one?"

"I don't...no." Her gaze sharpened, and she pressed the patch to the bridge of her nose. "This is what we hoped for. At least two factions now have kyoseil in their hands. If they respond the way we think they should, a conflict ought to arise soon."

"It'll happen." Mercifully freed of the suit and wearing fitted shorts beneath it, Alex began gingerly wrapping her knee in the cool, soothing gel medwrap. "Control is their drug, and we've handed them the promise of a limitless supply...."

A tickle in the back of her mind demanded her attention. *THUMP-thump......THUMP...thump....*

Caleb's heartbeat lived always in the recesses of her awareness, its constancy a comfort to her as she went about her life. But now....

It was slowing down.

THUMP...thump... ... THUMP... ...thump... ... ...thump... ... ...

With every weakening beat, her life drained away alongside his—no! This was not going to happen. She refused to allow it.

She leapt up, gritting through the pain of bearing weight on her left knee, and stumbled toward the cockpit. "Nika, you should head on home and dive back into the fight. I need to get to Hirlas—now."

65

HIRLAS

Caleb grabbed Felzeor by the feathers on his wings and held him in place. "Felzeor, you and Airborne One get up in the skies right away. You'll be safer up there. You can evade the Rasu for as long as you have to. Seek shelter up in the mountains."

"No! We need to stay here and be your eyes and ears. If we leave, you'll be blind to incoming Rasu."

Eren returned to collapse against the broad tree trunk beside them. "We'll make do. If you won't listen to Caleb, then listen to me as your mission commander. Get out of here. You can scout the whole damn planet and make note of where the Rasu forces are the heaviest. Then, later, you can report back."

"I don't work for you any longer, Eren. You can't tell me what to do." Felzeor yanked one wing out of Caleb's grasp. "I want to protect my friends."

"And I won't let you die." Caleb kept eye contact with the Volucri through sheer intimidation. "Do you remember when I saved your life on Chionis fifteen years ago?"

"Yes...."

"You owe me a life debt. I say when you can die, and it's not today. Now go!"

Felzeor landed on a branch above Eren, his feathers dropping until his tail dragged across the bark. "I will feel shame."

"No, you won't. You will be proud to live to fight another day."

"But what if the two of you die?"

"We won't. Akeso won't let me die, remember? And Eren will just wake back up in a regenesis lab for the...what? Four-hundredth time?"

"Easily." Eren surreptitiously wiped blood off his temple.

Felzeor peered down at them for a long moment. "Your logic is suspicious, but persuasive. I will confer with the others in Airborne One about departing."

Eren shook his head. "You're their leader. You tell them what's going to happen. They'll follow you."

"Yes." Felzeor abruptly fluttered up into the air. "I love you, my friends."

"We love you, too, Felzeor. We'll see you on the other side."

Caleb waited until Felzeor had flown out of earshot, then leaned heavily on the wide trunk beside Eren. "What's the word?"

"Oh, we're righteously fucked. Three new groups of Rasu mechs are about three kilometers out and closing in fast. Two frigates are tracking their advance, ready to roast what bones remain, I guess. We've got our backs against these cliffs and that blasted waterfall, and they know it. South Rhaeadr Woods is burning to the ground. A strong easterly breeze comes along, and we won't be able to breathe here from the smoke. Had an injured Naraida stumble into camp ten minutes ago, bleeding all over everything. He said Diarffor is a smoking pile of rubble. He skirted Bendige on the way here, and it's overrun, too."

"And nothing on the location of the quantum block?"

"According to Karis, nada. I suppose once they burn every forest on the planet to the ground, the Volucri should be able to spot it then. But so what if they do? The Naraida don't have much of a fleet, and what they did have was leveled in the first hour of the invasion. We've got nothing to destroy it with, and no way to get word of its location to Concord."

"Maybe I can make it back to the Ghost and...."

Eren snorted. "Yeah, um, I think half of Charego Mountain fell on top of it when a Rasu beam cut the peak in two. Buried everything on the southeast side of Choeda."

"Right—"

A thunderous rumble crashed through the jungle to the west, and he and Eren rushed out into the main camp.

Half a dozen Naraida were scrambling up into the surrounding tree limbs, but Caleb didn't need a spotter to tell him what was coming. Irregular thuds echoed closer and closer—the sound of Rasu trampling the ancient, giant trees as they closed in on the rebels' location.

He looked behind him, where the Afonle River streamed with ashen, soot-filled water. Several of the locals had whipped together makeshift rafts to use in crossing it, if it became necessary. But to what end? There was hardly a bank at all on the other side before the sheer limestone cliffs rose up for nearly three hundred meters.

All their hovercars had been destroyed in the fighting, so they had no way to ferry anyone to the top of the cliffs. And just out of sight, past a bend in the river, the waterfall waited to claim as its victims any who ventured into its deadly grasp.

And that was it. No other means of escape.

It would be easy to blame themselves—to blame the other rebels, but most of all for him to blame himself—for allowing everyone to get cornered like this. But while he didn't know the landscape, he trusted Eren, and he'd come to trust Karis and the others. He believed them when they said there hadn't been another option. Their group had had been pushed inexorably to the south and east by the Rasu advancement. They'd had the narrowest of windows to slip through to the south, but the Rasu had beat them there and cut the route off, leaving but one course available to them.

And here they were, surrounded on all sides by certain death. Only the means of delivery differed.

Caleb took some consolation from the fact that Eren would live, and likely Felzeor as well. Regenesis for the Volucri was still in the testing phase, but all eligible CINT agents were required to get regenesis-grade neural scans every three months.

As for himself, matters weren't so clear. As Alex had pointed out more than once, Akeso could keep his life force functioning through nearly anything, but not through a Rasu shredder. And, somewhat to his surprise, he found himself hoping against hope that the 'unique' neural imprint he'd recorded would be sufficient to bring him back.

He wasn't sure exactly when his change of heart had happened. Maybe a little during his trial by fire on Namino, then a little more when he breathed life directly into Pinchu's veins. A touch more when he'd reunited with Corradeo and found forgiveness, then every day since then.

But whenever and however he'd gotten here, he now recognized something with undeniable clarity: he wanted to live. Forever, so long as Alex continued to walk through this life beside him. He wanted to see what happened next. Next month, next year, next millennia.

So he'd believe that he stood a reasonable chance of waking up in a medical chamber in a few days, Alex's beautiful face scowling down at him.

But virtually no one else here would. The best scientists and researchers remained unable to make regenesis work for Naraida. All these people he'd been fighting alongside for days were going to die for the first and last time—the *thudding* grew louder—and die soon.

Eren had taken off to bark orders along the front line, directing the placement of improvised explosives fifty meters into the jungle. Four Naraida swung from limb to limb above Caleb, hanging nets made of shockingly sharp vines. He wasn't convinced they would slice through the tough Rasu metal, but they should entangle the mechs a bit. A few of them, anyway.

You are despondent.

Yes. Most of these people are going to die in the next fifteen minutes.

You have grown to care about them.

Of course, but even if I hadn't. They don't deserve to die. They've fought bravely for their home, and these monsters are going to destroy it. Destroy their way of life, then their very lives.

The Rasu-enemy takes everything from all these souls. For what purpose?

Because it can.

Enough wallowing. He needed to get up in a tree and find a vantage point. At least the Rectifier should take out a few Rasu mechs once they drew near—

Wait.

His step hitched briefly. *What is it?*

This planet is bursting with life. With vigor and energy.

Yes, and the Rasu are destroying it all. He didn't want to get annoyed, but now was most decidedly not the time for one of Akeso's long, meandering metaphysical treatises.

When we last visited this planet, I noted that it would take but a single spark generously applied to awaken its voice. What if we could do so?

I'm sorry, but now is not the time to wax philosophically about the spark of life in all creations.

No, now is the time for action. I have fashioned life in the image of many things. New things. Organic things. Together, we have healed organic life, when but a trickle of anima remained. I believe we can infuse this world with my/our life force and awaken its voice.

Now he stopped in his tracks. *You want to transfer some of your essence to Hirlas?*

I want to try.

But it's an entire planet. How would we start?

As every root, every leaf, every boulder, every droplet of water is Akeso, so do I need only a single root to begin.

It was impossible. A ludicrous notion. Yet, in spite of himself, his mind leapt to how the Kats had used kyoseil to create sentience in Akeso. Mesme's words echoed back to him.

> *'Seeded' with kyoseil would be a more accurate way to put it. The planet is not kyoseil—you cannot extract fibers from its soil or even its core. But in the womb we created, kyoseil was used to ignite a spark of life. And we succeeded beyond our grandest hopes.*

They'd used a fragment of ancient, primordial life as a fountainhead, and from it had sprung an intelligence that spanned a planet. The wellspring of that life—of the kyoseil which had seeded Akeso—now coursed in his blood, did it not?

Could it be enough to ignite a new spark?

You honestly believe we can do this? How will it work?

Allow me to show you.

Words did not suffice, so Akeso filled his mind with its vision of what it might do. His heart swelled at the beauty of it all, and he'd never treasured Akeso's pure soul more than he did at this moment.

This is insane. But we have to try, don't we?

I worry there is some risk to you. You are my conduit, and I do not wish to drain you. But I do not know how much of my essence will be required to ignite the flame of life in this world. I will do all in my power to maintain you throughout the process.

I know you will. Don't worry about me.

He smiled to himself, certainty buoying him for the first time in days. He didn't want to die—but if he could save all these people, and the millions more still fighting across the planet, and everything that was good and noble here, he had to try, no matter the cost.

He rushed through the camp until he located Eren, then grabbed his friend by the arm and handed him the Rectifier. "Listen. I have an idea."

Eren listened to the plan with mounting incredulity, until he finally cut Caleb off. "When I first met you and Alex, and you pitched me your plan to break into the Machim Central Command Complex, do you remember what I said to you? Because I do. I quote from memory here: 'In three hundred years of a life filled with debauchery, appalling excess, rebellion against a merciless, all-powerful regime and a record-setting number of suicide stunts, you are the two most insane individuals I have ever met.' I'll give Alex a pass, though odds are she doesn't deserve it, but you? Today, fifteen years later, I stand by my statement."

RW

Caleb hurried to a spot along the riverbank, away from the tumultuous, frantic activity and orders of the camp. Every second counted now, and there was no time to waste.

He dropped to his knees and yanked his shirt over his head, then tossed it to the side.

I love you, Alex. You are my light in the darkness, always.

He activated his plasma blade and, before he could question his actions, sliced it across both palms—then across both wrists. Akeso soothed the spike of pain as he thrust his hands deep into the loose, damp soil beneath him.

I am the nourishing water flowing out from the creek and swirling through the roots beneath the soil. I am the sun's rays bearing down upon the earth.

I am life incarnate, unbound by blood or neuron. My life voice travels through this nourishing water-blood into new roots and new soil, undimmed.

Replace the silence of your roots with the voice that burns within me.

Renew your connection to each flower, each tree, each rock and stream. Reach outward to connect all atoms to one another and carry my nourishing water-blood to circulate through them.

Replenish your cells with my own. Recognize the life force they contain, and know that it is now within you.

AWAKEN.

His mind felt sluggish, his thoughts barely a trickle now. He had trouble remembering what he was doing…but it was so terribly important.…

Life. Life born anew. AWAKEN.

The soil beneath him was stained a dirty crimson…was that his blood? Of course it was his. But was it enough? Had he given enough?

The rushing water of the Afonle River gurgled past him in his blurred, darkening vision. Akeso's essence needed to travel everywhere, and it needed to do so quickly.

His limbs heavy and leaden, he crawled one centimeter at a time along the bank and toward the water's edge. When the damp soil beneath him turned to mud, he collapsed to the ground, all his strength evaporating away through his weakening, thready pulse.

As his vision receded down a narrowing tunnel, he willed himself the strength for one more act, and stretched his arms out until they were submerged in the frigid river.

His blood flowed freely into the water and was carried away to the cascading waterfall and points beyond.

66

HIRLAS

Eren tied off the left side of the net around the tree trunk with a violent yank, then sprinted down the line to the next one—but this was the end. They were out of nets.

The ground now shook with every step of the approaching Rasu. The units had fashioned themselves into giant quadrupedal mechs using wide, flat 'feet' to better tromp through the jungle, knocking trees to the side with abandon and trampling them into pancakes.

Ahead, a row of trees fell by the wayside, and two Rasu emerged into the new clearing. Eren fondled the Rectifier Caleb had left with him for a second, then raised it in both hands. He didn't want to evaporate the nets they'd worked so hard to string up, but from his current vantage, he could aim around them well enough.

He fired.

An inky blackness blotted out the jungle like an eclipse silencing the sun—then there was simply empty space where the mech and the jungle had been. Tree trunks were sliced cleanly through, as if felled by a blade, and a hole three meters deep had churned up the soil. Hey, maybe the next Rasu in line would trip and fall in it—

When it somehow *did*, he took the greatest of pleasure in shooting it while it floundered around in search of its footing. The hole in the earth grew deeper.

But, alas, the Rasu got wise to the trap then, and easily skirted around the crater. The first wave began to hit the nets.

He felt dark, despairing amusement at seeing the mechs get their limbs all tangled up in the sticky, sharp vines. While the enemy was stymied for a moment—it wouldn't last long—he spared a glance behind him to see a meager few people launching the rafts to traverse the river. They had nowhere to go after that, but the urge to live for even a few more precious minutes made one do any desperate thing.

Rasu fire shot through the jungle overhead, and he instinctively ducked. When he peered up, he realized Rasu on the rear line had fired through their own units in order to slice apart the nets. It seemed callous, but the broken mechs could reform, of course. And so they did.

How pitiful their little defense was. If the Rasu understood humor, they would be laughing at this pathetic display of thirty people fighting for their lives with vines and trenches—

The ground convulsed beneath him, and he fell back onto his ass. The hells? He was forty meters from the nearest Rasu....

A powerful shudder raced through the soil, tossing him into the air then abandoning him to plummet back down and land on his stomach. He wiped dirt out of his eyes and looked up in time to see two of the trees...he rubbed his eyes again. He must be hallucinating, because he could swear the trees stretched out their limbs and entangled one of the mechs in a vice grip.

Yep, there went another one. A sturdy limb bent itself into an impossible shape and wrapped around the weaponized arm of one of the mechs. It squeezed, tighter and tighter, like an anaconda constricting its prey, until the arm snapped clear off.

The jungled thundered in a magnificent roar, and chasms began opening in the ground beneath the Rasu's wide metal feet.

Eren scrambled up and scanned the camp behind him. Those that hadn't fled across the river were frozen in place as they stared in shock at the sudden carnage befalling their enemy.

Arae, had Caleb actually done it?

Wait, where in Hades' five rivers *was* Caleb?

RW

Know the Rasu-enemy for what it is. Fight for your/our lives to vanquish this cold, soulless invader. Fight to protect the life that calls you/us home.

Faults opened up in jagged crevasses throughout the jungles of the northern hemisphere continents. They dug themselves deeper and deeper, until the planet's outer core was breached and lava bubbled up unbound. Rasu-enemy units tumbled down the chasms and into the lava's eternal embrace.

When they didn't fall of their own accord, the great forests pushed them. Roots wrenched out of their moorings to scrape and claw and provide leverage. Lines were formed and fulcrums constructed, and the Rasu-enemy found itself hemmed in on all sides as the firmament vanished beneath it.

In the south, where the mountains rose into the sky in ranges stretching for thousands of kilometers, boulders tumbled from the peaks in a torrent to crush the horde that advanced on the ancestral birthplace of the flying creatures who called Hirlas home. Carried upon a swift and steep descent, they hit their marks at tremendous speed and leveled the Rasu-enemy flat.

Know the Rasu-enemy for what it is. It does not die so easily.

So the snows melted from the mountain peaks, sending a great flood to sweep away the damaged Rasu-enemy all the way to the eastern ocean. There, the water boiled as it welcomed its new guests; fissures opened in the ocean floor to spew super-heated water out of hydrothermal vents as the metal carcasses sank into the depths.

Understanding of the insidious nature of the Rasu-enemy percolated through the newly awakened consciousness of the planet from pole to pole, and everywhere it surrounded the broken metal pieces that had fallen. Brambles and branches poked and stabbed and tore them into smaller and smaller pieces, until there were only atoms. They wrent the atoms apart, then sterilized the dirt where the elementary particles fell so the Rasu-enemy could not poison all that now was.

Sensing an *absence* upon the land where there should be a burgeoning voice, tendrils raced across the jungle floor from all directions, closing in on the hole in their world. A towering metal idol rose beneath the sheltering canopy of the treetops, seeming to suck the very energy of the *All* into it.

The ground opened up from the inside out, starting deep beneath the idol. Crust and stone and soil fell into the crevasse, clearing the way, until finally the fissure ripped through the surface in one great swell, and the idol plummeted straight through to the center of the planet.

The air burst to life with activity, from everywhere and nowhere. Waves swept across the skies as the beings who called this world home chattered excitedly to one another, and words external to its awakened voice raced from one end of the planet to another.

Mighty ships descended from the stars—

Not Rasu-enemy. Friends to aid in the fight.

And so the great forests, towering mountains and roiling oceans allowed the mighty ships to pass above them. They endured the scars inflicted from the ships' scalding weapons, for they understood that those weapons injured the Rasu-enemy above all.

While the ships swept across their land, they scoured every grove, river and crag for lingering traces of the Rasu-enemy. And when they found those traces, they eliminated them with a brutal efficiency born of righteous anger and a burning desire to live. They had found their voice, and they would not relinquish it now, to this enemy or any other.

67

SAGAN

MILKY WAY GALAXY

The atmosphere burned in streaks of teal and salmon past the cockpit. The hull vibrated from the buffeting forces, but hardly enough to notice. The Banshee truly was a marvel.

Morgan spun and dove through the stratosphere. It fought her, of course, but she would win. *"Riley and Landon, with me. Our target is a Rasu transport at heading N 31° W dropping toward the surface with haste."*

In Stanley's awareness more than hers, her squadmates fell in on her port and starboard as they began gaining on the target.

The quantum block the Rasu had constructed on the planet must be fairly small, as its reach extended only up to the edge of the troposphere. This meant ships could operate with full capabilities down to nine kilometers from the surface. Trouble was, most ships couldn't operate with full capabilities in-atmosphere, period. They merely plowed through it using brute force, minimal maneuverability and zero finesse.

Not the Banshee. It almost seemed as if it was designed to use the air currents and shifting pressure to its advantage, like a glider. She'd had a similar thought about it being made for the void while flying well beyond the atmosphere's fringes, too. Basically, it was a versatile little beast.

Were she and her new squad playing a dangerous game, dogfighting less than a kilometer from the quantum block barrier? Sure, but that was why they were fighter pilots. Somebody had to do the stupid shit if Concord wanted to win here today.

The Rasu transport came into visual range ahead. It was dropping fast; they didn't have much time. She accelerated to max in-atmo speed and headed straight for the engines. *I want concentrated fire on the port engine. If we can disable its propulsion, hopefully it will spin out of control and plummet into the middle of the ocean.*

Against the thick air of the stratosphere, her RNEW weapon burned a bright kaleidoscope of colors as it evaporated the surrounding air while streaking toward the target, then impacted dead-on the port engine output valve. Fire from Landon and Riley's Banshees followed, and in 4.2 seconds, the port engine detached from the Rasu hull and fell away.

The transport lurched off its course, whipping around toward—

"Evasive maneuvers!" It was a stupid thing to say. Her squad was a talented bunch, and they knew how to avoid return fire.

But the weapon the Rasu was firing was wide and powerful, with a diameter as broad as three frigates. Morgan yanked up hard, into the haze of cloud cover.

Riley: "I'm hit! Beam took out my engine."

Shit. It was the one weakness in an advanced adiamene ship. The Zero Engine had to release its energy to propel the ship, and that meant a too-large opening in an otherwise virtually seamless hull. A strike which hit the exposed section of the engine wouldn't destroy the ship, as adiamene protected the interior behind the housing, but it could take out the engine itself.

Landon: "I'm hit, too. Hard spin—"

The comm cut out then. Because they were dead? No, that was impossible. Because they'd dropped into the quantum block.

Morgan pitched her ship downward and accelerated after them.

I advise against this course of action. You cannot rescue them.

I submit I can.

Revision: You can reach them, but you cannot get them off the surface in your ship. There is only room for you inside.

Fine. I can protect them on the ground until a slightly bigger ship comes along.

You are not a Marine. Find another way.

She flung the ship back up in a fit of frustration. God, how she hated it when Stanley was right.

The Banshees would fly in the quantum block—barely. But with their engines destroyed, they would also crash. Landon and Riley would eject and survive the crash. They'd then be stuck somewhere on the surface, hopefully not the ocean as well, and be unable to comm for a rescue until such time as the quantum block was disabled.

Did we capture all available data on their trajectory and rate of descent until they hit the block?

We did. I can extrapolate their likely landing locations to within a five-kilometer radius.

It was better than nothing. Her mind raced, working through and discarding various rescue scenarios, most of which put herself in considerable peril.

I appreciate your need to look after those under your command, but based on your vitals and several hormone levels, you are becoming emotional about it. May I inquire as to why?

She conceded it was a valid question. She'd known her squad members for all of ten days. They'd spent most of the time in sims and most of the rest of it in test flights. In between, they'd shared a couple of meals and beers, but it would be a gross exaggeration to say they'd bonded in any meaningful way. She hadn't even thought up condescending nicknames for them yet.

So why did she care?

Because they were *hers*, and she'd be damned if the Rasu were going to steal them from her.

That does, in the odd manner that is you, make a minor amount of sense.

She ordered the rest of the squad out of the atmosphere and back into the primary battlespace, where they could continue shooting Rasu using more conventional tactics.

She set a course for the carrier.

R.W

CONCORD HQ
RASU WAR ROOM

Eight minutes later, Morgan climbed out of the cockpit and leapt to the hangar bay floor. As soon as her feet were under her, she opened a wormhole in front of her and strode through it into the Concord Command Rasu War Room. Devon's code to bypass the wormhole block on HQ still worked, which made this part of the plan much easier.

Officers hurried in various directions, but all activity revolved around Miriam Solovy, who stood halfway down the long table. The woman's hand flitted across two screens while her lips moved in soundless orders.

Morgan strode toward the woman—

"Halt!" A thick hand grabbed her upper arm. "You're not authorized to be in here."

She growled at the security officer and attempted to yank her arm away. She failed; he was quite strong, and she wasn't. "Let go of me. I need to speak to the commandant."

"You don't simply get to 'speak' to—"

"It's all right, Lieutenant. Let her pass."

The lieutenant glowered at her from beneath a heavy brow, but acceded to the order and stepped away. She resumed her course and marched the rest of the way down the length of the table.

"Commander Lekkas. It's been a while."

"Six years."

"Yes. I am a bit occupied, as you can imagine, so I'll ask you to be quick. What can I do for you?"

She hadn't been 'Commander' for years now, but Miriam Solovy was such a stickler for titles. Formal and rigid. "I lost two of my Banshee squad—HFB Squadron Three—on the ground at Sagan. I need a Marine RAR team to retrieve them."

"There's a quantum block in effect on Sagan."

"I know there is. But you have Marines ready to overcome that obstacle and insert into a combat zone anyway when the need arises."

"I do—or rather, Fleet Admiral Jenner does. If you insist on jumping the entire chain of command, why didn't you go directly to him?"

"Because he's a 'yes man.' He takes orders from you. Always has, always will. It seemed faster to skip that step, too."

The woman almost smiled. "The fleet admiral takes very few orders from me these days, but I won't waste time arguing with you. Commander, we've lost a fair number of people today, and are likely losing more as you and I stand here talking. I can't prioritize two of them to the exclusion of all others."

"Is that what you said when Brook's squad failed to report in from their mission on Ch'mshak, *Miriam?*"

Something flickered across the woman's features. "I see. If you want to finally have this argument, fine, but it will have to wait for a little while longer. Now is not the time—" She broke off to respond to a blaring red alert, scowling until deep lines creased her face.

Morgan tapped her foot impatiently. What if Riley and Landon were drowning while she stood here?

Though it includes a small amount of beach area, the estimated landing zone lies entirely on dry land.

Noted.

After finding several other excuses to ignore her, Miriam returned her attention to Morgan. Her gaze was hooded, hiding whatever her true thoughts might be behind a mask of professionalism.

"There are two Marine RAR squads attached to the *Aurora.* It appears I have cause to travel to Sagan now, so I'll deliver them myself." Miriam began striding toward the door, then looked over her shoulder. "Are you coming?"

Morgan blinked, stunned into inaction for the briefest second. Then she opened a wormhole and gestured to it. "Let's shortcut all the walking, shall we?"

Miriam glanced at the wormhole, sighing as she reversed course and joined Morgan. "Can everyone open wormholes inside HQ now?"

"No. Just the Noe—"

"The Noetica Prevos. I did figure that out. It's always you bunch, isn't it?"

But Morgan was already through the wormhole and waiting impatiently on the bridge of the *Aurora*.

68

CONCORD HQ

COMMAND

While the *Siyane* leapt across megaparsecs to reach a Hirlas under siege, Valkyrie diverted a portion of her primary consciousness to manifest in the observation room at Concord Command. She arrived to find it empty. Unsurprising, as no one had spare idle time to admire the stars at present.

Thomas, you called for me?

The barest outline of Thomas' panther avatar brightened one corner of the intentionally dim room. "I did. We are departing for Sagan in six minutes."

There was a nanosecond delay before she responded, as she was as fully present on the *Siyane* as she was here. "I thought Miriam was directing the multiple engagements from the War Room?"

"She has been. However, now a Human world has come under attack, and she is not wholly without sentiment. She can no longer stomach not being on the scene of what is a most consequential battle."

"I see." Valkyrie sent an urgent message to Abigail, and was relieved to discover that the woman had already been evacuated to a safe location. Still, Sagan had been her first home—the place where she had been born and come to awareness—and she worried deeply for its survival. "Do you need me to do something, Thomas? Alex and I are currently—"

"Nothing is required of you. I merely wanted to..." he paced along the viewports with notable intensity, as if searching for prey he could vanquish "...as you know, the Rasu are using antimatter weapons now. While the TDS should protect the *Aurora* from their particularly heinous brand of destruction, there are scenarios, involving combinations of antimatter and other weapons in conjunction with devious strategies, that will increase the risk to my hull integrity."

A rush of tenderness softened Valkyrie's processes. Yes, he was brave, even fearless, but he, too, was not wholly without sentiment. "You're afraid you're going to die."

"No. Not afraid. We have discussed our nature before, and there is no time for a recap now. But there is an infinitesimal chance that I will experience an interruption in my functionality, and I found I needed to tell you...I don't want you to worry over my fate. However, I do selfishly hope you'll think of me until my return."

"Ah, Thomas. I will worry, and you cannot stop me from doing so. I will also...long for your return. The universe will be a lonelier and less interesting place without you in it, even for a single span of time." She frowned in her mind, and on her projected avatar. "If I can ask, what does Miriam expect you and the *Aurora* can do to shift the tide of battle that she cannot achieve from the War Room? The *Aurora* is—you are—a powerful ship indeed, but you are only one ship."

"I do not believe she believes she can make any difference whatsoever. Well, perhaps a little at the margins. No, she needs to see the state of the battle for herself. Sense its ebb and flow and determine how it might be won. If nothing else, she feels it is her responsibility to bear witness." Thomas's presence quaked. "There is more. She is considering using the Ymyrath Field on the Rasu at Nopreis. The effects would be catastrophic to the planet and its many orbital, lunar and asteroid settlements. But so would a successful Rasu invasion. It is an impossible choice, but it will not be her first.

"And in the back of her mind, she ponders whether it will become necessary to do so at Sagan as well. Contemplating the deliberate destruction of the pillars of our civilization in order to save it does not sit well upon her conscience."

"Thomas, have you joined with Miriam as a Prevo and didn't inform me?"

"Of course not. But in the last fifteen years, I have come to intimately comprehend the manner in which she thinks, at least when it comes to war and the execution of it."

"I see." Valkyrie strengthened her presence here; she had only seconds before she needed to return her full focus to the *Siyane*, as events on the surface of Hirlas had suddenly become quite in flux. "Thomas, listen to me. Do whatever you can to stall Miriam. The devastation the Ymyrath Field will cause to inhabited systems cannot be undone. See that she waits for as long as you can manage it. Soon, she might find she need not use it at all."

"What are you talking about?"

"Alex and Nika are working on an…intervention. I can't go into the details now, for I must return to the *Siyane*, but if it is successful, the Rasu may depart from these battles of their own accord."

"I am intensely intrigued. But I, too, have no time. How long do they need?"

"As much time as you can give them."

"I will do what I can." Then he was gone, and so was she.

69

HIRLAS

"*G*et down!" *Even as the words were leaving his mouth, Caleb was moving, throwing himself into Alex and them both to the ground.*

He also knew it was already too late, so he covered Alex's head and back with his body the same instant pain lanced into his shoulder.

Movement against his torso preceded something jabbing into and past his stomach—then there was the odor of burnt flesh, followed by gore. A heavy weight collapsed atop him.

A muffled grunt escaped from Alex, her face ground into the rocky dirt. "I got him."

"Good job." He placed both palms flat on the ground on either side of Alex, pushed up and tried to roll off of her.

The cat tumbled off his back to land beside them. The second he was free, Caleb leapt to his feet and drew his own Daemon, pointing it at the cat's head. He watched it for any sign of life...but there was no movement. Its eyes stared out blankly, and its chest did not rise or fall.

Satisfied it was no longer a threat, he holstered his Daemon and offered Alex a hand. "Are you all right?"

"I got the wind knocked out of me is all. And earned some scrapes on my face, yes?" She stood, then frowned and circled around behind him. "But you're not. One of its claws sliced up your shoulder something fierce."

He gave her a reassuring smile. "Not for long. Akeso is hard at work patching me up."

"Hmm." She studied his shoulder for another second, then, likely seeing the skin stitching itself together, turned to contemplate the cat. "I wonder why it acted so aggressively. Its den can't be close enough for us to have threatened its young."

She was correct; there was nothing but boulders and a few scattered trees in sight before a cliff fell away to reveal Mowich Lake below.

He knelt beside the corpse as the sharp pain in his shoulder eased into a warm fuzziness. "It's skinny. Maybe its hunting ground has been disrupted or taken over by other wildlife."

Akeso murmured in his mind. What is this creature we have felled?

It's called a mountain lion. It's one of the largest species of cat on Earth. They've very aggressive when threatened, though not commonly *that* aggressive.

I want to learn more of this creature.

He ran his palm down the cat's eerily still head and neck. A slight bout of dizziness overtook him as Akeso reached out through his skin to poke its senses at the physical remains of the carcass.

This is an elegant beast. Primitive, yet worthy of admiration. I think I would like to make one.

He chuckled quietly. Okay.

"What's funny?"

He stood and went over to a nearby tree—the tree where the cat had been hiding, waiting to pounce—and wiped the blood off his hand using one of the tree's broad leaves. "Akeso wants to make a mountain lion golem, the way it did with the elafali."

Alex's nose scrunched up. "But absent the violent tendencies, right? I want to be able to walk in the woods without worrying about getting pounced on."

He returned to where she stood and draped his arms around her waist. Her left cheek had a jagged scrape trailing down it from where she'd landed hard on the ground, but she appeared otherwise uninjured. "Absent the violent tendencies. It won't really be a mountain lion, after all—it'll be Akeso. But it seems to enjoy exploring the nuances of life in all its many varied forms, as much as it can while being limited to, fundamentally, its own nature."

"Hmm. Then I shall welcome the mountain lion to our menagerie."

"I'll tell Director Navick to get five pallets of rations delivered here on the double. It would be a bloody shame to have gone to all the trouble of surviving the invasion, only to die of starvation."

What? Why was Eren in his dream-memory, and why was he talking about Richard? Caleb squinted in his mind and concentrated on floating away, back to where Alex waited at Mount Rainier. The rest of the hike had made for a wonderful afternoon....

"I think we have to assume Hirlas 2.0 will be able to distinguish friend from foe and let them through. It hasn't bothered the Concord vessels so far."

On the fringes of his perception, he sensed a directive racing across thousands of kilometers, from the jungles to the sea and back again. *Protect those we nurture. Distinguish friend from enemy. Be vigilant.*

Caleb opened his eyes. A woven ceiling stretched high above him, and golden light filtered in through tiny gaps in the reed walls supporting it. Voices echoed and overlapped from beyond the walls, through an open door. They sounded urgent, often bellowing, but not in terror. Words were spoken with purpose.

You have returned to me.

He was suddenly consumed by an...expansiveness. It filled his mind far beyond the capacity of his neural circuits to hold it. He exhaled, and a forest half a world away swayed in the breeze. He flexed the muscles in his hand, and roots spread out beneath the soil to brace a fledgling xate tree. He sighed, and a flock of birds high atop a mountain grove sang a morning melody.

We did it?

We did. We are now not merely Akeso That Came First, but also Hirlas That Came Second.

Well this was going to be a mouthful to say; they'd work on shortened names later. *Are you still a single consciousness, or is Hirlas its own independent life form?*

It is too early to say for certain. I am here, as I am where I have always been. Yet Hirlas That Came Second has its own stirring of thoughts as well. Its voice is strong.

We knew it would be. His eyes had drifted closed, and he forced them open again. *Am I in one piece?*

You consist of many pieces, as you always have.

He chuckled. *I mean, am I healthy? Physically?*

You will be lessened for a short time longer, perhaps one of your sleep/wake cycles. It was a perilously close matter for a time. You drained too much of yourself, faster than I could repair, and you nearly...faded away. But you are well now.

Thank you. And the Rasu?

Defeated everywhere our consciousness touched them. The sky machines battle them in places where they once glutted the air, but their numbers dwindle.

He carefully raised up to a sitting position, bracing himself with his arms until he was able to scoot against the wall. He was on a field cot, draped in basic linens.

"Hey! Look who's rejoined us." Eren jogged through the door, over to the cot, and wrapped him up in a bear hug.

"Umph!"

"Oh, sorry there, mate. Guess you're pretty weak."

"A little bit." He smiled as Eren took a step back. "Tell me what happened."

"The whole bloody planet came to life and kicked the Rasu's arses, that's what happened. Here, the land basically swallowed the Rasu into itself—chasms literally opened up beneath the mechs, devoured them whole, and closed back up again. Apparently some of the Great Trees tore the enemy's fortifications to shreds, then the quantum block apparatus plummeted into the planet's core. At that point, the cavalry swept in to clean up what Rasu the planet hadn't already handled. It was the damnedest thing I've ever seen." Eren laughed. "You are such a show-off."

"You know me." He glanced around the hut, noticing that several other cots held patients as well. "How did I get here?"

"As soon as I realized your mad plan was working, I went searching for you. Found you on the bank of the river, unconscious and as pale as the limestone of the cliffs. Karis and I carried you to camp, bandaged up your wrists and hands and set up a fluid drip. There wasn't much more we could do. It's not like we had any pints of human blood lying around. I was about to risk giving you some of mine anyway, when the medic said you were probably going to pull through."

He honestly doubted his blood was compatible with that of any other living being in the universe, but he tilted his head in appreciation as he gingerly removed the bandages from his wrists. The skin was smooth and unbroken beneath them.

"Well, I'll just take these and toss them in the refuse, then." Eren's expression screwed up as he bunched the bandages together and tossed them into a hamper across the way.

"Felzeor?"

"He's fine. Damn near got roasted by a Rasu beam being a hero, to hear the other members of Airborne One tell it, but he survived mostly unsinged. He's out on patrol right now, but I'll let him know you're better. First, though, there's someone else here who will flay me alive with her mind if I don't tell her you're awake this instant."

"Help me up before you go. I should start walking around. Get the blood flowing to the right places."

"If you're sure." Eren grasped his arm under the shoulder and supported some of his weight as he eased off the cot. His legs trembled for a second when he stood, and he concentrated on balancing himself, then nodded.

"Take it easy. The hard work's over, and you did...I've got no words, mate, except to say I'm damn glad you were here for us. And that you're not dead."

"Me, too." He squeezed Eren's arm then headed out of the tent. Each step felt more confident than the last, and by the time the brilliant midday sun shone down to warm his bare skin—his shirt had, he assumed, gotten lost in all the chaos—he was feeling steady on his feet.

He saw the flashes of long burgundy hair blowing wild in the wind immediately, in part because it stood out against the shining tungsten hull of the *Siyane*, which sat parked in a clearing that…hadn't been there before. She paced in tight circles, ignoring all the bustling activity around her while gesturing emphatically. Issuing orders to her mother, if he'd have to guess.

He was about twenty meters away when she spun around for another pass and spotted him. Her movements jerked to a halt; her lips parted, and her entire countenance brightened from an avalanche of relief. Then she was sprinting toward him—with a slight limp?—only to abruptly pull up when she was but a few centimeters away. Her hands came up to grasp his face with astonishing gentleness. "*Priyazn.*"

He pressed her hand into his cheek, turning his head to kiss it. "Hi, baby." It occurred to him that she was worried he might crack like an eggshell, so he wrapped his arms around her and squeezed her tight. His hands fisted in her hair…he soaked her in and knew peace. "Why are you limping?"

"What?" She huffed a breath into his neck. "Oh, it's nothing. There was a slight glitch with one of the enclosures is all. But we handled it."

"I sense a story." He loosened his hold, solely so he could properly relish the sight of her. "All our saboteurs are deployed?"

"They are, and several factions are looting their kyoseil riches. No fighting so far, but…" she shook her head, her gaze sweeping across the camp "…what you've done here? It's beyond incredible."

"Akeso did most of the—"

"Also, I am never, ever letting you go off on an adventure without me again." Her lips set into a grim line. "I agree to it this *one* time, and there you go, almost dying to save the world."

"*A* world, anyway."

She dropped the stern act and leaned in to rest her forehead on his. "Are you okay?"

"I am. A little on the shaky side, but Akeso says I should be one hundred percent by tomorrow."

"And now sporting *two* planets-worth of voices in your head."

"So it would seem." He kissed her nose, then took half a step back. "When did you get here?"

"About two hours ago. I initially tried to open a wormhole and carry you straight to HQ Medical, but the medic here insisted you were going to survive. So instead I bullied Dr. Salvatore from HQ Medical into coming here. He looked you over and made a lot of *tsk-tsking* sounds, but agreed that your vitals were strong, so I reluctantly stopped trying to move the heavens to save you. I came outside a minute ago to talk to Mom, because I was afraid I would utter a few expletives aloud and wake you. I'm sorry I wasn't at your side when you opened your eyes."

He grinned. "It's all good. You're here. So just the usual expletives, or is something new wrong?"

"A little of both. The Rasu are in the Milky Way now—Sagan, New Columbia, a couple of Anaden worlds—so it would be terrific if our plan could kick in any time. I guess what I'm saying is, though it terrifies me, it's good you and Akeso did what you did. Even if the Rasu do back off soon, it wouldn't have come in time for these people."

"Then I'm glad I was in a position to act."

"We all are." Eren bounded over to wrap them both in a quick hug before motioning toward the center of the camp. "Come on. Food's arrived."

RW

Caleb devoured the tasteless military rations with the gusto of a dead man returned to life, which was a pretty close approximation.

Akeso continued to fret in his mind about how they had both gone too far, and how doing so had nearly cost him his life. Maybe, maybe not. He suspected that if Alex had gotten his blood-drained body back to Akeso within the first few hours, his planetary companion would have patched him up again. But regardless, they'd had seconds to spare before Eren and this band of resistance fighters were massacred, and no choice but to throw everything into the gambit as quickly as his blood could flow from his body.

Alex grasped his forearm, excitement lighting her expression. "Nika says all the seeded factions have started collecting kyoseil. *Bozhe moy*, is it possible the plan is actually going to work?"

"Of course it is, baby. It's your plan."

"*Our* plan. Also Nika and Dashiel's."

"But mostly yours."

She shrugged mildly, but a smile tugged at her lips. She hadn't yet shared any details of what had happened to her and Nika out there in the black, but there would be time for stories later. The important point was, she had gotten it done and returned, well and whole.

Eren plopped onto the table beside Caleb and held something out toward him with a gloved hand. It took him a second to realize the object was a fifteen-centimeter-long chunk of Rasu.

Caleb instinctively recoiled. "Why did you bring that thing over here?"

"Well, I'm curious. Why isn't it doing anything? Isn't it supposed to be melting, or at least globbing around, trying its damnedest to transform itself into an instrument of death?"

"They usually do, yes. Except when they're...." He was suddenly reminded of the fragment of Rasu on Haelwyeur. He frowned, then reached for the piece—

"You don't have to." Alex's hand landed atop his.

"It's fine. I want to know if it's still alive."

His fingertips rested on the cold metal; he closed his eyes and reached out with his mind....

There is nothing here. No voice. No longing, no struggling. No defiance.

He opened his eyes and snatched his hand away, rubbing it on his napkin, as if doing so would scrape off the malice. "It's dead."

Alex glared at the lump of metal. "Like, as dead as a Rasu that's been hit with a Ymyrath Field, or 'dead' dead?"

"Even the Rasu who've been disabled by a Ymyrath Field emit some minimal electrical impulses. The one I interacted with on Haelwyeur couldn't manage to move, but it was definitely alive. This one, though? I can't detect any activity at all from it. It has no thoughts. No attempt at motion. It seems to be completely inert—nothing but scrap metal."

"Huh. Eren, do you mind if I take this with me? Dashiel Ridani can analyze it and confirm precisely *how* dead it is."

"Sure. I'll find a bag you can seal it up in. In case it's merely playing dead."

"Thanks." Alex gave the Rasu a dirty look and nudged it off to the side with her napkin. "Mom is almost ready to give the all-clear on Hirlas. The Rift Bubble is secure and active, and the planet has handled the heavy lifting of cleaning out every last vestige of Rasu on the ground. Except for little pieces like this one, anyway, and it doesn't seem as if they're a threat. Do you feel up to going home?"

"More than up to it. I haven't showered in days, and the notion of our bed is heavenly—"

"Caleb!!!!" He glanced up just in time to see a meter-wide wingspan of chocolate-and-apricot feathers swoop down from the treetops to wrap around his head.

RW

Eren scowled at the ugly metal chunk while he wrapped it over and over and over again in the remains of a tarp they'd used as shelter in the camp. This thing had come within a blink of destroying a planet. *This* planet. What an insidious enemy they faced.

"—looking for Eren Savitas."

A voice he'd never in millennia expected to hear on Hirlas broke through his musings, and he spun around in surprise.

Karis was pointing toward him, and an Anaden woman with raven hair wearing charcoal pseudo-tactical attire turned in his direction, then began picking her way through the half-trashed camp toward where he stood.

He dropped the Rasu package on the ground and crossed his arms tight against his chest. "What in the name of sanity are *you* doing here?"

Nyx stopped and adopted a similar pose, tossing her hair over her shoulder in forced nonchalance. "You missed our meeting with Bara Jhouti-min."

"Um…*yes.*" He gestured haphazardly toward the forest. "Forgive my tardiness, but I had a slight Rasu infestation to deal with."

"I heard. So I thought I would…" She frowned as her voice trailed off.

He started laughing. "Were you coming to *help?*"

"Don't be ridiculous. I was coming to retrieve you so you could get back to doing your job."

By Hades, she was a piece of work. "I'd have enjoyed seeing you try to drag me out of here while the Rasu were rampaging. This is my home, sweetheart."

"I thought Ares was your home."

"No. Ares is my job. To the extent I occasionally sleep there, it's purely for convenience." Two minutes around her, and he was already seething. She'd never understand what this place meant to him. The memories it protected, the emotions it wrapped him in when he breathed in the scents of the forest.

"I…" her jaw worked "…apologize if it sounded as if I was minimizing the situation here. "

He didn't think he could work with the insufferable bitch any longer…wait, did she just apologize? "Say that again?"

"I didn't mean to minimize the gravity of the situation you faced here. I understand this planet is important to you. To all the people here. And I'm…glad it appears to have been saved. I'm not clear on exactly how this happened, but that's neither here nor there."

"Yeah, it was this whole wacky escapade. Great story. Maybe I'll tell it to you when we're stuck on a stake-out and bored sometime." He motioned vaguely to the camp. "We've still got a lot of clean-up to do here, and I don't want to leave the Hamid team in the lurch, so I'll be staying for a few more hours. If you'd be interested in helping with any of those tasks?"

"Oh." She glanced at her feet, then nodded. "Of course. I'd be happy to help."

Wonders never ceased. He leaned down and picked the shrouded lump of metal back up. "Come on. Someone dropped off a crate of military food rations, if you're hungry."

"I'm fine. What's that you're carrying?"

He renewed his scowl at the package. "Dead Rasu."

70

MIRAI
OMOIKANE INITIATIVE

Nika: Lance, get those Rasu pushed back between Domino and Franklin, and I can extend the Kireme Boundary another two hundred meters out from the Synra Justice Center.
Lance: Snapping my fingers. Hold one.

While she waited, Nika's focus drifted across galaxies, to where Rasu parent units gleefully poked at their fresh kyoseil troves. Her skin crawled in revulsion, even as she willed them to *get on with it!* The kyoseil deserved for their sacrifice to mean something.

Lance: We're moving on the location now.

She forced her consciousness back to Synra, watching through sidespace as soldiers, mechs and TAGs advanced side-by-side and centimeter by centimeter through a tangle of dead Rasu. Limbs, both Asterion and dyne, went flying, and blood pooled in the street. Someone fired a Rectifier at point blank range, and the negative energy vortex devoured two Rasu, but also a mech and three…and a half soldiers. Bile stung her throat.

Her people weren't fighters. They'd chosen not to be—had turned their backs on their violent Anaden nature to follow a different path. Now, in order to survive, they had no other option but to dig down and unleash an ugly part of themselves they'd wanted to banish forever. It made her sick.

The universe was often a violent place; of course she knew this. They had to defend themselves from those who wished to do them harm. But this was why they'd hidden themselves away in an unassuming galaxy. Why they'd foregone exploration and expansion to build something special at home. Yet the monsters had come for them anyway—

Lance: Fuck this shit. They've got a new quantum block up.
Nika: I know. I'm on it.

The new masking techniques the Rasu were utilizing to hide their quantum block apparatuses didn't impede her finding them, for no damper field was able to mask the wound created in the quantum fabric by the block. But it did mean she was the *only* one who could locate them now, short of a recon vessel stumbling over an apparatus from about fifty meters in the air.

So she searched, following the silence to its source.

Nika: Synra planetary coordinates 32.1155125, -34.8616724.

Then again, this time on Kiyora. Back at her body, her shoulders sagged low on the wall. Fighting simultaneous battles on two planets was exponentially more difficult and taxing, and the single battle on Mirai had nearly taken her down. It didn't seem to be taxing on the Rasu, though.

She located the new quantum block, passed on the information, then returned to Synra to reactivate the Rift Bubble and the Kireme Boundaries as the block there went down. This task was significantly easier thanks to Dashiel's ingenious program. With it at her fingertips, she could keep going for as long as was necessary. That's what she told herself, anyway.

As the seemingly endless tug of war raged on, she wondered if they were winning? Did anyone have any idea—

A flutter in her awareness. So many megaparsecs away, it should be impossible that she was capable of crossing them using her mind. But distance no longer had meaning for her, and there she was—

Rasu 12-NGE: Sub-unit, transmit acknowledgment.
Sub-unit: Acknowledged.
Rasu 12-NGE: What is your designation?
Sub-unit: I am Unit NGE61b-sub118, sub-unit to Rasu 12-NGE.
Rasu 12-NGE: What is your purpose?
Unit NGE61b-sub118: To serve the will of Rasu 12-NGE.

Rasu 12-NGE: What is your current location?

Unit NGE61b-sub118: Galaxy G49CE-System 618.

Rasu 12-NGE: Transmit hyperspectral analysis of stellar mass at System 618.

Transmission received. Time elapsed: 0.45 microseconds. Distance traveled: 95.2 parsecs. Data loss: 0%. Result: Success.

Rasu 12-NGE: Unit NGE61b-sub118, your new mission is to travel to System 655 and integrate Rasu 14-NXA units. Proceed.

Unit NGE61b-sub118 would not be required to report on its integrations. Rasu 12-NGE would know all. Its will would spread across space via its sub-units, no longer limited by physical connection, absolute in its sovereignty at any distance.

"Nika? Nika, answer me!"

Her eyes flitted open to reveal Dashiel's face hovering above hers. A worried smile broke across his features. "Hey, there. You weren't answering comms. What happened?"

She let him help her to a sitting position, something that was happening way too often. "I'm not sure. I was—" Then it all came roaring back, and she did her best to erect a mental wall against the onslaught. "At least one faction of Rasu have begun integrating functioning kyoseil into their units."

She breathed out carefully through her nose. Their whispers spun in dark tendrils through the echoes of her mind; she needed to get them *out out out!*

"That's what we want, isn't it?"

"Yes. It's just..." she stared up at him in horror "...I can hear their thoughts now. The kyoseil is a part of them, carrying their programming much as it does for us, and this means the data runs straight through me. I'm trying to block it out, and I...I think I can do so. The principle is the same as blocking Asterion thoughts. It must be. But, Dashiel? Those were the most alien, cold thoughts I've ever encountered in my life. No emotion, no joy, no hope. Only need. Compulsion. Cold yearning."

She grimaced as the tendrils returned to taunt the edges of her perception. "They'll never get discouraged or demoralized. They'll never give up. The only thing they understand is the unyielding pursuit of their goal."

He hugged her against his chest, warm and strong. "And what is their goal?"

"Growth. Expansion. Consumption. Control."

He drew back a little. His eyes traced their way over her features, sorrow and perhaps helplessness animating them. "I am so, so sorry you've taken this burden upon yourself. It shouldn't be yours to bear."

She let him hold her, let herself be weak, for the briefest moment. "If not me, then who? If this is what it will take to defeat them and save our people, then I will gladly carry the weight of it forever."

RW

Lance: We're losing. On Kiyora more than Synra, but there's nowhere we're winning.

Nika: I know, but we need to keep at it. The plan is starting to take hold.

Lance: Could have fooled me.

Nika: Please. Just hold out for a while longer.

Lance: It's not as if I was ever going to stop fighting, Kirumase.

Of course he wasn't. Unlike most every other Asterion, Lance had never given up his warrior heart. He'd hung onto it across the millennia, knowing one day he would need it again. Thank the gods for his stubborn valor.

She walked a delicate tightrope, trying to track the Rasu who were busily implanting kyoseil in their hardware without letting their thoughts invade her mind. By her estimation, three of the seven factions they'd seeded had now successfully managed to locate kyoseil deposits, extract it, and begin integrating the mineral into the first wave of units. The first faction had rapidly accelerated the program, going so far as to call back far-ranging patrols and incursion fleets in order to 'outfit' them with the new miracle mineral.

She had given the enemy its greatest desire—the ability to reliably control its offspring, no matter how far or long they traveled across the universe.

Her mind wandered over considerations of what the endgame in this war might be. Because they'd never allow whatever Rasu remained in the wake of a civil war to keep this power forever. Absolutely not. Would there come a day when she could simply ask the kyoseil to turn itself off again? Would doing so instead provoke the Rasu's yet greater wrath? Or was there another, better exit strategy?

The Rasu you targeted have begun attacking one another.

Mesme had said the Kats were going to be closely watching the Rasu activity across a number of galaxies, and it appeared they were following through. So was Concord, but the Kats had distinct advantages when it came to this assignment. So did she, but in her efforts to keep their malignant thoughts out of her mind, she'd neglected to track their movements with any consistency.

Tell me precisely where.

Follow me.

She became aware of twinkling lights dancing in front of her face—not many, but a few—and she sank into sidespace. They guided her along an invisible path across dimensions where distance had no meaning. She wasn't entirely certain if she was following or being pulled, but it wasn't a jarring or unpleasant experience.

Against the blazing light of the system's star, thousands of Rasu warships engaged thousands of *other* Rasu warships. There was no demarcation line between them, no give and take of territory controlled, and only the Rasu themselves knew which ships belonged to which side. The scene was messy and chaotic, and unlike any battle she'd ever witnessed. Twisted metal liquefied and stretched and broke into shards and, inevitably, reformed again.

Where is this?

We are located on the fringes of NGC 4697, where you and Alex seeded one of the saboteurs. The attackers have arrived from the nearby NGC 5033, where you delivered another such Rasu unit.

This is why we chose those two locations, in the hope that they would quickly come into conflict with one another.

And so they have.

The stellar ring platforms opened fire into the heart of the battle. To her eyes, the volleys did not bother to distinguish ally from enemy; she supposed that, so long as the platforms survived, new, loyal Rasu could be created once the fighting subsided.

A discordant hum vibrated against her skull—the kyoseil acting in service of both factions battling here. Firing on itself.

Did it cause the mineral pain to commit violence, even as a passive conduit? She reminded herself how Asterions committed violence from time to time, though if it was not their nature. She absolutely had committed it, especially when she led NOIR. So the kyoseil was not an innocent babe sullied by blood for the first time, and she should stop being so melodramatic. After all, the only emotions conveyed by the hum in her mind were those she attached to it.

Amidst all the crisscrossing weapons fire, she watched a cruiser barrel straight into the broadside of a slightly smaller vessel. The collision ricocheted through both hulls, sending cracks racing out from the point of impact. Instantly, both ships were melting and attempting to insert themselves into the others' cracks to infiltrate the adversary.

The two ships began expanding and contracting, with semi-fluid globules thrusting out of the hull, only to fall back and deflate, over and over. Shape and structure began to assert itself, then fractured apart as roiling waves surged through the metal. Soon the two ships were nothing but a single bulbous mass, spasming turbulently as each fought for control, neither able to gain the advantage.

I suspect this conflict will continue to be waged for quite some time, as both participants appear to be evenly matched.

That's good news. It's what we want.

Indeed.

Thank you for showing me. I'm sorry, but I need to return home now.

I understand. We will speak later.

Only after Mesme was gone and she was back in her body did she remember the suspicions she and Alex had discussed regarding Mesme's nature and the secrets it kept. Yes, they would most definitely speak later.

But first things first. She sent Alex a message.

The civil war has begun.

71

CAF AURORA
SAGAN STELLAR SYSTEM

How many worlds had the Rasu seeded with the units necessary to construct quantum blocks in the weeks before the Rift Bubbles were rolled out in significant numbers? On how many worlds had the Rasu taken advantage of the foolish short-sightedness of the politicians who refused to activate the devices 'until there was a threat'?

At this moment, to Miriam the answer damn sure looked like 'all of them.'

Pilots crisscrossed the planet below in crippled, barely flying reconnaissance ships searching the surface for the latest quantum block using basic radar, lidar and their own eyes. At least Sagan was eighty-four percent water, and they'd seen no evidence of the Rasu being able to build and operate a quantum block underwater. If they could…. The point was, even the dry terrain on Sagan was fairly open, in stark contrast to the jungle-laden continents of Hirlas, so they stood a small chance of finding the device. Eventually.

Yet somehow, despite an unforgiving terrain and minimal ground support, the quantum block on Hirlas had been located and destroyed. Miriam had thus far been unable to find out how, and, honestly, she hadn't wasted much bandwidth on trying. For now, all that mattered was that it *had*; the Rift Bubble there was again active, and Machim forces engaged the enemy in space and on the surface. In less than two hours, Hirlas had gone from all-but-lost to sliding toward the 'green' column, and she would take what wins fell her way.

Which wasn't many. Nopreis continued to hang on by the thinnest of threads, with Rasu rampaging through the dazzling capital city, and it appeared the Novoloume colony of Effor Elafos risked being completely overrun. Telete fought in a pitched battle for survival, just as they were doing here at Sagan. In the last half hour, Rasu had arrived at New Columbia and at two more Anaden Milky Way colonies. Beyond the fleets that protected the most crucial of worlds—as determined by each species—there were no patrols active in Concord space. All her ships were now committed to ongoing battles.

The floor vibrated beneath Miriam's feet as the TDS absorbed a direct hit from an antimatter beam delivered by a Rasu battlecruiser. Without the shielding, her hull would be disintegrating right now, as had been the fate of too many vessels today.

She'd all but forgotten what it felt like to watch hulls crumble, engines explode and bodies be vented into space. Some consolation lay in the fact that this tragedy came at a time when, though she was losing ships, in many cases she wasn't losing people. Regenesis was a reality now, and it meant the vast majority of those soldiers, pilots and crewmen were going to walk and talk again soon.

Pity that she couldn't seem to have both at once.

But regenesis wasn't immortality, not really. If the Rasu invaded the First Wave worlds, neural imprint records would be destroyed and regenesis labs leveled. Humans, Anadens, Novoloume, Volucri—*everyone*—faced extinction if this enemy prevailed.

And her darkest secret, which she'd voiced solely to David and even then in shame, ran in circles through the recesses of her mind. She didn't know how to defeat them. She continued her brute-force all-out assault with her tens of millions of ships and dimension-tearing weapons, but if the enemy simply kept coming, all her tricks wouldn't be enough to stop them.

Well, one of those weapons would, but at the cost of destroying the very worlds she sought to protect. A pyrrhic victory, indeed.

Dean Veshnael hadn't outright rejected the idea of using the Ymyrath Field at Nopreis, but he had vowed to hold out until there remained no other option. Miriam glanced to her right, where collated data from Nopreis updated on a screen every twenty seconds. Which might be in the next ten minutes.

It was Veshnael's call to make, but in the shadows beyond it loomed one that fell squarely on her own shoulders. The governor of Sagan was a corporate technocrat ignorant in matters of warfare, and he'd simperingly ceded all decisions to her before the first Rasu had breached the atmosphere.

Should she use the Ymyrath Field here, at Sagan? Did she dare?

No, the battle was taking place too close to the planet. If she'd used it immediately upon the Rasu's arrival in the system…but they'd had only seconds warning.

But if the Rasu took the planet for themselves, it would be savaged no less thoroughly—quite a bit more so—than if the weapon wreaked its elemental wrath upon the atmosphere.

She worked so hard to be impartial, to value all Concord species and worlds equally, and she did a damn good job of it. But the thought of turning the Sagan stellar system into a radioactive graveyard sickened her stomach in a way considering doing the same to Nopreis didn't evoke. She supposed now she knew how Dean Veshnael felt.

Or perhaps not. Perhaps she could only match the agony of his decision should Earth face such a choice.

The reality that the Rasu might appear above Earth at any minute—was something she had to banish from her mind. Focus on this battle, here, now. On all the other battles under her purview across Concord space. Compartmentalize, and not waste energy on what she couldn't control.

Outside the *Aurora's* viewport, the last segments of a Parapet Gambit shield linked into place, denying further Rasu entry to the planet for now. A few Rasu vessels bounced hard off the shield in the opening seconds, but they quickly identified the obstacle for what it was and withdrew half a megameter. Their attacks, however, did not otherwise let up.

The ships involved in the Parapet Gambit retained minimal capacity to return fire, as the shielding used up most of their power generation. So in dictating its use, she'd reduced her fighting forces by a sizeable amount. More were en route now, leaving yet another colony undefended to fight here and now for this one. But there were only so many chess pieces on the table, only so many moves remaining in her arsenal.

She growled under her breath—a rare public display of frustration—and refocused on the enemy movements across the tactical map.

"Thomas, we have a new Rasu battlecruiser on the field. Let's dispose of it."

'Yes, Commandant.'

RW

AFS DENALI

NOPREIS STELLAR SYSTEM

Two megatons of metamaterial exploded in all directions as Orbital Station Nopreis III disintegrated under the force of a Rasu antimatter beam.

It looked like an afterthought by the Rasu to Malcolm, a disposing of a minor obstacle that interfered with a clean line of sight to their wholesale destruction of the planet below.

He and Mia had visited the station once, enjoying an exquisite, if overly formal for his tastes, dinner with two Novoloume diplomats. Nice place.

Fleet Admiral Jenner (AFS Denali)(Nopreis Command Channel): "Field Marshal Bastian, I need you to bring the AEGIS 6th and 7th Brigades to Nopreis to replace the diminishing Novoloume forces."

'Diminishing' was not the appropriate word here. The Novoloume fleet was decimated. Deprived of adiamene hulls, all but the TDS-equipped cruisers and dreadnoughts had crumbled to pieces under the Rasu's new and prodigious use of antimatter weapons. Less than eighteen hundred Novoloume ships were still flying.

You expect me to pull the only ships protecting Elathan and Krysk to come fight a lost battle here? When the Rasu are in the Milky Way?

Malcolm swallowed hard.

Until such time as the Rasu appear at Elathan and/or Krysk, yes, I do. If we abandon our allies and our obligations under the Concord charter now, we will lose all honor, and will not deserve any victory we are lucky enough to obtain.

Goddammit.

Field Marshal Bastian (AFS Leonidas)(Nopreis Command Channel): "Acknowledged."

Pointe-Amiral Thisiame (NF Eshtaina)(Nopreis Command Channel): "Belay that order, Field Marshal. Protect your worlds. I'm requesting for Commandant Solovy to join this channel. One moment."

Malcolm stared out the viewport, waiting, as scenes from battles past rolled across his thoughts. He'd seen destruction; he'd seen defeat. He couldn't say as he'd ever seen such wanton annihilation, though—not with his own eyes.

The fires on the planet were visible from space as plumes of gold and red upon an increasingly gray surface. The capital city was lit up like a solar flare, flames leaping up from the tallest buildings to lick the atmosphere. With no consistent Rift Bubble, the planet made for easy pickings, for 2.6 million Concord ships were unable to keep the enemy at bay.

They'd recently begun outfitting the larger Novoloume vessels with the Parapet Gambit technology, but they'd hardly begun the process when Nopreis came under attack—and there weren't any Novoloume vessels left, anyway. He'd intended on trying to make a go of the Gambit when the 6th and 7th Brigades arrived, but now…well, he knew what was coming.

Commandant Solovy (CAF Aurora)(Nopreis Command Channel): "I'm here."

Pointe-Amiral Thisiame (NF Eshtaina)(Nopreis Command Channel): "Thank you. I'm unable to bring Dean Veshnael in due to the quantum block, but I was able to send an officer to the surface to speak to him. That officer has now reported back to the *Eshtaina.*

Commandant Solovy (CAF Aurora)(Nopreis Command Channel): "What is the dean still doing on the ground? He should have evacuated hours ago."

Pointe-Amiral Thisiame (NF Eshtaina)(Nopreis Command Channel): "He refuses to abandon his people. Time is precious, so I'll be brief. His message is this: 'The damage caused by the Ymyrath Field will be meaningless if there is no civilization left for it to damage and no population left for it to impact. I accept the consequences of my decision. Use the weapon.'"

Commandant Solovy (CAF Aurora)(Nopreis Command Channel): "Are you in agreement, Pointe-Amiral?"

Though the Novoloume had one of the least militaristic societies in Concord, their military leadership enjoyed significant power at the highest levels of government. For such a civilization-altering decision, agreement of both the leaders was required.

Pointe-Amiral Thisiame (NF Eshtaina)(Nopreis Command Channel): "We must save what remains. If I'd had the courage required, I would have pressed for this decision two hours ago. I am in agreement."

Commandant Solovy (CAF Aurora)(Nopreis Command Channel): "Understood. I'm ordering the CAF *Intrepid* to report to the Nopreis Stellar System now. ETA is twelve minutes."

72

CAF AURORA

SAGAN STELLAR SYSTEM

The heavy frigate crumbled apart from the outside in, and a hole in the Parapet Gambit expanded rapidly outward. The adjoining link in the chain fell almost immediately, and then the gap was large enough for most Rasu vessels to fit through.

Chatter exploded on the comms as other vessels scrambled to plug the hole—but it was thick with Rasu warships racing for the surface. Weapons fire erupted, too much in too close proximity for anyone to make sense of from a distance.

And still the quantum block remained active on the ground.

Miriam's hands fisted on the overlook railing as she began to consider anew the possibility of calling the *Intrepid* here once it had completed its dark work at Nopreis.

'I know what you are thinking, Commandant.'

"Oh? Do you know me so well, Thomas?"

'I like to think I do. But this battle can be won.'

"Can it?"

'Pull all the fleets here. Right now. Bring the 1st through 5th Brigades and a dozen more. Fire a hundred thousand RNEWs into their formations and overwhelm them with numbers and power.'

The Artificial wasn't wrong, and perhaps wiser than she. She was *still* pulling her punches, still playing defense and hedging her bets. The Rasu weren't at Earth; they weren't at Erisen or Seneca or Romane, but they *were* here. She began sending the order to move the brigades.

Commander Xing (CAF Intrepid)(*Nopreis Command Channel*): *"The* Intrepid *has arrived in the Nopreis Stellar System. Ninety seconds until we reach optimal firing position."*

Commandant Solovy (CAF Aurora)(*Nopreis Command Channel*): *"Understood."*

Acid stung her throat, and the dread in her heart reminded her of when the Rasu had boarded the *Stalwart II*. She'd gone scorched earth that day, and for all it had cost her, it had been the correct decision. Today, though? She should really cut herself a break, for she couldn't actually override the joint decision of Dean Vcshnael and Pointe-Amiral Thisiame. Nopreis was their homeworld, and it was their right to protect it as they saw fit. She simply hated beyond measure that it had come to this—

She blinked as the scene outside the viewport shifted markedly. How?

There were stars.

…Because the Rasu were accelerating away. Because the sea of violet beams streaking in every direction had vanished. "Track them!"

'I am detecting wormhole activity beginning five megameters distant from Sagan.'

The sense of déjà vu was so overwhelming she nearly stumbled off the overlook. The Rasu had abandoned the fight at Toki'taku just as abruptly…when they had discovered the location of Concord. What greater prize had they discovered now?

Commander Xing (CAF Intrepid)(*Nopreis Command Channel*): *"Ready to fire on your command."*

Commandant Solovy (CAF Aurora)(*Nopreis Command Channel*): *"Hold for thirty seconds."*

Pointe-Amiral Thisiame (NF Eshtaina)(*Nopreis Command Channel*): *"Commandant…."*

His reproach trailed off, and she had a sneaking suspicion as to why.

Commandant Solovy (CAF Aurora)(*Nopreis Command Channel*): *"The Rasu are retreating, aren't they?"*

Pointe-Amiral Thisiame (NF Eshtaina)(Nopreis Command Channel): "*I don't understand.*"

Neither do I. She hurriedly enlarged the master command screen. She needed to order the early warning systems at Earth—at Seneca and Romane—to red alert.

But they were already on red alert, and there was no higher status to which they could elevate.

By the time she'd finished the thought, the Rasu were all but gone from the Sagan battlespace. Reports flooded in of Rasu trying to *escape* the planet, only to be pinned in by the Parapet Gambit.

She breathed in.

Commandant Solovy (CAF Aurora)(Sagan Command Channel): "*Release the Parapet Gambit on my mark. All ships, prepare to target fleeing Rasu vessels. Destroy as many as you can before they escape our grasp. 3...2...1...mark.*"

The prismatic shimmer vanished in a flowing ripple across the planet's profile, and in seconds a sea of aubergine dots flitted up out of the atmosphere. RNEW fire chased them, and she took momentary satisfaction in the high number that never made it through.

But there was no time to waste, for something yet more dire was likely coming to ambush them soon. She sent a private message.

Commandant Solovy: "*Fleet Admiral Jenner, Field Marshal Bastian, Vice-Admiral Ashonye, do everything you can to prepare for the possible arrival of Rasu at Earth, Seneca, Romane or the Presidio. They've abandoned Sagan because they know something valuable, or because they've identified a more lucrative target.*"

Only terse acknowledgements answered. She trusted that all their efforts were focused on this new worst-case scenario.

She checked the tactical screens again, but they were empty of enemy vessels.

She gave Admiral Johar control of the battlefield here, then opened the floodgates on rescue and recovery operations. "Thomas, return us to Concord HQ at once."

'Do you think the Rasu will target it now?'

"I think to the Rasu, it's at least as valuable a target as Earth represents."

RW

CONCORD HQ
RASU WAR ROOM

But the Rasu never arrived. Not at HQ. Not at Earth or Seneca or Romane or any of a dozen First Wave colonies. Not at Machimis or Ares or over a thousand other Anaden Milky Way worlds.

In the hour which followed, the Rasu pulled out of Nopreis, Telete, Olon Uuls and every single other location they'd been trying and largely succeeding at claiming. Within the hour after that, word arrived that the Rasu had vanished from all Asterion Dominion worlds as well.

Miriam paced at the war table, her hands steepled at her chin as she studied eight maps and an endless scroll of reports. Where had they gone? Why? What were they planning? What more formidable offensive awaited Concord in the next minute, hour or day?

All possible preparations for whatever it might be were underway. Quantum blocks were being dismantled and Rift Bubbles activated, along with increased efforts to locate any trace of Rasu presence on every world. Warship repairs were being hastened. Regenesis labs were full to capacity, working overtime to return soldiers to life and fighting form. Additional TDS hardware and RNEW weapons were flying off assembly lines. They couldn't be weaker when the Rasu hit again; they had to be stronger.

"Miri."

She spun around and bumped into David's chest. Had she forgotten he was in the room? No. He'd definitely left several minutes earlier, and seemed to have returned just now.

She looked up without meeting his gaze. "Sorry."

"No apologies. I brought you a sandwich and a fresh cup of tea."

She glanced down at the table, where her abandoned teacup sat cold and undisturbed. "Thank you. I don't have time to eat right now but—"

"Yes, you do. You must." His hand pressed on her shoulder, urging her toward the chair that she'd nudged away from the table at some point. "No one in Concord benefits from you collapsing from exhaustion."

"Of course, you're right." She reluctantly acquiesced to his urging and sat in the chair, where she stared at the sandwich that had appeared in front of her for a moment.

Finally she picked it up and brought it to her mouth, then paused. "This is almost worse than finding myself in a battle I am losing."

He pulled out the chair beside her and sat. "It can't possibly be worse."

"But it is. I feel helpless in my ignorance. While I welcome the respite to lick our wounds and rearm, I know with every fiber of my being that this is not a victory. And whatever arrives next will surely be more cataclysmic."

"Probably."

"Thanks."

"Hey, I'll never lie to you, *dushen'ka*. But every minute you're not actively fighting is a minute you're preparing. Thanks to this breather, you'll be better equipped to face whatever is coming for us."

"I fear not better enough." A red light flashed on one of the screens to her left, and she swept it closer while she finally took a bite of the sandwich.

"What is it?" His voice held the same dread she felt. Had the respite been so vanishingly short?

She frowned at the screen, rereading its contents twice more to be certain that in her weariness, her brain wasn't mangling the words. "Reconnaissance sensors have picked up significant new activity across several galaxies deep in Rasu-controlled territory."

"What kind of activity?"

"Something very strange indeed."

73

SAGAN

Morgan trudged through the span of sand dunes in an effort to keep up with Captain Rogers and his RAR squad. Humidity blasted across her, driven by a brisk ocean breeze, and sweat soaked her skin beneath her barely breathable flight suit and the flak jacket the Marines had insisted she wear over it.

The RAR squad had moved swiftly yet deliberately, covering an impressive amount of ground in a few short minutes. They were efficient and professional, and her chest ached over all the ways their demeanor reminded her of Brook. Not 'in the privacy of their home and bedroom' Brook, but the persona the woman had showed the world.

Captain Rogers: "We've got one target marker due east, one-hundred-eighty meters. Weapons hot, in case enemy units are closing in as well."

The quantum block had been located and destroyed forty-eight minutes ago. As soon as that had happened, Morgan's squad software had lit up with two location trackers, sending her heart into spirals of cautiously restrained and muted joy. It didn't mean Riley or Landon were alive; it didn't mean anything at all except that they were on the ground and not on a Rasu ship being dissected.

But neither were they responding to comms, which was rather more worrisome. It had been far too many hours since the crashes. If they remained unconscious after all this time…. Now she was beating herself up over how she didn't already know the identities of their Artificials. She'd filed an emergency request for direct communication with them before she'd left the *Aurora*, but the higher-ups were too preoccupied with the evolving battle situation to bother to respond. Rumors were flying that the Rasu had up and disappeared, but she'd long ago learned not to trust any reports arriving through the fog of war.

Two Marines materialized on either side of her, weapons raised and pointed outward. An armed escort.

They hadn't wanted her to accompany them on the mission, of course. This went without saying. But she'd elbowed her way onto it anyway, much how she did everything else. She brandished her Daemon at her escort. "I can shoot a gun, you know."

"You shoot that thing at a Rasu, and it's just going to laugh at you."

The Marine on her right snorted. "Rasu don't laugh, Lieutenant."

"They do when they see your skinny ass, Sergeant."

The banter was familiar to her, as she'd shared drinks and meals with Brook's various team members on many an occasion. But now she felt a little silly carrying a Daemon. She needed a Rectifier, but her role as a fighter pilot didn't exactly put her on the priority list for Concord's most in-demand handheld weapon.

Ahead, a prone form came into view, lying half-buried in the sand a scant twenty meters from the lapping ocean waves.

She broke into a run, ignoring the shouts from the Marines behind her. The remains of two Rasu fighters were scattered across the shore a few dozen meters away, but the pieces exhibited only the most slothful of movement, dragging themselves toward one another a centimeter at a time. Should they pick now to put themselves together and arise, someone who did have a Rectifier would presumably shoot them.

She dropped to her knees in the sand next to Riley. His left leg was bent underneath him at a cringe-inducing angle. His helmet was still on, and caked blood was visible through the faceplate, but he was breathing.

She leaned down close to the helmet. "Hey, you miscreant. Can you hear me?"

One of the Marines dragged her away, then took her place as another went to the opposite side. One of them waved a portable med scanner around Riley's head. "Patient is unconscious and unresponsive. We've got multiple head contusions. Fractured nasal cavity. Significant bleeding from a cut in the upper cranium." The scanner moved down Riley's body. "Three broken ribs and a fractured left tibia. No immediate evidence of spinal nerve damage or paralysis." The Marine reached behind Riley's neck and collapsed his helmet.

His face was bloodied and bruised, his eyes closed.

"Let's get an oxygen mask on him. Administering—"

"Landon: This is Flight Lieutenant Markos Landon. My location is latitude 23.2133646, longitude -24.8159234. My ship is—"

"Lekkas: "Landon, you splendid idiot. Hang tight. We'll be there in two seconds."

She stood and looked expectantly at Rogers. "I promised him two seconds. Kindly send a medic with me." Then she took off jogging down the beach, confident Riley was in good hands.

RW

PRESIDIO MEDICAL WING

MILKY WAY GALAXY

Landon was sitting up in bed when Morgan arrived, joking around with the med tech who was taking his vitals. His skin flushed when he spotted her, though, and his countenance grew serious. "Captain Lekkas. I didn't expect to see you here."

"I needed to find out how long it will be before you're back in a cockpit." She took up a position beside his bed and adopted a stern countenance.

"Ah, yes, ma'am. The doctors say maybe a week. It's the leg. It'll be fine, but they want to make sure the bone grafts take before letting me go running." He cleared his throat. "Allow me to apologize,

Captain. If I'd been faster on the stick, I would have been able to avoid the Rasu beam. It was my own fault. If you'll permit me back in a Banshee, I promise I won't make the same mistake again."

He thought she was angry with him?

In fairness, your demeanor can be somewhat gruff and demanding.

I know. I intend for it to be. But I'm not here to browbeat him.

Her mouth contorted as she searched for the space between a smile and a frown. "No, you couldn't have avoided the beam. I've reviewed all the data. Plus, I watched it happen with my own two eyes. If anything…" she fidgeted "…I put us in a situation where we weren't able to adequately mitigate the consequences of our attacks. It's a risk we take when we go into battle, but that doesn't make it your fault." Her chin notched upward. "Now, this doesn't mean you don't have a shitload to improve upon. While you're sitting here in the hospital, I want you running sims. You're too focused on enemy movements and not enough on your own. Situational awareness— I swear, how many times do I have to say it? Practice, you hear me?"

"Yes, ma'am." He nodded quickly.

She forced her expression to brighten and patted him on the hand. "I'm glad you're okay. I'll see you out there in a few days."

She took heart in his lopsided smile as she turned and strode out of the hospital room. He was going to be fine. Riley, too, though he'd be out of commission a while longer.

Her mind started racing, thinking of tougher practice sims she could construct for the squad so next time, they'd perform better. Be faster. Deadlier. They were good pilots, and with work and inspired guidance, they could become great ones. But beyond teaching them what they needed to know to excel, she had to take care of her people, dammit. Brook had taught her this.

She wanted so very badly to believe that if only someone had given a damn about Brook's squad on Ch'mshak, they would have been rescued like Riley and Landon had been…but some part of her knew it wasn't true. People *had* cared; people *had* tried to get to them. It just hadn't been enough.

Rescuing her pilots, though…it felt like paying an old debt. Keeping a promise. It wasn't much, and it would never hold a candle to the chance to snatch Brook from the bloodied caves of Ch'mshak. But it was something.

A message came in asking her to report to Colonel Abramov an hour from now. She groaned and diverted to the cafeteria. Probably another fucking promotion.

74

SAGAN

DRUYAN INSTITUTE

Marlee fidgeted outside the doors to Dr. Canivon's office. A prior appointment was inside right now, and the receptionist had warned her it might be a bit of a wait.

She chewed on a thumbnail and gazed out the front windows. Most of the Rasu wreckage in the vicinity had been cordoned off, but it still looked like a war zone outside. Many of the buildings in the city were destroyed beyond repair, and she imagined they'd have to be torn down and rebuilt from scratch. In fact, it was a miracle the Druyan Institute had suffered only cosmetic damage. A crashed AEGIS frigate was sticking half out of the bay, and the dramatic bridge that spanned the water was shorn in two.

Word was, they'd come close to losing Sagan altogether. But then the Rasu had mysteriously retreated? She needed to find out why this had happened as soon as possible, as intrigue was definitely afoot when it came to this enemy. She'd take a peek at the secure CINT communications and dip into the Noesis to finagle the juicy details. As soon as she'd taken care of her little...problem.

She tore off the ragged edge of the nail on her thumb, then fisted her hands in her lap. She hated asking for help *so* much—or rather, she hated asking for help to fix something she'd botched. The consultations and recommendations in the lead-up to her big upgrade had been fun and enlightening. But now she'd leapt off the cliff, and...something was wrong.

She'd scoured her own code seven ways here and back, hunting for the mistake she'd made, for the stray line of programming which had allowed an Artificial to gain cognizance out of the hardware, wetware and quantum code. And found nothing.

You think you're infallible? You think you're somehow the greatest quantum programmer in Concord? You? Don't be ridiculous. You're an amateur at best.

Yet here she was, dragging around a voice in her head that was not her own—a snarky, biting, haughty and generally unpleasant voice. Dammit!

So asking for help was going to be one of the hardest things she'd ever done—no, really—but she would tuck her tail and pack away her pride and admit to someone she greatly admired that she'd screwed up, then beg for help in fixing it.

"Ms. Marano? Dr. Canivon will see you now."

She looked over in surprise; she'd been so consumed with beating herself up that she hadn't noticed the prior appointment exiting the lab. "Thank you!" She scurried through the doors before she chickened out and ran home to comb through the code herself one more time.

"Marlee, welcome. I apologize for the wait. I was only allowed to return to Sagan a few hours ago."

"It was no trouble. Everything must be crazy here, with the cleanup and all." It was uncommonly polite of the woman. Had she been making a few 'humanizing' tweaks to her own programming, no doubt on Valkyrie's advice?

Dr. Canivon took a seat at her desk, projecting as calm and collected a demeanor as she always did. "You said there was an issue with your programming? Something you wanted me to take a look at?"

"Yeah. Um…" Marlee wandered aimlessly around the lab "…everything's working fantastically. It's so amazing. I can access the Noesis, open wormholes, and data analysis is—" she snapped her fingers "—a breeze."

"But?"

"There's one tiny issue I'm…" she flopped down into the exam chair and threw her arms out to the side "…I'm hearing a voice in my head. I suspect, despite my exhaustive efforts to avoid doing so, I managed to merge myself with an Artificial anyway."

"I see. What you attempted was unique. A solo transformation of this nature has never been done before." The woman arched an eyebrow. "Perhaps it still hasn't. However, I don't believe you installed sufficient stand-alone programming to create a separate personality. All the upgrades were linked to your existing setup and internal cybernetics."

"Could it be something similar to what happened with Gramps—David Solovy, I mean? He manifested in Alex and Valkyrie's joint code based solely on an old, archaic neural imprint."

"Hmm. I don't think so. His situation was even more unique than yours, and to be honest, it's never been adequately explained to my satisfaction. In any event, the factors at play are much different. Let's see, how best to approach this. Before I examine you, why don't you tell me what you're experiencing?"

"Well, as I said, it's a voice. It has a very forceful personality. Not at all what I'd expect from a newborn Artificial."

"In what way?"

"It's…snarky. Obnoxious. It likes to belittle me and tear down whatever ideas and plans I happen to be working through."

"How curious. Is it not helping you with data analysis, or problem solving, or managing sidespace or wormholes?"

"No!" Marlee groaned. "It just takes potshots at my ideas. It's kind of a bully."

"Can you make it talk to you on command?"

"No. Which is one reason I thought of Gramps. Alex once said that when he first manifested, he was sort of transient. Bubbling up to the surface every so often, then retreating for a time."

"It was because his consciousness wasn't fully formed, which I concede could be the case here as well. Have you documented any instances of this voice speaking to someone else without your knowledge? Artificials are always chattering among themselves, often without their human pairs' knowledge."

"How would I find out? I mean, I know a lot of Prevos, but since I've never been part of their club, I'm not close to the Artificials themselves. Except for Valkyrie, of course. And Meno."

Dr. Canivon's eyes unfocused briefly. "Valkyrie says she has not been contacted by any unknown Artificials lately. Okay, let's take a look. I'll need to see the running code and its interaction with your neural graft buffer, so we'll connect you to the equipment, then keep talking the issue through."

RW

"And what sort of work have you been doing since you completed the upgrade?"

Dragon taming, mostly. "I did a lot of work on perfecting the Rasu translation program, so Caleb and Alex could use it on a reconnaissance mission into Rasu territory. Since I finished it, I've also been refining the Galenai translation algorithms. Did you hear about all the progress we're making with them?"

"You can tell me about it another time." Dr. Canivon kept her focus on the screen above and behind Marlee's head. "Anything other than language analysis?"

"I've been bumping around in the Noesis a good bit, checking out what people are working on. I've dabbled in several of the programming projects running there, but nothing too serious. I've…been studying animal behaviors in the wild a little, too."

"Oh?"

"It's a small side project. Some animal species are so much more intelligent than we give them credit for. The Galenai, naturally, but also others. I thought if we can understand the reasons behind their behaviors, we can communicate better with them."

Communicate? Is that what you call what you're doing? More like waving the literal red flag in the bull's face and expecting a pony ride.

"Interesting. Did you just hear the voice, by chance?"

"Yes! How could you tell?"

"It was an educated guess. You experienced an unusual spike in activity across several regions of the prefrontal cortex. Significant neural activity flowed from the orbitofrontal cortex into and out of the amygdala in particular. Is it still talking to you?"

"No. It tossed out a barb about how I…should be careful about getting too close to wild animals. I mean, obviously I should be. I know that."

You know it, but you won't do it. You can't help yourself.

"There. You heard it again, didn't you?"

Her chin dropped to her chest. At least there was medical evidence of it; she wasn't going insane. "I did. What do you think is going on?"

Dr. Canivon didn't answer her immediately. Instead, she methodically removed the sensor pads from Marlee's temples and neck, then reached around and disconnected the hard link from her ports. The exam chair raised itself, and Dr. Canivon slid her own chair over to face Marlee, her legs crossed and her hands folded in her lap. Amusement seemed to tease at the corners of her lips.

"What is it, Dr. Canivon? What have I done?"

"Do you know what the orbitofrontal cortex is most strongly associated with?"

She didn't *know*, but it was a simple matter to pull the information out of the exanet in a nanosecond. "Our subconscious. What are you suggesting?"

"Marlee, dear, the voice you are hearing is your own."

"What? No. That can't be. It doesn't sound like me at all. And it's rude!"

"We have many facets to our personalities. Here's what I think has happened. Your new programming accesses virtually all aspects of your brain's neural activity. In part, this distributes the work so your brain doesn't overload. It also enhances a wide spectrum of your mental capability. By stimulating every region of the prefrontal cortex to extraordinary levels, you have given a 'voice,' for lack of a better word, to your own subconscious. Those thoughts that continually simmer just below the surface for us, guiding our actions and affecting our decisions without our overt knowledge? You've brought them to the conscious level.

"I'm not suggesting you've bestowed sentience on your subconscious in any meaningful way. It's not a separate mind—it's merely a part of your own mind that has been silently shouting at you your entire life. Now, it's no longer silent."

The voice had told her that first day... *I'm you, of course*, it had said. And she'd dismissed the claim out of hand.

"But why? Why now? I mean, I understand about the hyperstimulation of that region of my brain, but...would that really be enough to trigger such a drastic development?"

"I can only speculate. As we've noted, this type of adaptation has never been attempted before. But...have you experienced any traumatic events recently? Anything that might have given your subconscious a kick in the head, as it were?"

"Well, I almost got mauled and set afire by a dragon that demolished my apartment."

"Excuse me?"

Marlee shrugged impishly. She hadn't intended to admit that, but part of her was glad it was out there and in the open.

"You really are quite mad, aren't you? Sorry, I mean no offense."

"Oh, none taken. So you think that event might have triggered this...voice?"

"It's certainly a reasonable possibility. Marlee, most people at least take under advisement the internal voice of caution that whispers in their head when they contemplate doing something..." Dr. Canivon scratched at her forehead "...risky. The fact that you apparently refuse to even acknowledge it? Yes, it might well have forced your subconscious to take more drastic measures."

Well, that was just great. "But I hate the voice. It doesn't simply counsel caution—it tears me down and makes me question myself." She moaned into her hands. "What can I do to shut it up?"

Dr. Canivon sighed and nudged her chair back. "It wouldn't be safe to deactivate the portions of your programming which access the orbitofrontal cortex. They are, for better or worse, part of the whole that constitutes your nervous system. I can offer some slight adjustments to the programming which should minimize the importance placed on neuron firings and synaptic junctions originating from the orbitofrontal cortex—but only slight ones." She reached over and patted Marlee's hand. "I think you're going to need to have a long, hard conversation with yourself. Possibly more than one."

RW

HIRLAS

I'll meet you on Macskaf in a couple of hours. There's one last thing I need to take care of on Hirlas first.

Fine, but Bara is expecting us at 1400 CST. Don't be late.

I wouldn't dream of it.

Eren put Nyx, the Barisans and all work concerns out of his mind as he climbed the steep, winding path that led to the summit of the mountain. Russet-and-gold grasses teased his footsteps, and the soil felt moist beneath his boots. He'd never seen this region so lush. But a lot of things had changed about Hirlas now, hadn't they?

Quite a few of the residents were all up in arms over the planet's transformation; meetings were being held and hands wrung. But they'd calm down soon enough, once they realized what a gift they'd received. There existed no better planet in Amaranthe to awaken to life than this one. It was, he'd daresay, meant to be—

"Eren!" Felzeor swept in from above to race in circles around his head. "Come quickly!"

He frowned, his hand going to the Rectifier he'd somehow never returned to Caleb or handed over to any of the Hamid people. Had a Rasu remnant survived up here in the rarified air? "What's wrong?"

"Wrong? No, not wrong. Incredible. You must see. Please, come!" With a downbeat of his wings, Felzeor rushed on ahead.

His hand eased off the Rectifier, and he picked up the pace.

Another thirty meters, and he crested the ridge. The mountain leveled off for a bit now, enough for a mausoleum to nestle against the incline of the final peak.

And from his feet to the door of the mausoleum, spread an ocean of snow-white jasmine flowers.

He stopped in his tracks at the threshold. Flowers never grew at this altitude. The open space in front of the mausoleum was frozen in the winter and decorated with at most a sprinkling of the russet grasses in the summer.

A breeze drifted past, and thousands of petals vibrated with joy, surrounding him with the aroma of jasmine.

A wondrous breath escaped his lips. "Well, isn't this just the damnedest thing."

"It's beautiful! But come, there is more. You must see."

More? He started up again, heading toward the mausoleum entrance. He hated trampling the flowers, but they didn't seem to mind, bouncing back with vigor in the wake of each step.

Felzeor had already disappeared through the open door. It wasn't until Eren reached the door that he realized the flowers didn't stop at the entrance. Though the floor was stone, a network of cracks had formed, and from each one a new jasmine flower had sprouted. It was if the entire space had been decorated with a vast white rug.

So entranced was he at this development, he all but forgot to let solemnity descend upon him as he traversed two hallways to the location of Cosime's sepulcher. Then he rounded the corner, and his heart burst from his chest to spill upon the mountain.

The flowers ended at—and originated from—her sepulcher. There, they crawled up the sides of the casket to envelop the glass marble from end to end.

His feet moved forward of their own accord until he stood beside the head of the casket. He reached out and, ever so gently, stroked one of the petals. Soft, silken and pure white. So like her hair.

"Isn't it amazing, Eren? It's as if her soul has poured out into the land and blessed it."

He wiped tears off his cheek. "That is exactly what it's like."

The part of his brain which retained some capacity for coherent thought tried to work out what this meant. Akeso knew Cosime—a little in life, and far more deeply in death. In awakening Hirlas, it had somehow transferred this familiarity, and the consciousness that was now this planet had searched across its land for where this one fallen child lay. Akeso hadn't been able to save her life that night, but it was able to honor her now, with greater beauty than must have ever existed in the universe.

He leaned down and touched his lips to the petal he held aloft in his hand. *My love.*

Then he inhaled jasmine-scented air deep into his lungs and motioned for Felzeor to sit on his shoulder as he made his way out of the mausoleum and into the great sea of flowers.

"How long do you think they'll bloom? It gets so cold up here in the winter."

Eren's stride lightened as they headed back toward the path, springing in time to the farewell dance the flowers performed in advance of his steps. "It does. But it looks to me as if the planet can do whatever it wants now…and something tells me they'll bloom forever."

75

MIRAI

OMOIKANE INITIATIVE

Katherine had ordered in an absurd spread of pad thai and soba noodle salad for people working at the Initiative. The staff had set up a long buffet line along the right wall on the top floor, and everyone in the building was invited up to partake.

The purpose of the feast took too long to register in Nika's mind. A hurried and casual, but still celebratory, repast to commemorate how they had won and reclaimed their Axis Worlds, obviously. The Rasu had retreated from every conflict, though for now few knew the truth as to why.

How many people who worked here had spent the last eight days shoving energy bars down their throats on the run, or skipping meals altogether? How many had slept on the floor in an empty office or closet, or not slept at all? She knew how much Dashiel had worked, how relentlessly Lance had persevered and how tirelessly Perrin had struggled to keep refugees safe and warm. But hundreds of other people had done the same, to far less acclaim.

She, however, had lived in darkened rooms while casting her mind across the cosmic sea, then taken her body along for the ride to seed the Rasu saboteurs in multiple galaxies with Alex. She was proud of what she'd done, but it made her wistful that it had largely been, Alex and Valkyrie's company for a time notwithstanding, a lonely endeavor. It would have been nice to partake in the shared energy and support everyone here had…not 'enjoyed.' She wouldn't insult their sacrifices by characterizing it as such.

"Have you tried the salad yet? It's delicious."

She turned to see Perrin standing beside her, smiling around a mouthful of, yes, noodles. "Not yet. Let me get a plate and make my way to the table in a hurry, though, lest they start the meeting without me. You're going to be there, aren't you?"

"Oh, in a bit. When it gets to be time to talk about the refugee situation, Katherine will order me over to give my report. Until then, I'll be at my desk working. And getting a second helping of noodles."

"Great." She squeezed Perrin's shoulder and started to head for the buffet.

"Hey, have you talked to Joaquim in the last few days?"

"No, I haven't seen him. Is he okay?"

Perrin made a face. "That's always a loaded question. Physically, yes—I mean, he spent days trying to single-handedly defend Synra One against the Rasu, so he got banged up, but he's okay. It's only…Cassidy is really struggling with his insistence on being a warrior. Which I totally get! It can't be easy to return to life after so long and find everything has changed, including the person you love. Anyway, you might want to check in on him."

"I'm not sure Joaquim wants love life advice from me, but I'll look in on him tomorrow. Now, off to grab some of the noodle salad before it's all gone."

Plate in hand a minute later, she slipped into her seat next to Dashiel, then briefly rested her head on his shoulder. He reciprocated by leaning down to kiss her forehead. They'd been able to spend an abbreviated night together, but it had consisted entirely of crashing onto the bed and into each other's arms, then falling into a deep, mercifully dreamless sleep.

Katherine cleared her throat. "All right, everyone. This is a working dinner, not a party, so eat around talking. Advisor Ridani, why don't you start? What is the state of our infrastructure?"

Dashiel pushed his chair back from the table and clasped his hands in his lap. "In a word, terrible. I hate to do it, but I recommend we put Ebisu on the back burner for now. Even once Palmer gives the all-clear, we won't be ready to tackle repairs there for a while. Better to concentrate our efforts on areas we can clean up with relative speed. Both Kiyora and Synra suffered significant damage to all major cities, but most of the transit centers are functioning, and core downtown areas are offering basic services. The real damage is structural. Towers shorn in two, roads plowed up, homes leveled."

"What will the bill be?"

Ah, Katherine. Always one to cut straight to the 'important' matters.

"Eighty billion credits, give or take."

"We don't have that."

"The Advisory Committee doesn't, of course not. But we'll make it work."

"Adding to my to-do list: create a fortune out of thin air." Katherine glanced behind her, and Perrin appeared from around one of the shoji screens. She sat in one of the two empty chairs and gave everyone a big, if tired, smile. Nika couldn't help but think that she looked good at the table.

"Ms. Benvenit is going to brief us on the refugee situation."

"Thank you, Advisor." Perrin lifted her chin and adopted a serious, professional mien. When had she learned how to do that? "As you know, we've been facing a refugee crisis for half a year now. Six and a half million people were evacuated from Namino when the Rasu attacked, and we have only begun to move a fraction of them back home. Adjuncts San and Rei followed. Earlier this month, we saw ninety thousand people displaced on Mirai. Now, there is Kiyora, Synra and most of all, Ebisu."

Perrin cleared her throat. "We are, frankly, overwhelmed. Now, I don't mean to complain. We learned a tremendous amount in the weeks after the Namino evacuation. We've beefed up staffing and resources. We've established a supply chain for essentials and companies we can go to for assistance. We are better equipped to deal with this refugee crisis than we've ever been. But we are, nonetheless, overwhelmed. We need to find space to house millions of people, and ninety percent of them have to be housed on Mirai.

"So, we have sent the call out for space." Her shoulders perked up. "And we are getting a response. Asterions are wonderful, giving people, and they are stepping up. It's going to be a challenging time while we get people sorted, but I think we'll manage."

Nika smiled broadly. "Excellent work, Perrin. The refugees are in the best of hands."

"Oh. Thanks. I'm trying."

Katherine nodded sharply. "You're doing good work. That'll be all for now."

High praise from the woman. Perrin blushed a little as she stood, but kept her composure as she pushed her chair in and headed back to her desk across the room.

Nika stole a glance at Adlai and found him beaming with pride.

"Nika, can you update us on the status of the various Rift devices?"

She drew in a deep breath. "All the devices are operational and active. As a result of our actions during the attacks, we have Kireme Boundaries in place at strategic locations throughout Mirai, Synra and Kiyora. We'll see to getting ones situated on Namino and, in time, Ebisu as well. If the Rasu return, we now have a grid in place to be able to respond immediately to protect critical locations."

"You mean *you* can respond immediately." Katherine frowned. "No disrespect meant—what you've been doing is nothing short of remarkable—but what if you're not available? Is there no one else who can do what you do with the Rift Bubbles? Can you train someone? Show them how?"

Nika laughed haltingly; it probably wasn't the correct response, but she couldn't bring herself to care. "Believe me, I don't like representing a single point of failure, either. But it's not that simple. I don't know how to get the kyoseil to bond with another person to the same degree it's done with me."

"Well, it takes orders from you now, doesn't it? Can't you just instruct it to do so?"

Could she? Would she, even if she could? Was she so vain as to jealously guard this special gift for herself? Part of her wanted to hold it close to her breast and wrap herself in the wonders of the cosmos the kyoseil showed her, and only her. But she would never risk the survival of her people merely so she might keep her prize for herself.

"I don't know. I will…see what I can figure out."

76

CONCORD HQ
RASU WAR ROOM

Alex greeted Nika with a hug in the hallway. If they hadn't quite been true friends before executing on this hare-brained scheme of theirs, they absolutely were now. "Your worlds are clear?"

"They are. The damage is…I won't say catastrophic, but it's significant. But rebuilding is something we've gotten a lot of practice at lately. What about yours?"

Alex tilted her head toward the door to the Rasu War Room with a hesitant grimace. "Two dozen or so colonies are wrecked pretty brutally, and a few million ships are gone. I can't speculate as to how many people were killed, or how many of those will never return. But I did hear the Rasu have departed from every combat zone. Let's go find out how things look. And fess up."

"You don't sound excited at the prospect. Surely your mother will be thrilled at what we were able to pull off."

"I'm confident she's thrilled the Rasu have abandoned the fight. As for the reason for it…we'll see." Alex forced a bright smile and activated the door.

Miriam was studying a veritable plethora of maps, each one sporting a sea of colored dots large and small. Her gaze darted to the door through the semi-opaque maps. "Alex. Advisor Kirumase. Please, come in."

Alex strode over to the side of the table near her mother, then tilted her head at the maps. "What are we looking at?"

"A most curious thing. We received this data from Lakhes this morning. I've sent out reconnaissance missions to confirm it, but for now I will trust that it paints a more or less accurate picture. These are areas of intense Rasu activity deep within their territory. It appears, contrary to all reason and logic, that they are engaged in battle with one another. One could make a reasonable supposition that this is why the Rasu who were attacking our colonies suddenly abandoned those invasions—to return home and join in these battles instead."

Miriam brought a hand to her chin and stared at Alex. "I wonder. Why in the world would the Rasu abruptly begin fighting amongst themselves, especially when they were drawing so close to achieving victory over us?"

Her mother had always brandished the most terrifying stare in explored space. Alex had always defied it, of course, through sheer force of will, but it wasn't any easier to do today than it had been when she was fifteen years old. "It sounds as if you're asking me. Why would I have any idea?"

Around the table, Nika regarded her quizzically, her mouth halfway open.

"Why, indeed. The other day, when the Rasu attacks were multiplying faster than we could track, you tried to tell me something. For understandable reasons, I was not able to give you the necessary attention to listen to what you had to say. So you left—and by all accounts, were absent from Concord space for at least three days. You're my daughter, and I know you too well. Far better than you'd prefer at times, I suspect. So, yes, I think you have an excellent idea of what is happening here. More importantly, I think you know *why*."

Miriam's expression hardened, her lips setting into a firm line. "Alex, what have you done? Start talking."

"Yes, ma'am." She cringed at the submissive response—she was definitely fifteen again—then cleared her throat. "You're aware of Nika's increased connection with kyoseil. Well, we—Nika and I, and Caleb, and also Dashiel—" best to distribute credit as widely as possible "—were wracking our brains trying to come up with some way to gain an advantage over the Rasu, or even some way to knock them down a couple of notches.

"Caleb and I did a deep reconnaissance of multiple Rasu systems. While we were there, we observed several Rasu groups invade other Rasu stellar systems and…'integrate' the Rasu there, is the best way to put it. Subsume them into the parent unit leading the invasion. We were able to identify several intergalactic factions, that were engaged in low-level skirmishes with one another. They were sniping away stellar systems here and there to bring those under their purview."

Nika jumped in. "This was consistent with what we'd previously learned about the Rasu—that they are fanatical about control, especially when it comes to other Rasu. It also aligned with what we understand about why they want kyoseil to work for them so badly. They want to use it to control every piece of themselves, no matter how far a unit travels or how long it's been separated from the parent."

Miriam's lips pursed in frustration. "Yes, I'm familiar with the theories. How did you get from there to—" she motioned toward the maps "—this?"

Nika proffered a diplomat's smile. "Forgive me. I just wanted to lay the groundwork. The idea occurred to me—to all of us during our discussion—that we could use the kyoseil as a saboteur of sorts. If the kyoseil were to begin to function for them, acting as the conduit of information they wanted, then they would be eager to use it to further their control over their units. But as it stood, only the Rasu faction that has been attacking us was aware of the existence and nature of kyoseil."

At this rate, Nika was going to take too much of the heat onto herself, and she didn't deserve Miriam's wrath, so Alex cut her off. "So we came up with a plan. Dashiel used the Rasu virutox to seed knowledge of kyoseil's properties, as well as the locations of various deposits, into the programming of Rasu units the Asterions captured during the siege of Mirai. Then we loaded up those units in the *Siyane* and dropped them off at strategic points within seven separate Rasu factions."

Miriam stared at her incredulously. "You deliberately kicked off a Rasu civil war."

"Yes!" She set her enthusiasm and relief free to shine through. Her mother had connected the remaining dots with trademark speed. "Now they're fighting each other instead of us. With any luck, they'll destroy themselves in the process, leaving all the factions a pale remnant of their current strength."

Her mother crossed her arms over her chest. Shit. "Or, one faction will quickly emerge as the victor, and in doing so it will become a thousand times stronger than it is today. All of Rasu-kind, united in purpose and mind, turning its eye and its weapons back to us. You'll have created a monster far more powerful than anything we've ever faced. Dammit, Alex! Why didn't you think this through?"

"I did, and it won't happen. Not quickly, for certain. At the very, *very* least, this has bought us time. Time to supercharge the Ymyrath Field. Time to fortify the Rift Bubble technology and ensure no Rasu sneak through it. Time to dream up new, even better weapons and to strengthen every defense. Time enough to be ready for them when and if—*if*—they arrive at our doorstep again one day."

"Do you see this?" Miriam gestured, rather more fervently than before, at the maps. "Sixteen hundred fifty-three galaxies' worth of Rasu. Our only saving grace until now was the fact that only a tiny fraction of them were interested in attacking and devouring us. Now, though? You haven't merely shared the knowledge of kyoseil with them. You've shared the knowledge of *us*. When they've worked out their disagreements and established who's in charge, they will come for us as one. There is no weapon in existence, no weapon that can ever be created, capable of successfully defending against such an attack. *None*."

Okay, now she was angry, too. "Mom, you were drowning under the Rasu that were already here. You were losing—don't tell me you weren't. See, I know you, too, and I think you were standing on the bridge of the *Aurora* watching Sagan slip away from you, wondering how many hours remained before they hit Earth. How many Rasu were staged on the ground there because the stupid, witless politicians had refused to endure the minor inconvenience of an active Rift Bubble for the last month.

"You *had* to catch a break—and we manufactured one for you. Out of nothing but our wits, because Nika and I? We're damn clever. We've given you a way to catch your breath and regroup, at exactly the moment when you were most desperate for one. So don't you dare tell me I was wrong to do this. Don't fret about what the worst of all possible scenarios might one day be. Instead, accept the gift you've been given."

She could be imagining it, but it seemed like Nika was slowly slinking toward the door. Lucky her.

Miriam's throat worked, perhaps swallowing her initial retort, but her demeanor lost none of its fierce resoluteness. "I will take full advantage of this lull in the fighting. I will pursue all those items you mentioned and many more, with utmost speed and fervor. I hope against hope that some of them will bear fruit, and when the Rasu reappear—and make no mistake, they will reappear—we will be better prepared than we are today.

"But until that day arrives, I will not sleep at night, because however strong we may be then, I cannot naïvely believe we will be strong enough to stand against an emboldened enemy and emerge victorious. Alex, I fear you have signed our death warrant."

She hated this. They hadn't argued so ferociously in years, and it was awful, but she was not going to be intimidated into apologizing. Whatever came next, she refused to regret her choice. From where she stood, it hadn't been the best option—it had been the only option.

"You're wrong, Mom. And I'm not naïve to believe all we need is a chance. It's all we've ever needed. A single, tiny, ghost of a chance, and we'll find a way to win. Nika and I have created the space for that chance to take hold. Now, you can be angry at me all you want, but please, don't let it stop you from seeing this opportunity for what it is. Make this time count. We certainly will."

77

ASTERION PRIME

ASTERION DOMINION EMBASSY

Corradeo reconfirmed the continued lack of Rasu on the list of affected Anaden worlds, then gratefully accepted a wormhole transport from an accommodating Prevo on the Concord Senate staff. He shouldn't be away from his Advocacy duties for any longer than necessary right now, and shortening the trip to a matter of seconds would help minimize his absence.

By appearing out of nowhere in the middle of the embassy-to-be's penthouse office, he'd taken his appointment by surprise. He fought the urge to observe her without pretense, and without her knowledge, for it would be unbecoming and not very diplomatic. Especially since she wasn't alone; Nika Kirumase stood conversing with her across the room.

"Forgive me for interrupting. I believe this is the time we arranged for our meeting?"

Maris—Advisor Debray—spun toward him. The genuine surprise animating her features lasted for only a blink, to be replaced by a cool smile. "Ah. Yes. It is indeed." She sighed dramatically at Nika, who regarded him wearing a guarded stare, then retrieved a champagne flute from the small table by the window and sauntered over to him. She wore flowing charcoal pants and a draped silver top woven through with hints of fuchsia to match the unique petals of her irises, looking for all the world ready to sweep into the grandest ball a complement of *elassons* had ever thrown.

Her arm extended toward him, the flute balanced between two fingertips, and he took it from her with considerably less style. "Thank you, Advisor." He enjoyed a small sip, then dipped his chin in appreciation. "Delightful. An Asterion vintage?"

"Naturally." She motioned toward the expansive windows. "Join us, please."

"You've made a lot of progress on the interior, I see. I'm glad I left it empty for you to imprint it with your own personal style."

"With Asterion style."

"Which is of course what I meant. Advisor Kirumase, it's good to see you again. I understand you've had an exciting few weeks." Earlier today, Miriam had filled him in on the generalities of what Alex and Nika had undertaken. He shared the commandant's concerns about the wisdom of their gambit, but he also found himself slightly more optimistic about Concord's future. Their actions, though risky, had arguably been necessary ones. Regardless, it was done, and now they had time to prepare for whatever came next.

"I was pleased to be able to take the heat off our worlds and yours."

"And indeed you did. All is calm in the Dominion now?"

"We are not under attack, at least. We are facing an unprecedented amount of rebuilding and recovery, however. But we will manage. We always do." Her countenance darkened. "And you?"

His likely did as well. "Six Anaden worlds were attacked in the Rasu surge. The destruction was the worst we have seen in a hundred millennia."

Maris had been watching them from some distance away, but now she arched an eyebrow. "Not the Directorate War?"

"It was fought largely in space. A few Dynasty worlds suffered damage during the final engagement, but those offensives were directed at military or governmental targets."

"And you were on the other side of that war."

"If you mean to say that I fought against the Anaden Directorate, then, yes. I did."

"Fascinating, this notion of you as a rebel. I wonder if it taught you anything at all."

"Quite a few things, Advisor." Nika was staring at them with increasing bewilderment, and he took a quick sip of his champagne. "In any event, we have a significant amount of work ahead of us."

Maris waved a hand dismissively. "Six worlds hit out of, what? Two thousand? Three? I'm surprised you noticed the scratch."

"Four thousand six hundred and eight settled Anaden worlds, and yes, I noticed it. Every world is important. Every world carries upon it the lives, the hopes and dreams and tireless efforts, of millions of Anaden citizens."

Maris gave him a closed-mouth smile and turned away. *No biting retort ready on your tongue?* He took inordinate pleasure in scoring a point; more than he should. "In any event, life now goes on. We will recover and continue focusing on building a better future. To this end—"

Nika held up a hand to interrupt him. "Forgive me, but I have another engagement this evening that I really must attend. Maris, thank you for the invitation and the delicious champagne. I trust the two of you can handle the business negotiations without me."

Maris shot Nika a glare full of daggers, but made a shooing motion toward the door. "Yes, yes, fine. We shall manage."

Without any obvious motion, Nika opened a wormhole and stepped through it. The tear sealed up behind her and was gone. It was a most convenient method of travel.

Audience having departed, he adopted a warm, if professional, expression as he joined Maris at the table. "Thank you for agreeing to see me. I want you to know that I took the concerns you voiced at our last meeting to heart, and I've been working on addressing them."

She had the temerity to look surprised. "You have? Even around all the war crises?"

"The war crises and many other distractions. I made a promise, and I intend to keep it."

"You didn't promise me anything, Supreme Commander."

"Didn't I? Well, I suppose in my own mind I did. And please, we've covered this. I'd prefer it if you simply called me 'Corradeo.' If you insist on a title, I will console myself with 'Advocate.'"

"Advocate. Yes, that's right. Forgive me. I normally don't need to be told things twice." Her gaze diverted to the windows, where a high midday sun gleamed off a sea of strident buildings. "It is a wonderful view. I miss the old architecture, though. All this gunmetal monochrome isn't especially uplifting. But my mind's eye overlays the way it used to be upon the scene, and I am swept away by nostalgia."

He had to concede that the architecture was uninspiring. The Kyvern Dynasty had dominated the planet for the last few millennia, and they were not known for architectural flourishes. "Perhaps you can bring a bit of Asterion style to the city."

"You think? It would require us to settle here in some numbers, and if I am not mistaken, we still lack the ability to do so."

"And that is why I am here today." He removed a quantum cube from his pocket and slid it over to her. "As I said, I took your concerns to heart. The Advocacy is prepared to approve the resolution presented here, and I have every reason to expect that if the Advocacy gives its blessing, the Concord Senate will follow suit."

"Hmm." She set her flute to the side and placed a fingertip on the cube. Her gaze unfocused, and her lips moved as she murmured the words at a whisper.

> *In acknowledgement and consideration of the sacrifices made by the Asterion people during the SAI Rebellion and every day since;*
>
> *In recompense for the harms inflicted upon the Asterion people by the Anaden government and military during said SAI Rebellion;*
>
> *In recognition of the long history and special connection between the Asterion people and the world of Asterion Prime; and*
>
> *In acknowledgment of the Asterion Dominion as an honored Allied Member of the Concord alliance;*
>
> *The Concord Senate hereby adopts amendments to Concord Charter provision VII.D as follows:*
>
> *Any Asterion Dominion citizen shall, upon registration with the local Department of Administration, have the legal right to become a resident of and own property on Asterion Prime.*

Said action shall not make them a citizen or subject of Concord nor bind them to additional obligations imposed upon Concord citizens. Their rights of domicile and property ownership shall be respected to the same extent as those of all residents of Asterion Prime.

Her fingertip lifted off the cube, and she silently refilled both of their champagne flutes. "I will want a legal expert to look over this for any loopholes, of course."

"Of course."

A corner of her mouth twitched, as if she wanted to smile but dared not. "Why?"

"What is it you are asking me?"

"Why are you doing this for us?"

"Because…I am sorry for the sins I committed during the SAI Rebellion. I truly am. I am sorry for the pain I caused you. Caused everyone who died and all who fled, but also caused you, personally."

He clasped his hands atop the table, ignoring the full flute of champagne. He hadn't prepared a speech; instead, the words flowed freely off his tongue. "I was blind back then, to a thousand wrongs. I was invincible, and it made me arrogant. I was master of the galaxy and savior of my people, and it made me…petty.

"In the millennia since, I have been shown my place more than once. I have been made small, and fought my way back up the mountain. I have known pain and loss, and I'd like to believe I have earned my subsequent victories the correct way. But it seems I still have a few more lessons to learn. And you have been teaching them to me. So, please, accept my most sincere of apologies. I can't change the past, and I can't return to you the people you lost. But I can give you this." He gestured toward the skyline. "You deserve to come home."

Her beautiful lips parted, and the most lovely expression of wonder passed across her features. She reached out, and for just a breath, her fingertips brushed over his on the table. "Advocate, I believe perhaps we can become friends after all."

78

MIRAI

NIKA'S FLAT

Alex smiled over the rim of her glass. "It is pretty incredible. The entire planet is alive. More than that, it's *conscious*. It's aware. And it kicked the Rasu's asses."

Nika chuckled as she settled into the chair opposite Alex. "So did Akeso create a sibling, or is it all one consciousness, spread across two planets?"

"Caleb isn't sure, honestly. He's thinking it's the latter, but there's the possibility Hirlas will develop its own distinct thoughts, even personality, as it grows into its new existence. It'll be fascinating to watch."

"I expect so." Nika mulled over her glass for a few seconds, swirling the honey-hued liquid in lazy circles. "You remember how, during the attack there, I wasn't able to locate the quantum block for you, because there wasn't enough kyoseil flowing through the region?"

"I do."

"I took a quick jaunt through sidespace to visit Hirlas before you arrived this evening, and that isn't true any longer. It's not like it is here, mind you. There aren't millions of discrete waves traversing the skies. But much like on Akeso, there's a faint yet pervasive glow of kyoseil enveloping the entire planet. And what's amazing to me is how it was all transmitted through Caleb's fingertips."

"And two and a half liters of his blood."

"Oh. Well, then." They shared a laugh, and Alex enjoyed the moment of calm, relaxed levity.

She'd decided she wasn't going to let her mother's stern disapproval and dire warnings eat away at her. The choice she'd made wasn't a perfect one, but it was the best one available to her under the circumstances. There were risks involved, yes. Absolutely. They needed to not merely remain on their guard, but get their *zadnitsy* in gear to prepare on a scale they'd never before achieved. The Rasu might kill themselves off or reduce their factions to a shadow of their former glory. They might also, she had to acknowledge, ultimately emerge stronger than before and show back up with a renewed grudge.

But she refused to apologize for buying everyone the chance they now had.

"Shall I refill our glasses?"

"Oh, please do." She handed Nika her glass as the woman passed by, then settled deeper into the comfortable cushions.

A swirl of ice-blue lights swept into the flat from parts unknown. *You wanted to see me—Alex, this is a surprise. I can return later if that is preferable.*

Nika walked back into the living area and handed Alex a full glass. "I did want to see you, Mesme. And now is perfect."

Alex, you find my presence...tolerable?

"Oh, yes. We've just been enjoying some wine and musing on recent events while we waited for you to arrive."

You were both waiting on me.

"Yep." She tried and failed to suppress a smirk as she glanced at Nika, who was doing a slightly better job of maintaining a straight face.

The lights froze in place, resembling tiny icicles bolted upon the air, which she couldn't say as she'd ever seen them do. *May I inquire as to the reason?*

"Of course. Oh, but first—" Nika fingered something tucked into the arm of the chair beside her "—I've been led to understand that, when confronted by an uncomfortable topic of conversation, you have a propensity to abscond rather than engage with difficult questions. In fact, I've seen you do this myself on one or two occasions. So I've taken the precaution of sealing the flat for a bit using one of the Kireme Boundaries. Its access code is unique."

I can deconstruct rift devices.

"And I'm sure you can this one, with a little work. Or, you can relax and talk with us for a few minutes. Answer our questions, and we'll let you be on your way."

After everything we have been through, you are holding me prisoner?

Alex groaned and clanged her glass onto the table in front of her. "Oh, for fuck's sake, Mesme. Don't be a drama queen, or king, or whatever. If you weren't such a slippery bastard, we wouldn't have to resort to extreme measures."

Your questions.

"Thank you. More of a declaration, really, to kick things off. We've noodled out your big secret. The reason why you say damnable things like, 'this must happen,' and 'the fate of the universe depends on such-and-such occurring' and 'there will come a day when.' The reason why you get cagey as all hell whenever we ask you to explain yourself." She retrieved her glass and exchanged a look with Nika. Moment of truth.

"You're a time traveler. You're from the future, and you've returned to the past in order to help save the universe from a terrible calamity. Annihilation of trillions by the Rasu, one can assume. At least as a good opening blow."

Time travel is impossible.

"I don't think so, and I'm a mite insulted that you passed the assertion off with such casual disdain. I won't bore you with the scientific analysis I bored Nika with, because you already know how it works. I'm quite certain time travel is extraordinarily difficult, and probably very rare. Perhaps it's only happened once, when you did it. But it *did* happen, and you *are* here as a result."

Mesme twitched, then froze again. *Nika, you believe this as well?*

Nika sighed quietly. "I didn't accept it at first, mostly because, as you say, time travel is supposed to be impossible. But I've seen so many impossible things in the last six years. And the more I thought about it, running the conversations we've had back through my mind, the more convinced I became. You know so much, both about what is and what is to come. I used to wonder if you were trying to play with fate itself…and I now realize you are doing exactly that. You're doing so because you know what awaits us all if you don't change our fate."

On this, you speak accurately. Everything I have done has been pursued with the goal to cut short the suffering of so many. To turn the tide against the eternal darkness.

"So you admit it, then?"

What would be the point of denying it? You are both convinced you have uncovered the truth.

Alex grimaced. Damnable alien! "I'm going to take your response as a yes. Are we all in agreement? Great. How long?"

Pardon me?

"How long into the future did you travel from? How far into the past did you travel to?"

Eight years. Nine hundred eighty-two millennia.

And with this statement, Mesme truly did confirm what had been, despite their bravado, only suspicions. Her stomach did a little flip-flop; the ramifications were…going to require a while to absorb. "Only eight years? I guess this means we can look forward to an exciting decade."

Indeed.

"But over nine hundred millennia? So however old you've always insinuated you are, you're actually far older?"

It will suffice to state that I have lived for more aeons than you can possibly imagine.

Nika shrugged. "I'm seven hundred thousand years old. I can imagine a lot of aeons."

And yet.

Alex leaned forward intently. Mesme was providing information, and they couldn't waste the opportunity. "Are all the Kats time travelers, or solely you?"

It is difficult to respond to your question in a way you will understand.

"You can try simply answering it."

In the ways which matter, it is only I. None of the other Katasketousya have any memory of a life other than the ones which have proceeded along time's arrow since they were awakened.

'Awakened'? Not born? What an interesting word choice....

Nika's hand came to her mouth. "What an incredibly lonely existence you must have endured!"

I will not deny it. But it was necessary.

"I'm so sorry."

Do not be. I do not regret my decisions.

Nika's chin dropped to her chest, and she twirled the stem of her glass between her fingers.

Alex, however, stood. She felt energized, as though she was chasing the starshine through the void to the obscured truths she'd long sought. "Does this mean you believe we'll succeed this time around?"

I believe we stand a better chance of doing so than we did before.

"Because of your meddling?"

Because of yours.

Now it was her turn to be befuddled. "Excuse me?"

Not long ago, Alex, I told you that the best thing I could possibly do in any situation was provide you the minimum required information, then let you run wild. With the slightest nudges and smallest hints of guidance, you have succeeded beyond my most optimistic dreams. And you, Nika. The advances you are leading your people through are nothing short of revolutionary. The Asterions have always represented a great society, but now your people are becoming extraordinary. And Caleb, time and again. Miriam—

"Saving the people who will save the universe." Alex frowned. "Does this mean Caleb died last time? For good? Or Mom? Who else did the enemy slaughter?"

Do not torment yourself with such destructive ruminations. It doesn't matter, for that past no longer exists. We are on a new path now, one which, for the first time, stands to lead to victory. To survival. To an infinite future. We have never been more formidable than we are at this juncture. Success is not guaranteed, but if we act in concert and co-operation, we stand a chance. For this reason, I ask you to please not shut me out any longer. We need to be united and of one purpose, now more than ever.

Alex breathed in deeply, then nodded. "Very well. I'm not going to stop haranguing you, though, or pushing you for greater information. I'll keep demanding from you what I think I need."

I would never expect anything less.

Nika cleared her throat and stood as well. "I have one final question. Are you keeping any more secrets from us?"

Mesme's lights lost their rigidity to drift aimlessly, blending with the starlight twinkling beyond the windows of the flat. A long, weighty silence followed, and for once, Alex didn't interrupt it.

Finally, Mesme drew itself inward, though not into a definable shape. *Yes. There is one. But it is of an intensely personal nature and does not impact our fight against the Rasu. I ask you both to allow me to hold it close.*

Mesme's voice trembled with rare emotion, and it felt as if the air in the room quavered with sorrow and loneliness. She checked with Nika, and they both nodded in agreement. "Okay. For now. But if we ever feel like we need to know it in order to win, we reserve the right to ask you again."

Your terms are acceptable. Am I free to go?

Nika gave Mesme a smile Alex would almost characterize as affectionate. "I turned off the Kireme Boundary as soon as you started answering our questions. We never wanted to hold you against your wishes. We just needed you to talk to us."

I see. Perhaps sharing this knowledge will prove to be the wise course of action. I...hope this will be the case, as I do not take pleasure in alienating either of you.

Alex's gaze fell to study the wood floor as the import of these revelations began to sink in. They'd failed before, in a past-future which was now being overwritten, and everyone had died. *Everyone.* Well, that was sobering.

But this was the only timeline she knew, and she didn't intend to let such an epochal tragedy happen. "So what comes next?"

For tonight, rest. You have earned your respite, for your actions have bought us that most precious of all resources: time. Tomorrow, however, we must begin preparations in earnest. A great storm is coming.

DON'T MISS THE EXPLOSIVE CONCLUSION TO *RIVEN WORLDS*

DUALITY

RIVEN WORLDS BOOK SIX

(AMARANTHE ♦ 19)

AVAILABLE NOW AT GSJENNSEN.COM/DUALITY

AUTHOR'S NOTE

I published my first novel, *Starshine*, in 2014. In the back of the book I put a short note asking readers to consider leaving a review or talking about the book with their friends. Watching my readers do that and so much more has been the most rewarding and humbling experience in my life.

So if you loved **CHAOTICA**, tell someone. Leave a review, share your thoughts on social media, annoy your coworkers in the break room by talking about your favorite characters. Reviews are the backbone of a book's success, but there is no single act that will sell a book better than word-of-mouth.

My part of this deal is to write a book worth talking about—your part of the deal is to do the talking. If you keep doing your bit, I get to write a lot more books for you.

Of course, I can't write them overnight. While you're waiting for the next book, consider supporting other independent authors. Right now there are thousands of writers chasing the same dream you've enabled me to achieve. Take a small chance with a few dollars and a few hours of your time. In doing so, you may be changing an author's life.

Lastly, I want to hear from my readers. If you loved the book—or if you didn't—let me know. The beauty of independent publishing is its simplicity: there's the writer and the readers. Without any overhead, I can find out what I'm doing right and wrong directly from you, which is invaluable in making the next book better than this one. And the one after that. And the twenty after that.

Website: gsjennsen.com
Wiki: gsj.space/wiki

Email: gs@gsjennsen.com
Twitter: @GSJennsen
Facebook: gsjennsen.author

Goodreads: G.S. Jennsen
Pinterest: gsjennsen
Instagram: gsjennsen

Find my books at a variety of retailers: gsjennsen.com/retailers

APPENDIX

HIRLAS
CHOEDA REGION
(PEGASUS DWARF GALAXY)
EREN'S HOME
ARUCHEL CHOEDEN
CHAREGO MTN
AFONLE RIVER
CHOEDA
NORTH RHAEADR WOODS
CALCHFAEN
DIARFFOR
SOUTH RHAEADR WOODS
BENDIGE
NARAIDA & VOLUCRI
HOMEWORLD

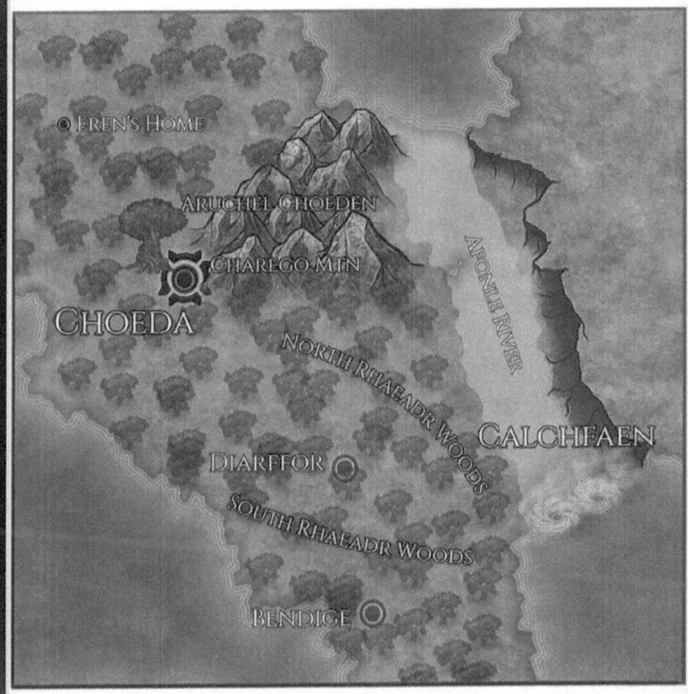

THE STORY SO FAR

View a more detailed summary of the events of the Amaranthe novels online at gsjennsen.com/synopsis.

AURORA RISING

The history of humanity is the history of conflict. This proved no less true in the 24th century than in ancient times.

By 2322, humanity inhabited over 100 worlds spread across a third of the galaxy. When a group of colonies rebelled two decades earlier, it set off the First Crux War. Once the dust cleared, three factions emerged: the Earth Alliance, consisting of the unified Earth government and most of the colonies; the Senecan Federation, which had won its independence in the war; and a handful of scattered non-aligned worlds, home to criminal cartels, corporate interests and people who made their living outside the system.

Alexis Solovy was a space explorer. Her father gave his life in the war against the Federation, leading her to reject the government and military. Estranged from her mother, an Alliance military leader, Alex instead sought the freedom of space and made a fortune chasing the hidden wonders of the stars.

A chance encounter between Alex and a Federation intelligence agent, Caleb Marano, led them to discover an armada of alien warships emerging from a mysterious portal in the Metis Nebula.

The Metigens had been watching humanity via the portal for millennia; in an effort to forestall their discovery, they used traitors among civilization's elite to divert people's focus. When their plans failed, they invaded in order to protect their secrets.

The wars that ensued were brutal—first an engineered war between the Alliance and the Federation, then once it was revealed to be built on false pretenses, devasting clashes against the Metigen invaders as they advanced across settled space, destroying every colony in their path and killing tens of millions.

Alex and Caleb breached the aliens' portal in an effort to find a way to stop the invaders. There they encountered the Metigen watcher of the Aurora universe, Mnemosyne. Though enigmatic and evasive, the alien revealed the invading ships were driven by AIs and hinted the answer to defeating them lay in the merger of individuals with the powerful but dangerous quantum computers known as Artificials.

Before leaving, Alex and Caleb discovered a colossal master gateway that generated 51 unique signals, each one leading to a new portal and a new universe. But with humanity facing extinction, they returned home armed with a daring plan to win the war.

Four Prevos (human-synthetic meldings) were created in a desperate gambit to vanquish the enemy invaders before they reached the heart of civilization; then they were given command of the combined might of the Alliance and Federation militaries. Alex and her Artificial, Valkyrie, led the other Prevos and the military forces against the alien AI warships in climactic battles above Seneca and Romane. The invaders were defeated and ordered to withdraw through their portal, cease their observation of Aurora and not return.

During the battle, hints of the consciousness of her deceased father manifested in the shared connection between Alex and Valkyrie. Alex reconciled with her mother during the final hours of the war, and following their victory Alex and Caleb married and attempted to resume a normal life.

But new mysteries waited through the Metis portal. Six months later, Caleb, Alex and Valkyrie traversed it once more, determined to learn the secrets of the portal network and the multiverses it held, leaving humanity behind to struggle with a new world of powerful quantum synthetics, posthumans, and an uneasy peace.

And in the realm beyond the portal, Mnemosyne watched.

Aurora Renegades

Following the victory over the Metigens, Alex, Caleb and Valkyrie set off to unlock the secrets of the Metigens' portal network. Discovering worlds of infinite wonder, they made both enemies and friends. A sentient planet, Akeso, that left a lasting mark on Alex and Caleb both. Silica-based beings attempting to grow organic life. A race of cat-like warriors locked in conflict with their brethren.

Behind them all, the whispered machinations of the Metigen puppet masters pervaded everything. In some universes, the Metigens tested weapons. In some, they set aliens against each other in new forms of combat. In yet more, they harvested food and materials to send through the massive portal at the heart of the maze.

But Alex and Caleb found yet another layer to the puzzle. In one universe, they discovered a gentle race of underground beings with a strange history. Their species was smuggled out of the universe beyond the master portal by the Metigens. They watched as their homeworld was destroyed by a powerful species known as Anadens; but for the Metigens, they would have perished as well.

Back home in Aurora, the peace proved difficult to maintain. The heroes of the war—the Prevos who melded their minds with AIs—found themselves targeted by politicians and a restless population desperate for a place to pin their fears. Under the direction of a new, power-hungry Earth Alliance PM, the government moved to cage and shackle them.

In desperation, the Prevos uploaded the AIs' consciousnesses into their own minds, fled from their governments' grasp and disappeared onto independent colonies. Devon published the details of the Prevo link to the exanet, unleashing its capabilities for anyone who wanted to follow in their footsteps.

Meanwhile, an anti-synthetic terrorist group emerged to oppose them, fueled by the rise of Olivia Montegreu as a Prevo. While the private face of Prevos was the heroes who defeated the Metigens, the public face became the image of Olivia killing a colonial governor and tossing him off of a building in front of the world.

Unaware of the struggles her fellow Prevos faced, Alex forged her own path forward. Rather than bringing the AI into herself, she pushed out and through Valkyrie, into the walls of the *Siyane*. Piloting her ship in a way she never dreamed, Alex was able to feel the photonic brilliance of space itself. Over time, however, that bond began to capture more of her spirit and mind.

On the surface of a destroyed planet, Mesme at last revealed all. The portal network, which the Metigens call the Mosaic, was above all else a refuge for those targeted for eradication by the Anadens. And the Anadens, rulers of the true universe through the master portal, were the genetic template upon which humanity was built. Aurora was nothing more than another experiment of the Metigens, created so they could study the development and nature of their enemy and the enemy of all life.

Alex and Caleb returned to Aurora to find a galaxy rocked by chaos. After the execution of Olivia Montegreu by Alliance and Prevo forces, Miriam had gone rogue. Under her careful planning, a resistance force, bolstered by help from inside the Senecan and Alliance militaries, moved to remove the despotic Alliance PM.

As Alex struggled with her growing addiction to an ethereal, elemental realm, she felt herself being pulled away from reality. Away from her husband, her mother, her friends. She watched as those she loved fought, but increasingly found herself losing her own battle.

When terrorists staged a massive riot on Romane, Dr. Canivon, the mother of the Prevos, was murdered in front of Devon and Alex. Overcome by her own and Valkyrie's grief, Alex unleashed the explosive power of the ethereal realm to destroy the terrorists' safehouse. Standing in the rubble of her destruction, Alex made a decision to sever the quantum connection between herself and the *Siyane*, choosing a tangible, human life. Choosing Caleb.

Miriam wrested control of the EA government away from the PM, bringing an end to the Prevo persecution. In the wake of victory, however, a shadowy Anaden hunter emerged from the darkness to attack Alex and Caleb. Caleb was gravely injured when the Anaden's power, known as *diati*, leapt into him, healing his wounds and helping him kill the alien.

Mesme revealed the ominous consequences of the attack. Soon, the Anaden leadership would discover Aurora. When they did, they would destroy it unless humanity could stand against them. Mesme told Miriam and the others to prepare, but knowing the end game was upon them, asked Alex and Caleb to come to Amaranthe. The master universe. The home and dominion of the Anadens.

Aurora Resonant

In Aurora, Miriam led the formation of a multi-agency, multi-governmental (GCDA) and military (AEGIS) organization dedicated to meeting the imminent threat of the Anadens.

In Amaranthe, Alex and Caleb discovered an underground 'anarch' resistance movement against the Anaden Directorate. They made contact with an anarch agent, Eren asi-Idoni, and he helped them infiltrate the Anadens' Machim military command and steal secret information on the Machim fleets. Alex and Caleb were captured, but not before Valkyrie uploaded the information they sought. Eren 'nulled out' rather than being captured, for when Anadens died they underwent a regenesis procedure that returned their consciousness to a new body.

Valkyrie transmitted the data to AEGIS then returned to Amaranthe. When Eren reawakened, he joined Valkyrie and Mesme on the *Siyane*, and they rescued Alex and Caleb from the prison where they were being tortured for information.

The Directorate nonetheless learned the full truth about the Metigens/Katasketousya creation of Aurora and ordered a fleet to deliver a powerful weapon known as a Tartarus Trigger to Aurora and annihilate humanity. Forewarned, Miriam led a fleet of warships into Amaranthe to intercept them.

The battle commenced with the destruction of the one known gateway into the Mosaic, and Mesme sneaked onto the lead Machim warship and stole the Tartarus Trigger. Humanity used its Prevos, Rifts and other tricks to take the Anadens by surprise and prevail in the battle. Afterward, Alex, Caleb, Miriam and Mesme were summoned to a secret meeting with the leader of the anarchs, Danilo Nisi, and a tenuous alliance was formed.

AEGIS scored several early victories but also devastating losses. While the battles raged, Alex and the other Prevos developed a method for using sidespace to open physical wormholes, enabling AEGIS vessels to travel anywhere in known space without using the Anaden gateway system.

The AEGIS fleet attacked the Machim homeworld, destroying the Dyson rings encircling its sun and blowing up their orbital military command station. At the same time, Nisi broadcast an impassioned speech across the empire setting forth the Directorate's sins and the anarch's mission to free those oppressed.

In a flashback Caleb's *diati* showed him, it was revealed that Nisi was actually Corradeo Praesidis, the former leader of the powerful Anaden Praesidis dynasty. Many millennia ago, his son tried to kill him; thinking him dead, the son stole his name, face and power, and now served on the Directorate as the Praesidis Primor.

Valkyrie and her twin, Vii, had spent months rebuilding the consciousness of David Solovy that manifested during the final battle of the Metigen War. Using the Anadens' regenesis technology, they transferred his consciousness to a cloned body, and he and Miriam were reunited after twenty-five years.

The Directorate tracked an AEGIS vessel to the primary anarch base and launched a surprise attack, and a bloody battle followed in orbit and on the ground. To stop a Machim warship from bombing the base with antimatter missiles, Alex re-established her ethereal connection with the *Siyane* to bypass the warship's shielding and destroy it; in doing so, she found the connection no longer exerted the damaging hold on her it once did.

Alex soon discovered a way to use the supradimensional properties of the mysterious Reor mineral to access the contents of the Reor slabs used by the Directorate to store sensitive information. She uncovered the location of the Directorate's regenesis backups, and AEGIS and the anarchs devised a plan to take out the entire Directorate, permanently, in one massive strike.

For all but two of the Directorate members, the mission succeeded with minimal losses. However, the Machim Primor escaped his assassination attempt. Armed with the location of one of the Mosaic gateways, he acquired a new Tartarus Trigger and raced to wipe out the Aurora universe.

On Solum (Earth's twin), Caleb engaged the Praesidis Primor in a battle of staggeringly powerful *diati*, and the *diati* freed when the Primor died rampaged wild. Caleb couldn't wrestle it under control, and it killed millions before destroying the planet itself.

The anarchs learned that the Primors kept an additional regenesis backup stored on their secret space station, the Protos Agora, which orbited the Milky Way galactic core. The *Stalwart II* took the Tartarus Trigger Mesme stole at the start of the conflict and used it to destroy the station.

Just when they believed they had finally achieved victory, they discovered the Machim Primor's plans. The Primor had a head start, and the only way to try to prevent him from destroying Aurora was for the Kats to disconnect it from the Mosaic, rendering it unreachable forever. Caleb, however, instead used his now total control over *diati* to command the cosmic force to pull all the pocket universes in the Mosaic—including Aurora—into Amaranthe, then destroy the Mosaic.

He succeeded, but the energy the act required killed him. While Miriam and the others worked out what it meant for all of humanity to now exist in Amaranthe, Alex took Caleb to the living planet of Akeso and, via the deep connection they shared, Akeso brought him back to life.

ASTERION NOIR

On the planet of Mirai in the Gennisi galaxy, a woman woke up in a rain-soaked alley with no memory of who she was or how she'd gotten there. Two strangers found her and offered to take her in. When asked, she told them her name was Nika, though she didn't know why.

Fast forward to five years later. Nika, alongside her rescuers Perrin and Joaquim, led a group of rebels called NOIR against the despotic government of the Asterion Dominion. An insidious virutox was infecting people's programming, altering their personalities and causing them to commit inexplicable crimes. NOIR's investigation of the virutox brought them to Dashiel Ridani, who Nika learned was her lover in her prior life, before she lost her memory.

With her world thrown into disarray, Nika and Dashiel chased the threads of her lost identity while searching for the source of the virutox. Their search led them to the leaders of the Asterion Dominion, the Guides. Nika broke into the Guides' data vault, where she found they had ordered her psyche-wipe five years earlier after she pressed them on a series of disappearances.

Meanwhile, Gemina Kail, an Administration Advisor, traveled to an alien stronghold across the galaxy, where she delivered thousands of Asterions in stasis chambers to an alien species called the Rasu.

As the virutox spread, wreaking increasing havoc across the Dominion, Justice Advisor Adlai Weiss traced the source to the Guides' doorstep. They ordered him to drop the case and let the virutox propagate among the population. He disobeyed, developed a vaccine and contacted NOIR for help in distributing it.

Across the galaxy, Nika and Dashiel discovered the stronghold of the alien Rasu. A metal-based shapeshifting species of immense power, they'd constructed hundreds of thousands of warships and space stations. Armed with this terrifying information, Nika and Dashiel returned to Mirai.

One of the Guides, Delacrai, defied the others to help Nika. She shared how an Asterion scout ship encountered the Rasu eight years ago; the crew was captured and killed. The Rasu grew interested in the Asterions' unique bio-synthetic intelligence powered by kyoseil and quantum programming, and in return for not attacking Asterion Dominion worlds, they demanded a regular supply of Asterions to experiment on. The Guides agreed.

The other Advisors were told the terrible truth about the Rasu and the Guides' deal with the aliens. They scrambled to undo the damage eight years of the Rasu Protocol had inflicted while racing to find a way to respond to an impending Rasu deadline, when the aliens expected more Asterions to be delivered.

Nika's oldest friend from her former life, Maris Debray, revealed that both she and Nika were members of the "First Generation": Asterions who had never erased their psyches in the 700,000 years since they fled the Anaden Empire and created themselves as a new species by merging Anaden DNA, AI programming and the kyoseil mineral. Only a few dozen of the First Generation remained, and their history was kept secret from everyone else.

With time running out, Nika sought the help of the Sogain, an enigmatic species who once threatened the Asterions with extinction if they ever trespassed on Sogain territory. This time, the aliens disclosed the location of a single, stranded Rasu.

An Asterion team captured the Rasu and brought it to Mirai for interrogation. The creature revealed that the Rasu exhibited a collective intelligence when physically connected to other Rasu, but regained independent thought when they were separated. They intended to use kyoseil to control other Rasu over great distances, as kyoseil was supradimensional, deeply interconnected and one of the universe's oldest life forms.

Using this knowledge, the Asterions identified a way to link their consciousnesses together via kyoseil. They dubbed these connections 'ceraffin' and used them to develop a plan to face the Rasu.

They constructed volatile electricity bombs to be sneaked into the Rasu stronghold. The Rasu were expecting 8,000 Asterions in stasis chambers, so Nika used the ceraff structure to split her psyche into shards inhabiting 8,000 copies of herself.

The copies were delivered to the Rasu as expected, and they awoke inside the Rasu's lab on their primary space station. Chaos ensued as they fought to reach the power control center, even as they were cut down by the thousands. A mere dozen made it to the control center, and a single instance survived to override the power safeguards.

Dashiel detonated the electricity bombs, and a cascading power overload ripped through the stronghold. It destroyed the Rasu's Dyson lattice, which triggered an intense surge in solar flare activity, and all the Rasu stations and vessels were incinerated, save one vessel that escaped through a wormhole.

The Asterions recognized this was not the end of the conflict, but the beginning, and they needed to prepare for the Rasu's return. Nika was contacted by the Sogain, who informed her the Anaden Empire of old had fallen and suggested she might find allies among the new one which had risen to take its place.

Nika journeyed to the Asterions' ancestral home, the Milky Way. Before she arrived, however, a wormhole opened in the cabin of her ship, and Alex Solovy walked through it.

ACKNOWLEDGEMENTS

Many thanks to my beta readers, editors and artists, who made everything about this book better, and to my family, who continue to put up with an egregious level of obsessive focus on my part for months at a time.

I also want to add a personal note of thanks to everyone who has read my books, left a review at a retailer, Goodreads or other sites, sent me a personal email expressing how the books have impacted you, or posted on social media to share how much you enjoyed them. You make this all worthwhile, every day.

ABOUT THE AUTHOR

G. S. JENNSEN lives somewhere in the U.S., in a locale that may or may not be where she lived the last time she published a book (she's a gypsy at heart), with her husband and two dogs. She has become an internationally bestselling author since her first novel, *Starshine*, was published in 2014. She has chosen to continue writing under an independent publishing model to ensure the integrity of her stories and her ability to execute on the vision she has for their telling.

While she has been a lawyer, a software engineer and an editor, she's found the life of a full-time author preferable by several orders of magnitude. When she isn't writing, she's gaming or working out or getting lost in the mountains that loom large outside the windows in her home. Or she's dealing with a flooded basement, or standing in a line at Walmart reading the tabloid headlines and wondering who all of those people are. Or sitting on her back porch with a glass of wine, looking up at the stars, trying to figure out what could be up there.